Whiskey Tango

Whiskey Tango— A Romantic Suspense
Copyright © 2016 by Shay Lawless

ISBN-10: 1-940087-18-X
ISBN-13: 978-1-940087-18-4

I0692722

21 Crows Dusk to Dawn
Publishing, 21 Crows, LLC

Cover Photos:

© Can Stock Photo Inc. ghoststone
© Can Stock Photo Inc. Noltelourens
© Can Stock Photo Inc. Artofphoto
© Can Stock Photo Inc.angiepics
© Can Stock Photo Inc. Sergwsq
© Can Stock Photo Inc. AlexMax
© Can Stock Photo Inc. josnik

SHAY LAWLESS

CHAPTER 1

GOD SQUAD

I came face to face with him on the same night I got arrested. Colt Lucero. Yes, that's his real name. It sounds like a stage name for a hot, male porn star. And yeah, most of the girls volunteering at Abraham Wesley Outreach, where he works part-time as an outreach volunteer, follow him around with drool running down their chins. He is hot. He's too hot, actually. He has this cocky swagger and it turns even the too-churchy women's heads until they nearly break their necks craning to watch him walk away.

He's white button-up shirt, black tie, khaki pants and a too-perfect face. He's the kind of guy the rich Holy Trinity Church girls who live in the upscale brick homes over on the north side get their moms to ask over for supper. They call him perfect. But everybody I know (who lives on the south side in the little paint-peeling white houses with rickety fences and old brick apartment buildings with crappy cars parked out front) calls him God Squad.

Comically, he wears the name like a badge of honor. Well, at least he did until I told him the reason everybody on my side of town gave him the nickname three months ago when he moved here. My town, it is Hensley Grove, Kentucky. Our claim to fame is being the home to the largest domestic turkey and the place where the Cannon Bread Mill once stood until eight years ago when it closed down. Unofficially, and to the horror of our local tourism department, we were also pegged by *Celebrity Magazine* in 2011 as having one of the highest murder rates in the United States. I suppose that's why God Squad is here.

"You know why they call you God Squad, don't you?" I ask Colt Lucero. I'm leaning back in the brown, metal chair with my feet kicked up on the dingy white top of the plastic foldout table. It's not an easy feat to hide the panties in the stretchy maroon cocktail dress I'm wearing. But I'm trying to shove on a broken heel into the little post that once held it. I keep pushing myself back, and the nubby rubber floor protectors on the bottom of two of the chair legs are worn down to nothing. The metal sticks out, grinding a dry and grating trail across the floor. I note with some satisfaction it also makes the police officer posted at the door grit her teeth and rub her arms to push away the chills.

"No, I don't, Raeanna—it is Raeanna, right? Or do you go by Tango?" Colt rolls his eyes impatiently upward toward the ceiling. They are an odd color of blue and so dark, they almost seem navy shining beneath the orange-yellow fluorescent lights in the dingy interrogation room at the Hensley Grove Police Station.

"Everybody calls me Tango except Poppy and Anna."

"Okay, Tango—"

"Do you want to know the reason, God Squad?"

"I'm sure you're going to tell me." He's got a New York drawl that clashes with my southern Kentucky twang. I only notice I hang on to the end of my own words when he talks and cuts his short. The sound of the two colliding might be as cruel on the ears as the grind of my chair legs on the concrete floor.

"I am." It's kind of funny. This guy is known for being really laid back, sweet, patient, and gentle. But within two minutes of face to face talk with me, he is already running his hand through his freshly cut, short black hair and grinding his perfect, too-white teeth ragged between his jaws. His fingers are tapping on his knee and his leg is jumping up and down.

My foster mom, Anna, who raised me always hard-sighs like she is exhaling a pumpkin and tells me I have that effect on people. "You have a bit of a mouth on you, Raeanna," she says with her eyes closed and her head slowly, methodically moving back and forth. "You could be a little more ladylike sometimes."

No, I mean, I've tried. And it isn't like whatever I'm thinking comes spilling out of my mouth like raw sewage. It took me a long time to get here. I didn't talk much until I was seven or eight—too much drama in my life. I just think I've spent the last eighteen years trying to catch up for all that quiet. So I wiggle the elastic hair tie off the brownish hair I've got piled on top of my head. I waggle my neck to let it flow down with a bit of haughty swagger to meet his pompous air. Then I slump back in my chair with arms folded, tell Colt Lucero what he needs to know right now:

"The God Squad was the original committee formed to figure out which endangered species got put back on the not-endangered list, you get it?" I make a wild blink of my eyes that my foster brother used to describe as cat-like and not in a nice way when we were kids. He used to bark like a dog and chase me across the living room. "They could doom a species or save it." I am just the opposite of what Colt is used to dealing with on the upscale, subdivision side of town where he lives. He commutes each day to the south side to help what the preacher at Holy Trinity likes to call the *poverty stricken south-siders.*

I'm a kind of an in-your-face type of person. Some folks would call me poor white trash because of my mom and dad and where I came from. It doesn't help that I've got long, dark hair and I add in violet highlights to match my abnormally violet eyes. I've got a tattoo of a tiny black star the size of a thumbprint on my back. I wear red lipstick, tight dresses, and when I'm in a foul mood, I douse my fingernails black. The only things all-American I don is a face full of freckles and a rainbow-colored snap bracelet from the 1990s that I flop on my too-skinny wrist once in a while. My daddy told me it probably belonged to my mama.

"No, I don't get it."

"When you come knocking at somebody's door," I make a grand sigh, drop my gaze and my expression, "they are either sitting in jail or you're going to redeem them by making them do community service with your stupid mission. Which will it be for me? Are you going to tell them I'm worth saving or let them send me to hell—?" I pause for the dramatic effect. "I mean, jail?"

I probably shouldn't have been so mean to him while I dab an icepack wrapped in toilet paper against my black eye. He's obviously my only hope of getting out of here. Because, by God, I've tried the alternatives. I attempted to bribe Rachael Updike at the front desk with my last crumpled dollar and a half-chewed pack of bubble gum I dug out of my purse. She is in her mid-fifties and has red-orange hair stuffed in a bun on top of her head and a thousand freckles donning her smile-less face. She rolled her eyes. When the line was at its peak of eight or nine reprobates like myself, I had a good clue the oh-holy-hell-he's-hot, dark-haired man in the suit two people behind me was trying to get into the restroom because he kept looking all antsy right and left, fidgeting back and forth on his feet. I'd seen him before, couldn't quite place the exact location.

Such, I had an idea. It was launched by the 1930s black and white gangster movie I'd watched by myself last night on TV at two in the morning. And the fact that the mysterious, fidgeting man was actually wearing a fedora in Hensley Grove only made it that much more enticing. A fedora? Who wears those anymore? And surely not here. Anything outside a camo ball cap and a hunter orange shirt could get a person shot if walking the wrong road at night. But he looked 1930s and he looked gangster and I was bored and wanted out of here.

I zoomed past them all, jumping up and down like I was going to pee my pants until Rachael gave me the restroom key with a muffled curse beneath her breath. "Tango," she told me using my nickname because I really believe everybody thinks it is my real name. "You're really irritating." Do they not think it out? What could Tango really be short for? Then, I slipped up beside the suit and tie guy that looked like he was probably in there with some organized crime family and probably rich as hell. I nodded coolly.

"Dude," I whispered. "You're with the mafia, right?" I dangled the key near his hand and he looked down. Our fingers almost met. "You look a bit New York City to be anything else. You know, the hat," I patted my head and he reached up self-consciously like he's just realizing how out of place it is right now against the dirty t-shirts, neck tattoos and scuffed tennis shoes. "So here's the thing, sweetheart," I said to him, made a stealthy look right to left. "I won't tell anybody. It's our little secret. You get me out of the joint and I'll give you—*the key*."

"The key to what?" he states softly. He's got an accent. It is deep and I lean in. "Madame, someone stole my wallet." Maybe he wasn't with an American crime syndicate. Maybe he's from South America or—Switzerland or— I'd probably seen him on the news after a mob warfare.

"Yeah, the bathroom key?" I dangled it higher like he couldn't see it in the first place. "Oh, well, you are in the official dead body dumping capital of the U.S. Maybe you know that and that's why you're fidgeting—oh," I stop and exaggerate revelation. "Maybe—that's why you are here. You didn't hear that from me." I looked around. Yeah, there were some pretty creepy looking people in here. "Don't kill me. I won't tell anybody. I figured you were mafia and had to go to the bathroom. I figured I could befriend you and you could break me out later."

He just stared at me like I was nuts, then Rachael told me to either go to the bathroom or she was going to send me back to a holding room. I rolled my eyes. "Come on, Rachael, I'm just trying to lighten up the mood in here," I whined loudly. "This waiting room is *soooo* boring."

So after being ushered to a room by a no-nonsense cop, who got mad at me because I followed far enough behind in the darkened hallway that I could hide a few silly ballet jumps (with a broken shoe heel) whenever he turned, I'm in the holding room where Rachael told me I might have more fun.

I've got nobody else to call. But I feel I have a good reason to take some of my anger out on somebody else. I'd had a terrible, horrible afternoon spiraling ever-so-quickly downward so I almost feel like the toes of my black heels are settled precariously on the very threshold of hell. Well, the high heel of my left foot. I lost the heel to my right shoe somewhere in the yard of the subsidized apartment I shared with my boyfriend—excuse me, ex-boyfriend—while his new girlfriend dragged me kicking and screaming by my hair off the front porch and down to the buckled concrete sidewalk. So I have just a wee bit of the disposition of a rabid tomcat tonight.

Don't get me wrong. It hadn't started so badly. I'm almost finished with my four years of art school. Neil Wright, my art instructor at Field's Community College sets up a visual arts show at the Hensley Grove Town Gallery, a local mini-mall, every year for his graduating seniors. It was today. And it's a big thing. Ten of his most talented students get chosen to set up their projects, show them off, and sell their art. Families pour in for support. Well, everybody else's family rushed in for support. I sat there with my stupid artwork I'd dedicated every non-working hour I wasn't at my job at the diner or watching my three year-old all alone. Nobody I knew showed up. Not a single family member, not a friend. Not my boyfriend who was still my boyfriend at five in the afternoon.

And he's the reason I'm sitting at the police station. I asked him to come to the art exhibit every day for the last month since I found out my work was being shown. Every day, he sat on the shabby couch in our apartment, arms folded while he waved a hand for me to move out from my spot between his knees and the TV.

"Listen, Kev," I'd grumbled. "Everybody else has half a million family members coming. Tia Wilson has her mom and seven of her sisters flying in from Florida. I got Poppy and you. You're my boyfriend. I shouldn't have to tell you the things a boyfriend is supposed to do." Poppy had been my foster dad since I was six. Besides Anna and their kids, he is still about the only family I've got. He and Anna, are in their early seventies. Still, they manage to take in a couple kids and maintain their support for those of us who had worked our way outside their nest.

"Yeah, baby, then don't tell me. Whatever. It really sounds boring. Art is boring. Do you need to me to stop in to get the grade? I got three bucks. Just buy something from your stuff and say I bought it. How about I just stay with Mia?" Mia is my three year-old daughter. It should have been a big, red flag right then. Kevin's idea of watching my kid is sitting her in front of the TV while he takes a nap, then complaining for two days about having to babysit her.

"Art is boring?" I asked him. "Because dancing is art and you like my dancing."

"Are you going to dance at the show like you dance for me?" He'd smiled like a dirty old man, wiggled his eyebrows. "Because you could get good money for that down at Chippy's Strip Club. Skip the art show. You ain't gonna make a cent there. Go get a job at Chippy's. You'd make helluva good tips there."

Still, the crappy attitude wasn't the reason he is my ex as of two hours and fifteen minutes ago. It was because he didn't show and two other people that I don't like so much did come. Which, again, I probably should have expected. And if I'd found him lounging on the couch half-drunk with his buddies watching a ballgame, I probably would have forgiven him. Again. But, he just doesn't show. Then I start to get pissed, bummed out, and worried, all at once because Tyrone Edgers who makes these weird clay models of chickens has thirty people show up and his grandma pays him three-hundred dollars for a figure of a horse-man-chicken.

"So part of our modern art grade is to attend this boring show," a silky voice wafted to my ears. "I think it is stupid they make us do other classes than dance."

I had been desperately tapping messages into my cell phone to my boyfriend when Alexandra Edward strutted up to where I was sitting, her long, ballerina legs barely hidden by the slit in the maxi-skirt she's wearing. I call her Mean Alex sometimes because of her snippy attitude toward me. She's got fine, white-blonde hair that barely makes it to her shoulders and she's what I call model-pretty—curiously abnormal facial features and super tall and skinny. Her stiletto heels make her another foot taller. I have to crane my neck to look up. I always feel like an ugly little toad staring up at the beautiful princess.

Taylor Peirce, Alexandra's doppelganger with raven-black hair, has been her sidekick since fourth grade. She sidles up beside Alexandra and latches on to her arm. There's usually four of them. I look for their illustrious leader, Delia Childs, and the dark-haired girl who is usually latched to her arm, Hannah Lafferty. Delia's the leader of their pack, quietly malicious. It makes me sore to say, my boyfriend calls her drop dead beauty queen gorgeous with her sandy hair, big boobs, and the pointy features of an elf.

Alexandra, Taylor, Hannah and Delia are in the performing arts program at the college. Believe it or not, Hensley Grove has one of the highest rated dance and contemporary arts programs in the U.S. Delia's had it out for me for twelve years since we both took dance classes at Denise Beller's Uptown Dance Studio in town and I beat her out of the part of the princess in the annual pageant. I half expect her to lunge from the shadows at me like a demon sorceress, wait for her to slip up beside the other three and ram my ego with her bitter remarks. She's not there. Nor is quiet Hannah who is the only one of the four who is majoring in both modern dance and ballet.

I usually envy Hannah. She's what I dreamed of becoming growing up, that tie between the freshness of modern dance and the deeply rooted charm of ballet. She's usually donning a t-shirt with *Adrien Moreau, Mon Chéri* on it. Her hero. He is the equivalent for the modern ballet dancer of a teenage boy band to a twelve year-old. Believe it or not, I heard she's got her room covered in posters of him. And yes, they do make posters of famous ballet dancers.

"So that sounds pretty simple," I muttered, looking back to my phone. "I have to use my hard-earned skills to pass the class. You just have to look dumb and show up. Makes perfect sense to me."

"Quit being so dramatic, Tango. At least I show." Taylor rolled her eyes. "You never attended the last two dance courses for the performing arts degree. You have become what Shane calls one of his greatest failures." She wiggled her head back and forth arrogantly. "You know the rules. Dean Paulson told everybody that even you visual art majors have to be a part of the final competition in less than six weeks. If you don't attend, you will not get your visual arts degree either. Are you going to be one of Neil Wright's greatest failures too?"

I just stared at her. *The contest.* Everyone at the school banks their entire college career on this competition. It's called the Edna Fields Performing Arts Contest and it is offered to all the students. The only problem for the visual arts students is that it is difficult to blow away a judge with one or two drawings settled on a bland table in the sterile Thomas Banks Visual Arts Center. The performing art students, on the other hand, get a beautiful stage that had been donated by none other than the famous ballet dancer and actor Edna Joyce Fields. And, surprise surprise, someone in the performing arts—dancing or theatrical department has won for the last seventeen years.

"No, Neil Wright said the art students just had to be in the exhibit here," I corrected her. "Then we don't have to be in the stupid competition because we're never going to win against performers."

"And Dean Paulson said he wasn't bending the rules for any professors or their students. It was just a rumor that Neil got permission. Everybody has to compete."

"Well, I could stand up there and flip you off in my old blue jean shorts and a ripped t-shirt and look better than you in that stupid little tutu of yours doing fat-girl glissades across the stage," I jumped up and made a funky hunched-over duck walk two steps up and two steps back before I plop down again.

"You're such a bitch, Tango."

"Yeah, well, so are you. By the way, where's the rest of your coven? Out buying brooms?"

Her eyes got dark then. "None of your business." I

saw her looking at my three paintings on display. All three are different forms of perspective illusion.

"Yeah," Taylor snickered. "It is so much harder to pick up a camera and take a picture of—of some drugged-out woman smoking a cigarette and looking out a window."

"Well, the drugged out woman is my mama. That's the only memory I have of her, standing and looking out a window. She left me when I was little," I divulged, shrugged her off with a subtle roll of my eyes. It is true. Mama was tall with a dark complexion and she was skinny. I was only two or three, but I clearly recall her image, brown hair and an upturned nose. I can smell the faint tinges of rose perfume and cigarette smoke wafting in the air. She was beautiful.

"I like to think she's seeing beyond what her life was like right then," I sighed. "Maybe thinking about the horizon and where she could go from there. And it isn't a photograph. It's a Trompe-l'œil, a painting that's three dimensional. If you put it on a wall, it looks like there's a window there." It is difficult to tell what is real and what is painted. They both just stared at it for thirty seconds with pinch-pucker lips like I'm lying.

"Oh, my God, this is so boring." Alexandra finally faked a yawn into a cupped hand. "I'd rather fail my class than sit here and stare at this junk. Let's go look at the clay chickens."

I pushed my hands to my head and screech in exasperation with them. Taylor jumps and Alexandra turns to give me a pickle-lipped glare. "You're crazy, Tango."

"Say it to my face, bitch," I called back, wagged my hand like I was waving her back. Neither return.

"Um, I just did," Alexandra spat at me. She's right. It made me irritated. Oh, and that's where I saw the mafia guy. Now I remember. He was standing in the shadows of

Nina Long's sculpture of an angel riding a moose. His body was facing the moose, but his head was turned back like he was capturing the conversation. He had a *that-woman-is-crazy* kind of stare before he whipped his head back around like he didn't want to get eye contact with the nutcase.

I was overwhelmed with pity for myself for ten minutes after they finally left. I picked up my artwork, tossed it in a box and plunked it in the dumpster behind the Hensley Grove Town Gallery. Then, with the threadbare mindset of a damaged doll tossed into the Goodwill bin mixed with the irritated outlook of a rabid raccoon that just got kicked, I headed toward home to find out if my boyfriend was perhaps lying dead in the parking lot in front of my apartment building. That's why he didn't come out.

I found out the real reason Kevin wasn't at the art exhibit when I pushed my key into the lock and opened the door. Surprise. He was far from dead. In fact, he was donning his brand new boxers I bought him last Christmas and chasing a naked Sophie Wells, who works with me at Joe's Home-style Diner, around our cruddy apartment.

I should have walked away. I could have just grabbed up my clothes, stuffed them in a couple plastic grocery sacks and been on my way. I didn't. I'm the one that signed the rental agreement so I couldn't. And because I've got a bit of a temper. I walked into the living room, grabbed up a lamp and started swinging it like a Louisville Slugger all over the apartment. I had trashed everything belonging to Kevin in the living room and was working toward the dining room when five feet seven inch and one-hundred and fifty pound Sophie tackled me, all one-hundred and maybe two pounds and five feet six inches, like a hulking professional football player tackles a prissy ballet dancer and started slugging me. Kevin, bless his evil soul, grabbed my arms and tried to pull me away from her and she kicked me in the face.

CHAPTER 2

PREPARING FOR A TRIPPLE CHOCOLATE NIGHT

That's how I got the black eye and the bloody nose that I'm still swiping with a tissue while I'm staring Colt Lucero in the eyes. It is four hours after the cops took away the makeshift Louisville Slugger and five hours since the art show fiasco.

"So, God Squad, I take it Gil sent you out here to try to glue me back together, fix me." I reveal I know my foster family's secret. I'm broken and only a miracle worker sent from heaven, like Colt, can duct tape me back together. Gil is my foster brother I've lived with since I was six. I knew he was buddies with Colt, figured he had sent him. Gil was always trying to protect his dad from us evil foster kids. I think if he had his way, we would have all been like dandelion seeds with their little parachutes dispersed to the wind, then killed off with weed killer before we could reproduce.

"Raeanna, he sent me out here to tell you that he couldn't be here. He got your messages off your Pop's phone, But your—Pop—couldn't come."

"Poppy," I correct him. "I call my foster dad Poppy."

"Yes, Poppy." He is trying to reach his hand out like he wants to lay it on my wrist, comfort me. I eye him with the glare of the evil witches in any fairy tale right before she turns a princess into a frog. I pull my hands away, push them to my waist.

"Your Poppy's over at Community Hospital. He had a seizure."

I stand straight up. I'm not used to being confined. I

don't know why I think I can just push my way past Colt. However, when I hear Poppy is sick, my mind just goes left of center.

I lose all the shitty attitude right then. Colt rises with me, pushes a hand out to try to stop me at the same time the cop that is standing at the doorway snaps to attention. She is tickling her gun. I am trying to figure out how I can get out the door without getting shot.

"Tango, stop." Colt is trying to comfort me with a soft, assertive tone. "Don't get crazy, think it out."

"Don't—get—crazy? Crazy is my boyfriend screwing somebody behind my back, wearing the underpants I bought him for Christmas, and me walking into the apartment that I rented in my name and finding him screwing her tonight. Crazy is being kicked out of *my* apartment by his new girlfriend. Crazy is making me come down to this shithole and me getting spanked for doing nothing but coming home to check on him because I thought he might have been dead in the parking lot because he walked into the middle of a drug deal. That's crazy," I growl, dark eyes staring at him. "I need to pick up my kid from the babysitter. I need to get to the hospital. I need to be with my Poppy."

"And you can't," Colt almost coos like a mama sweet-whispers to a child on the verge of a tantrum. "You're being detained until all this—" He pauses and has the audacity to wave his fingers around his face. "Angry-crazy goes away."

"Angry-crazy," I spit back at him, hot eyes staring bolts of lightning into his.

"Yes," he says softly, but firmly. "You've got to quit taunting the police officers—I mean, who does jumps and flips down a police station hallway?"

"Nice, Lucero. It was a grande jeté and a double back

stand. I was trying to lighten the mood. Is that what I am? Angry-crazy? No, I'm just a little livid. However, I can actually show you angry-crazy if you want and I can do it right now. Get me un-detained!" I scream it. I know I shouldn't have. However, six minutes after I had left for the art show, Kevin had dropped Mia off at Kelsey Riddel's two rental rooms down from my place. I only know this because she has texted me twenty times telling me she has Mia and she's sick of it. If I don't get there in ten minutes, she's going to drop my sweet, innocent three year-old off on the curb. And I guess Kevin had been dumping Mia off a lot while he was *doing* Sophie when he was supposed to be babysitting my little girl. Because Kelsey's impatient voice screamed at me it was the last time Kevin was going to dump Mia with her. And Poppy, he is the only person in the entire world who understands me, has supported me through a lot of crap, and always has my back. And when I finally get to return the favor by being there for him when he's sick, I am stuck in a stupid police station with an idiot who calls me angry-crazy.

That's when the cop starts screaming at me to sit down. I don't like people yelling at me. It puts me in an even worse place than I am right now. For a moment, I think my head is going to explode. I can't think of anything but figuring out a way to claw through the cement walls and get to Poppy. The cop, she comes up and shoves me down hard on the chair. Colt is squatting down next to my knees with his elbow resting on the table, trying to tell me to calm down and I'm starting to panic, feeling my breathes just shoved out of my chest.

Breathe. I can't breathe. I think it is one and a half minutes of holy hell gasping for breath and getting ready to break loose when I take in a deep gulp of air and turn to Colt.

"Oh, this is going to be a triple chocolate night," I whisper to myself. It was.

"Triple chocolate?" Colt shakes his head, looks at me, and looks at the cop like they are code words to stop my panic attack.

I scrub my eyes. "Um, triple chocolate. When I used to have a bad day, Poppy would get me chocolate ice cream, chocolate syrup and a brownie to make me feel better. I guess we use it as a code word now. Triple chocolate days are the bad ones. God Squad, I need paper and a pencil, please. Drawing. It calms me down," I beg the man sitting in front of me. He scrubs a hand across his face. Then he makes a wavering turn to the police officer at the door. "Can she have a paper and pencil?"

"What the hell does she need that for, to stab you?"

"Therapy," I grunt-stutter. "It helps me relax."

Colt talks the cop into giving me paper and a pencil, assures her that I'm not going to go crazy and start stabbing people with the nubby eraser while he goes down to try to convince the police to release me and talk Kevin out of filing charges. Five minutes pass, then ten. I'm sitting there holding the pencil, staring at the blank sheet of white paper and taking in deep breaths like Poppy showed me to do when I was six and trying to deal with all those things that went bump in my night. I know I'm too far gone this time to draw, but just knowing that blank sheet of paper is there comforts me.

"—so his eyes were bigger, wider?"

I can hear the voice in the room across the hall slipping over chubby cop's shoulder. In fact, I can see the girl who is sobbing. She has short sandy-blonde hair swollen eyes. It is Delia Childs. I catch a glimpse of her face and it is still flawless like the fake picture-perfect complexions of actors when they cry for the camera. She doesn't have the puffy pink around her eyes and her nose isn't red. She just looks like she went outside in a misty rain and twirled around and she's got sprinkles on her cheeks. I decide right then if I was a superhero, she would be my archenemy. Of course, she would be the pretty one that just stands there with hands on hips and hair being blown by the wind on a tall new building. I would be a dark superhuman squatting in a puddle of dirty water in the gutter near the subsidized apartment buildings. I choose to wear a hoodie because my hair gets all frizzy with even the slightest hint of humidity in the air.

She has refused to let them close the door even while her mom, her aunt, and a skinny female officer with thumbs hooked to her belt hover around her. I now know her given name, Adeline, because I keep hearing the three of them repeat it—*Adeline, it's alright. You're going to be okay. Adeline, if you can give us a good idea of what he looks like, maybe we can find him.*

She has been attempting to describe a man to a frumpy-looking sketch artist that keeps scratching his head and holding up a paper. I can see his artist's rendition of the man he keeps holding up to her. It looks more like a mixture of himself and the aunt. It bugs me. He's not a real sketch artist. Hensley Grove is too small to have someone on the payroll for that. He's probably the guy that took a painting class in high school and who shows old ladies how to draw oranges and apples at the senior center. He appears to be more interested in the clock on the far wall behind them. He'd rather be anywhere but here with a bawling girl trying to draw a picture of a man he can't see and she obviously doesn't want to remember.

And me, I've got a blank piece of paper, a pencil and a clear image of the man popping up in my head.

"He had a round face. And pink cheeks." Shit. I'm almost embarrassed that I'm listening and conjuring up the image. "His jaws looked like that kind of dog that—"

"A bulldog," her mom offers. Delia nods her head.

"He had gray hair."

Shit, I don't need it. But there it is, the bumbling and jagged pieces of puzzle she is putting together for me in my head and what is roaming around in my mind. I watch the way she widens her eyes. I know the man's eyes must be wide, buggy. I see the way she puckers her lips, pushes them out when she is desperately trying to describe him, but can't quite seem to bring them from her mind to her tongue.

Delia waves a hand over her head to show he's got a thick mop of hair. She doesn't think she remembers. Somewhere in the back of her mind, she does. I know it. I can read it in every movement of her lips, every wiggle of her nose, every shift of her body in the chair. She just needs someone to take the images rambling aimlessly around her mind like pieces of puzzles that have fallen to the floor, pick them up in her expressions, and fit them all together.

I am still drawing when Colt Lucero comes back into the room.

"Hey." He pokes me on the shoulder. I blink, look up. "They are going to let you leave. You're being released. Your boyfriend isn't pressing charges or anything. He smelled like marijuana. I pointed that out to him. It seemed to change his rabid disposition."

I blink at him. I know my face must have been blank. I had been so engrossed in the drawing, I forgot where I was. I felt deflated, tired. "You'll take me to pick up Mia and see Poppy at the hospital?" I mutter. "Or do the cops? Maybe you can take me to my car." We walk from the room. I say nothing when I make a quick detour, slap the drawing on the table in front of Delia. Her eyes go wide as I walk out.

CHAPTER 3

EVERYTHING I OWN TOSSED TO THE APARTMENT PARKING LOT

Poppy's laying in a sterile pale-yellow room in a metal hospital bed with white sheets. He's got an IV in his arm and the lights are dimmed to make the room look gray and desolate like some post-apocalyptic warzone. The constant beep of a monitor hits my ears even before I step inside the doorway. The sound makes me shiver.

Nobody else is there but his son, Gil, who is sitting in a maroon vinyl chair with his skinny, khaki pants legs crossed and a laptop resting on his knees. The nurse tells us everyone has to leave so Poppy can get some much-needed rest. I am sure the only reason Gil has stuck around is to hold some imaginary cloves of garlic and a wooden cross between me and his dad, ward me off like a vampire or a witch trying to steal his dad's blood, soul—or his wallet.

"Well, look what the cat dragged in. Something Tangoofy. I sent you a thousand text messages, Tango," he says. He's always making more out of my nickname than he needs to do. He's even come up with what he calls his urban street lingo that he calls Tangonese for the stupid stuff I say. "Dad started asking for you six hours ago." He doesn't even look at Mia who is riding my hip and wearing an old maroon t-shirt for pajamas. It must have been Kelsey's twelve year-old son's shirts because it has FIGHT CLUB scrawled on the front in indelible marker. The back is tied up with a bread loaf twist tie to keep it from falling off her scrawny, three year-old shoulders. She has my frizzy, but fine, brown hair and it is running tangled knots down the back. I can tell she has been anxious about something because the little rat's nests on the top mean she's been twirling strands over and over with her teeny forefinger.

I also know Gil doesn't see his buddy, Colt, who is kind of wavering back and forth in the shadows outside the door. "Where have you been? Out drinking?" Gil is two years older than me and really uptight, strung up like a piñata ready to be slammed with a little league baseball bat. He coaches varsity high school soccer and junior varsity basketball and he teaches English Literature at Hensley Grove High School. He's also always had a chip on his shoulder about me coming to live with his mom and dad when I was six. He was the miracle baby that came twenty years after his parents had married and tried desperately for nineteen years to have kids. He was spoiled rotten and seven years old when I came along. He gripes it's because I'm poor white trash. Not so. He's got jealousy issues. I'm the only girl out of fourteen boys on both his mom and dad's side. They spoiled me silly when I was little, took me to ballet and soccer and gymnastics and bible school.

"Shut up, Gil," I grapple with the urge to kick him. "I had car problems."

"Yeah, because your car is a piece of crap and you can't afford something that runs because you don't have a big girl job—"

"I don't have a big girl job, *asshole*," I hiss back while I slide up beside Poppy's bed. "Because I have been putting myself through college unlike you who got your six years paid for on the mommy and daddy GI bill. And I actually have two big girl jobs. One is at Joe's Home-style Diner and the other is going to college."

"Don't curse, Raeanna," Poppy's voice is low and gruff. He had looked asleep; his eyes were closed until he spoke. Still, he gives me a weak smile.

"I'm sorry, Poppy," I say with a soft grin in return, then I turn to jeer at Gil. I note that he is peering out the door and noticing Colt wavering there like he's not sure if he should come or go. "I just had a cruddy night."

"Yeah, not as cruddy as dad," Gil mutters giving Colt a wave with his fingers. "But it's always got to be about you, doesn't it?"

"Sweetie, I missed your show," Poppy ignores his spoiled son who is hopping up and shaking Colt's hand. "How'd it go?"

"Good," I lie, cupping a yawn in my palm.

"Did you sell the painting of your mama looking out the window?" He raises a hand, wiggles a knobby knuckle toward the dresser next to him. "My wallet's up there, I think. I set aside money to buy it. I just couldn't get there. Had one of my seizures—"

"Mom took your wallet, Dad," Gil corrects him. "You can't leave it here. Somebody might steal it." He makes a point of dropping his head toward me like he is pointing out exactly who will pilfer his money. Then he turns to Colt. "Thanks for giving Tango a ride. We were kind of busy."

"How's he doing?" Colt asks. I can see Gil eyeing him up and down. Colt is sopping wet like I am, his clothes sticking to his skin. The rain was pouring when we came out of the police station and has not stopped since.

"He's doing better." Gil shrugs. "He used to get these all the time. They put him on meds. He must have forgotten to take them. Mom says we'll have to get him one of those plastic pill cases so he can remember when to take them. Wow, is it raining out that bad?"

I cringe hoping Colt doesn't divulge the entire reason we are sopping wet. I know Gil knows I was at the police station. Poppy doesn't.

"Yeah, buckets," he says. "I got her here as fast as I could."

Inwardly, I sigh in relief. Then I look down at Poppy. I see his eyes go to mine. Something is up. If he didn't take his meds, there was a reason.

"Yeah, if she wasn't out partying and getting arrested, she could have been here three hours ago. He shouldn't be up," Gil spits out and I groan, see Poppy's eyes get wide. I turn, stare lightning bolts at Gil who is rolling eyes at me like I'd been playing video games instead of picking up Mia and trying to get my car started for the last half hour. I don't tell him just forty-five minutes ago, I'd been standing just a step outside Colt Lucero's car and staring into the front lawn of my apartment building. It had begun to downpour, tiny droplets of late spring rain beating on the roof of the car behind me. The apartment's just a stone's throw from the main road and there's a big old billboard with lights on our side of the street. It illuminates the entire front of the building.

"Crud." I'd felt like crying standing in the parking lot. I didn't. Any tears that ever flowed from my eyes were long gone when I was a kid. I learned early that crying only made my daddy irritated. He had me for the first six years of my life before I went to Poppy and Anna's. When he got annoyed with my conduct, he smacked me. Punishment reinforcement. That's what my Psych 101 teacher called my daddy's reaction to what he considered bad behavior. My reaction was always a little cringe after he'd slapped me upside the head. Even grown up, I still have a funny way of wincing whenever I feel like crying while I'm in the process of shoving emotions away.

So I cringed. Then I stared at three big mounds of all my stuff tossed out of the upstairs apartment window and laying in piles in the yard. Everything that could have been broken was broken—the lamp Anna got me for Christmas, my candles, and my little clay figures I'd made. Lying in a sopping wet line were my clothes and artwork, assorted bottles of spray can paint. My sketchbooks were saturated, my paintings ran rivulets of blue and green and all colors mixed to a black on the sparse grass. My charcoal pencils, paintbrushes and fixatives were all ripped to shreds or busted.

"I've got a couple plastic grocery bags."

I could hear Colt telling me that while I stood there feeling like my whole life was getting flushed down some huge toilet bowl. I followed his steps, the rain making little gray pock marks on his white dress shirt. He stepped in a dingy puddle on the curb, looked at his foot, and then just shook his head. I'm sure he probably paid two-hundred dollars for those expensive, leather shoes. Still, he just looked up and gave me a wane smile.

Colt opened up his trunk and was dumping out whatever he had in those bags. He shoved one at me and started grabbing up what was left of my life and stuffing it inside. When it was too full to hold it, he simply started grabbing armloads and walking to my car. About the time I was on my third march from lawn to car, I hear Kelsey screaming at me from the stairway while she trooped downward with a half-asleep Mia in her arms. While I'm dishing out my last ten bucks in quarters and crumpled one -dollar bills in babysitting money, and shoving it in Kelsey's hand, I heard Colt call to me from the curb near my car.

"Raeanna, you need to come here a second."

It was pouring rain when I made my way in numbed silence to where his voice had come. I couldn't see his face. However, I could see the rigidness of his silhouette against the shine of the billboard lights. I stood there for a minute taking it in—my tires were flat. When I shined my phone at the passenger side, I could see the most brilliant color of florescent orange with CRAZY BITCH written in six year-old's scrawl along the back door.

"It's alright." I came up beside him, stared hard at the paint running down the side of my old car. My paint, that is, from the spray cans that were laying empty between the front tire and buckled curb. That hurt. They were my lifeblood, my therapy when things got bad. To the utter disappointment of the local police, I secretly paint artwork all over the buildings in town when I get upset.

I just shrugged. What else could I do? Obviously my ex-boyfriend wasn't done with me. "This is what's called white trash break up," I related to Colt. "It's part of the whole experience on the south side." He twisted his head slightly, looked at me like I'd said something completely out of his realm of understanding. Then when I forced up a smile, he realized I was trying to make light of the situation. My bumper was completely bashed in and my taillights were smashed like somebody had taken a baseball bat to them.

"You want me to call the police?" he asked me. The cringe in his eyes let on that it was the last thing he wanted to do, sit around on the south side of town in the pouring rain waiting for cops while girls in oversized t-shirts and dollar store pajama pants peered out the apartment windows at us.

"It was a piece of crap anyway. Can you take me to the hospital to see Poppy?" I don't know why I asked. I knew he wouldn't let me walk there. There's something about his stance that told me he didn't have a choice, like maybe Jesus would take away some of his steps to heaven if he didn't and he'd have to jump a bit to get there.

"Yes, of course."

CHAPTER 4

HENSLEY GROVE'S URBAN LEGEND AND THE MYSTERIOUS SUITCASE

So that's where I am now, sitting by Poppy with six inches of makeup I'd doused on my face along the ride. He doesn't look like the usual jovial man I know. His gray hair is mussed and sticking up on top and his wrinkly face looks pale, almost gray. He's tall, and his skinny legs end with pale feet sticking out of the sheets at the far end of the bed.

"Did you scratch your face?" Poppy asks me twice before I come up with a lie. I'm usually quicker with fibs.

"Yeah, I slipped on the concrete in the rain, hit the car door with my face."

"Did I hear you were at the police station?"

"Me?" I screw up my face like the idea is preposterous. "What would I be doing at the police station?" I laugh a little too heartily and note that Poppy is giving me a suspicious gaze. He smiles at Mia who is almost asleep with her head resting on my shoulder. She yawns in return. "I've got car problems. Gil is just being, well, Gil."

He tells Gil to go for a walk, take a break because I'm here. Gil hesitates, but Colt nudges him, tells him he needs a coffee. We watch their shadows fade on the cold linoleum floor of the hallway, then Poppy snatches up my hand.

"You know how hard it is for an old man to be treated like a child by his kids?" Poppy grunts at me.

"Well, no," I laugh quietly. "But I'll say *yes* just to dig my elbows into Gil."

"I didn't take my meds. He was right," Poppy divulges quickly. "Listen, I don't have a whole lot of time—"

My eyes widen. He says it like he's dying and my heart makes twenty flip-flops inside my chest. But he screws up his eyes and gives me a warning glare. "I'm not dying, Raeanna. Jeez-o-Pete, how old do you think I am?" *Jeez-o-Pete*. It's a classic Poppy saying. He has a million of them he uses instead of cursing.

"I'd wager you're about, let's say, a hundred and fifty?" I make a questioning face and shrug, then I bob my head up and down with a teasing smile. "Oh, you didn't really want me to answer that."

Poppy makes a big deal of rolling his eyes. "I'm not dying. Gil was right. I didn't take my pills. But it was an emergency. You can keep a secret. I know you can. Out of all my kids, you're the one that bottles everything up the most—tears, troubles, love."

"If you're trying to flatter me to boost my self-esteem, you're going about it the wrong way. I don't bottle up love," I argue. "I just dole it out in small increments."

"Well, yeah, you do. For years, I've been trying to get you to stop. But now, I'm kind of glad I didn't."

"Really?" I ask him with a little shock in my eyes.

"No, not really. What kind of dad would I be if I wanted you to bottle things up? But I do need your help, sweetie. And it is a big, big secret."

"Here." He thrusts yesterday's newspaper at me. It's folded in half and I scan down the articles to where Poppy's old fingers are jabbing. "Read this. Out loud."

I eye him carefully while he scoots up in the bed. I lug Mia up on my hip, realize she's fast asleep in my almost-numb right arm from holding her. "*Famed Dancer to Visit Local College*," I read the title, then slip to the article. "Celebrated ballet dancer Adrien Moreau, of Academy of The Dance with the Conciergerie Ballet Company, will be an honored guest instructor for two weeks—" I stop, nibble my lip, and squirm in my seat. "Poppy, my days of ballet dancing are long gone. Did Anna give you this? She needs to pack up the dream I'm going to be reborn as a dancer. I'm a different kind of artist now and—"

"No, no, sweetie." He rolls his eyes, pokes his finger in the air. "Not that. Go down farther to the picture."

I wave the paper in the air because it is crimped and I'm one-handed with Mia in my arms. "Move over a little. I've got to sit down. My arm is asleep from holding her."

I push myself up on the side so I'm sitting next to him. I take in the picture of what appears to be a brick wall of the rundown back side of the old Cannon Bread Mill and the hillside behind it running into the Rocky Fork Creek. There is also the back of a female police officer with her arms akimbo standing on the broken asphalt of an old parking lot above the water. Even though her gun belt and protective Kevlar vest hidden beneath her shirt give her bulk, she still isn't much bigger than my five feet and six inches. She's tiny and has her brown hair cut short like a man's.

"I know her. She goes to your church, doesn't she? What's her name?"

"Her name is Chloe Murphy. She just got moved up to a conditional detective position at the Hensley Grove Police Department. Ben James retired and they are trying her out. Anna sings with her in the choir at Holy Trinity. She's a nice young lady and you would know that if you went to church with us more often. Please, just read the article before your brother comes back."

My brother. Poppy never slips *foster* in front of any of his family's names when it comes to me. As far as he's concerned, he raised me. I'm his kid. I appreciate that, but it catches me off-guard. I've got a family out there somewhere and it feels strange sometimes feeling like I belong to his family with all their flawless, perfect lives to my broken one. They are so different from me.

I sigh. "*Shedding New Light on an Old Mystery*," I read the title slowly. "Oh, no, not this again," I mutter, look up and catch Poppy's eyes. He just gives me a solemn bob of his head.

"Yes, Chloe gave us a heads up so it wasn't such a shock when it came out again," Poppy says softly. "I'm sure you heard the news. There was a murdered girl found along the creek bank just below the train trestle. Well, they believe it was a girl. They said the body got caught in the slats of the trestle and got hit by all three trains coming through after midnight. There wasn't much left of her. It was on all the local stations just yesterday."

"No," I mutter. "Who was it?" I get this funny sinking feeling in my chest. I think of Delia crying at the police station. She and Hannah weren't at the show tonight. No, surely it couldn't be Hannah.

"They haven't released the name yet," Poppy replies. "But every time there is a homicide, they drudge the other four murdered girls up and try to tie them all in together. Then your daddy's name starts coming up."

"Well, I haven't seen my daddy. And he's like seventy -eight. I don't think he could outrun a girl even half his age," I tell him. I can feel the hair rise on my arms in irritation. It is mixed with the muddy awareness that Hannah Lafferty might be dead. I remember sitting in the back of my daddy's car when he took me for rides. He hung things from his rearview mirror like little prisms and chains with charms and they would shine. I thought he was magic. "So they can't pull him in this time. It's a bunch of bullcrap because the cops can't solve the cold cases here. My dad, he's a lot of things. But he isn't a murderer."

Not everyone agrees with me. Every town has an urban legend, a twisted tale sewn together like a spider's web and whispered behind closed palm from one person to the next. Hensley Grove isn't any different. Once in a while when there is a lull in the usual high-end gossip, our little piece of lore gets drudged up from the muck where it had settled since the last time it was big news. Most people could either choose to roll eyes at the legend or gobble it up. I don't have that luxury. I'm tangled into the legend. I'm not quite the spider that weaved the web, but I was certainly spawned by him and forever, I know, I'm trapped there and dragged along with him.

The whole messy web started back twenty-four years ago. It was November fifth and an early winter storm had pushed through southern Kentucky. A single engine plane heading for Nashville crashed into the already-crumbling stone bridge over the Rocky Fork Creek on Black Street, between High Street and Second, and sunk into the murky depths of the creek. There were supposedly four men on board. At least that's what the airport attendant reported had boarded the plane. Only one body was found miles away where the fork of our creek dumped into the bigger Cumberland River. It was a man that had been hired through a temporary job agency as a security guard two days earlier. What he was guarding, no one knew. The rest of those on board, they assumed, were all killed, sucked into the flood-level waters that eventually led to the Cumberland River. Three days of searching brought up nothing but one small empty overnight suitcase and one duffel bag of men's clothing.

But that's where I come in to the picture, or at least my dad does. The wreck happened three blocks from an apartment my dad was sharing with a friend. He was one of the first at the scene. Three bystanders attested to seeing a mid-size man with bushy, black hair and a round face standing within the yellow plastic tape they used to cordon off the accident area and looking into the water. He had a slight limp to his right leg while he eased around the cordoned off area and a scar on his right cheek. Both of those injuries my daddy had received in a motorcycle wreck in his teens. Two observed him leaning over and then, carrying off a bag from the wreckage that night. A bag. The family of the pilot stated that he had been awakened at one in the morning and was offered a substantial amount of cash to fly the plane. As the rumor progressed from town to town, the amount also grew to be as high as a million dollars.

So, my daddy's been in jail for breaking and entering more times than I can count on my right hand. Everybody thinks he took the money from the plane wreck. So, when anything criminal comes up like the death of young women when he was around, he's about the only criminal who spent hard time in prison, everyone assumes he had something to do with the murders.

Nevertheless, there is one nice thing about growing up in a town where everyone knows everyone else. Even though it is whispered around every dining room table about these little skeletons in my closet, nobody says them aloud or to outsiders. I am one of their own, regardless of my sordid hereditary. And it is too easy in a small town to trace the path of the gossip and find out who has said it.

"Poppy, he didn't steal the money. I honestly think the butthead pilot bailed out a few hundred feet above and just left whoever was on board to crash and burn. That was a theory, you know." I know. Because I've looked into the plane wreck myself just out of curiosity, and maybe to clear my name from that web. Most people don't know it, but it has become somewhat of a closet obsession with me.

"Oh for God's sakes, Raeanna," Poppy grunts. He isn't one to hold back. "They saw your dad leave the scene with a bag. The last time he got out of jail, he completely disappeared. That was three years ago. He's probably on some Caribbean Island spending the money. But just read the rest, would you?"

"You know that offends me," I sniff at one of Poppy's favorite sayings. "You always tell me that the apple doesn't fall far from the tree. Are you saying I'm going to be a criminal too?" He's always muttering it under his breath when I tell him something stupid Kevin has done. Kevin's dad hung out with my dad. They both got caught breaking into a house on High Street ten years ago. He figures Kevin's going to head that direction too.

"And that offends me, young lady," Poppy snaps back. "I may not have sired you, but I raised you. You're from *my* apple tree. Even if you're a lemon some days with that sassy attitude."

"Sassy and sired." I roll my eyes. "Really, Poppy? I'm not an animal and people don't use those words in this century."

"Would you rather have me say you didn't come from my loins?" Poppy grunted sarcastically.

"Ew, my gosh, that's disgusting. You don't have get so mad at me, Poppy." I feign a whine, give him one of my classic disgruntled glares complete with eye roll and head waggle. Then I grumble, turn my attention back to the article. "It says: *Standing on the brink of being a ghost town since the Cannon Mill shut down eight years ago, the population of the town of Hensley Grove, Kentucky appears to be dwindling. However, the crime rate is what concerns many who live there. It is on the rise. It equals* that of cities ten times its size. Quaint and peaceful on the surface, Hensley Grove holds some dark secrets in its past. On a chilly November night of 1992, a plane crash in the Rocky Fork Creek left federal agents baffled when only one body was found weeks later in the Cumberland River. The plane was thought to have been carrying a large sum of money that was never uncovered. Added to this mystery, over the span of less than sixty years, four young women have been found murdered within the boundaries of the town. Long thought to be the work of one person, the serial killer was never found. Never have the two been tied together. But one unseasoned, but ambitious, young woman wants to look at the case with a new set of eyes and perhaps bring some of the town's sordid history to a close. She's Hensley Grove's newest detective on the oldest town cold cases. But this small town cop has big town ideas when it comes to solving the cases and making the streets of this small town safe once again. Detective Chloe Murphy is planning on spending many hours working on this case whether it is at her home office or on the job at the Hensley Grove Police Department. However, some new discoveries found during the demolition of two Cannon Mill outbuildings along the waterfront are tossing some new clues into the puzzle. Whether they just add to the mystery or shed new light on a series of murders, only time will tell. At first thought to be a mass burial of animals from the local dog pound, bones unearthed along the waterfront are now thought to be human remains—blah, blah, blah." I finish and turn my head to Poppy. "And the point to me reading you this is—?"

"You need to tell the police if your daddy comes knocking at your door," Poppy drops his voice, looks around as if anybody else was in the room. "And you need to make it clear you don't know where that money is and never have known if the police start asking questions again." He reaches up the arm with the IV and pushes his hand to his head. "Raeanna, you need to be careful. Don't walk outside by yourself, don't—"

"Poppy, I'm not scared. I can take care of myself." I sit up, turn to stare at him hard and long. He looks scared and I don't know why. I think of my real daddy and all's I can conjure up right then is the memory of the dank, dark cabin we lived within outside town for as long as I can remember. The smell of wood smoke and lantern oil makes me shudder still. I don't remember much, but I remember always feeling scared there because we were so alone. Not so anymore. I watch Poppy's shaky hand come out and latch on to my own.

"Please, Raeanna," he says softly. "Just once, listen to me. Don't—don't be like—"

"Okay," I interrupt him. I know he won't say it aloud and I know he will just stop there, let the words sit in the air like hot tar melting on asphalt. He wants to say *your mama and daddy*. I sit there, stare at him hard. I've got a daddy who spends most his time in prison and a mama who abandoned me. Everybody knows that part of me and I know when they look at me, they think whatever made my parents do what they did is genetic. I'm not to be trusted. Sooner or later, I'm going to explode into some big ball of crazy and abandon Mia, rob a bank, and kill somebody.

"Just lay low for a while, take those summer dance classes you promised you'd make up so you can finish your degree. Maybe you can meet that Mister Moreau in the paper. It would make Anna happy."

I stare at him hard. Finish my degree? A pang of irritation creeps up my spine. My classes would be finished if the dance instructor, Shane Delgado, wasn't such an ass. I feel my heart drop, while my gaze does the same thing toward the floor. He doesn't trust me. Nobody trusts me. Still, I don't say anything. I just let it bang off me like the angry wasps banged into me last week when I stood under their nest. It's easier.

"Poppy, me and the dance instructor don't get along," I tell him. "I may never finish my performing arts degree. That's why I went into visual arts."

"Sweetie, sometimes you've just got to—what are the words you kids use nowadays? Oh, yeah, suck it up."

"Suck it up." Yeah, that was pretty much what I was doing four years ago on my knees in front of Shane that got me into that mess so I couldn't finish my classes. "I know Anna wants me to finish what I started. I get that. But, Poppy, it isn't just getting from start to finish like a race. It is more like I was sculpting a figure and it shattered into a thousand pieces partway through. I can't finish it. I can't find all the pieces. It can't be fixed."

"Nothing broken can't be fixed," Poppy gives my hand a little squeeze, lets his eyes slip toward a sleeping Mia. "Shane Delgado is just more sensitive than most. You hurt his feelings. He had a lot of dreams invested in you—

"Oh, my God, Poppy!" I groan. "You always make it sound like I broke everybody's dreams."

"I'm sorry, hon. I didn't mean it that way. Just—just give him some respect. He'll come around." He makes me feel guilty and I pull away, roll my eyes. He doesn't try to stop me. He just smiles. "Please fix it. Finishing your degree will open up a whole new world for you. Two dance classes, that's it, right? Then you're finished?"

"Yeah, I guess." I swing my legs around again so I'm lounging beside him. Mia is sucking hard on her thumb and makes a soft coo when I shift. We both stare at her, then share a smile.

"Except for those sky blue eyes, she looks just like you," Poppy says softly, patting her head. "Oh, by the way, I need you to run up to Gil's attic and check for an old suitcase for me." Poppy says it so casually, later on I will contemplate if my world as I knew it took a direct hit-twist in the opposite direction it was heading because of the low-key appearance of his request, or simply because I did as he asked. "It's called a Tringle Double Case and it has a little gold emblem on the front that says *Tringle*."

"Can't Gil get it for you?" I give him a questioning gaze. Gil's house used to be Poppy and Anna's house. They moved farther outside town so Anna could garden and now they rent the house to Gil. I know they still store some of their stuff in the attic and the garage.

"Well, I'd rather this suitcase thing is our little secret for now. Put it somewhere safe in your house. Just tell him you're digging out some old pictures for an anniversary present I'm giving Anna. Tell him you're using them to paint some kind of picture."

"Yeah, sure," I say softly, yawn. I'm trying not to speculate what is inside the suitcases. Old porn magazines he doesn't want Anna to know he owns? I start to give him back his newspaper and hear Gil's murmurs slipping up the darkened hallway.

"Rae, don't tell anybody about the suitcases, alright?"

I open my mouth to speak, I don't get to reply, just solemnly and silently bob my head up and down.

"What are you doing laying down in bed," Gil utters, coming around the corner, a small Styrofoam cup of coffee in his hand with a mist of steam slipping over the cuffed border. "You're weird. You're not planning on camping out here. They won't let you stay especially with the kid."

"I was just reading him the newspaper, idiot," I

retort, pushing myself up with one elbow so I didn't awaken Mia.

"I suppose she told you she got kicked out of her apartment," Gil rolls his eyes. "He doesn't have any money with him, so don't ask for any."

"You got kicked out of your apartment?"

I wanted to kill Gil right then. He acted surprised like he thought I'd been blubbering to Poppy about my problems.

"Oh, come on, Tangolandish, you really didn't know Kevin had been screwing around with Sophie Wells for the last ten months? Everybody knew that. Everybody." Gil plops down in the vinyl chair again, waves his hand at Colt. I'm waiting for his friend to start in on making fun of me. Oh, what the hell. They always thought it was something of a game—big tomcat catches the little mouse and they all bat it around.

"Gilbert Baldwin, do not use that kind of language around a young lady," Poppy reprimands him. Then he turns to me. "You broke up with Kevin? I'm sorry, honey."

"I don't see any ladies around here," Gil mutters beneath his breath.

"Quit being a shit, Gil. I've had a cruddy day." I push off the bed, wiggle Mia around and stand up straight. "Poppy, I'm leaving," I say. "You need sleep. I'll stop by before work tomorrow and bring you a hot chocolate. Text me about that um, painting."

He bobs his head up and down, smiles softly at me. "And you don't go out after dark and lock your doors."

CHAPTER 5

HOW TO TICK OFF THE CHIEF OF POLICE

"You afraid you're going to get your hair wet, pretty boy?" I am rolling my eyes at Colt who is jog-walking after me down the wet hospital sidewalk. The parking lot lights make a mess of the shadows and for a moment, there are two of him. His feet are splashing in the puddles and he is carrying a black umbrella over his head. I think of Poppy. It isn't because of Colt. It's because whenever I screw up (and I do it often), he tells me I'll look back on it someday and laugh. It's another one of his classic Poppy sayings that he thinks will have a profound effect on me. And right now, I'm bent against this new onslaught of what I will hopefully and fondly one day call Biggest Screw up Day Ever. I'm juggling the heel to my shoe in my left hand and trying to adjust the step on my right foot where the heel should be. The wind is kicking in and the lightning is sparking above my head. Mia's tucked into my chest and sniffling a gooey green snot on my dress.

"Uh oh, got some of those fair tendrils wet, princess?" I ask him, reach up and try to wiggle my hand in his hair. He's a bit too tall and I miss and nearly cuff his cheek.

"I brought the umbrella for you and your little girl," he says flatly, gives me a scathing twist of his lips. Funny thing, even when he tries to come off as being sarcastic, he just looks that much prettier.

"Oh." I feel kind of stupid when he shoves it in my hands.

"Gil said you can crash at his house tonight. I told him about your car and your boyfriend."

"Why does everybody keep calling Kevin my boyfriend? It's ex-boyfriend. And gee, thanks, God Squad," I return blandly. "Because I wanted Gil to have more ammunition to shoot at me."

"Gil cares about you," Colt tells me with a shrug. "Where else are you going to go this late? It's—" he lifts his arm, looks at a watch on his wrist. "Wow, it's midnight."

"*Wow*." I shake my head. "You really use that word?"

He doesn't get to answer. Gil pulls his car up to the curb next to us, rolls down his passenger side window. "You and Mia can't walk with some creep slinking around this town—"

I jab a thumb at Colt. "That's no way to talk about your friends."

"Tango, you know what I mean," Gil gives Colt a half-slant eye roll to let the other man know he doesn't agree with my smear of his meaning. "And you can't sleep in your car tonight, Tango," he calls out. "Not outside the apartment with your crazy boyfriend inside. Hell, for all you know, he murdered that girl." He twists his head around, peers upward at me. "You do know that some girl's body was found out at the tracks, don't you? She's dead."

"He's my ex-boyfriend," I retort. "And I think the general consensus at the apartment complex is that the nickname Crazy Bitch has already been taken by me. It was written on my car. Maybe it was me who murdered her."

"Yeah, whatever." Gil nods his head like he doesn't care. "But I'd be careful who you tell that to considering the source. Just crash at my place. It's late. If I leave you out in the storm, Dad will kill me."

~

"Mama, I love you," Mia's soft voice is curtailed only by a yawn and a cupped hand to her lips an hour later. We'd just settled down into the bedroom that was mine when the house was

Poppy's, staring at the ceiling. She's tucked into my arm and we're listening to the rain on the roof above our bed. It's two in the morning. The room is a pretty color of pale green with a fluffy, flowery green comforter and a lime green lamp and lampshade on the olive bed stand to my right. Anna basked my room in pretty frills and ballet dancers. It has become Gil's guest bedroom, but remains the same. There's stencil dancers along the tops of the walls and framed paintings of tiny girl dancers all around the room. There's three walking up the wall of me posed and lacing my ballet shoes when I was seven, then ten, and fifteen. And she still has a little roll of athletic tape and a box of Band-Aids on my bed stand I used to wrap my feet in every night to help my bubble blisters heal. It only stands to remind me of regrets of my past. I try to close my eyes and not think about them. But I blink, look down at my toes sticking out of the blankets and the blisters, corns and bunions on my ugly dancer feet won't let me.

"I love you, too, baby." I tear my eyes away and reach out, roll my hand across her fine hair. My heart aches that she has been getting dumped at somebody's house I hardly know. She started crying in the car on the way to Gil's. From what I can piece together, Kevin told her it was a secret staying with Kelsey. She couldn't tell me. I'd wondered why she was so quiet when Kelsey shoved her into my arms.

I swear to myself I'll never get another boyfriend. They just seem to get in the way. Maybe this is a sign, a warning. Maybe the next boyfriend will leave Mia sitting next to a pool by herself or something. I shudder, then watch her eyes close and a soft smile curves her lips. I can't sleep, though. It's nothing new. Night is when the bad things start slipping into my head. Unpaid bills and daddy's fist. The swimming pool with Mia's tiny hands slowly sinking from the surface. Kevin and Sophie's wide eyes when I walked through the apartment door. And not being the prima ballerina of Anna's dreams. I close my eyes, think of different things like Poppy taught me to do, try to push the cruddy day away.

It's difficult. I just go over the shitty events of the day over and over and wish I could toss and turn but can't because Mia's shoved into the cleft of my arm. I pause momentarily to try and find any part of it I can use to wipe out the bad. I recall Gil and Colt jumping into the garbage dumpster behind the Hensley Grove Town Gallery to salvage the sopping remains of my art projects. They held them up. I didn't think I could rescue them. My mama's image was distorted to the point she looked like she was wearing a long, black gown. Yet, I couldn't tell the two men that watching them standing waist deep in spaghetti and half-eaten hamburgers from the food court.

My phone dings and I lean to the right, grab it off the bed stand before it wakes Mia. I see the picture of Sophie pop up. I stare at the picture. Sophie is pudgy and pretty with long, bleach blonde hair and thick eyelashes. She's doing a funny wave at me with a peace sign. In the background, Kevin is photo bombing her with his middle finger raised. I snuffle sarcastically to myself. Why didn't I see that coming? They both got along a little too well. They were both too pretty for me, this little dark thing that is always hunched over a drawing with ugly calloused toes, too backwards to say the right thing at the right time.

I'm sorry. Please don't hate us. It was a momentary lapse of judgement. Sophie's text message says. *We got drunk watching the game—*

How do you answer that? If you're emotionally broke like me, you feel the normal humiliation and infuriation, but you start to tap in an: *I'll think about it.* Because I know they are the only ones in the world that understand me, that know most of the scars, that put up with the awkwardness and anger issues and inability to know how to love the way normal people love—then all of it is wiped away by the sound of knuckles to the bedroom door.

"Tango." It is Gil whose voice interrupts my self-destruction. He sounds grumpy and tired while his words cut through the silence. "The cops are outside. They need to talk to you."

Just as quickly as Gil speaks, my worries dissipate like condensation from a boiling pot of water vanishes toward the ceiling and are replaced with a whole new set of uncertainties and doubts.

"The—the cops?" I stutter. God, it is past one in the morning. My cruddy day couldn't possibly merge with the next, could it? The door opens a crack and I see Gil lit up from the hallway. He's got on brown pajama pants with little horses on them and his feet are bare. "Please hurry, their lights are illuminating the entire street."

I sit up in bed slowly, gingerly slide a sweating and sleeping Mia out from beneath my arm. Gil just gives me this irritated gaze, backs up while I push through the door in my almost-dry shorts and a tank top.

They think at first I'm lying about the image I drew for the girl at the police station.

"Is this a joke?" A cop, with a bulbous nose and plastic over his Smoky Bear hat to deter the rain, asks me. I recognize him from high school. His name is Gabe Reynolds. He's short and chubby-buff. He used to be on the football team, but I think he spent most of his time on the bench flexing his muscles for the freshman girls. He has chicken leg arms—kind of thick toward his shoulder and skinny toward the forearm until they end in tiny hands. He is using one of those tiny hands to hold up the picture of the man I drew for the girl at the police station. "You can get in a lot of trouble for this, Raeanna. I remember the crap you used to pull in high school. You're not in high school anymore. There are people's reputations at stake, good people."

"Why'd you draw this?" She's the skinny cop on the front page of the newspaper Poppy showed me. Her narrowed, suspicious gaze settles on me. Her name is Chloe Murphy. She could pass as a boy with her short brown hair cut just above the ears and her masculine stance, legs splayed and arms folded across her chest. She goes to Poppy's church, Holy Trinity, and volunteers at the food pantry with him on Wednesdays. I'd call her elusive just because she seems like some kind of loner. I never see Chloe hanging out with anybody. She's always by herself. "Just tell us this was a joke and we'll forget the entire thing," Chloe barks at me flatly. "I got feelers out on you and they say you're a bit of a wildcard, Baldwin. You're a stray pup just waiting to pee on the carpet when the new owner isn't looking. Just tell us the truth. We'll let everybody know it was a joke. But if you don't, there are going to be consequences. Big ones." Her radio burps loudly before I can answer. It is strapped to her scrawny shoulder and she holds up a finger and steps down Gil's walkway to the sidewalk along the street.

"It wasn't a joke," I mumble to Gabe who is watching his partner walk away and not appearing to listen to me. "I just drew the dude exactly as Delia Childs described him. I could hear her from the other room. I could see what the artist was drawing and it didn't look anything like what she was describing." I look behind me into Gil's house. His girlfriend, Layla, is peering at me from behind the couch. Colt was sleeping on the couch, but he is now sitting on the armrest closest to the doorway in a pair of Gil's borrowed pajama pants and a white t-shirt. He's rubbing the early morning stubble with his fingers.

"Tango, that's Chris Peirce," Layla says while my eyes pause on her. "Taylor Peirce's father. Her sandy-colored hair is in ringlets on her neck and she's got the biggest boobs I've ever seen on a woman. I make an effort not to talk to them like everybody else does. She's pudgy, short, and her voice is soft and melodious. Eyes. I look at her eyes. They are brown, maybe? I don't know. They are lost to the shadows. So I focus on her voice. It is almost like the velvety sound of an organ playing inside a closed church while you stand outside. It matches her sweet and wholesome demeanor. "He's the chief of police." She should know, she's an administrative office manager for the city.

"What can I say? Then it was him." I shrug. Gil is shaking his head next to me. I see Colt look up, catch his gaze. There's something short of an eye roll between them.

"Maybe you saw him when you went into the police station. Or maybe Delia got interviewed by him," Colt suggests with a toss of his hands. It's kind of haughty. I roll my eyes at him. He really, really annoys me and almost as much as Gil irritates me.

Just as I turn back to Gabe, his female counterpart comes marching back up and waving her hand at me.

"Alright," Chloe says. "You and your husband, you've got to go with us."

"Husband?" I laugh sarcastically. "There isn't anybody that could ever fill those shoes. But, if you're talking about my boyfriend. He's an ex-boyfriend. If you put me in the same room with him, I'll rip his eyes out, latch on to his balls, and pull them up until they are wrapped around his neck. And then you're going to have to arrest me because I'll strangle him with them." I look at Chloe for support. I get nothing but a flat-line gaze.

"Damn," Gabe says. "That's cold."

"Listen, I'm just saying." I latch on to his eyes because he seems at least slightly supportive. "I caught him with another girl. The knife he stuck in my back is still in there, the wound hasn't healed yet." I sigh. "It doesn't matter. He wasn't anywhere near me tonight. He isn't involved."

"He wasn't with you at the station?"

"No, that was—" I stop, almost jab a thumb behind me at Colt. Then I veer, fake-rub a tickle on my nose. I'm thinking they are going to take me back behind some bar and beat me with a baseball bat or something to cover up for their boss. Dead. No use dragging Gil's buddy into this with me. "I was by myself."

"No, it says here you were with a gentleman with dark hair, blue eyes—"

"Nope. That wasn't me," I insist.

"It was me."

Everybody's eyes turn back to Colt who is standing up and trudging across the room. He looks pale. Maybe he knows we're both going to be murdered behind a bar.

"No, it wasn't you," I lie, turn around and wave a hand at him. "Don't lie."

But he goes past my hand and nods to Chloe. "It was me. I'll go. But is she under arrest? Where are we going?"

The two cops look at each other. Their faces are doused in blue, then red from the police lights. "We can't tell you. It is—confidential."

CHAPTER 6

DANGLING 100 FEET IN THE AIR

"Tell them the sketch you did was a joke or I swear to God, I'll jump."

It is only confidential because Delia Childs is Chief Peirce's daughter's friend. Or, they are trying to murder me. I'm not quite sure which one it is yet. I am standing a hundred feet up on the rusted metal walkway high atop the old Hensley Grove water tower. I can hear the gritty paint and bits of rust crackle beneath a pair of two-sizes-too-big tennis shoes I borrowed from Gil's girlfriend. Colt and I are roped together. I know this couldn't be proper procedure sending two completely untrained bystanders to the top of a damaged water tower and quite possibly, to their death.

I have to guess that something the south side of this town lacks isn't just ample police patrol as my old neighbor, Missus Finch, complains heartily on Friday nights. It is also a guidebook on the proper techniques of saving lives and perhaps *not* using civilians in a dangerous manner to do so. Then again, I'm wondering if the two officers below are perhaps just setting us up so it looks like we fell as payback for my drawing of their boss as a prime suspect for some robbery or murder.

However, I'm not so worried about me. Colt's usually tan face is a funky shade of olive green and with every deliberately sluggish and awkward step up the rusty ladder, he looks down and says: *Aw, man, I think I'm going to throw up.* And Delia Childs, who is threatening me, is perched precariously on her rear on a rickety metal maintenance catwalk jutting three feet out from the walkway that goes around the entire tower. It is better suited for the occasional pigeons that have pooped all over the water tower and not an angry, hundred and twenty pound girl who appears to be way past drunk while she wavers back and forth in the shadows.

I blink at her, but my head turns to the shadows below me and toward Colt just as he makes it to the top of the ladder. "Hey," I call to him softly. I am already two steps along on the walkway. There's no place for me to latch my carabiner this time because the railing is rusted away and dangling mostly-detached and outward at this point. So I tell Colt to latch his to the top step. "And if she lets me get to the walkway," I tell him trying to say it quietly enough Delia can't hear. "Unlatch yours and try to stay close."

"And we won't be attached to—anything?"

"Well, yes and no." I shrug. "What do you want from me? I don't know. I left my book on *Rope Climbing and Saving Crazy People* at home. I'm flying on my own with this. They told me to come up here and try to talk her down. I am the worst person to put in this position. She's been my archenemy since like our fourth grade ballet class. It is like sending in a superhero to save the bad guy."

"Or the other way around?" Colt utters.

"What the hell?" I gripe, shaking my head. "Regardless, they've got guns. I don't. What's a girl to do? Besides, the last time I was up here, there was a railing." I point upward, jab a thumb to the huge painting of a green alien standing over a futuristic idea of what Hensley Grove will look like in a hundred years. On one street, there's a huge X to denote the next key in my follower's treasure hunt. Last time I checked on my social network page, I had eighty-nine. That's not bad for a town with a population of less than five-thousand.

He chews on this a minute. I guess he figures out I

did the graffiti. I probably should think it is funny that the cops below me don't know and the same two with their arms crossed one-hundred feet from me right now spent the better half of two hours cursing and chasing me down the night I painted it. They still don't know *that graffiti bastard* was me. "And don't tell anybody it was me," I add. "I'll deny it. But there's a railing on the little deck Delia's sitting on. Latch on to the rail if there's an emergency."

"I don't like heights."

"Really," I snap sarcastically, give him an eye roll. "I wouldn't have figured that, God Squad. You look so self-possessed right now with your legs shaking so badly they are rattling the entire water tower."

"You don't have to be so caustic, Tango. I just can't go any farther. But I can help you talk to her."

"How about if I just tell her not to jump. That's a no-brainer."

"No, just talk to her. Ask her stuff. Tell her you've had a crappy day too. Let her know she's not alone."

I stare at him. Colt may have been clinging to the stairway with a look of utter horror on his pale, pursed lips. But there is something in the way he nods to me, something in his eyes making me believe he is being truthful.

"Okay."

"Is that you?" I hear from the little catwalk. It looks like a rickety gangplank off a pirate ghost ship with metal bars all the way to the end. I'm about twenty steps away from her. I take five which is where I have to stop because the rope between Colt and I pulls stiff. I look down, he is clinging to the carabiner latched to the banister of the stairway like it is an umbrella in the middle of a monsoon.

"Well, look who it is—Whiskey Tango." She is sitting with her legs dangling on the catwalk, her hand lazily settled on the railing. "I got to say, I figured they couldn't talk you into coming up here. Did they threaten you with a gun or a baton? Oh, no, I know what. Did they offer you, a coupon for one free handful of the pot in their evidence locker?"

I grit my teeth against her spiteful words. I can see the city all lit up with little twinkling lights behind Delia. It's pretty and cozy and a stark contrast to the uneasy mood here. The wind is blowing. I can't think of anything to say. My words seem to fade as soon as I say them. There isn't anything to stop them. One step to my left and I'm standing on air. "So that's all I have to do to get you down from here, sign a paper saying I sketched the police chief as your suspect and it was a joke? Because you know how that's going to end for me. I'm going to look like an idiot or get arrested or both."

She sniffs a laugh. "You already look like an idiot, Tango. Everybody's sick of your stupid, high school pranks and big mouth. You don't need help from me getting there." Then she shifts and wavers. "You shouldn't have done that to me. It was mean. Hannah Lafferty's dead, you know that, right? She's all dead and—dead. You put that picture in my head and I really thought you were being truthful." She's got a bottle of something that looks like rum in her hand and the sweet scent slips up between us. "And do you know who you drew? Taylor's dad. What the hell?" Sweat breaks out on my forehead. She's dead drunk.

"Listen, I just drew what you described." I blink in the darkness. I'm a little shaken about Hannah. I figured it was her, but hearing it was different.

"You don't think if it was him that I saw with Hannah, I wouldn't have just said it was him?"

I am afraid to say something wrong, terrified. Oh, I feel my face flush, my heart do a little double-step. I watch her chin drop, see her eyes close slightly. That wasn't what she was hoping I would say. It isn't a good sign.

"I don't know. I didn't think it looked like him."

"I thought maybe you'd seen—seen Hannah with him. I thought maybe he was really the man who—who did that to her." She sounds almost distraught like suddenly we didn't share something she wanted so badly to share with somebody else. Or maybe, she's just lying to save her butt.

"No," I mutter. I remembered what Colt told me to do and I look down at him. He is fumbling with the carabiner like he is trying to either work up the courage to release it and come up, or practice taking it off so he can run like hell back down that ladder.

"Listen, Delia, the reason I was in the police station was that I had a shitty day, too, you know? I mean, my best friend didn't get murdered—" I try to take a step forward, but the rope between me and Colt stops me. I don't want to say murdered. I just stop. "You know. But I had some paintings in Neil Wright's art show and nobody came to see them. I went home, caught my boyfriend screwing one of the girls I wait tables with at the diner."

"Oh, my God, shut up. Isn't that just another day for any of you poor white trash living on the south side? Everybody knew Kevin was screwing Sophie Wells since Halloween last year. They showed up at party at the bar dressed like Adam and Eve and she had on nothing but three leaves. What part of him trying to take the leaves off her with his teeth all night did you not get?"

"I wasn't there. Mia had an earache—"

"So do you want me to drag it out and explain to you why you don't have a boyfriend or should we just let it rest in the air there?" she spits. "Listen, I got enough problems. I don't need some loser dishing out more on my plate." In the moonlight, I see her throw her head back, close her eyes tightly shut. The rum bottle, she holds up in the air toward me. "Or maybe you want to trade me places, drown your problems? Because if there's a competition on which one of us is the biggest loser, I think it is you."

She must like this free ride on dishing all her hatred at me. I can't fight back. I just stand there thinking we'd all be better off if I just walked across and gave her a little shove with my hands, hurried the whole process up a bit. Then, just make my way down the ladder and leave. But the image of Anna and Poppy with shamed faces reading in the Hensley Grove Tribune tomorrow that I made the cowardly move of stepping back down the ladder thirty seconds before Delia's body was tossed toward the ground keeps my feet steady. I see her lean slightly to the right. I follow her gaze toward the ladder.

"Who is that?"

"Just the poor dude that got stuck coming here because he was picking me up—" *at the jail*. I don't add the last part. I just stop there. "Poppy had a seizure and was in the hospital. His name's Colt. Don't ask him to wave. He's clinging to the ladder like it's a nice set of tits."

"Colt?" She laughs a little. I push the hair back from my face. "Oh, I know Colt," she says, her eyes making a lazy jog behind me. Then she says hello to him like she's just passing him on the street.

"So I'll sign the paper. Will you come down?" I ask her bluntly. "Please and thank you."

"Damn, will you cool it?" Delia hisses. "I'm trying to decide and you keep interrupting me. It's like blah, blah, blah with you, Tango. Just go away. You annoy me." As her words get more intense, I see her face starting to screw up like she's working up the courage to do something to make it all go away. I know I should say something, anything. I don't know what to say because I'm terrified this is the moment I should be having just the right words or she's going to jump. I can see it in the shift of her eyes like she's sizing up the length of time from catwalk to ground before she dies. I see it in the upward tip of her chin now like she is unwavering in making the plunge. My eyes veer desperately backward to Colt. He must have seen how wide they are. I am scared.

"Talk to her, Tango," I hear Colt tell me with a hint of desperation. I just nod numbly.

"I don't know what to say to you to stop you from jumping. I know I felt like crap tonight. Sometimes I feel like it would be easier to deal with things if I was dead. I mean, four years ago, I thought my life was over. I thought I'd screwed everything up getting pregnant. But my Poppy, he says that once you've hit that bottom, there's nowhere else to go but up."

I'm thinking maybe I can get closer to her. I turn, ask Colt to maybe unlatch his carabiner, but I notice he is already doing it and has taken a step to the walkway. I realize right then that my tummy has that excited tickle. I assume he has the same thing. But for me, it is good. It is an adventure. To Colt, I think it is like he is staring death in the face.

"Do you really consider what you're doing now better?" Delia's voice is cold, slices through me like a butter knife trying hard to dig into a tough steak. "I mean, what do you do, Tango?" she asks me. "You work at a diner for minimum wage and live in a dirty welfare apartment building. You had everything all of us wished for since we were old enough to walk and you tossed it out the window. Now, you're nothing, nobody. Well, except for that stupid little girl that's tied you down. Wow, we all saw that coming. You're a loser just like your druggy mom and your criminal dad. You're a washed up ballerina that's too old to start again, too young to quit."

It hurts. It's not fair. She knows all the buttons to push on me and she's banging them hard with her fist. I can't reply with the same amount of enthusiastic, hostile banter we usually toss back and forth. I just stand there feeling little, my eyes veering slowly back to Colt who is begging me with his eyes not to let loose on her. But obviously singing her a sweet lullaby isn't working.

"Well, okay, that's enough, Delia," I finally spout through gritted teeth. "You've had your free token to crap talk me tonight. You're holding me hostage here and my patience is about nil to none right now. Don't be stupid. I said I'd sign the paper. Let's go."

"Oh, okay," she says with a snotty air. "You know what? Hannah hated you more than I do. You know what I'm going to do for her? I'm going to punch that stupid nose of yours. Come on, Tango, let's fight it out. For Hannah."

"Are you insane?" I ask her and take a step back. "I'm not going to fight you, here or even down there." It is obviously the wrong thing to say because I hear Colt grunt his disapproval at the ladder. That's when Delia pushes herself to her feet. I watch her falter, then take a step left. Delia is trash talking me beneath her breath, waggle walking like a drunk duck toward me.

"Oh, shit," I whisper. "Delia, stop. Please." Then, my heart nearly jumps into my throat. I see her waver. I see Delia look down and then shake her head slightly.

"Oh, no-no-no. Don't look down," I whisper. Vertigo. She'd gotten up too quickly. She reaches out a hand as if to catch herself. She is going to die. There was nothing but air between herself and the little railing.

"Oh, Colt, you got to hook on to the railing." It is all I can whimper while I bolt toward Delia. It is a stupid, stupid move and I feel my rope snap hard between myself and the man behind me. He has no clue what I am seeing, Delia ready to lose her balance and fall.

I run. I just take off and run as fast as I can down the walkway. There are six steps of the ten that I have without any pull. Then there is one as the rope between Colt and I snap to a tautness. Then while I watch Delia lounge backward, her hands wildly waving in the air to shouts and screams way below, I leap like a drowning swimmer toward her. Three steps. My hands are waggling crazily in the air. My upper body makes it past the walkway. My legs bang off the metal and wood. I dive downward, feel one arm latch around between shoulder and neck and the other, around her waist. It is an oh-shit moment, the kind you realize that maybe the choice you just made was a stupid one because it is going to hurt like holy hell in a second, but it is too late to change while nothing but air lays between the ground and your head.

Still, I feel her body smash into my own. I feel my arms wrap around just beneath her armpits and my legs, I just circle her waist and hold on, and hope to God Colt remembers to latch the carabiner to the railing. Then, in the blackness, we silently fall downward.

CHAPTER 4

FALLING

"You didn't have to say that word."

I am dangling ninety feet above the ground. The rope swinging Delia and me back and forth like a pendulum has almost come to a standstill. I stared death in the face. I believe I have a right to curse. I feel Delia's fingernails ripping shreds into my shoulders. I think my spine is now in a thousand pieces from the jolt. And Colt Lucero has the audacity to reprimand me while he dangles upside-down six feet above me. So I flip him my middle finger. "Screw off, Lucero."

Okay, I said the *F*-word. Actually, I screamed it, drew it out to its fullest capacity right around the U, and let the CK lounge in the air for at least to the count of ten during the initial jolt when the rope stopped. Delia and I came to a complete standstill after going a hundred and fifty miles per hour downward. I think the jar to every bone in my body warranted some curse while we swing back and forth clinging together with every fiber in our bodies.

Apparently, Delia thinks his remark is funny and giggles. I think she is just drunk-happy. I don't know. Her breath reeks of rum. When the rope begins to lower slowly toward the ground, she starts to cry, then sob until my shoulder is wet with her tears. By the time my feet touch the earth again, she is hysterical and laying in a ball on the ground. Her mom is hugging her while I sit on the ground trying not to think how sore I'm going to be in the morning. Colt nearly cuffs me in the head with his feet. We have to wait for someone to come up and unhitch his carabiner, otherwise we would have dangled there forever.

"I think I broke me," I mumble.

"You are nuts, Tango. You are completely bat-crap crazy." Colt keeps telling me while we descend. I get as far away from him as I can once they unstrap me from the harness. It doesn't matter. Tara Whiting is an EMS and she ambushes us to make sure we aren't hurt. Colt takes off his shirt to expose this huge scuff mark between his shoulder blades. Tara's trying really hard to focus on the scrape and not the chiseled perfection of muscles on his shoulders and back. She's blinking wildly. And I've got to say, that boy might be lean, but he is damn near the most perfect paintable specimen I'd ever seen. I just want to mold a statue out of the perfectly sculpted body.

"Dang, bud, you can be my muse." I reach out, poke his shoulder with my finger. "You've got to let me Picasso you."

He laughs, looks up at me with a half-smile. "I don't—I don't know what that means."

"You inspire me. To paint you. You'd be a perfect model for—something."

"Yeah, that's not happening," Colt mutters, his smile drops instantly. He almost sounds insulted. Which, of course, offends me because it is like telling me I'm a poor artist.

"Your loss." I shrug his comment off. "I might be famous someday—"

"By illegally painting graffiti on government property?" he jabs a thumb toward the water tower. "The only thing that's going to do is get you arrested—again."

"Will you shut up?" I hiss. "And who are you to judge me? You're a freaking evangelist for the Abraham Wesley Outreach Program, Lucero. You don't think we've dealt with stupid religious fanatics before? You dumbasses are a dime a dozen trying to convert everybody in town because you think we're all poor and stupid," I yell at him. I watch him lean his head back and roll his hand through his hair nervously. Something about the way he does this makes me feel bad for him. He's lonely. I know that. He might fool everybody else, but I know he has no clue how to relate to people outside his rich boy norm. So I drop my voice, push my hands out to put a stop to the conversation. "Cease fire. Can you get the cops to give us a ride back to Gil's? I'm afraid Mia's going to wake up. She freaks out if I'm not there at night. And I've got to get to work in a few hours. I need some sleep."

The Tringle Double Case was a pair of leather suitcases made in 1949 that could be locked together. They were personally designed by a small company in Oxford, England for the exclusive use of the Demast Shipping Charters as a gift given to certain, affluent clientele who had chartered their ships for family use. There were only forty-two made.

I found this bit of information hardly pertinent when Poppy texted it to me at three in them morning: *Rae—don't forget to get the Tringle suitcase at the old house.* I wasn't going anywhere fast. As promised, I signed a formal statement declaring my stupidity that the picture I'd drawn was a bad joke and I was sorry. It was demeaning at best. It didn't help I was stuck leaning against the hood of the cop car while Colt sweet-talked Delia into going to the hospital. It took nearly forty minutes and he promised he'd ride along with her. No matter my back was ripped to shreds and I caught the drunk witch before she hit the ground.

Later, however, when I am sorting through the mounds of junk in his attic, I find myself searching up the image of the suitcases online so I can pinpoint the exact location of Poppy's mysterious treasure he needs me to pilfer from Gil's.

"Tango, what are you doing in the attic?"

I didn't think I could get away with sneaking into the attic without Gil knowing. We both have to leave for work at the same time and the attic has a pull-door from the ceiling that opens up into a stairway. The spring arm assembly makes a loud creaking sound. I am so sore from falling last night, I can hardly move too, so I basically crawled up the attic stairway. He sticks his head out of the bathroom with a towel around his waist and a toothbrush stuck into his mouth.

"I'm getting something for Poppy," I yell down.

"He asked you to get it?" Gil mumbles through the brush and white toothpaste foam. He looks like a rabid dog. "Because I don't remember him saying anything. And whatever is up there isn't any of your business."

"Because I'm not *real* family?" I gruff back. "Because you're standing there almost naked. If you aren't related, that creeps me out."

"Don't play that card, Tango," Gil huffs. His hair is still wet and curly around his head. There's more toothpaste foam on his chin. "Your track record isn't so great with doing stuff for your *real* family and leaving Poppy ten bucks lighter in his wallet."

I am standing at the edge of the attic looking down. I ignore his remark. Ug, it is like a sauna up here. Yes, he is right. I did steal money from Poppy to give to my dad. But it was when I was eight. I was vulnerable then. Not so much now.

"Gil," I mutter while I flick the little string for the attic light on and off. It is dangling in front of my face while I peer around the miniscule room. "It was a million years ago. And I'm getting this for Poppy."

"What is it?"

"Wedding stuff. Pictures," I lie. "He's planning something for his anniversary."

"Yeah, I don't believe you." He shuffles away and starts to shut the bathroom door, then opens it again. "Hey, what happened last night? Where'd the cops take you?"

"They wanted me to sign a statement that I drew the sketch to get back at Delia for something." It wasn't quite a lie. Just not the entire truth.

"Wow, really? That was really low, Tango. You do realize that your credibility has hit an all-time low."

"It was what she described."

"Yeah, you keep those lies for dad," he told me. "Why'd they need Colt?"

"They thought he was my husband." At least that part was true. Gil thinks this is hilarious and laughs loud enough I hear him even after the door is shut.

"Oh, screw you," I mumble. "He's not that far out of my league." That makes Gil laugh even louder because he heard me and he finds the very thought ludicrous. I forgot, teachers have the hearing of bats.

It doesn't matter. I forget all about him for the next hour while I fumble through mounds of old magazines, countless boxes, and baskets and trunks with sweat pouring down my forehead and the middle of my back.

Bingo! I find it twenty-one minutes before I have to get to work, a huge old suitcase with a leather handle. But there's only one and I text Poppy this. He promptly tells me he knew that: *Rae, it's fine. I only have the one. Don't let anyone see it.*

None-the-less, I grab up the one he asked me to get

and drag it downstairs and enclose it in a black garbage bag so it matches all my clothes I washed at four this morning at Gil's. Then I wake up Mia and get her dressed.

Gil, Colt and Layla all look up from their silent breakfast of toast and blink at me. Colt doesn't even look like he's in any kind of pain. They are all dressed and picture perfect, coffee cups in their fingers.

"Gil, can you drop me off at work? Well, and just a short stop at the sitters?" I plead to my foster brother. "I've got to be there in eighteen minutes."

"You're going to make me late."

"For frigging what?" I ask him, holding my arms out. "It's summer. What do you do in an empty school in summer?"

"Summer school."

"Oh," I nod. "I'm begging you. You can drop me within a mile radius and I'll get there."

"And then what?" Layla asks me. She is giving me a soft smile. "Sweetie, where are you going to go after work?"

"Kevin goes into work at three. I'll catch Rocky and have him go with me to the apartment." Rocky is about six feet and eleven inches and three hundred pounds of part-time bouncer at Don's All-Nighter Tavern. "I'll get the manager to change the locks and I'm going to get rid of his junk and put mine back in. The lease is in my name."

"And you think that's going to work?" Gil asks me.

"Yeah, Tim Young, he's the guy who runs the apartments. He's always telling me to look him up when I don't have a boyfriend anymore. He'll take care of me."

"You know how stupid you sound right now, don't you, Tangonut?" Gil's narrowed eyes tell me I must have sounded really ignorant. Layla and Colt stifle smiles. "He's not wanting to help you out, Tango. He's figuring you'll exchange services for rent."

"Will I will," I shrug. "I can clean apartments after people leave—"

"Gil!" Layla gasps, loses the smile. She gives me this sorrowful gaze like I don't deserve the comment. With her expression in mind, I think it out a moment.

"Oh, yeah, right. Wrong services," I mutter, realizing exactly what had been offered up and got the fleeting image of me giving ol' Tim a silent blowjob in the hallway while I hold a broom in one hand and a dust pan in the other. "I'll figure something else out."

"Oh, that ought to turn out well," Gil mutters.

"Gil, please leave her alone." Layla looks over and smiles awkwardly at Colt. But Gil isn't going to let it go. He swings his head around to stare at his girlfriend who is getting ready to say something. She is nervously wrapping a finger around her hair, a habit that she gets when she feels like she is stuck in the middle between me and Gil and wants to stick up for me.

"Well, she put it on herself with the pictures, babe." Gil motions my direction with a wave of his hand. "There isn't a guy in a thousand mile radius that hasn't seen the Tango porn. Sometimes I don't think she's capable of making a good decision."

Tango porn. I grit my teeth. Now my face is red, while my eyes swing upward and anywhere but the three faces staring at me. That's what my foster brother calls the pictures Calvin Reed took of me for his final art exam. They weren't that bad, just me naked laying on a grand piano in partial darkness, somebody's old car, his brother's motorcycle and in a bunch of places we had to sneak in after dark.

"It isn't porn, Gil." I narrow my eyes, feel my hands in fists. "It is art. And Calvin got an A for it."

"Yeah, I bet he did. What'd you get? A sense of satisfaction that when everybody looks at you now, they know what's underneath all that black you wear?" Gil laughs softly. I see Colt's eyes going back and forth. I assume he thinks Gil and I are going to break out in a fight because he stands up really quickly, bumps the table with his hip. When the cups and plates stop tinkling, he looks straight at me. "Um, I can help change a lock," Colt offers. "Heck, I'd do it for a cup of coffee." He's looking from Gil to me with a half-grin on his lips like he's trying to be funny. I feel like an idiot enough now realizing he was joining in on Gil's antics. He's not. I hate Gil's friends.

"Oh, my God, you've seen it too?" I shake my head, look upwards, and try not to scream. "It's art, God Squad. And I'm not servicing you either." I bring my head down, glare at him with cold eyes. He starts to protest his intentions and Gil pushes out a hand.

"I'll make it easy on everybody. I can grab you a grocery cart from the Jenson's Grocery, put it in the trunk of my car." Gil waggles his toast toward me. "You can get a head start on being a basket lady. I don't think Hensley Grove's had one since Crazy Rita got hit by a car on Main. A couple blankets, a dead cat, and some garbage and you're on your way to a new life."

"Go to hell, Gil," I scream at him. "Just go to hell!"

CHAPTER 8

RUSSIAN MAFIA IN HENSLEY GROVE

"Hey, Six Cups of Coffee Going on Seven, you want one for the road?"

There's this guy who has been coming into Joe's Home-style Diner where I work for about two weeks. He sits as far away from the other customers as possible. You see, the restaurant still has the same look it had in the 1950s when it was built—retro white tables with chrome rims and red vinyl chairs. There are booths with little juke boxes, and the counter is laminate with the old glass salt and shaker bottles on top. Disturbingly, I'm wearing Joe Timberline's idea of a soda shop uniform which is a baby blue flare skirt that exposes far too much of my scrawny legs and is way too short for the Sunday crowd, a pair of black and white saddle shoes, and a soda shop cap.

There are a few dark corner booths for those who like to flirt it up a bit with a date. This is where the guy sits who orders all the coffee. The people who come here, they could have been pulled from a 1950s painting. They fit right in. Not him. He's always wearing dark sunglasses even in that booth.

So, the guy who orders the million cups of coffee in the corner a couple days of the week always has sunglasses, a newspaper and his computer and a beanie hat over his head. His hair is fine and comes to his shoulders. And I finally realize today he's the guy from the police station who got his wallet stolen. He does everything he can to be inconspicuous. He is maybe a few years older than me and I can see the muscles bulging under his shirts like he works out. I think he is a famous actor maybe. He does have the too-pretty look of a model on the cover of a magazine. Or—or maybe he's some kind of mafia dude hiding out. Yeah, I like that better.

But if he's trying to fit in with the crowd at Joe's and look inconspicuous, he's going about it the wrong way. I tell him that, too: "Hey, just saying, if you're trying to hide out from the mob or the cops, you're not blending well. Although the ploy pretending you got your wallet stolen and using it to get into the police station to obtain top secret information from Rachael Updike was a smart move. Didn't see that coming. But what I'm saying is this: buy a pair of jeans and a t-shirt." He looks up from his newspaper, tugs his sunglasses down a bit and blinks twice before curling up his lip.

"No, I'm not hiding out from the mob." He's got sweet eyes that aren't too big and these full, heart-shaped pouty lips that turn down at the corners and gives him a kind of sad, melancholy look. He's got the perfect arched nose and I think Anna would tell me he's walked straight out of one of her night time soap operas if she saw him.

Ah, but he has a deep accent, maybe Russian. "Oh, maybe you're a spy—oh, oh! Or even better, you have a lover here." I look around for his matching ensemble in a deep red dress.

"What are you doing?"

"I'm looking for a Russian woman of about twenty-five or twenty-six, your lover, right? She would be wearing a sultry red dress cut up to here." I scoot into the chair beside him, juggling my coffee and tug up my dress. I can see his brow furrow and know beneath the black lenses, he is rolling his eyes at me. "She is married and her husband works for the Russian mafia and you have to fly here to meet her in Hensley Grove, Kentucky home of the largest domestic turkey weighing over sixty pounds." That last part is true. It is our claim to fame, I suppose. "But flying a million miles to hide out here, it is nothing. You would do anything for your sensual-lipped, dark-eyed beauty, right? You would walk four-hundred miles in a desert. You live her, breathe her. Without her, you can't sleep at night, can't eat. But the lack of eating is not a problem for you because you ordinarily weight five-hundred pounds. Her love keeps you anorexic and still, she loves you being chubby. It is an endless cycle of hell for you. But—but here, you two cross paths. One of you walks out the door first, takes the quick route to the Main Street Quality Motel where you'll rendezvous beneath the SWIMMING FOR GUESTS ONLY sign. The other waits until all is clear and follows a different path, down the alley and past Jenson's Grocery and the dollar store."

"Why wouldn't we just meet at the motel?" he asks me with a twist of his own quite sensual lips. "And why do I have to be the fat one?"

"It's more romantic?" I shrug. "And you're fat because I say you're fat." Then I raise a finger. "No, no, I've got it. That's what brought you here, this is your secret meeting place, the place where you first met. I am the go-between who holds the messages each of you sends to the other. They are sweet notes, poems and love letters and maps to your next exotic destination with a twist. That is, you have to come here to know the next place for your romantic tryst—"

"Tango!" That's Joe yelling at me. "Quit hassling the customers and get back to work!"

"Hang on, Joe, I'm going to be an assassin in a minute," I yell at him, wave my hand in the air, but I'm still eyeing the Russian mafia dude and he's eyeing me. "She must be beautiful and mysterious. You are risking your life for her." I widen my eyes, lean over the table. "She knows at any moment her husband will find out and send a hundred men for you to fend off with—no, two-hundred bearing swords, knives, and semi-automatics." I lift up the cheap plastic table cloths Joe puts on the tables and peer beneath. There's just a small leather duffel bag. "Oh, or maybe a sawed-off shotgun." I snap my gaze back up to the table. "Do they have sawed-off shotguns in Russia or are they only found in Kentucky. I've got an aunt that uses them to chase away the bears on her front porch. Maybe you are packing a pistol."

"No gun," he tells me with an annoyed gaze and a hinting flick of his newspaper to get me to leave. I tear my eyes away, make a slight spin in my chair. "So where is she, your beautiful lover with eyes of blue and hair of—I don't know, copper? Because I want to be the one she hires to kill her cruel and abusive husband, the assassin."

"The assassin." He shakes his head. "Yes, I know you. You're the crazy girl from the police station." He's all nice dress pants and suit and tie and everybody else is jeans and t-shirts and baseball caps. He stops staring at me and points to his laptop sitting unopened in front of him. "Is there Wi-Fi here?"

I laugh. "You're kidding me, right? At this diner?" He doesn't think it is so funny.

"I am not surprised. I come here for home cooked meals and it is—" he waves a hand. "Fried burgers and French fries and not as the name implies—home-style. I miss home. I want—"

"Borscht?" I ask him. I'm kind of proud of myself for knowing that soupy mixture from a chef show I watched the other afternoon.

"What?" he asks, shakes his head. "No, beef stew."

He says he had to catch a flight and doesn't know the

time it leaves the airport. I stand up and take out my receipt book and write on it. Then, I hand him the piece of paper. I believe he thinks I am trying to pick him up. He shakes his head and pushes it away with a thank you, but no.

"Pretty mafia boy, it's not my phone number," I tell him. "I've got way too many men in my life right now wreaking havoc on it. What I'm lacking is a little excitement and romance." I cock my head to the side, think about it a moment. "Actually, I can get that from a book online for three bucks and put it down for two days without feeling guilty for ignoring it because it would rather watch football in the first place. The paper has my login, username, and password for my internet connection. Have at it."

He peels his sunglasses down a bit and peers at the paper. Oh, baby, he's got puppy eyes. He is pretty. Short brown hair and warm eyes the color of the dark brown sugar Anna uses to make her chocolate chip cookies. I'm sure I could come up with a multitude of fake rendezvous with him before I went to sleep at night.

And I tell Anna about him when she meets me in the parking lot of my apartment. Well, I tell her about the mysterious Russian stranger that shows up at Joe's Home-style Diner in Hensley Grove and not the details of how I would mentally ravish him for a few lonely nights. "You be careful about talking to strangers," she warns me. "He might start stalking you, Raeanna. Don't you watch the Saturday afternoon movies? There are lots of creeps out there. You don't want to find yourself dead in a ditch."

"Dead in a ditch. Well, no. I guess I don't." I don't remind her that I'd be dead and wouldn't care at that point. And I think I scared the poor guy more than he scared me. "Naw, Anna, I feel sorry for him. He's kind of backwards like Billy."

She is coming to check on me to see how I'm doing.

There's a hole busted in the wall of my apartment the size of Kevin's fist. There are dishes piled three feet high in the sink, trash on the floor, and beer cans everywhere. He'd obviously been partying with his buddies for the three days it took for me to sneak back into the apartment and pay Ralph Emerson sixty bucks to change the locks. I had to pay my neighbor, Rocky Merino (the part time bouncer and the guy whose dad owns Merino Car Repair in town) another two-hundred and forty bucks to bandage up my car so I can drive it. Such, my electric is shut off and I'm running on candles for lights when Anna and Gil come for a visit three days later.

"Why is it so dark in here, honey?" Anna has brown-gray, shoulder-length hair and she's short and skinny. She reaches out, flicks the light switch three times and stares up at the ceiling light as if by denial, alone, the electric will be magically restored. I suppose it is worth a try. I've tried all the other four stages of grief—anger, bargaining, depression and finally, acceptance while Mia and I ate cold hotdogs and pink Kool-Aid.

The little light cover is dirty brown and has bugs in it. "Do you need new bulbs?" She looks young for her age, which is probably close to Poppy's age, and she always wears pretty, trendy dresses. She has always been kind to me, but perhaps a little standoffish. It was Anna who took me to the ballet classes three to five times a week for nearly eleven years. She tirelessly supported me, advocated for me, and helped me get into the college. I was just three years and three months into a college scholarship in ballet and seven months into seasonal touring with the Ballet Theatre of America when I got pregnant with Mia. I almost felt like I broke her. Anna kind of stepped back raising me then. I let her down and she is cool around me most of the time.

"They turned off the electric." I dismiss it with a wave of my hand while I grudgingly light a couple candles I have been saving to read a book with at night. Candles are expensive and I've got until Friday before payday. "No big deal. I'll get it back on Friday. It was one of the things Kevin was supposed to pay." She appears to make light of it with a smile, but I see her looking around the bare room. I know she is seeing me twirling around some huge stage for crowds of thousands in a tutu, then seeing me in a pair of old jean shorts and standing on an ugly green and brown carpet in a low rent apartment with Mia banging on my left hip for another cracker. I've got nothing left but one of the hand-me-down couches I got from their old house, a fake wooden stand with a TV on top of it, and a round dining room table with four mismatched chairs around it. Oh, and to complete my living room suite, there's my ten dollar yard sale sofa table and twelve black garbage bags with Kevin's left-over party trash and his clothes against the far wall.

"Poppy Ray wanted me to come over and check on you," she says. "He's supposed to keep it easy for a couple more days." She and Gil are standing just inside the doorway staring into the room like they are waiting for a cockroach to come rambling through. "Did you have a party last night?"

"Or a murder?" Gil adds smugly.

"No." I follow their gazes to a red stain on one wall that I missed when I was cleaning. "Kevin did before I moved back in. I think the boys had a catsup fight." Or at least, I hope they did. I didn't find a body under my bed. "You want to come in for some—water?" I realize I have no food or drinks in the refrigerator. Everything went bad and was dripping green off the glass shelves when the electric got shut off.

"Water?" Anna looks me up and down. "Sweetie, do

you have food for you and Mia?" She steps past me and I cringe, open my eyes wide at Gil for support because I know she's heading into the kitchen.

"Of course," I lie. And yes, she goes right to the cabinets and opens them. Empty. Then she walks past the bowl of soapy bleach water I was using to clean the refrigerator, tugs open the door and peers into the dark depths and the nothingness inside.

"You can't live like this." She turns, closes the refrigerator and lets her arms fall to her sides. "You can't. Poppy and I do our best to support your desire to be an artist." And I know she is wanting to say I had my chance to be a real ballet dancer in a troupe that would be touring the world. But I got pregnant, lost it all. She doesn't, instead she just sighs deeply.

"I know," I say before she reminds me in a roundabout way I'm a loser by looking at the lights again.

"But, honey, what are the odds you'll ever make money at painting? I know it is your backup—" She is looking hard at me, but her gaze is soft and gentle even before her eyes slip down to Mia who is now kicking me with the toe of her worn tennis shoe. "You work, go to college, and you support your boyfriend. You've got a little girl."

"Well, he isn't my boyfriend anymore," I tell her. "And he drives trucks."

"When was the last time he drove a truck, Tango? It's been six months, I think." Gil shakes his head. "He's an ass and a bum. He's not even Mia's dad. And in two weeks, just like you always do, you'll get back with him and you'll be sitting right here just like you've always done."

Anna holds up her hands to ward off Gil's verbal blows. "Raeanna, you know, Gil talked to the principal at the high school yesterday. He said they are hiring some custodial workers there. The job is full-time. And before you answer, your degree isn't going to waste. You can paint and draw on your off time."

"Tango, it's what we all do, settle for something less," Gil interjects. "Do you think I really wanted to teach? I wanted to pitch for the Reds. I knew the odds were one in a million that I'd go past college playing ball."

"Maybe I want to try to be that one in a million," I mumble. "I've got a job at Joe's."

"Honey, you had your chance at being one in a million," Anna says softly. I know as soon as she says it, she wishes she hadn't. I chomp my jaws shut tightly. It is suddenly silent. I know she lacks at words. Still, she holds out her hands to her sides. "I'm not being mean, just honest. I just don't think you get second chances, sweetie. And now, you're busy with other things." She looks over to the floor where Mia has changed her attention. She is now shoving a dress on a doll, then banging the head on the couch. They always make me feel small and foolish like a four year-old asking to jump in the deep side of the pool and I can't swim yet. But I don't care. I want to dive in the deep end. I really, really think if I kick hard enough and hold my breath long enough, I can make it to the top.

However, I don't expect any of them to understand. They all had everything handed to them. They never had to survive a week on a box of stale cereal and a baby bottle of generic ginger ale. I did when I was four and more than once. It kind of builds a certain desire to accomplish more than what the deadbeat daddy (who left me in the fold up playpen for three days unattended while he was in jail for fighting at a bar) achieved in life.

Anyway, the only person that gets me is Poppy. He's the one that kept getting me to draw the scary stuff in my head, get it out on paper. Then we'd burn it in a little fire ring behind the house. Then he started keeping the papers because he said they were so good. About the time I'd lived with Anna and Poppy Ray for a year, the dark things hanging around my mind had turned to butterflies and flowers and slightly strange fairies and odd unicorns with three butts.

They are both looking at me with sad, knowing eyes. I'd once heard Anna tell a lady at church my dad probably kept me alive for the welfare check he got for taking care of me and he got half of what it was worth buying food with it and reselling the food at a quarter of the worth. Anna just nods and gives me a fake smile that she knows I know is bogus just for the sake of mom-guilt.

"You'll think about it?" she asks me. "We'll put in a good word for you at the high school." She turns to Gil and wiggles her fingers. "Sweetie, run out to the car. Get her the application and the number she needs to call." Of course, Gil does what his mom tells him to do. Still, I get the idea that his departure was planned. As soon as he slips out the door with a side gaze to his mom, Anna turns and stares me dead in the eye. "I talked to Ruth who sings in the choir with me. She has a son who is a nice young man. He—"

"No, Anna. I don't want to be fixed up on a date if that is what you're getting at," I tell her, shaking my head back and forth. "I don't need a husband so I can pay bills—"

"Sweetie, it is never too soon to find the right man to fit into your life." She leans over and gently pushes the hair away from my eyes. I know I tip slightly to feel her touch. I also know I put on the brakes when I realize I am doing it and step away. She takes note of this like she always does, smiles softly like I hurt her feelings.

"I thought that girl they found on the riverbank was you, Raeanna. I thought—" She is crying and I don't know what to do. "Well, I should have been around more for you.

I should have helped you find a nice man to settle down with and I didn't. I just stood back, didn't think it was my job to guide you in that direction." She sniffles while I push my hair back from my face over and over again in some nervous attempt to cope with her crying. It is just that every time she sniffs, I hear my dad's hand slap on my face. "I failed you."

"No, no you didn't." I reach out and touch her arm gently with my fingers. I failed me. I know that. I just know if I tell her that, she's going to cry harder. It is awkward for a minute or so in the silence. We both look up when Gil slides through the door, waving the application papers in his hand.

"Raeanna," Anna says softly. "You need to find someone who treats you nicely, who works. Would you do it for me?" She takes the papers from Gil and slides them into my hand. "Just one date. That's all I ask—"

"Anna, no," I mutter. "I don't want to date anybody right now. I don't need a guy around to make me feel whole."

"How about halfway," Gil mutters. "Or at least a quarter to cover the bills."

Anna ignores her son, just stares at me, and she sighs deeply. Then she pulls a tissue out of her purse and starts dabbing it at her eyes. Crap. I should have known it was a trap after I bob my head up and down way too hard.

"Okay, yes. I will, Anna. If you'll stop crying, I'll go out with him."

CHAPTER 9
ALMOST GETTING CAUGHT LETTING THE EX KNOW HOW I FEEL

Gil calls me at half past six, yelling at me and asking me what I said to make his mom so upset. I just said she wanted me to go out on a blind date with one of her friend's sons. Then he starts trying to fix me up with every one of his buddies. I get it. Everybody knows Kevin is going to come back and they are trying to show me there's better guys out there and hope one snatches me up before Kevin's knuckles knock on my door.

Kevin doesn't have any place else to live. He will bum a stay at one of his so-called friends for two or three days, maybe a week until their wives or girlfriends have enough of him drinking beer and setting up a homestead on their couch and he'll get kicked out. Then he'll come back to me with his sad eyes and begging to let him stay until he finds someplace to rent. And always in the past, I'd let him stay until he crept back into my bed again.

Not this time. I vow to myself that it isn't going to happen. I'm not that needy and he has to grow up. So for my last twenty bucks, Rocky Merino stands with Mia on his shoulders and plays watch-out for me while I climb up the ladder to the vacant billboard across the highway and paint a picture of me from neck to blue, ripped-up jeans and my middle finger standing straight up in the air. Rocky. He's huge and has short red hair and freckles. Most people take one look at him and their eyes get wide with fear because he's so big and so fierce looking. Really, he's as sweet as a big puppy dog as long as you don't make him mad. He'd walk in front of a firing squad for anybody.

I figured, if Kevin came, he'd see that image on the billboard, know my answer to his coming back. I didn't need to respond to his gravely, begging voice at my door. And the image was good. Even Rocky said so when I stepped back and flipped the billboard lights back on and stared up at the mirror image of my skinny arms in the wife-beater t-shirt, knobby knees, and then my wrinkle-knuckled middle finger. "Damn, girl, that looks like you took a picture of you." And he is right. It does.

The only problem I have is Missus Finch in Apartment 7B who sees the lights come back on for the billboard and calls the cops for the obscene gesture gawking at her from her balcony.

"Crap," I mutter at Rocky who is laughing so hard at the steps beneath her, I don't hear the car pull into the parking lot until it douses us in the lights for a split second. I mean, Missus Finch is screaming at the local police so loudly about the new billboard she believes is placed there by a local business, her voice is echoing down over the traffic on the main road.

My concern, however, isn't the cops this time. It is the voice I can hear talking as the car shuts off. It is God Squad. And he has four people stuffed into his vehicle who are climbing out. Surely, he isn't coming to the Little Pine Estates Apartment Complex to see me. Who else could he possibly know here?

"Rocky, Rocky. Buddy, we've got to get inside." I try to smother my huge friend's stifled laughter while I push him up the stairway with both my hands. Mia is giggling even though she has no clue what is going on. Rocky's got on cargo shorts and a t-shirt, and his pudgy-buff arms are bulging out the sleeves. He moves as slowly as an ant on a piece of toast with peanut butter. I get this awful feeling in the pit of my belly that we're going to get caught. If it isn't by Missus Finch, it will be Colt Lucero or the cops.

"Rocky, you've got to sit on the couch and just act normal," I tell him. "I'm begging you. Watch a ballgame like you've been here the entire night. I've got paint on my hands. I've got to wash it off."

"I was out—running," I tell Colt who is standing on my second floor breezeway eight minutes later. "I work on my art in the evening and sometimes, I need an artistic break." He is asking me why I am out of breath, sees the paint stains on my fingers. And, by God, I see him eyeing the police car pulling into the parking lot to check out Missus Finch's call. There is a small crowd gathering and following her finger pointing to the billboard. Colt's eyes drop to my feet. I'm wearing lime green flip-flops with speckles of red, yellow and blue on my bare toes.

"You run in those?" he asks.

"It's all I've got, Lucero. And it isn't any of your business. What do you want?" I narrow my eyes at his friends behind him. There are two young men dressed in khaki pants and white button-up shirts. They are churchy-looking boys holding boxes and smiling too widely with perfect white teeth. I cringe when I see Alexandra Edward and Taylor Peirce are among them, pushing up against Colt's back like he's a knight that's going to protect them from the wicked witch at the door. Their eyes are darting from me and then toward Billy Thompson, my next door neighbor. He's about twenty-two and a bit on the paranoid side. He takes classes over at the college and has an incredibly high IQ. He also has long hair, a beard and I have to constantly tell him not to stare at me when I'm walking up the stairs because it freaks me out.

Alexandra and Taylor are clinging to each other like

they are in a war zone. Colt still hasn't answered my question because Alexandra is pumping his arm to look at Billy whose mouth is slack while he stares at them. Now Colt's eyes are kind of wide.

"What do you want, God Squad?"

"Oh." He turns his attention back to me. "We were right down the road on Baker Street hanging out at Taylor's grandpa's house. He's really funny. We thought of you. We brought you a couple boxes from the food pantry at the mission. Your—brother—" He pauses and tries to read my gaze to see if his title for Gil is correct. I remain expressionless. "Well, he said you were having a difficult time—" He wags a thumb behind him and gives me a big, toothy grin like his Holy Roller pals. "Gil said you were dead broke and food poor. So we're here to help you out."

I could have killed Gil right then. He knew exactly what he was doing when he told God Squad I was needy. It is another one of his intentional underhand maneuvers to make me feel inferior. I feel the warmth start in my cheeks and spread out hot-red to my neck. Okay, it isn't bad enough that he announces how poor I am to everyone in the hallway, but that he brings me handouts from some donation box like the ones in front of Jenson's Grocery Store in town makes me livid with embarrassment. Then, to top it all off, he drags my archenemies down here with him just to rub it in.

"No, I don't want it. You need to leave," I say, trying to stifle my temper while Colt thrusts a box at me with canned vegetables inside and a loaf of bread with a perishable date that expired yesterday. I breathe in, breathe out. I feel the irritation seeping up from the tingle in my wrists, along my arms, and then my shoulders.

"Oh, God, this ought to be good."

I turn slowly to see Rocky pushing himself up from

the couch, a slight smile scooting across his lips when he says that. I know he sees the expression on my face. My jaws are churning, my eyes are wide. I think he's probably seen it before because he's cracking his knuckles like there's going to be a fight. When he isn't helping his dad in the family car shop, he's a bouncer down at Don's All-Nighter Tavern. I've seen him bear hug more than one drunk idiot out the front door and on to the sidewalk. But I hold out my hand, ward him off for the moment. He stops and I turn back to Colt and stare him dead in the eyes.

"Tango, come on, there isn't anything wrong with accepting the kindness of others when you are down—"

"Down?" I lean forward, push a hand on Colt Lucero's chest and give him a little shove. "You think I'm down? No, buddy, down is when you hit the bottom and there's no way out. I'm out and climbing." I bite my lip, hold back a bit because I know Gil is going to hear this like second-hand smoke later from his friends. "It's like this, God Squad. Listen and listen well. I am not poor. I do not need your donations. I do not accept charity from a bunch of bible-thumping, arrogant, sons-of-bitches who think just because they have a mommy and daddy to support their every dream and desire, they are better than me. You are not." I take another step toward him, put out my hand against his belly and gently push him back another step. "In fact, just because you wear the starched shirts, the ties and the pleated 1950s business pants doesn't make you better than me or anybody else in this apartment." I watch his eyes veer downward toward his pants. "It just makes you look out of place and like you're trying to be better than everybody else. I've got news for you. You're not." I take another step and he automatically walks back and bumps into Alexandra, steps on the toes of her sandals with fake bling all over the upper. "I can't speak for anybody else in the apartment building, but I don't want any of your do-good, goody two shoes, second-hand shit that nobody else wants or needs and you think I want because I live here. And you think it's a dump. It isn't. It is home. I'm better than that and so is everybody in here. So you can take your boxes of canned lima beans that the grocery store donated because nobody else bought them and the expired box of powdered milk somebody snatched out of the cabinet because the bus was waiting and the kids were collecting donations for the poor to earn a free pizza from Big G's Pizza for the classroom that day. You can take your haughty attitude and your castoff rummage sale junk that didn't sell and your hand-me-down rotting fruits and vegetables, and SHOVE IT UP YOUR ASSES!" I stop, take in a slow breath. "Just divide them up among yourselves accordingly."

I am about to slam the door when the cop comes up the stairway.

"Is there a problem up here?" He has a hand on the gun at his belt. I know it is freaking out God Squad and his gang because the two boys have paled to a creamy white. Oh, it is Gabe Reynolds again.

"No, we were just leaving." Colt swings around, bumps the box into Taylor's boobs who squeaks in pain.

"Hey, Gabe," I say. I see his eyes scanning all of us and stopping on me.

"Not you again." Officer Reynolds stops next to me.

"You say that like it's a bad thing."

He grunts like it is, but doesn't say anything aloud. "You don't know anything about the sign out there, do you?" he asks me, veering slightly to the right and pointing a finger across the highway. "You see anybody over there tonight?" Colt and his friends have come to a complete halt and everybody's eyes turn in the direction of the cop's hand. And I know everybody in that group has seen my work, knows that's kind of my thing.

"Oh, my," I say. "That's offensive. Are advertising agencies allowed to put that stuff on billboards?"

"No," Officer Reynolds answers flatly. He narrows his gaze at me. Everybody's eyes go from me to him. "I think the general consensus is that it was painted by someone who goes to the art college and who also lives nearby. Maybe somebody who has been known to do this before."

"Well, that's disturbing." I scratch my head, look back to Rocky for some backup. "You don't think it was me, do you?" I try to look surprised, push my hands behind my back. Rocky, he's just looking smug like he's waiting for a comedy to play out.

"I've been here with Rocky the entire time."

"And running, right?" Colt Lucero pipes up. He's got a mean streak to him, I just found out. I see it in the self-satisfied cock of his chin right then. "I think Tango, here, just got done running."

"Running." Officer Reynolds doesn't believe us. But I know for a fact, he isn't going to disrespect Colt right now in front of everyone by insinuating he's a liar.

"Yeah, running."

Two minutes later, I shut the door behind me.

"Rocky, what's up with you?" I am standing with my back to the door, holding up my hands.

"I don't know." He shrugs, looks me in the eye. "I'm just not so into lying to God Squad. He's nice. He sends business to my dad's shop."

"You're kidding me, right?" I groan. "Is there anybody who doesn't like him? I mean, he isn't nice all the time. He got mad at me the other day at the police station."

"You know, Tango, that doesn't surprise me," Rocky mutters. "That doesn't surprise me at all."

CHAPTER 20

CREEPY BILLY, MY BEST FRIEND

"Christ Almighty, Tango stop! Breathe, dammit!"

I don't recognize Rocky's voice for a second. He's holding my arms and shaking me hard. I hear Mia crying next to me. I see his red hair. I'm like not connecting who he is at first, then I take in a deep breath. It's a horrid gasp like I haven't breathed in years. I can see Greg Pauly and Billy Hazel standing behind him looking like a clown just jumped out at them.

"Hey," Rocky says gruffly. I blink at him. I see Mia blinking at me. She is kneeling next to the couch with big tears in her eyes. Rocky's eyes are wide. "Are you there?"

"Yeah—yeah," I stutter. "Bad, bad dream." I remember. I went over to Rocky's to watch some TV. He and his friends got tired of watching a sappy romance with me and went in, started playing poker. I remember tucking Mia into the blanket with me. We must have fallen asleep.

"You were bluer than a cloudless day in July." Greg Pauly's got a bit of a southern accent. He's from Tennessee and drives trucks to Toledo. He stops a lot at Rocky's and stays the night. He's always saying hi to me when I leave for work in the early morning. But these kind-of strangers staring at me like I've got six ears and four sets of eyes make me miss Kevin. He just let my stuff bounce off him. In retrospect, it was probably because he was bouncing himself off Sophie.

Rocky makes me some warm milk and gives me a couple ibuprofen for my headache. When I'm finished, I wash the chipped cup in the sink and head back to my lonely apartment, tuck Mia into her own bed. On my way in,

I'd seen Billy Thompson sitting on a baby blue, webbed aluminum lawn chair. So after Mia goes to sleep, I leave the front door open and slip outside beside Billy. He's hunched over with a baseball hat on and a pair of binoculars in his fist.

"You know that looks creepy, right, Billy?" I say softly. It is two in the morning and quiet except for the crickets and an occasional car on the highway. He looks up at me. I see his thick glasses shine in the parking lot lights.

"What'd they do to you in there?" he asks me.

"Nothing. I had a bad dream. Rocky made me warm milk when I woke up."

"What do you dream about?"

"Scary stuff sometimes. I fell through the ice in Rocky Fork Creek when I was like two or three, almost drowned. I still hear the crash of the ice breaking and feel the water all around me. I hold my breath at night sometimes. I suppose I remember it."

"You know that sounds creepy, right?" Billy says and I can see a flash of white teeth when he smiles. I chuckle softly, sit down beside the chair. I pull my knees up, hug them with my arms and lean my back against the wall. We sit there in silence. Once in a while Billy takes his binoculars and looks out toward the highway.

"So, is it going to scare me if you tell me what you're looking at, Billy?" I finally ask him.

"Yes. Probably. Dead girls."

I feel goosebumps rise on my arms. "Dead girls. Like ones you buried across the highway?"

"No, Tango, don't be weird. Somebody else did."

"Well, that's a relief."

"No, it isn't. It shouldn't be a relief," he tells me with his nasally voice. "Because I wouldn't kill you. I like you.

But we don't know who might be raping and killing girls out there. Maybe they don't like you. Then, they would rape and kill you."

"What is your sudden interest in dead girls, Billy?" I ask him. "Can I give you some advice? If any cops ask you about dead girls or—or anybody being dead, you don't answer them like you're talking to me right now."

"I know. Because it's creepy." I know he is rolling his eyes. "They found a dead girl along the highway. "Lucinda Delray with the Tri-City News Station on the TV tonight said that a motorist coming down the state route saw something tan in the grass. He stopped. It was a dead girl. She was naked and bloated and rotting in the sun. She had flies on her, I bet. That makes six dead girls."

"Six dead girls?"

"Yes," Billy says, scans the skyline like a Navy Seal inspects the horizon before he begins his crusade. "There was one in 1958, one in 1963, one in 1972 and one in 1983. Then the girl who was at the river. Lucinda Delray didn't say anything about the others. I looked them up on my computer."

"Is it really like a—serial killer? Poppy had me read something that mentioned a serial killer in the newspaper."

"I don't know. I just know the cops believe they were all killed within a twenty mile radius of Hensley Grove even though they were from as far away as Michigan. I can't find a connection on the dates." He drops his binoculars to his lap. "My mom says I have tunnel vision. I focus too much on one thing. She says if there are four round objects in front of me and one square one and I have to push them through a round hole, I choose the single square one that won't fit and try to figure out how I can make it fit. It may not be the one I should focus on. So I'm keeping my options open. I still think it's a serial killer."

"Okay, so let me ask you something, Billy." I nibble my lip, think about my daddy. I know it is whispered he killed those girls just because he went to jail so many times for other offences. I suddenly get this idea that maybe I can figure out who the real killer is and clear my daddy's name, clear my name. I'm sick of everybody looking at me like I've got some disease just lying dormant in me and ready to wake up so I can kill people. I can't tell you how nice it would be to toss that back in Delia Childs' face, not have everybody staring at me when I walk down the street and know they are whispering that I'm Dell Smythe's kid. "So have you dug up any of the possible suspects? Could you dig up a list of people that might have killed these girls?"

Billy seems to contemplate this thought. "I'll have to think about that. Is it a test?"

"Maybe," I say. "Can you get me a list of the girls killed too?"

"Yeah, if you want. Don't tell my mom. She'll be mad. I miss my mom."

"I miss Kevin." I sigh. Billy doesn't judge me. Or maybe he just doesn't even care. He doesn't look at me like I'm a girl or anything. I watch him bring up his binoculars, scan the horizon for dead girls again. Curiously, I don't find this strange tonight. Sometimes I think he is my only real friend.

"Mom says I have to go to the Fields Acapella Club dance. I have to be in the acapella club because it is the only one that will take me so I can be in the competition and get my final grade this semester. I don't want to go. It is to meet people." He throws his head back, groans. "I don't like meeting people. The girls are either too fat or too skinny. I don't like it at all. I don't want to walk in there alone and try to meet people."

"I'll go with you if you want." I pat his arm. He looks

at my hand with puckered lips like a mosquito just bit him.

"No, I don't want to go. They are trying to get me to sing at the Edna Fields Performing Arts competition. I don't want to sing in front of a bunch of people I don't know."

"*Arrr*" I growl, hold my palms to the sides of my head in frustration. "That stupid competition!"

"It is stupid. The dance performers have won every year for seventeen years. Why bother, I ask them? You know what they say? Maybe this year, we'll win." He rolls his eyes. "The odds are slim, Tango. They are nil to none."

"Okay. Well, *I* support your desire to not even attempt to twist fate. Are you going to be out here for a while?" I ask him. He nods, shoves his glasses up his nose.

"Fate doesn't have anything to do with winning the competition," Billy states. "Shane Delgado said he'd quit if his girls didn't win every year."

"That's just a rumor," I tell him. But I know and he knows it is probably true. But it occurs to me the ultimate way to cram a knife into my ex-teacher and ex-lover's back is to win it with art. And yet, even while I think it, the thought sounds ludicrous.

I sigh. "If I run into my apartment and get my drawing pad and a blanket," I ask Billy. "Would you keep me company? I don't want to sleep."

"Yes. That's cool. You're good at art stuff. It looks real when you draw, not like at the museum. Can you draw me a picture of something like a cat? I want a cat and we're not allowed to have cats."

"Cool," I chuckle at him. I'd rather get Billy a cat when he tells me that. I smile to myself and look up to see him cramming his finger into his nostril. "Yuck, we don't pick noses, Billy," I whine at him. "It's not cool." And I don't think it's strange that I could easily call him my best friend.

CHAPTER 11

WAITING TABLES AT JOE'S DINER

"Shhh." I have a brown paper bag in my hand. I slide it on the table in the rear of Joe's diner. Russian Mafia is there today, incognito as usual. "It is top· secret." To demonstrate the importance of this, I had written TOP SECRET on the bag in different colored markers with the same kind of graffiti letters I use to paint on the brick walls. This, I poke with my forefinger to make sure he doesn't miss it. "It is from your lover. She could not come. It was too dangerous." I lean in. "My boss, they call him Joe. That's not his real name. He murdered the real Joe and moved into his position. He sells body parts out the back door now and works for the FBI. That's how I knew the Russian police followed her in Texas so she took a flight to Rio to escape them. He gave me the inside info and I gave him my left kidney to get the information to find your beloved. But I would give my own heart for you two to meet." I point to the sack. "This will keep you alive until you meet her in Rio. But if anyone finds out, he'll kill me—"

"Tango, order up! Where the heck are you?"

"Oh, no, he is on to me! Godspeed to you, Russian Mafia! May you find your love!" I whisper loudly and spin on my heels to make a quick retreat toward the front of the store. I'm in such a hurry, I bump my hip on the corner of a table and it hurts bad enough to yelp and spew out a few curses. Crap, it is Sunday morning and it is all church people whose eyes get wide while I rub away the ache. As if they have never cursed stubbing a toe or bumping a head.

I hear a chuckle and turn my head sharply when I return to a walk. I can see Russian Mafia peeking into the bag with a little smile playing on his lips. Anna makes a thick beef stew from a recipe she got from her mamaw and I asked her to help me make some last night. I also pilfered three of her breakfast croissants and stuffed them in aluminum foil and laid them on top.

Everybody's chattering softly about pieces of Hannah Lafferty's body being found underneath the second High Street viaduct and train trestle, so mangled that it is only discernible by swatches of her hair. Another body was found along the highway.

"Hey."

I think the worst part of the buffet is carrying out the trays of meat and plopping them into the buffet warmer. I have to slide them between the glass sneeze guards. The infrared heat lamps above burn my upper arms and the metal base where the trays sit scald my fingers. The buffet is also near the far side of the restaurant and I have to slip through the other server's tables to get in and out. The other server is Dana. While she takes great pride in culling out every last penny from the wallet of the horny churchy guys back there, the women on her shift tend to get overlooked. So when I have to dump the trays, I always get caught by some wife who doesn't have her wallet open and needs a glass of water or another handful of the tiny half and half creamers.

So I cringe when I turn toward the female voice at my elbow. It blends in with the chaotic commotion of a hundred voices competing with three bawling babies, bald-headed, five foot tall Joe screaming that an order is up, and the TV blasting Sunday sports above the counter.

"Yeah, what do you need?" I know it is a little curt when I see the brusqueness in her eyes. I should have seen her there, recognized the girl that had been sitting on the catwalk of the water tower.

"I just wanted to say hi."

"Hi, Delia" I mumble, trying to make up for not seeing her there. "I—I didn't see you." I make a quick swing of my eyes around the table, take in the reason I'd avoided this part of the restaurant. It's the younger crowd with a bunch of tables all shoved together to fit a myriad of different denominations, most of them from the college, of same age people. They chat it up over coffee for hours. I don't think church ever even comes up in any of the conversations I've overheard. Gil's here. I cringe. Poppy and Anna usually have a quiet lunch at the house in the summer. However, Gill, he always squeals on me about not going to church. And I've been avoiding Reverend Greene at Holy Trinity. He wants me to paint a wall on the education part of the church building facing the alley, something church-worthy and inspirational. He wants to cover up the cusswords some of the kids have written there. I've got nothing coming to mind when he asks me to inspire him with my art that he says Poppy dotes all over.

I'm starting to get a little headache just above my temple. It isn't a good sign. Whenever I get a little ache like this, I wonder if I have some sort of deadly genetic condition that was passed down from my mama's side of the family and then, to me. I know I'm leaning on the table a little hard thinking about this. I try to think of something good, push the scary away. I used to shove in the image of Kevin, know I'd at least have him to wake me up when I screamed at night or listen half-heartedly when I told him about *the bad stuff*. And at least I could shove myself into his chest and feel safer while he snored overhead—

"—come with us tomorrow? Please."

I'd spaced out into the realm of some imaginary world and being spooned by Kevin in a fluffy bed of clouds. I'm blinking at Delia who is smiling impatiently at me.

"Tomorrow?" I ask. Everybody at the table snickers.

"Too much partying, little sis?" Gil asks me from the far end. He reaches out his hand and pokes a finger at a shopping bag. It is settled in Colt Lucero's hand. I wince. "She was telling you that she and Colt bought you a pair of running shoes. They thought it might not be a good idea you ran alone."

"I don't—" *Run.* I stop because I see the smug smile on Colt's face. I guess I did use it as an alibi.

"You don't need to run in sandals anymore, Tango. Like you were last week," Colt tells me, tosses the bag with a shoe box inside toward me. I catch it like a football, hear them all laughing like it's a joke. "You can run with us. Gil thought it might not be safe out there with you running all by yourself at night and in flip-flops. You needed a bodyguard from all the criminals, gangsters, and lawbreakers defacing property and stuff." Smart ass.

Joe is yelling at me from the kitchen. I can see a line at the cash register. I nod, give him a wave. I am hugging the box to my chest wondering if it really has shoes in it or maybe a dead rat or something as a joke.

"You almost killed me, you know that right?" Delia has her hand on my wrist. I wince. I kind of have a thing about lingering touches, although everybody complains I'm constantly poking, prodding and nudging them. Her voice is low so nobody else can hear.

"I wasn't the one standing on the edge of a water tower catwalk with a bottle of rum," I muster in return. I hear Joe yelling at me and I wave a hand, use it as an excuse to bumble my way to the kitchen.

At three-thirty, I get a break. Joe doesn't have a breakroom. It's more like an old table out behind the restaurant. It's hot and in the sunshine and it stinks because the dumpster is back there. I have to take out the garbage when I go and I'm tossing the black sack into the dumpster. It's heavy and I'm leaning back and trying not to splash the soda I've got in my left hand while I start to swing the bag in my right.

"Let me get that." It is Colt again and he's holding out his hand, palm up to take the bag. I'm not quick to give it up, but I set it down, take a step back.

He snatches it up, makes an easy basket into the dumpster. "You on break?"

"Yeah," I say cautiously.

"Okay, I didn't want to get you in trouble again," he tells me. "Your—what do you call Anna? Mom?"

"My Anna."

"Okay, Gil says Anna's worried about you. She doesn't want you to go back with your ex so she's trying to fix you up with a bunch of her friend's sons or something. He kind of brought up me asking you out. They are all going out for supper. You want to go with me? Maybe it will get them off your back."

I stare at him hard. "Why—would you do that?" I ask him brusquely. "Listen, God Squad, you can't persuade me to go out with you and your friends. Delia's never done anything nice for me. She's only nice to me when you're around. I know a joke when I see it—"

"It's Colt, Tango. You offend me when you call me God Squad."

"Okay, Colt, if you we are going to broach the subject of name calling," I say hotly. "You offend me when you call me Tango. If you aren't in the zone of what Tango stands for, it is far worse than God Squad."

"Tango's your last name."

"Baldwin is my last name. Raeanna is my first name. Tango stands for Whiskey Tango which means white trash," I say flatly. "Every time you call me Tango, you are calling me white trash."

I think there is a moment there that he looks like I just set off fireworks between us. He gets a strangely stunned twist of his lips, takes in a deep breath and stares hard at the ground. It is silent until he stares at me like he's seeing me in a whole new light.

"Um, well, Raeanna, I—I didn't know that. Everybody calls you Tango." He stops like he's thinking out the ramifications of what he just said, swallows hard and goes on. "I assumed it was your last name. You were adopted by Ray and Anna. But I didn't think you took their name. Listen, never mind, you're just way out of my comfort zone. I don't mean any offence. You are just—way, way out of my comfort zone." He throws his hand into the air above my head for show.

"And you kind of throw me off my happy place, so what the hell?" I snap back.

"You've—got a happy place?" He asks me with a smart-alecky twist to his lips.

"Yeah, okay," I grit my teeth, stare hard at him. He thinks that's funny. I just grunt, walk over to the picnic table and plop down.

"Why do you think it's a joke?"

"The tennis shoes?" I say before I take a long suck through the straw.

"You deserved that. You lied to me. You lied to the cops. You manipulated me, made me lie to the cops and look like an idiot in front of everybody who was standing there." He sits down beside me, folds his hands at his knees. "Everybody knew it was you. Now my credibility is as ruined as that billboard."

"That billboard looked good." I shrug.

"The painting was good, the foul image of you flipping somebody off was not." Colt fiddles his fingers at his knees.

"It was for my ex-boyfriend, who deserves to see every bit of it when he drives past every day."

"His loss, Raeanna, is that he doesn't have you anymore. I bet he's feeling that pain right now. But the thousands of kids that go that same route did not deserve to see it. The city covered it up with a sheet this morning so all the people driving to church didn't have to look at it. And if you clean it up, I won't go down to the police station and tell them it was really you."

"You're kidding me, right?" I squelch a laugh. His face stays deadpan.

"Nope."

"You're a piece of work, God Squad," I grunt, push myself to my feet. I pick up the half-full soda and toss it in the dumpster. I pivot on my feet, pass the table.

"Go out with me," he just announces. I can't even wrap my head around his words.

"Go—out? Like and clean the billboard?"

"Well, no, go out on a date with me. Tonight. They are all making plans about going to the country club. You can be my date. It'll make Anna happy."

"You're funny." I look around for his friends. All's I can see is the back parking lot and the sun roasting off the pavement.

"Lay off, Lucero. I know you want to make Taylor or Alexandra jealous. I know nobody's going to make fun of you. On the other hand, I'm going to be the butt of the jokes for the next three weeks. Even if we weren't going to be their free entertainment tonight, I wouldn't go with you. You're just a little too—this," I wiggle my fingers at his starched white shirt and tie. "You're just too suit and tie, door-to-door Jesus salesman for me."

"You're telling me to lay off?" he retorted. I could see him grinding his jaws to force back the smile. "And you're way too much of that—" He stands back grandly, holds out both arms toward my 1950s-style skirt and goofy shirt.

"It's my uniform," I tell him dully.

"Well, whatever," he just says that like it is supposed to have meaning. "I'm talking about what's underneath." Then he rubs his hand to his face. "I mean, in your head. Why would you think it's a joke?"

"Dude, they call me Whiskey Tango. There's a reason for that."

"Are you white trash?" he asks while I feel the anger rise in my belly. It must show on my face. "And don't look at me like that," he goes on. "Just answer the question."

"No, but that's what everybody in my apartment building would say."

"That you're white trash?"

"No, that they *aren't* white trash either. But some of them, I look at them, and they probably are. Maybe I am too."

"Nobody with the gift of painting like you could be white trash. White trash don't go to college and they don't work their butts off like you do in there." He shrugs, gets up and walks around me to the door. "I'll leave. Take your break. Think about running with us sometime. It's a good way to deal with stuff."

He just looks kind of sad like a kicked puppy. Colt

stuffs his hands in his pockets, loses his cocky swagger. I guess it would suck digging the bottom of the dumpster for a date and having her turn you down.

"Yeah, God Squad, I'll go out with you." I didn't think he heard me, he'd faded into the shadows of the little portico around the door.

"Cool," he remarks. His voice is coming from the shade while the door makes a grinding creak when he opens it. He sticks out his hand and makes a geeky thumbs up in the sunlight. "I'll pick you up at seven."

The restaurant clears out before the supper crowd. There's about a half hour where there are only two or three people coming and going. My shift lasts until four and after I go back in, I snatch up the coffee, start making the rounds to see if a man at the counter wants to order. He wasn't there when I went out for break. I couldn't tell if Dana had bothered to take care of him.

I'm rocked when I snatch up a coffee cup and wiggle the half-full carafe in front of him. "Coffee?" I ask, then I stand there shaken.

He doesn't answer right away, just looks up. It is the man I drew for Delia. Chris Peirce, that was his name. I'd seen his face on TV. He wasn't in uniform, just sitting there in Sunday suit and tie. "Raeanna Baldwin. Well, Starr Smythe, if we go by your real name before your adopted parents changed it." He sits back a little in the bar seat, folds his arms. I feel my face flush, feel my heart pounding so hard in my chest, it aches. "A chip off your dad's shoulder, aren't you," he says in a soft, gravelly voice. I just stare at him, force my eyes to not look away. He scares me. There's something about him I can't quite describe leaving me with a sick feeling in my belly. "That was quite a joke you played on me at the station," he says. "But just so you know, I don't take kindly to jokes that hurt me, mar my reputation. I'm chalking it up to college pranks and not that you're trying to cover for somebody. Because we know you wouldn't do that, would you? I know your friends, your accomplices. And I know you don't want to end up like your daddy. I'm watching you."

I can see the top of Joe's balding round head staring at me from the swinging door on the far side of the kitchen. He steps back when our eyes meet and I'm sure he's bailing on me. I just plop the coffee cup down, stand back. Then I hear Joe yelling from the little window across from me. "Tango! Order up!" he yells it. I know there's no order. I blink, though, and recover quickly. He's slapping a plate with God-knows-what on it.

Chris Peirce slips out of the stool, slaps a five down on the counter. "You grew up at Ray Baldwin's, didn't you?" Again, I don't answer. "I thought so." He pokes a finger at the five spot sitting on the counter while I start for Joe's window. "Here's a tip for you. Run."

CHAPTER 12

MEETING COLT'S EX-WIFE—WHAT?

"So this is how Colt is playing it out, huh? I should have seen that coming. Did he pay for your services or did his mommy set this up?"

I am standing just outside the women's bathroom at the Salt Springs Country Club. I'm waiting for Delia to finish washing her hands. She had dragged me away from the table with a scathing glare, claws around my wrist, and an excuse she didn't want to go alone. Alexandra Edwards and Taylor Peirce follow us with their eyes all the way to the door. Then Delia whisper-screams at me over the sink for five minutes telling me that Colt is on a pity date with me because Anna asked him to take me. Alexandra Edwards has a huge crush on Colt and I better not try to steal him from her. I stare at her smugly, don't say anything. Then I just turn and walk out the restroom doors.

That's when I hear the woman's voice. I look up, see a brunette dressed in what I can only assume is a five-hundred dollar dress and low pumps. She's wearing a hat and gloves. Her pink lips are pursed and she has this self-assured swing of her shoulders when she says each word.

I look right to left, thinking that maybe she's talking to somebody else. We've only been at the country club fifteen minutes and I think I've been accosted visually by every woman in the place for being with Colt. I think it is funny. I'm the only one that doesn't want to be with him. However, Anna calls me as soon as I get off work and she already heard from Gil that I'm going out with Colt. She's almost making wedding plans. I can't hardly tell her I think he's a dick after watching her sad expression burned into my brain the other day when she opened the empty cabinets.

Colt had picked me up at precisely six-forty-five. He'd stared at me really funny when I slipped out the door and met him on the step.

"I wasn't sure if I should dress like my friends or dress like your friends. So I kind of cut it down the middle," I told him. I was wearing a cocktail dress Anna helped me pick out for an art exhibit six months ago. It was a black off-the-shoulder lace. It was tight and Anna told me I ought to sell six pieces of art wearing this little number because the dress was sexy and it showed off my curves. I did sell two. Then I put my hair up in front and let little tendrils dangle down my back. That's what I figure his friends would wear. But I like the sexy stilettos Anna thinks are a bit risqué. And I like a bit more makeup than most with deep cherry red lipstick. That's the *me* part of the outfit.

"Um, yeah," he answers. And you know what? I don't really care if he's too stuck up to answer. I shrug it off. Then I kind of think it's funny. He's got on jeans and a t-shirt and a jacket.

"Is this okay?" he asks me. "I usually ask my mom or my sister. They aren't around. I'm winging it here."

"Colt, you could put on a plastic garbage bag and the girls would be chasing after you," I laugh. And again, he looks at me funny. Has he never heard somebody laugh out loud?

So I'm a little discombobulated. That's what Poppy calls it when he feels awkward and unsure, a little off-kilter. The ride to the restaurant was quiet. He's got a nice car and I can't think of anything to say but ask him what size the engine is. What a stupid thing to ask. But that's what Rocky and I talk about when he comes over and sits in front of my TV and watches shows with me. Kevin just talked about wrestling or baseball. It didn't matter. Colt didn't know.

I'm not sure if I'm overdressed, underdressed, or if the small talk around the table is what a joke it is that Colt Lucero and Raeanna Baldwin are going out tonight. I really don't know any of these people except for Delia, Alexandra and Taylor. It's just weird that nobody's saying anything about Hannah. I know it is because they are walking on eggshells around Delia. She keeps crying, dabbing a blue Kleenex to her eyes and nose.

Alexandra and Taylor just keep staring at me hard, pushing their heads together. I've got nothing in common with Colt so I just sit there quietly wishing I was anywhere but here. Especially now, waiting for Delia to come out of the bathroom because I think the woman facing me is calling me a prostitute.

So this is how Colt is playing it out, huh? I should have seen that coming. Did he pay for your services or did his mommy set this up? I don't know what the woman means. There's only a sharply dressed maître d' looking with bored detachment toward us. "I have no clue what you're talking about," I return. My eyes are veering toward the bathroom door, wishing Delia would come out. The other two girls have vanished. "And if you are implying I am being paid for any services, I would suggest you not do that because it sounds like you are calling me a whore. Who the hell are you?"

"I'm the girl Colt married for two weeks, then the one he left because he said he made a mistake."

"Oh, that explains it." I just stare at her. It didn't blow me away because I figure, everybody's got stuff in their locked closet they don't want folks to know. Mine is full of all sorts of stuff. Of course, it wasn't my idea to go snooping around anybody else's, and certainly not Colt's. I just didn't know the guy that well, didn't see anything more than eating dinner with him tonight and hoping to avoid him for whatever time it took for him to move on to another town. I just don't like feeling like I'm somebody's assignment, something broken that needs to be fixed.

She is looking me up and down from the tip of my toes to the top of my head. I stare hard at her in return.

"Hmmm. He seems pretty forgiving," I tell her. "You must have really screwed something up to lose a guy like that."

"Oh," the sound just peeps out of her lips. She almost slams into Delia when she pivots on her feet and high-tails it through the bathroom doors. Sobbing. I can hear it while Delia's eyes go from me to the bathroom doors.

"I don't want to know, Tango, what went on right there," she whispers to me. "You are a piece of work. I can't wait until this evening is over." Then she looks up over my shoulder. I see her face pale. "Oh, no, it's the owner of the country club." Delia says this like we're going to get kicked out because I made the woman cry. I can see two well-dressed men in suits walking directly toward us. One is tall with thick hair and the other is a bit dumpy with a black comb over.

"It's okay, that's my Uncle Lion," I tell her. He doesn't have a beard now, but he did when I was little. I thought he looked like a big, old lion. "He's my foster-dad's brother. He's alright." And he usually doesn't want to have much to do with Poppy and his family, which includes me. I guess you would call them estranged. Uncle Lion, his real name is Bill, got the country club in his father's will. I don't know why, didn't ask. I just know Poppy never talks about his family. But it's not a huge town and between church and family functions, we'd see them a few times a year.

"Well, you're all grown up," Uncle Lion says to me. He snatches up my hands and holds them out, looks me up and down. "How's your poppy doing?"

"Fine." I'm not going to broach any subject that might be controversial with Poppy's family, so I chitchat it up about my school. Then he drags me and Delia into his office and shows me a couple paintings Anna has given him from my exhibits.

"I wondered what she was doing with all of them," I laugh. "They aren't her kind of art. She likes flowers and gentle brooks and sandy beaches. She implies mine are a bit on the dark side." The one we are staring at is a three-dimensional view of a window. Outside, a couple kids are walking in a muddy creek.

"Amazing. Simply amazing." The man beside me reaches out, touches the canvas, and pokes a knuckle at it like he's going to knock on glass. "It looks like a real window. If those kids moved, I wouldn't be surprised. They look—alive."

"That's why I like this one while I work," Uncle Lion says to the man. "I can pretend I'm not here at all." He turns, points to his desk. "Check this one out. This is my favorite joke."

All our eyes go to the small cigar box laying there. Within, are a few cigars, a pack of bubble gum, and a set of keys. "Have a cigar, Walt," Uncle Lion says. Walt reaches out, bangs his hand on the canvas. It isn't an open cigar box at all. It's just a painting.

"Yeah, I was mad when I did that one," I told my uncle. "Everybody kept stealing my gum."

They laugh and I poke a finger toward the hallway, tell them we probably should get back to our group. Delia's mouth is shut tightly, her anger for the moment subdued.

"Before anything is said—" I hover by my chair moments

later. Colt looks up to watch Delia sit down, then turns to me. "I didn't say anything that would make most normal people cry."

"What?" Colt hops up, pulls the chair out for me. And yes, I took note of it while I sit down. It is nice. Poppy does it all the time for Anna.

"What, you ask?" I watch Colt sit. "Thanks for warning me about your ex. She's quite a piece of work and she's sobbing in the women's restroom. By the way, it would have been nice if you would have given me a heads up that I'm a revenge date. I walked right into that trap. I should be the one crying in the bathroom. She called me a whore."

"You didn't—hit her, did you?" Colt asks me.

"Of course not." I shrug. "I didn't need to. Right about now, she's kicking her own self from one end of the restroom to the other for whatever she did to *not* deserve you."

Colt's head tips to one side. I think he wants to either slide under the table or ask me what I meant. However, his phone rings and he picks it up, answers it. He looks at me, holds up a finger and slips out of his chair. I see him heading for the foyer.

Okay, six times, he does this even before we order. It occurs to me that he's trying to get out of the date long before he lingers over the back of my chair and asks if he can talk to me a minute. It really doesn't matter. Whatever polite conversation we had over my vegetarian plate and his huge steak was gone halfway through on his seventh time to the foyer.

"I have to leave." He leans in and tells me in the hallway. "I can take you home or I'm sure somebody else can drive you back. One of the families I'm working with is having an issue."

CHAPTER 13

WATCHING GOD SQUAD GET THE CRAP BEAT OUT OF HIM

"You don't know what you're getting yourself into, God Squad," I'm telling Colt that while he drives down High Street toward my apartment. He hasn't said anything about his ex-wife. Nor has he apologized for her verbal abuse. I guess he just figures I'm okay with everybody thinking I'm that girl somebody would use to make an ex think he's sleeping around. "I'm just saying." He's not listening. I am just about to put my earphones on, listen to music because his conversation is getting a bit—dramatic on the other end.

"Bring him home, bring him home!" I can hear the woman screaming. "They are going to kill Zane! Please, Colt—" But it was kind of tough to do it quickly enough.

"I know these guys," I mutter. "If that's Zane Hill, he's over at Troy Matteson's house. They are partying. They have beer and pot and a bunch of big high school guys that like to gang up on people. Zane's a good kid from the north side that got in with the bad crowd on the south side. And Troy's parents, they don't care what those kids do. Troy's dad, he doesn't like anybody that might look like police. You look like police."

"I think I've got it under control."

"You'll just drive over there, talk some sense into the kid? Drag him back to the north side of town to mommy and daddy?" I ask him. "I mean, that's easy. He's seventeen and grew up on the North Side. Seventeen year-olds who grow up over there and come over here, they like to impress their friends here that they know suits and ties like you, right?" Wrong.

"I've been working with him, Raeanna," he tells me. Colt's nice to look at. His eyes look so blue against his black hair. "He's coming around. Listen, I shouldn't be talking about other people's private things. But Zane, he's talking about going back to church, stop hanging around Troy."

"He'll tell you anything you want to hear, Colt," I tell him. "He'll tell you anything that gets you and his parents off his back." I fiddle with my earphone. "Troy's mom used to work with me at Joe's."

"What are you saying?" He turns to look at me. I can tell he must have been listening a bit. He looks concerned.

"I'm saying that I can go knock on Tonya's door. That's Troy's mom. I can see if Troy and Zane are there." I look him straight in the eye. "Because I can tell you, dressed like that, nobody's going to answer the door."

"That makes me feel really comfortable letting you go the way you're dressed," Colt sniffs sarcastically.

"I grew up with these people, went to school with them," I tell him. "They might look rough, but I know most of them. They know me and Poppy." I pause, sigh. "Poppy used to take a pine tree and presents over to the house on Christmas Eve so the kids had stuff to open. Troy's dad, Kyle, he used to drink a lot and had a hard time keeping a job. He's quick with a fist if he's mad. And I've been to a few parties there with Kevin."

"Why did I know you were going to say that?"

At eight-fifteen, Colt pulls into Troy's driveway. It is a tiny white house with knee-high grass and broken bicycles strewn all over the lawn. Troy's dad answers the door. Kyle Matteson's got a beer in his hand and gives me a painfully long leer from my boobs to my feet.

"What you need, baby girl?" he asks through the lit cigarette in his lips. Then he tells me that Troy isn't there at the same moment, Troy comes up behind him.

"Zane's mom is trying to find him. She's worried."

"I don't know where he is. Maybe he's at Brian Young's. Why are you asking?"

"Listen, you two are inseparable," I say softly, ignoring his question. "I know that you know where he is."

"Even if I did, I wouldn't tell you," Troy mutters.

"Okay, is there a reason?" I ask him. "Because I don't understand why Zane can't call or something. Can you call his mom and just have him check in?"

Kyle starts to close the door. His son steps back. "Just leave it alone, baby girl. It's none of your business. We'll handle it here." He's a big man with lots of plump to his belly.

"His mom is worried sick. I listened to her voice on the phone. I heard—"

"Yeah, you heard nothing. A bunch of crap is what it is. I've seen the kid. Whatever they are feeding you and him—" He nods to the car. I can see Colt standing at the car with his elbow resting on the open door. "It's crap."

"What do you mean?"

"You know," Troy says around his dad's shoulder. "Everybody listens to his parents' side of the story just because his dad's a teacher and they go to church every Sunday. His dad beats the crap out of him, Tango."

"Robert Hill, the math teacher hits his kid?" I almost laugh, think it's ludicrous. I had Mister Hill for Geometry. He was strict, but never seemed to have a bad temper. Then I see a shadow shift on the stairway behind Troy and his dad. My eyes narrow. I see a kid, maybe sixteen or seventeen. He's skinny and his hair is well-kept. He looks like any American kid except for the bruises. His eye is black and blue. He's got that look I know, the one *I* get. The one that screams *I just can't take it anymore, just kill me if he does it again.*

"Zane, did your dad do that?" I ask. But he isn't looking at me. He's looking over my shoulder. I turn too, see Colt taking long strides to the bottom of the one porch step.

"What does it matter? He's going to talk me into going back. Tango, I can't take it anymore. I can't do anything right. I'm sick of making excuses, telling people I fell down the steps, got hit with a baseball—"

"Hey, bud." Colt has on a happy face, the kind that is supposed to pacify. It doesn't work here. It is too fake. "Your mom and dad, they need you to come home."

I don't know the exact point Kyle starts throwing punches. There was about five minutes of back and forth conversation where Colt is trying to persuade Zane to come with him. I keep saying to him, *wait, wait, you've got to listen to what he has to say.* He isn't listening and I suppose that's what ticks Kyle Matteson off. Because it is just like he is suddenly a male wolf and one of his pups is getting attacked. *Boom, boom!* The next thing I know, he's just waling on Colt. He gets three or four good punches in before Colt, who is taking steps backward finally falls on his rear on the little sidewalk. I know he's going to dive in for more and I feel my heart pounding in my chest.

"Kyle, stop now." I slip between, push out a hand and gently place it on Kyle's belly. "Please," I say softly just like Poppy used to do to me when I got crazy. "Stop. I think he might listen to what you have to say now." I see him look down at me and I look him straight in the eyes. "He doesn't understand. Tell him now instead of raising your fist because punching him all the way to the street is only going to get the cops here."

Silence. Kyle Matteson's face is red and angry and his

eyes are bloodshot. So I turn my head, see Colt starting to rise slowly. He's got his hands out like he's showing he's not going to fight.

"Colt, Zane's mom isn't telling you the whole truth," I tell him. "Her husband is beating him. Kyle's family, here, is trying to protect him." I know it is difficult for Colt to see past Kyle Matteson's old, dirty t-shirt and rundown house on the south side and think that Robert Hill, in his suit and tie, living in his cute little bungalow on the north side would be the bad guy in the story unfolding. But he looks me in the eyes, looks at Kyle, then I see him nod like he's surrendering to an enemy that he realizes may have been right all along.

"You know, I should have listened to my own intuition. I had a suspicion there was more going on." He lifts his hand, rubs his chin where Kyle left a red mark. "I listened to Ralph Edward at the Wesley Outreach Program, —" he acts like he's going to say more, doesn't. "I guess it comes down to this. He's not going to be safe here, Mister Matteson." He looks around me, then takes a step forward so he's within range of Kyle's fist again. But I guess it shows a bit of trust while he sighs. "His mom and dad's next move is to call the cops, drag him back. I talked them out of filing a missing person report just yet."

"I don't want to go to the cops, Colt." Zane is standing at the doorway. I can see Colt eyeing him. He almost looks sad while he stares at the boy. "They won't believe me. Even if they do, they'll send dad to therapy again. It doesn't work. Tango, you get that, right?"

I nod, see Colt staring at me like he's sizing up what my situation could have possibly been. "Yeah, I do." I turn. "So find him someplace safe," I say to Colt. "Surely you know of some place he can go where they can't get him, right?

Aren't there safe houses?"

"He's not leaving my house unless I know the boy's safe," Kyle growls. "I'll get out my gun, shoot the cops if they try to take him back to that crap for a dad. I don't trust the suit here. I don't trust—"

"Kyle, Colt's on your side now. He didn't know." I turn and face Zane. "You never told him?"

"I didn't. I figured he was on dad's side."

I turned back to Kyle. "You're going to have to trust somebody or you're going to end up dead on the front lawn because the idiot cops, they aren't going to listen to your side of the story. Then Zane's right back where he started. Colt can get him to a safe place. You can trust him. For me, alright? You remember my dad. I wouldn't do that to any kid. If you don't trust him, trust me when I say Colt will get him somewhere safe. I won't let Zane get hurt again."

CHAPTER 14

WORST DATE EVER AND THAT'S NOT
INCLUDING THE EX SHOWING UP WITH A
BASEBALL BAT

"Worst date ever, huh?"

Colt asks me that at Swirly's Ice Cream in Belleview three towns over at eleven o'clock. We're sitting on the curb because the ice cream parlor only serves from the window after ten at night.

"Well, it's your lucky night. I've got nothing to compare it to," I tell him. We just spent the last two hours driving Zane to a safe house. The boy sniffled in the back seat most of the way. He looked so lost and alone it almost killed me. I regret it now, but I had looked down at the little vintage rainbow snap bracelet I was wearing. It's probably the only thing I have of my own mama. But it seemed appropriate at the time to take it off my wrist, turn around in the seat and snap it on to Zane's wrist. *This was my mama's. It's always made me feel safe because I think maybe there's a little bit of her in it. Maybe it's magic.* I wanted to tell him not to toss it in the garbage once he got out of the car. The moment I gave it to him, I wanted to take it back. I couldn't. Now, I'm filled with regret.

"I've never been on a legitimate date unless you can call Kevin driving me through the fast food drive through equal to or in close proximity of a veritable date. Then I've been on a countless number, maybe four times a week. He isn't a *take your girl out* kind of man. We were together for two years."

"You're lying again."

"I'm not." I smile because his face is expressionless

and intense both at the same time. "But, okay, my first real date hasn't been that bad. What girl could ask for more? We almost ate at the nicest restaurant in the county. There was drama, a fight, plenty of comedy—that would be the initial expression on your face when Kyle threw the punch."

"Wow, I was not expecting that. That guy hit me hard. I saw lights." He leans over and bumps my shoulder gently. "You know, you're my hero," he says, raising his voice like he's imitating a woman. "You saved my butt."

"There's always a fifty-fifty chance that he'd either slam me too or step back. Tonya used to talk about how gentle he was with her, so I figured the odds he'd hit a girl were slim. He's really a nice guy under all that poor white trash." I swipe the napkin across my lips. "You should have been watching his eyes, his stance, God Squad," I tell Colt. "If you see a man's eyes get big, see him change his position so he can lean back, and he takes in a big breath, he's getting ready to punch."

"You've seen that look before?"

"My dad was a drunk." I reach around, touch the tiny star on my shoulder. Colt takes note of it.

"You know, you do that every time you say *dad*." He reaches around and touches his shoulder to display that stupid habit I have. He's right. I don't deny it or agree. "You ever talk to your dad?"

"No. His buddies come into the diner once in a while when they are out of jail, bum money for cigarettes and beer from me. I used to steal money for him and his friends when I was a kid. Five bucks here, ten bucks there from Anna's purse and Poppy's wallet. They still come to me for money when they're down. Every time they come, I ask them if they've seen him. They haven't." I pat my purse at my side. "Sadly, I keep a twenty in there just in case he does show up. I suppose I think maybe he'll stop by for some money like his buddies do. He got out of jail a few years ago. I talked to him on the phone. But I haven't seen him since I was little. Still, I'll run out of gas first before I use it."

"I couldn't imagine hitting a little kid," Colt says softly. "At least they got you out of there before—" He's quiet for a minute. "You know, before he really hurt you." We watch three cars drive past beneath the spray of a red stop light. Colt finally breaks the silence. "I didn't see it as a revenge date," he finally says. "I mean, in retrospect, I guess I saw it in my head as minor benefit if we saw Bella. Her family visits here in the summer a lot. Is that a bad thing?"

"I don't know where you come from, Lucero." I push myself to my feet. "But we're obviously from two different worlds. Where I come from, when you imply a girl's a slut, it's a bad thing. When you invite a girl along for the ride because everybody assumes she's going to look the part of the local slut so a guy can appear like he's a player to his ex, that's a shitty thing to do."

"Raeanna—" He jumps up, towers over me. "Stop right there. Please. It wasn't anything like that. Holy cow, that's not what I meant when you called it a revenge date. It's because you're pretty, the kind of date that makes the other guys jealous you're not hanging on their arm. It isn't because of the way you act or look or how people perceive you."

Pretty. I look at Colt. I linger on that word, taste it with my ears like it's the soft song sung by a heavy metal band that blows me away because it is so unexpected. Nobody ever calls me beautiful. Yeah, he's probably just covering his ass.

"Listen, it was Gil's idea. And not as a joke. I think he is trying to keep you from going back to your boyfriend, have you meet new people."

"And that's even better than a revenge date. A pity date. That's what Delia called it. I think what your ex called me was actually better."

"What did Bella say to you?"

I sigh. "She asked if you or your mom paid me for my services."

"Oh, yeah, she can be mean. Don't listen to her. Nobody else thinks that."

"Listen, it doesn't matter," I tell him, looking up. "I'm tired. Anna and Poppy already watch Mia when I go to classes. I hate to ask them to do it any longer. Take me home." I puff out my cheeks, let the air out slowly. "Chris Peirce, the police chief, stopped at the restaurant today. He freaked me out. I'm just jumpy."

"What?" He draws the word out. I just shrug, start to turn.

"He just said he'd be watching me. Because of the picture I drew of him. He's creepy."

"Raeanna, you need to go to the cops about him." Colt's eyes are really wide. "He's not stalking you, right?"

"Well, I hope not. Delia told me that the guy she saw Hannah with didn't look anything like my picture after she really took a look at it." I laugh sarcastically. "Besides, he is the cops, Colt," I tell him. "And no, I wouldn't call stopping in at the only sit-down restaurant in town after church stalking me."

"I think she's lying. I think Delia changed her mind when she found out it was the chief of police. She felt threatened." He reaches out, snatches on to my arm and I look down hard at it. I follow his hand warily. He drops his fingers, steps back.

I contemplate this while we walk side by side to his

car. "I'll watch my back." He opens the door for me. I try to act cool about it, but it blows me away that he does it. We listen to the radio on the way home and I wonder if he's going to walk me to the door, try to kiss me goodnight. I'm not sure if I'm ready to take that step yet even though I find myself happier without Kevin around. I chew on this all the way until we pull into the parking lot and I see his old, beat up truck sitting next to my parking spot. It's a rusty red and the door to the bed of the truck is down. Kevin is leaning against it. He looks up when we pull in. I can see him squinting at Colt's car. Somehow, he knew I'd gone out with Colt. I'm assuming Rocky's his informant.

"Hey, just when you thought this date couldn't get any better," I say softly. Colt looks over at me and I roll my eyes. "The ex-boyfriend shows up."

"No, really?"

"You know what, Colt?" I ask him. I try to keep a straight face because he's looking down at me in the light of the parking lamps like a dog with its paw caught in a trap. "The perfect white trash date for me would be two guys fighting it out in the parking lot of Little Pine Estates Apartment Complex. Shirts off, full-out punches. Then one goes down and begs me to stay with him while the other carries me off into the sunset. You think you can do that for me? I'll let you call me Tango."

"You're kidding me, right?"

"I am," I laugh. But it sounds chirpy like I'm nervous. "You can drop me off here. He's probably just hanging out with Rocky." I poke toward a parking space three cars down from Kevin's. "Regardless, he's not a fighter. Really, it was Sophie who dragged my face down the stairway." It is true. Kevin's too lazy to fight anybody, too laid back. I've never seen him throw a punch.

"I'm walking you to the door."

"Suit yourself." I wait for him to open my door. It's not just a treat. I want to rub it in Kevin's face that a guy I'd go out with thinks I am worthy enough to act like what Poppy calls a gentleman.

I never expected it. We walk behind the cars to get to my apartment because Rocky parked his motorcycle on the sidewalk. He always does it when Missus Finch, who is about ninety, drives to the store. Her spot is next to his and he's terrified she'll open her door on his bike or just plow right into it because she's half blind and parks sideways.

When we come around the back of the truck, I see Kevin reaching into the back. Out comes his arm with a baseball bat.

"Babe, what's going on?" He asks me this like I don't remember the surprised look in his eyes, the laughter when he keeled over in hysterics without a stitch of clothes in the living room with Sophie bumping bare naked into his butt. "We had a good thing, right? Who's this dude?"

"No, we didn't have a good thing or you wouldn't be doing some*thing* with Sophie." I stop, dead still. This is really out of Kevin's usual behavior. The only thing I can think of is that he's been doing drugs. Meth? Weed? I don't know. "Walk away, please."

"Hell, we ain't even broke up," Kevin waggles the baseball bat in his hand, swings it in a circle. "You're out screwing around already? You didn't get my texts? I apologized."

"Kevin, we broke up the second you started screwing Sophie, which was October of last year as far as I can get from everybody else who knew," I say slowly while I reach into my purse. The scent of beer is seeping through the air from his lips. "And no, I'm not screwing around. This is my friend and he drove because I'm still working on getting the bumps and bruises off my car that you did with the tire iron." Within, I have a bottle of SureFire Bear Deterrent which I bring out in my right hand. In my left, I take the cute, pink Double-Dare stun gun Poppy bought me for Christmas. "We can do this one of two ways. You can leave and he walks me to the door. Or you can move that Louisville Slugger a quarter inch in either direction and I'm going to douse you in pepper spray, bugger off your balls with my stun gun, then I'm calling the cops to pick you up off the ground."

"Can we at least talk?" Now he's giving me the sad eyes. "Please, Rae Rae." He holds up one hand, then drops the baseball bat back into his truck. "Please, please, please. Just me. I ain't gonna hit him. I promise."

"Back off a minute, let me talk to Colt."

So Kevin pats the back of the truck, gives me a long look. Then he paces around the far side. I can see his shadow lingering there.

"Didn't see that coming," I huff softly, not taking my eyes off that shadow.

"What do you want me to do?" Colt's looking down at me. I feel his hand on my wrist like he's ready to whip me back if Kevin lunges on me. "If you still want that perfect date," he says in a low voice. "I'm willing to give it a try. But getting my butt laid flat twice in a night in front of you is going to kill my self-esteem." He's kidding. I see his eyes sparkle there. "Even if I leave, I'm going to be thinking all night he's coming back. You want me to call the cops?"

No, I didn't. So I'm poking my finger on the phone and texting Rocky instead. "I'll get Rocky. He'll talk to him. He'll keep an eye out."

"You'll lock the door? Do you want to go to Gil's?"

"I've been with him almost two years, God Squad, he's never raised a hand to me."

It wasn't ten seconds later, I see Rocky coming out his door, working his way down the steps. He's got two buddies with him, big guys. It's only five minutes later, I'm safe up on my balcony looking out and watching Colt's car fade away toward the highway. Rocky's talking low and easy to Kevin, getting him back into his truck. Then my eyes just happen to slide up to the billboard and that stupid sheet still covering my art. Just then, I swear I see someone up there. I squint hard, notice the sheet wiggle back and forth, then waver in the air, floating downward to the ground below exposing the image I'd painted there.

I can't quite describe the feeling I got then. It was strangely wonderful and scary both at once. God Squad. The guy who about fainted at the top of the water tower had climbed up on the billboard and dragged the damn sheet off. And I know that picture bugged the crap out of him.

CHAPTER 15

BAILING BILLY OUT OF JAIL

Field's Community College was built in 1868. There were two separate schools then, one for males and one for females. In 1972, the two merged. The side for men was renovated and updated with a new dance theatre and art classrooms. The older section once set aside for women only, was turned into administrative offices. That is, except for the old theatre that is used only when there is an overflow of classes. And by me.

On Tuesdays, Wednesdays, and Thursdays, I sneak into the old dance theatre by sliding ten bucks into Barney Greene's withered hand. He's the janitor at the old section. He opens the front doors for me, turns on the lights of the beautiful old theatre with solid oak stage floor, red velvet seating, and thick gold-colored curtains. Every time, he flicks on the lights, he flings his arm out and tells me: *Dance, little girl, dance your heart out. Dance like the devil himself is trying to steal your shoes.* Then he lets me dance my heart out on the stage from eight at night until ten. I lay a little blanket down for Mia on the floor or get her comfy in a chair and she plays on my phone or watches a movie on my tablet. Then around nine, she falls asleep to the sound of her mama twirling and pirouetting to the beat of my cell phone hooked up to a portable speaker.

I love to dance. I just don't get to do it much anymore. I'm stuck in that endless cycle of work, school, kid, and home. I was one of only eight girls worldwide chosen for the Ballet Theatre of America before I got pregnant with Mia and quit. I've since forgiven myself. Anna, my foster family, and my dance instructors, however, have not exonerated me of my sins. My chance, they all know, is long gone. I'm too old for second chances, too busy with life for redemption. I'm like a loaf of bread left to mold on the shelf. I just exist. While mentally, painting the town in graffiti helps me cope with my emotional pain, it doesn't physically wear me down so I can sleep past all the stupid things I've done to let folks down. And it doesn't get rid of the scary stuff that sticks in my brain—like what happened this afternoon at exactly three-fifteen.

I get home after work and Mia was bouncing up and down to go to the bathroom next to my knee. "Mama, mama, mama—I gotta pee." I start to stick my key in the lock and the door just opens with my touch. I feel my face flush. Nobody else has the key to my new lock. I can't help but backtrack, think maybe I was in such a hurry this morning that I forgot to lock the door, shut it tightly.

"Hey, the cops were here today."

It is Rocky. He is sliding out the door to his apartment across from me. He's so big, he has to lean forward with his shoulders to get out the door. I turn. "Here? Why?" I ask. My hands are holding back Mia from going inside.

"They picked up Billy Thompson to question him about the murders an hour ago," Rocky said. He's got his keys on a long chain dangling in his fingers and he's spinning them around and around. "They took him down to the police station and he was completely freaking out. He kept yelling for you. I told him I'd get you. You'd already left work. You weren't answering your cell phone."

"Did they go into my apartment?"

"Not that I know of." Rocky towers above me. He furrows his brow, looks over my shoulder while I wag a hand at my partially open door. He runs a hand through his hair, pushes around me and walks inside. I follow cautiously, while he goes from room to room. My closet door is open, but otherwise, nothing seems amiss.

"Maybe you left the door open. You need to be more careful, Tango. Somebody here'll steal you blind."

I laugh sarcastically. "I've got nothing but an old couch and my clothes, Rocky." However, I know I didn't leave the door open. But I've got nothing in my apartment anyone would want, not even my purse. Not even Poppy's suitcase full of porn. It's still in the trunk of my car. I tried to jimmy the lock open and couldn't. I decided to drop it off at Poppy's. I just haven't had the time yet to do so.

I'm more worried about Billy, though. Twenty minutes later, I'm standing at the front desk with Mia clinging to my neck begging a frigid-faced Rachael Updike to let me talk to Billy. She keeps pushing up the glasses on her nose telling me he is being questioned and isn't complying with the officer's requests so they may detain him. I try to explain to her that Billy is autistic and she keeps rolling her eyes, holding out her hands. That's all she will tell me.

So I do the last thing I want to do and that's call God Squad, plead for him to wiggle his fingers at the officers and sprinkle some of his righteous magic on them. He doesn't find the picture I paint in his mind amusing and consequently tells me so before he sighs. "Tango, don't say stuff like that. I can't get involved in a murder case."

"Please," I use my softest, sweetest voice I can conjure up in my agitated mental state. I know what he really wants to say—he doesn't want to be associated with me. But I let it go. "Please, Colt, I won't cuss for a week if you come. Billy, he doesn't do well with new people and I know he's freaking out. It's what you do, right? Help people?"

"Oh, I'm Colt now and not God Squad?" He laughs at that, cynically though. It seems an excruciating amount of time before I see him push through the front door of the police station and step across the gritty linoleum floor. Rachael is all smiles now and leaning into the counter, poking her hair with the nubby eraser of the pencil she's holding and with a flirty expression like she's getting picked up by the hottest guy at the bar.

Rocky is chuckling, thinks it is funny when five minutes later, Gabe Reynolds comes shuffling down the hallway, adjusts his gun on his belt, and wiggles his fingers at me.

"You know you scare the shit out of him," Rocky mutters to me beneath his breath while I shove Mia into his arms. They are so huge, they completely engulf her. "So I highly recommend using your indoor voice so you don't get shot."

Indoor voice. It's what I always tell Mia to do when she starts singing too loudly in the apartment building. *Baby, use your indoor voice so you don't wake up Rocky. He's been working late nights.* Except Rocky always complains that I scream the words louder than Mia's voice could ever be so she can hear me over her own voice.

"What the hell—heck?" I am grunting with my finger poking Gabe's chest. However, I take his advice lightly when I walk into the little cubicle they have Billy sitting in. He's claustrophobic and he is literally shaking and as white as a sheet. I'm right in Gabe's face, realize that Colt is behind me and forty minutes into my deal, I've already broken it. "Sorry. I cursed," I turn quickly enough to mutter and wave a hand in front of me. "Work in progress," I tell Colt whose eyes are blinking scared rabbit like I'm going to come after him. Then I turn back to Gabe. "Listen, Gabe Reynolds, you've got no right keeping him here. He is afraid of enclosed places, he is autistic. Unless you want me to call every support, protection, and advocacy agency in the Midwest, you better release him. He hasn't done anything wrong."

"We received a call that he was stalking girls with his binoculars from the apartment balcony, Raeanna, you need to calm down." Gabe is pushing out his chest and then pushing out a hand. "Back off or he won't be the only one sitting in here, do you hear me? We're just looking at all angles. And we've stepped it up a bit since a second girl was found."

Well, he *always* stalks girls from the balcony with binoculars. He's just curious. He wouldn't know what to do with one if he got within a ten foot radius of her. I honestly believe he thinks I'm a boy. I don't say that, though. I don't get to. Colt comes sweeping up between us, puts a hand on my shoulder. "He's just doing his job, Tango. What do you want him to do? Billy needs to answer more questions."

"Like where he was on the nights when the two girls were found dead," Gabe says gruffly. "He won't answer me."

"Well, okay." I take a deep breath. I bite my tongue because Gabe is being incredibly cocky now he has Colt as backup. "Can I please sit with him while you ask those questions? Because I can help him answer them. I know where he was every night from 9 o'clock in the evening until two in the morning. With me. We sit on the deck because we both can't sleep. Then he goes to bed. I know he has gone to bed every night because I hear him take a shower through the walls after we sit on the deck, then I hear his bed creak when he lays down. He bangs his hand on the wall between our apartments to let me know he got into bed alright and I do the same back to him." I turn to Billy and look at him. "Isn't that right, Billy?"

"Yes. I knock once. She knocks back twice." Billy

stares at me. "Tango, can you yell at them like you do the mailman when he puts the wrong mail in your box and make them let me go home."

"We have his computer. It has page after page of serial killer information, lists of girls killed—"

I sigh. "Gabe, he's looking up stuff for me." I feel my face turn hot with embarrassment. I don't look at Colt because I know it just sends me farther down the ladder to hell knowing I'm spawned from Hensley Grove's most notorious criminal. "I asked him to do it. Listen, do we need to get an attorney? Because God's honest truth, it was me who asked him to do the research. It—it is creepy interesting. Just because we think it is creepy interesting doesn't make us creeps." I toss my hands out. "You know, and I don't even want to ask if you have a warrant to search his apartment—"

"He offered up the computer," Gabe tells me. He holds his arms out at his shoulders like he's stepping away from that situation. "He opened the door, let us in."

"And, Gabe," I growl. "He shouldn't have and you know the average person would not do that."

"I did not let him in," Billy hisses. "The mean cop had his foot in the door. I said *no*."

"The mean cop?" I ask. But I know. It is the chief of police. "Okay, is he under arrest? Because if he is, right now, he is going to ask for a lawyer."

"No."

"Then give him back his computer and release him," I say. I feel a little dizzy. Because I've got a good feeling that poor ol' Billy is sitting in here because of me, because of the picture I drew.

"My mom's going to be mad at me if she finds out I'm in jail. She's already mad at me because I said I'm not going to the Fields Acapella Club dance. The girls are either too fat like that cop," he points at Gabe. "Or too skinny like Tango." However, I feel shivers from his shoulders.

Gabe narrows his eyes at Billy, appears to ignore the criticism. "Chief Peirce, isn't going to be happy," Gabe tells me. "He's on his way into the station, cut his fishing trip out on the river short to sit in on the interview."

I turn to Colt. He's just staring at Billy who is sitting in the chair rocking back and forth with his hands clasped at his lap. He hums to himself when he's upset. It sounds like a lullaby. He's doing that right now.

"Gabe, have a heart," Colt's eyes work upward to the police officer who is eyeing Billy warily. "Tell your chief he was demanding a lawyer so you had to release him, would you?"

"Gabe, can you and Mister Lucero go for a walk a minute?"

Both Colt and I look up, then latch eyes to each other. He looks as unsure as me. I see Chloe Murphy standing at the doorway with her arms crossed. She nods her head toward the door. I see Colt start to protest, she shakes her head. "I'm not asking, Mister Lucero. Out." She nods her head toward the door, then moves aside to allow the men to exit.

"Listen, I caught the gist of what's going on here. And I'll take the fall for this one, have Billy released if you do me just a little favor, Baldwin." She closes the door with both hands. She's skinny, muscled where her Hensley Grove police uniform shirt sleeve stops above the elbow.

A little favor. My mind reels. She wants me to knock off someone? She wants me to snitch on somebody? I can't see how this is going to fare well.

"You know, Russel Adams just retired from his

detective position. They gave me his job temporarily to see how it works out. I know the reason the commissioners who hire did it. Because I'm a woman and the city has been pushing them to hire more women because there aren't any working here but me. And I know why the chief agreed. Because he thinks I'm an easy fail. You see, the chief plops cold cases in all the officer's laps to work on four or five hours of our work week. He gives the oldest and most difficult to the seasoned officers because he knows there's a better chance they'll get solved by them. Makes sense, right? He thinks it gives a look at cold cases with a new set of eyes, a different perspective." She leans her back on the doorframe, scrubs it back and forth like a bear scratching on a tree. "I'm good with that. I've been here three years. I know I've got a lot of learning to do. And I like a good mystery. Maybe, I figure, I'll solve an old robbery case and get a chance at becoming a permanent detective one day."

I'm just blinking at her.

"So, you can imagine my surprise when I get the biggest case in the Midwest slapped on my desk the first day I'm at my new position. At first, I'm thinking that the boss, he sees something in me and so I get a big head about it. Then I find out it was some big joke and I'm the butt end of it. He thinks a stupid woman isn't going to solve a case, starts calling me Cold Case. He gets a big laugh out of it with his buddies. Now, every time I walk into the room, I get called Cold Case and I know I'm stuck with that name until I retire twenty-two years from now."

"So you want to solve the case," I mutter softly.

"Yeah, stick it to the man. Isn't that what they used to say in the 1950s?"

"I don't know."

"But you do know, Baldwin, what case I'm working

on, don't you?"

I did. The murders of the girls. "I was six when I got taken away from him, Officer Murphy. I was a kid and stupid and—I don't think he did anything more than rob houses."

"And obviously, you're digging up information, too, although you did not allude to it five minutes ago."

I know what she is referring. I didn't mention the reason I was looking up information because Colt was there. I disregard it. Is it not enough I don't want anybody else to know about my relationship to an alleged mass murderer?

"I'm trying to prove he didn't do it, Chloe."

"Well, you help me. I'll help you. If you do it, I'll get Billy released tonight. You give me information that only you can give the police department. I'll give you what we have. Maybe we'll prove him innocent. Maybe, we won't."

She takes out a business card from her breast pocket and hands it over to me. "My cell phone if you need it."

So three hours later, I am dancing like the devil's trying to steal my shoes because I did what I could to get Billy out of the police station interrogation room. I get to shove aside the tears falling from Billy's eyes while Rocky and I drive him back to the apartment. I get to forget Colt chastising me for screaming at a cop and the humiliation of twenty minutes apologizing to Rocky for pulling him into the situation. Because I get this God-awful fear he's next in line for the Chief getting back at me for drawing that picture. I get to forget it all for one-hundred and twenty minutes of hardcore, break-ass dancing.

CHAPTER 16

FAKE BAND-AIDS AND the

MYSTERIOUS DANCER

I'm forty minutes after painting a drunk sprawled on the sidewalk behind the Don's All-Nighter Tavern and twenty-five minutes into my workout. Mia's tucked into a chair in a blanket at the old theatre and watching cartoons on my computer tablet. And her mama dances. Pirouettes, turns, and then to kick it up a notch, three jumps. I can't get it to fall together. I get two jumps in. Just as I try for the third, I plop on the wood floor like a fat kid doing a belly flop off the pool high board. It really isn't difficult. I just can't get high enough. I'm laying there on my belly, banging my head on the floor after seven attempts, hands in fists over my head. Mia is giggling at my tantrum, not comprehending it is real and not her mommy being silly.

"Your body isn't aligned correctly on the last jump so your weight isn't distributed properly."

I snap to attention, eyes wide. I hear the soft woman's voice and then the kind of sniff that comes after a good, hard sob. Nobody's supposed to know I'm here or Barney'll get fired. After hours, the college doesn't want to waste money on utilities. They don't want lights on or people working. And I certainly don't want anybody knowing I'm here like I'm trying to redeem myself of my past mistakes. I squint past the stage and into the filmy darkness and over the long rows of red velvet theatre seats. I see a thin shadow hunkered down back there in the rear.

"It's just me." It is Delia Childs. "After you bend—that last plié, you're leaning slightly forward so you can't get the height. It's a basic move. You should know it."

"What are you doing here?" I push myself up on my hands, turn my gaze to Mia who is craning her neck over the seat to see Delia.

"I should ask you that question in return. But I'm trying to get as far away from everybody else as possible," Delia answers. I hear her huff another dry sob. "I thought I found a hiding place in the old section. Not so, I guess."

"I can leave." I push myself to my feet, cringe inwardly at the ramifications of getting caught in here. If Delia tells anybody, I could get in a lot of trouble.

"What are you wearing?" Delia's voice cracks and she snuffles a giggle that trickles shards of glass in the air.

I look down. I've got on a raggedy black tutu and faded pink tights, and off-pink, worn-out legwarmers. I've got matching knit arm warmers because it is cold in the theatre even in the summer. My scrawny arms stick out like twigs. My outfit isn't that unusual barring the cut up t-shirt I'm wearing that Mia made me in preschool. It just doesn't match the strict guidelines of dancewear Shane Delgado demands that his students wear in his dance classes. It is far from the fresh new ones Delia is donning right now—black leotards, pink tights and pink ballet shoes—all from high end dance stores.

But I have a scar on my back. It is just below my left shoulder blade. It is about six inches in length and shaped like the side of the broken whiskey bottle that left the wound. Daddy dropped me on the bottle when I was two after I turned down his suggestion that I go to bed. I remember him holding my mouth shut while I scream-sobbed yellow snot and he taped up my wound with masking tape. Hence, the scar. Anna used to buy me tailor-made racerback leotards that stopped just above the pale white scar. I don't have the luxury of splurging on dance clothes now. A t-shirt hides my past. I roll my eyes, shrug.

She's one of Shane Delgado's chosen ones. I'm surprised she flew the coup.

"It's what I've got," I tell her flatly and wait for another snide comment. I'm assuming she's back to persecuting me since Colt isn't around. It doesn't come. Instead, there's another sob from the seats.

"I can't dance anymore. Nobody understands. They act like Hannah just went on vacation to Myrtle Beach and she'll be back. Do you know what that serial killer does to those girls? He rapes them, hits them with a hammer, then he cleans them out with bleach. That's what Taylor told me her dad told her. Except nobody talks about her because it's like if they do, I'll explode or something. I—I can't dance without her. Shane says to me today that he thinks I should use my anger and grief to make my dance better. Really? Really? God, he is an idiot."

Crap. I groan inwardly, let my shoulders drop. Although I agree with her, I'm not so good withy whiny, crybaby girls. Shane Delgado told me last week that unless I pass two of his classes, he won't let me graduate. He has held me hostage with this threat for almost four years.

"Um, it will come back to you," I mutter. "My Poppy used to tell me that it just takes time for wounds to our soul to heal. I suppose, Delia, if you are like me, your dancing comes from your soul. You just have to—"

"What do you know about that? Have you ever lost anybody you loved? Well, at least somebody that was worth losing," she spats at me with another sob. Suddenly, I'm the target of her anger. "I just want her back."

"Well, my mama left me. I don't miss her as much now like I did when I was little," I offer. "And Poppy told me those words when children's services would take me away from my daddy when he hit me. I don't miss him so much.

So that's what I know."

"You miss him at all?" Delia scoffs.

"He was my dad, Delia. He took care of me. He just scared me." I was getting ready to snatch up my purse, when I look down to Mia blinking up at me.

"Mama," Mia's soft whisper comes to me from her blanket. "She's crying. She needs a Band-Aid and a kiss." Oh, Mia's even got tears in her eyes.

"A Band-Aid isn't going to make her feel better, baby," I whisper hoping Delia didn't hear her words. "She hurts on the inside. Nobody can do anything about that."

"Yes, you can," she tells me in a soft voice. Her words still echo through the theatre specifically designed to carry voices. "Like the fake Band-Aid."

"What's she talking about?" Delia asks. I look at her, then follow her gaze to Mia who is dressed in a raggedy pair of pink pajamas with frayed hem at her ankles. She's got a lime green tutu around her waist and the mesh fabric is partially ripped away. On top, she is wearing her favorite t-shirt with a big teddy bear decal peeling off the front.

Delia sizes Mia up and down like she's a slimy, brown slug working its way across the sidewalk. I suppose in her world, little kids have matching pajamas. In Mia and my world, it's whatever I can grab when I stop long enough to make us a quick supper after work and before the janitor locks the door to the building here.

Ug. The Fake Band-Aid. Those are the pretend bandages I put on her skinned knees when I don't have a real one around. Of course, that's most of the time because I never have enough money for those little extras. I'm generic toothpaste and old toothbrushes, dollar store soap and hand-me-down bathroom towels. Mia's looking at me with her wide, unblinking eyes. I know if I tell her the stupid fake bandages don't work, my credibility with her is shot.

So I turn slightly to take in the oozy silhouette in the back of the theatre. "Fake Band-Aids are stuff that makes you feel better when you don't have the real thing. Like comfort food. Like painting for me." I see Delia rise, slip out of the shadows and into the dim lights of the aisle. "Hannah and I used to dance together. It was my—my comfort food, I guess. Now that she's—she's not here I can't dance. I don't want to dance and nobody gets it. Nobody understands that everything *dance* reminds me of her. I mean, you took the classes with us since kindergarten." She stops, shivers. "Oh, screw it. I don't even know why I'm telling you. You hated Hannah. You're probably glad she's dead."

"Why would you say that?" I've finally had it with her. "You have no right to say that. You come in and disrupt the only time I have to dance and give me crap. Go away."

"Why do you even bother to dance, Tango?" Delia growls. "It's a waste of time. You're too old to go anywhere and nobody's going to hire you except maybe at the strip club while you climb up a pole for a bunch of horny old men."

I stare at her, let my eyes roam down to Mia. She doesn't understand the words, but I know she gets that Delia is saying mean things to me. My jaws are churning. Delia comes into the light and I can see the pain in her blue eyes. I *feel* the pain in those eyes. I don't want Mia to see me fighting. I don't want her to see the things I saw with my dad so I take in a breath and let it out slowly, then I hold out my hand and wiggle my fingers. "Come dance with me, Delia," I say without expression in my voice. "I'll be your fake Band-Aid."

I simply throw her so off-guard that she stands there for thirty seconds blinking at me. She's expecting an angry retort. I can remember when I was nine with gangly legs, knobby knees, and frizzy dark hair, wishing so badly to have her perfect features, her long blonde hair. Even now, while I watch her doe eyes searching my own and even in their puffy red, I wish I was her. We're so opposite in character. She's usually well-spoken, I'm mouthy. Her blonde hair is fine and my brown hair is frizzy. She's light to my dark.

Then her head drops slowly and she stares at the floor before she takes six steps toward the stage and grabs my hand. I tow her up.

"Mia," I say, turning my attention down to the pile of blankets near the rear of the stage. "Go to my playlists and turn on some music for us."

So we dance to slow songs for a half hour and then fast for another forty minutes. We mix it up with ballet and modern dance and I even do some flips and end up crashing off through the curtains into the stage equipment. Delia barks a laugh when I come back through with a silly dance right through the curtains. Mia looks like she's enjoying picking the songs, playing mini-deejay.

We only have fifteen more minutes. I turn on one last song. I remember one of the old routines we used to do our first year and suggest we dance the same sequences. We feign having partners because neither of us have the muscle to lift the other. We tried twenty minutes earlier and ended up in a loose pile on the floor. While we dance in the shady depths of the old building, I'm thinking that maybe Delia's not so bad. I'm thinking that it is nice to have somebody to dance with and not be by myself all the time.

Then while I'm thinking these thoughts and fuzzing out while my body follows the music, I look over and there is a man dancing with us, picking up our steps in perfect synchronization. He's wearing a black tank top and workout pants so I know instantly, he's here with Shane Delgado or his classes. I'd never seen him at Field's Community College and he's got a dancer's body, the kind that tells me he takes his work seriously. He's tall and obviously well-tutored. He slides between us and slightly behind me but not before I catch a swatch of black hair and deep brown eyes. He sees me eye him, gives me a slight smile. Oh, shit. It is none other than Russian Mafia.

I turn away, suddenly shy and embarrassed. I should have known he was with Shane's class. I suppose I feel like this is my safe place here and suddenly, it is getting taken over by outsiders. Yes, outsiders in the plural form. I can hear voices in the back of the theatre where the audience sits. But I can't grind my teeth in irritation long. The part comes for a lift and I feel hands on my waist. I just go with it. Do I have a choice? I feel him lifting me up.

"So you are playing the part of the dancer, tonight?" I ask him. "Your lover has still not been found and you search among the villagers for her. Perhaps she is hidden here."

"You are a silly girl. Can you focus on the dance? Do a backbend on one hand, a cambré press lift?" he asks me while I swing around and upward. His accent is thick like peanut butter stored in the refrigerator. His hair is fine black and tied up in a bun in back.

"My question to you is can you lift me?" I return.

"I could toss you to—Rio, is it? I mean where my lover was last seen. I can do it with one hand and you can give her a note from me." He probably could toss me that far. He's well-muscled and toned like someone who doesn't just work out on equipment, but also focuses on the conditioning exercises for dancers. And, okay, yeah there isn't a single muscle in that bodysuit and workout pants that is hidden like it was in his suits at the diner.

"Don't toss me to Rio," I grunt while he lifts me and I fall back, let my hands drip down. "I think she is headed for London now. Her plan was foiled again." Perfect. It feels so good and he is steady, strong and confident like I remember

Shane Delgado being. "Okay, coming down." His voice is smooth, his movements well-orchestrated and athletic. He's more modern ballet than the old-school.

"How advanced are you?" he asks. "Do you trust me?"

"Did you trust I wasn't a spy and poisoned your food? Throw me something. I'll stop you if I can't do it. I'll probably puke on you first before I ever fall. And I'll trust you until you drop me."

"Nice to know." He smiles and his teeth are almost blinding white. "It was delicious, by the way. American, but homemade like my mother's." He has a genuine smile and a quick laugh.

He holds me there like I'm as light as a piece of paper, then brings me down to the ground. I fall into a natural stance and we dance forward in the same direction, fall into the pattern Delia is still dancing. Damn, he's good and fits me like a glove. I'm not sure how to take this. Usually the men I'd been paired with, other than Shane, were not so coordinated, experienced, and gentle. I feel he is going to great lengths to be in harmony with me.

"Let's see how strong you are." And he's talking to me, asking me if I can do this or do that. All intermediate dance jumps and lifts, a couple advanced where he has me run toward him and he raises me up and over his head in the bicycle lift. The whole time, he's talking and talking and I'm concentrating on what he says, communicating like I used to do with my partners. And he gives me a *holy shit* when we do a one handed presage lift. He lifts me with both his hands, then releases one. "Yeah, yeah, yeah—" I'm telling him so he knows I'm feeling comfortable. Maybe I'm not. I haven't done this lift in a few years.

"Okay," he says. "Look at me."

"Oh, you're kidding me," I mumble because I know it

is difficult. But I do it as he tells me, then I cross my eyes and stick out my tongue at him. I can feel him shiver a bit beneath my weight and I think he is trying to stifle a laugh. That's when I feel the tumble coming on.

"Tango! Stop! This is no time for being childish." It is Shane Delgado's voice behind me. I know he saw what I did and as we both shift forward, I feel us stop, see Shane's palm come out and steady my partner before he swings around and helps me to the floor. Then my old instructor is screaming at me about ridiculing one of the most beautiful of all ballet lifts and how I could have injured my partner.

Shane Delgado. He's like the perfect specimen of the male dancer. He's forty-something and muscled and he can charm the tutu off just about any dancer. At least, he did so with me. He's trendy blonde hair and blue eyes. He's always sweeping the bangs from his face with his fingers. He does so now while he stares bloody daggers at me.

"Do you know who you're dancing with, who you are mocking?" he yells at me. I can hear the muffled swish of clothes and know there are more than a few people in the theatre now, most likely his class. I can feel my cheeks heating up like I've opened an oven door and stuck my head a little too close. "Don't tell me you're that stupid, girl."

"Oh, screw off, Delgado," I hiss back. "I don't give a rat's butt who it is. You need to lighten up."

"Lighten up," his voice lowers while I turn my back to him, ready myself to walk out. "You don't turn your back on me."

I swivel around. "Like you didn't turn your back on me? Payback is a bitch, Delgado." Too late, I did exactly what he wanted, facing him again. I curse myself for turning around at all. If I was a cool woman instead of a hot-headed girl, I would have simply walked away. He just stands there. I see him quiver, know he is livid. Anna used to go on and on about how passionate he was when she'd watch my programs. She's such a fan of ballet, she goes to every one within a two-hundred mile radius, buys all the magazines, and even takes adult lessons at the Hensley Adult Career Center. However, if she called Shane passionate, I would call him fiery, raving mad. He used to scream at me so hard while he was teaching me the jumps that my ears would ring after class. I've had a stressful day. I came here to unwind. Instead, my happy, safe place just got invaded by all the people I don't like.

"I don't have to do what you say," I tell him softly. I take step backwards, lift up my chin and give him the smuggest smile I have. "Go to hell. You don't own any part of me anymore. I'm not in your classes. I'm not—" He cuts me off there.

"You're nothing. I know," he tells me with a haughty twist of his muscled shoulders. "And if Dean Paulson finds out you've been coming in here without permission, you're going to be in a whole lot of hot water."

I hold out my arms and turn to leave. "I don't care."

"But if you walk out that door, you will not be attending my class this upcoming fall. If you don't attend my class, you don't graduate. Do as I say. Respect your partner and finish the dance."

My eyes roll over to the man who had performed the dance with me. On the surface, he is cool and watching Shane without even the slightest hint of expression to let me know what he is thinking. I'm assuming he's already assessed my situation, taken in my tatty, threadbare clothes and wishes nothing more than to run like hell. Delia is standing behind him, her eyes as wide as fists looking from me to his back and then to Shane. Alexandra has sidled up beside her, white hair atop her head in a bun. She's holding her hand, whispering something to her like she's cooing a baby to sleep. Her fingers are pushing back her hair.

"Fine." I step off the stage and take the four steps to where Mia is settled into the chair. I tug my phone from her fingers and push on the spiciest revenge song I can find in the moment. Then I turn slowly and walk back up on stage.

It is quiet except for the music. There are probably six people on the stage and a dozen who had just come in the doors. I'm assuming they were all looking for Delia. She's such a drama queen. I step up to the stage again and stop coolly in front my mysterious dance partner and set myself with a grandiose, but graceful bow.

"Show me the way home," I tell him. For a minute and a half, I let him guide me around with his pirouettes and a handful of jumps and lifts. Then I turn and make small quick steps and stop just short of Shane. I hold my arms up asking him for a dance and his jaws are grinding so loudly, I hear his teeth gnash together. He turns me around and we dance across the floor while he starts to snap his own dance moves to me. Then, I suddenly turn my back on him and go into a full jump toward my other partner. I don't think any of them were expecting me to turn. Back and forth between the two, I go for another song. Shane is still calling out moves. Now he is jumping in to snatch me up when he feels I've danced enough with the other man.

I wrap my legs around the first man and play as passionate as I possibly can, then I turn during the last verse and start to do the same to Shane. He lifts me high and we turn, a perfect one-handed presage. He didn't see it coming until I turn my eyes downward to his. I smile, soft and sweet. Then I swing my leg around and bounce it off his head. Shane falters, caught off-guard. I see his eyes widen. I gently swing around him so his arms guide me downward belly to belly, a quick catch on his part to keep us from flipping forward. That's when my fingernails grasp holy hell on his back while my legs slide down his thighs. I take cherry red nails, let them rip hard and steady through his shirt and into his flesh from shoulder blade to hip.

He cusses, shoves me away when my feet hit the floor. We stand there face to face after I take the step back. My lips take on a mocking twist.

"Damn you, Tango," he growls between his teeth while I wiggle my shoulders and shrug. "Get out of here. You destroy the beauty in dance. Get out of here. Don't ever come near me or my classes. If you do, I will have you thrown off school property and I'll press charges."

But I'm already grabbing up my backpack and working my way to Mia. I can see her big blue eyes with thick, dark lashes blinking across the room at Shane Delgado's blue eyes with thick dark lashes. A matching set, they are. But if anyone else notices that, I don't know. I lift her up, swing my free arm high, and flip my middle finger at them all while I walk away. I yell the loudest *F-You, Shane* that echoes in the theatre and down the empty and dark halls. Already, his little coven of bloodthirsty dancers are honing in on their leader, lifting up his shirt, fussing over him. He pats Delia's hands away. "You don't own me," I grunt. "Don't try to screw with me."

Just as I am about to push through the doorway, I can hear my partner turn to Shane. "Where have you been hiding the diva here?"

And I can hear Shane's answer: "In the darkest depths of hell, I think."

I almost stop. The anger in my belly is bubbling, but I'm on the threshold of bursting into tears. The door opens for me and I see who is pushing it with one arm so he can give me a wide berth. Colt Lucero.

"I know. Work in progress," he mutters to me while I blink a bit stupefied at him and walk off into the dark.

CHAPTER 14

DEAD GIRL: SUSAN JAMES

When I was four, my daddy took me to a huge, tan house with big iron gates on the driveway. I remember the driveway because it was asphalt and freshly coated to a wet looking black shine. The pungent odor of the blacktop sealer slipped through the partially open window in the backseat and burned into my nostrils.

"Daddy needs you to climb through the window and open the front door. It's my boss's house and he wants me to pick up something inside. But I forgot to get the keys."

"Okay, daddy," I remember saying. It had always seemed daddy had a bunch of different bosses and a bunch of different houses he needed me to open. He was always good at forgetting to ask for the keys at work. So we got out of the car and walked in the shadows to the back of the house. He jimmied open a window with his hands, lifted me up, and I fell to the carpeted floor on the other side. It was only a minute later I would let Daddy into the back door still rubbing my knees where they ached from the fall. He made me stand at the back door while he rifled through each room. Then, when he found what his boss was needing, we left into the night.

By the time I was six, I was an old pro at just climbing through the window and rummaging through the house for valuables. I don't know if there was even a point where I went from thinking I was looking for something for his boss to comprehending we were robbing a house. I was just a kid and doing what Daddy asked me to do. It was more a treasure hunt for me. I thought it was fun, finding the booty while Daddy stood watch outside and waited for me to return with rings and money and just about anything valuable that could fit into a plastic grocery bag. And Daddy, he got a shiny look to his deep brown eyes matching the asphalt driveway when I found old coins or cash.

"So how'd your old man get caught?"

"Huh?" I blink out of my memory, swear I catch the faint scent of asphalt in my nostrils when I look up at Officer Chloe Murphy. She's dressed in informal work clothes—a pair of dark green pants and a polo shirt with HENSLEY GROVE POLICE written on the back. I'm telling her my story. It isn't because I want to do it. I don't have a choice. It was the proposition she gave me so Billy got released. "Oh, well, it was right after Anna and Ray Baldwin took me in. I started going to church with them. The Sunday school teacher read us a story about Zacchaeus, the tax collector who embezzled money from people. And she had this picture of him sitting in a tree so he could see Jesus when he came to his town. And Jesus was smiling and waving him down even though he stole money. Jesus looked so nice with a big smile and—until that moment, I didn't understand what we were doing breaking into houses. That the Jesus in the picture with the smiling face thought it was wrong made me worry he wouldn't like me. So the next time children's services gave me back to daddy, I went into the house and instead of ransacking it, I found a phone and called 9-1-1. You did say this was all confidential, right?"

"Yeah, if that's what you want." Chloe is staring at me expressionless. "It goes both ways. You don't discuss what we're talking about. Of course, I'll drag your scrawny ass to jail if you start chirping like a robin to everybody."

"That's nice to know." I don't trust her. I know she doesn't like me or trust me. But I've got nothing else, nobody else to toss information to me but Billy.

"So this is where they found Susan James in '58," Chloe tells me, lifts up a sheet of paper from the packet she is cradling in her right arm. "In 1958, your dad would have been about twenty-one. I've got his birthdate as around 1937. He's a pretty big guy. So at that time, he was perfectly capable, age-wise and size-wise, of murdering someone of Susan's stature." She is standing on the side of the road in the grass beside the first of two huge stone roadway viaducts running along High Street through town. To her right and where I am leaning is a sign bolted to the stone. It says: WELCOME TO HENSLEY GROVE. Such, everybody here calls this section the Welcome Viaduct. "It says on here she was twenty-two. She was last seen at nine o'clock at night leaving the Hensley Grove Public Library where she was the assistant librarian. She was found seven weeks later right about where you are—standing."

I know my eyes get wide. I shiver, take a step to the left. Chloe smothers a smile. "You mind looking at a couple pictures? They are kind of gory, something you might see on an R-rated horror movie. You're not a priss about these things, are you?"

"No, I'm fine," I lie, shake my head. She takes a step over. I see her watching my face while she exposes the black and white image of a dead woman sprawled on a small embankment beneath the very pillar we are standing alongside. Her face is contorted. She is wearing a wool jacket, skirt and tiny hat on her head. Her right arm is bent at the elbow with the hand cradling her head like she is laying out and looking at the sky. Her left arm is resting on her belly. Both hands have white gloves covering them.

"Look at the fingers of her left hand." Chloe pokes a finger at the picture. I squint, try to focus on a tiny, white object between her forefinger and middle finger.

"What is it?"

"A cigarette," she says. "Your dad, did he smoke?"

"Yeah, I suppose. Didn't everybody back then?" I know I cringe. I'm not a horror flick type of person.

"Susan's family and friends say she didn't." Chloe shifts a bit on her feet. "Do you know what kind of cigarettes he smoked?"

"I don't know," I force my eyes away from the woman and to her surroundings. "I remember the pack was red and white." There are six or seven men hovering above her in the picture, all are wearing 1950s suits and ties and have nondescript faces. One is squatting next to her in a gray suit and a narrow brim fedora hat. A second is kneeling down next to him with an old fashioned camera and taking a picture. Behind them, there are two more men, bystanders perhaps. One is holding the hand of what appears to be an eight or nine-year old boy. It is like a pose for an all men's club crime movie, creepy and like it is set to be published in a magazine. I let my eyes flow to the left and the old five story Baymont Hotel.

"Okay, you're not alright with it," she says. Chloe quickly flips a page and snaps the pictures away. She laughs aloud like it is funny.

"Don't act like I'm a baby," I mutter. "It is disturbing. How'd she die?"

"A hammer to the side of her head." Chloe pushes her fingers to a place just above her right ear. "There was a perfect imprint of the claw part, the neck, and the face of the hammer. It was one hit. The guy had to be strong. So you ever see any of these images at your father's? Maybe a photo of the woman when she was alive?"

"No." I'm honest. I know she doesn't believe me.

"Do you have any questions for me?" she asks and scoots up her pants to her flat belly. "Because I'm trying to be fair about this. I think it was your father. But I'm willing to be open about it. Not all of this is public information, like the cigarettes. But if you work with me, Baldwin, I'll tell you what I've got." She pauses, gives me a half-smile. "And I've got boxes and boxes cluttering my office. Well, at least for now. I'm assuming eventually, they are going to tie these two new murders in with the old and the feds will take it over. Say if you want to say."

I'm not a cop. I don't think things out like they do. So I just stand there. "Um, who are those men in the picture?"

She stares at me for a second, then blinks like she's confused I'd even ask it before she opens the packet again and turns it to me. "I'm not sure who some of them are, but I do know this is Ben Cunningham." She points to the man taking the picture. He owned the Hensley Grove Tribune, retired a couple years ago. Back then, he was one of the guys that wrote the articles on the murder. I've got the articles in a box. Now his son and grandson run it. Phillip King is the little guy in the scout uniform. He's right here." There is a boy standing on the outside of the picture with hands in pockets of a scout uniform. He is toeing the dirt with his shoe. "I'd say he was only twelve or thirteen. One of these guys was his dad. " She pushes her face in closer, narrows her eyes. She moves in closer and she smells like mosquito repellent. "The guy who is kneeling next to him, that was the police chief in 1958. I've seen his picture on our wall. He was Chris Peirce's grandfather. Oh, and if you look close, you'll recognize him." Chloe looks up at me, winces and points to the boy. "That's Chris Peirce. He was just a kid."

"They let him see the body?" I ask, shivering.

"It was a different time, you know?" Chloe shrugs. "I'm sure there were lots of people behind the photographer gawking at the scene. Tango, you'd be surprised at what people let their kids see and do—" She sees me eyeing her hard and sighs. "I guess I don't have to tell you that."

"I'm getting the feeling, though, even if he did do something more than robbing people, he had better judgment than these dudes," I tell her. "Can you get me a copy of the picture and write their names on it?"

"Yeah, sure, as long as you're not going on some vengeance trip—"

"No," I laugh. "I'm just trying to find a place to start. You promise me this is confidential, right?"

"Yes. And if you break the law, I am still going to arrest you even though we're doing this. I'll pull your ass over in a heartbeat if you're exceeding the speed limit."

"Well, that's nice to have a heads-up on. But your Chris Peirce came into Joe's diner where I work and threatened me the other day, Chloe. So as much as you believe it isn't him and it is my dad, I'm willing to go the opposite direction and say it is your boss."

"He was like seven or eight in the picture, Baldwin. I doubt he killed the girl."

"Well, he knows something." I push my hands out to my side. "My Poppy, he's all about trusting you guys, trusting the cops. He's middle class and drives five miles under the speed limit even when Gabe Reynolds doesn't have his patrol car parked down by the elementary school. Me, I watched a cop knock down our front door, drag my old man out of bed in the middle of the night three or four times because they wanted to question him. I see cops pulling over Rocky on his motorcycle because they say somebody with drugs was driving a vehicle like his."

"Cops are people, Baldwin. There's good and bad."

"Yeah, but cops carry the guns, Chloe, and have the law on their side even when the law is distorted."

She stands back and pushes her arms on her hips. "Billy Thompson's mom goes to Holy Trinity, same as your Anna and me. I didn't know until I was standing at choir practice the other day and she mentioned she had a son who had autism who sings at the college. I've been singing alto next to her soprano for three years and didn't put two and two together when Chief Peirce brought him down for questioning. His mom is all worried because he won't socialize, won't go to a singing thing at the school." Chloe rests her thumbs on her belt and rocks back and forth on her heels. "What's going on?"

"He takes classes and is in the singing group. His mom wants him to go to a dance so he meets people. He doesn't want to go."

"Why don't you take him?"

"I offered. He doesn't want to go."

"Listen, you take Billy to the acapella dance thing. I'll keep an eye out on the chief until this thing with the murders gets fixed. Hell, I'll sit outside your building and watch over you if you want."

I'm eyeing her curiously. "Why would you do this?"

"Because I want you to trust me. I want me to trust you." Chloe shakes her head. "Listen, Tango, I've got to be honest. There are a whole lot of people thinking you know where your dad is and where he hid some astronomical amount of money. You might have seen him murdering girls and just aren't telling us. You're like standing on a frozen pond in April and it is getting ready to thaw and crack. Do I trust you? Hell, no. But I know Anna and Ray. And I know if I'm standing here with you, you're less likely to be a suspect when all hell breaks loose. See where I'm coming from?"

"You think I'm the bad guy. You're playing warden?"

"Well yes and no. Regardless, I'm the closest thing to an alibi you'll have when the ice breaks. And you, you're the one who is going to think twice before you shoot me because I'm being nice to you."

CHAPTER 18

DEAD GIRL: LISA TATUM

"Okay, get dressed. We're going to your acapella dance."

I'm standing inside the doorway of Billy's apartment with my arms crossed. He is standing there staring at me, and blinking rapidly. I'm wearing a red dress and matching lipstick. I wave a hand over my face while Billy stares at me. "If the red is too much for you because of the autism thing you have, I'll go with a peach dress and peach lipstick. But you're going to the dance and I'm your date."

"I told you I didn't want to go."

"And I'm telling you that you either go with me or I'm going to get a fat girl to take you. A stranger. And maybe she'll try to kiss you and hold your hand. I won't do either."

"You're mean to me, Tango. I'm not going. I don't want to go with a fat girl or a skinny girl."

"Well, you are stuck with a skinny girl. That's me. Maybe while you are there, you will meet a girl that is between. You will go for one hour. Then we will come home. Period. It will make your mom happy and get the cops off my butt. Get dressed or by God, I will come over there and give you a great, big hug."

"You're dating a *dancer*?" This is coming from a pursed-lip girl with bleach blonde hair and arms folded across her chest. Her name is Malinda and she spits it out like a swallowed bug. She's wearing a fluffy yellowish shirt and when she wiggles her head back and forth with a haughty bit of attitude, Malinda looks like a pudgy puffed-up chicken trying to catch a fly. She is wearing thick glasses and keeps shoving them up the bridge of her nose. "So, Billy, what does a dancer got that I don't got?" We are standing in the small choir room and Malinda is literally six inches from my flat chest and poking a finger in the air between us. It is in the basement of the new college building. It is dark, damp, and musty down here.

"I'm actually not a performing artist," I interrupt Billy whose mouth is open like he is going to say something. "I paint." Because I know what he is going to say—*because you're fat*. Billy doesn't have a shut off valve. I tell him that all the time. Once I had a pimple on my chin and he pointed it out. I told him it was because I was on my period and to shut up. So every time I get a pimple, he asks me out loud if I'm on my period again.

"Yeah, right." Another girl steps up beside Malinda and rolls her eyes. Alma Bean. She's got eyes as wide as baseballs and a big nose. "You don't look like an artist with all that stuff going on—" she wiggles her fingers at my face. Stuff? I shake my head.

"It's called makeup and artists—" I tell her.

"I saw your picture on the wall in the dean's office with your little pink tutu—" When Malinda says this, it is in a high-pitched girly-girl voice and three more of her pit bulls coming shoulder to shoulder with her giggle. "You're one of *them*. You think you're all so much better than us because you're cute and skinny and someone in your group wins the Edna Fields Performing Arts Contest every year." Ah, the stupid contest *again*.

"Oh, my God," I groan, shake my head. "Why is it so important to win the contest? Only one person can win. And yes, you're right, it is always someone in the dance program. And I can also tell you that it will always be the student whose family is the richest in Shane Delgado's class. It's stupid."

The girls get quiet right then. It's kind of a stifled angry kind of quiet. "It's true." I shrug and start to list a few off with my fingers. "Amy Wells, Benjamin Harper, Tony Renault. Their parents are loaded. They can't dance worth crap."

"She's right." Malinda narrows her eyes. She looks at Billy who is tugging his beard nervously. I think Billy thinks there might be a knock down and drag out fight. I know for a fact, if he had to choose sides that it wouldn't be me he'd pick. He's probably already running through the statistical odds of one scrawny kitten in a dress overwhelming fourteen miscellaneous-sized pit bulls led by a slightly overweight alpha female wolf with curiously well-toned arms. Yep, I watch him shift slightly towards Alma Bean. I narrow my eyes at him and he does not move back.

"So drop the contest. None of us here are going to win," I mutter. "I don't hang with the mean girls."

Malinda mulls this over, nibbles her bottom lip. "Do you know how to do The Boot Scootin' Boogie?"

Sadly, I do. Poppy loves country music and he breaks out his old CDs at every family function. "Yeah, why?"

"Because we like to sing the song, but we don't know the dance—"

It is oddly fun hanging out with the acapella group. I can't sing. My raggedy-edged voice sounds like fingernails getting raked down a textured wall. Most of them certainly can't dance. When they are supposed to shift a bit sexy to the left, they bounce into each other with fits of laughter going right.

"You know, she could be our *in*," Malinda announces when we stop for pink punch puddled in Styrofoam cups.

"Your *in*?" I ask. "What does that mean?"

"You could dance while we sing for the competition. Then maybe we'd have a chance." All eyes are on me, a bit of hope tinging a certain tip to each head. "Or better yet, you could teach us how to dance and we can dance and sing."

"Well, for one, Shane Delgado and I aren't on good terms. You know the rumors. It has to be one of his girls that wins or he quits and we lose the entire dance program. I've shifted my attention to art. I could draw while you sang like those artists that do caricatures of people walking down the street. That's what is expected of me if I do the competition. I just don't think it would work."

We just sit there for a few minutes and chatter quietly when I get a call from Chloe. "Hey, you got ten minutes, I've got something I want to show you."

Ten minutes later, Chloe picks me and Billy up in her cruiser. "I've never sat in the front seat," I tell her when she lets me slide into the seat next to her in the cruiser.

"I bet," Chloe says a little too cheerfully. It almost sounds like she's making fun of me while I watch Billy slowly, quietly and warily settling into the back, his fingers walking the door like he's searching for the latch to get out.

"So what is so exciting that you had to break me out of the acapella club dance," I ask her. "Guilt for making us go?" I try to imagine her in anything but police clothes. I'm not sure I can muster her up in a church dress or even tomboy capris and a button up blouse. She eyes Billy in the back, then looks at me.

"No, actually, I'm trying to keep my part of the bargain," she answers with a stony gaze at me. "I've routed out a couple more of the sites where bodies were found. Thought you might like to come along, see what I've got."

It seems Lisa Tatum was twenty-three years old when they found her body at the Hensley Grove All-Stars Baseball Field. It was the summer of 1963 and a hot July 4th night when she failed to show up at her curfew time of eleven at night at her father's home on Ridgefield Drive about six blocks away. She had been last seen leaving the annual Fourth of July picnic at the company park owned by Cannon Bread Mill three blocks from the ball fields. However, a time could not be set other than it had started to get dark.

Her body was discovered behind a storage shed where the mowing and ball equipment was stored. A caretaker for the park found her body when he stepped behind the shed to dump trash from the stands into a garbage can located there. Her body appeared to be fresh without bloating, but with signs of rigor mortis indicating her death had been within four to six hours. There was a eight week time span she had been missing. She was found September 5th placed so her back was resting against the building wall, one arm on her knee and a cigarette in her fingers.

Her hair was still partially in a bouffant. Her sister said it took her nearly an hour to get her hair just right on top of her head each day. It seems she was picky. Lisa was wearing a ruby red velvet dance dress with a petticoat and heels she had been saving up to buy from her job at the local drugstore suggesting she was coming to meet someone.

"It might seem a little strange to visit the sites where the murder victims were found," Chloe tells me and Billy. Billy is dancing back and forth on his feet with bored detachment. He keeps telling me he hates sports, hates baseball. I tell him we aren't here to play sports, but to talk about dead girls. Now, he's interested. "I mean, the police combed the area for any traces of evidence. The only thing they found here was a half-smoked cigarette. They believed it was insignificant so the brand was not even written down. The caretaker wasn't sure if it could have been his. There were ballgames and hundreds of people attended them the weekend before. There was no such thing as DNA sampling back then so we'll never know." Chloe shrugs. "You can't solve a crime like this sitting in front of a computer. Coming here gives me a good feel for the murder. I can look around and see if there's anything the same as the other murders." She lifts a hand, points a finger to encompass the ball fields. "And such, I don't see anything. But maybe as the investigation progresses, I might note some similarities not visible at first glance." She takes out a camera then, takes a few shots. I watch, feeling kind of useless while I look left to right.

We walk the field. There is a concrete concession stand that Chloe states was also there at the time of the murder while she looks up and down at a picture in her file, appearing to compare the two.

"Pretty much the same as it was in '63," she notes, then gives a stern cock to her chin. "Except the graffiti." Her finger lifts and she points to a three foot high section of pink and blue artwork running along the back of the concession stand. There's a four foot baseball and bat painted into the center. "Man, I'd love to catch that sneaky little bastard." She rubs a finger to her nose, jabs her chin toward a palm-size black star edged in blue and pink. I turn enough to flash-warn Billy with wide eyes who has yet to remark on anything we are talking about. Now is usually the time he blurts out the truth. "See that star?" Chloe interrupts my fierce gaze at Billy. "That's his signature. He's got this crappy splotches of paint all over town and halfway to Cincinnati."

"Sneaky bastard," I repeat, tugging on my lower lip.

"Makes all of us good art students look like criminals," I mutter and absently pat the star on my shoulder. "Right, Billy?" I make a note to myself to avoid tank tops around Chloe.

"Well—" Billy throws up a finger, ready to say something I am sure will incriminate me. I cut him short.

"Yeah, okay, you're not an art student," I interrupt. "I'm just talking about any college students." Oh my God, that sounded so stupid. Chloe seems to shake off my artwork, turns to look at me. "Okay, how about we sit on this one tonight," she says. "Give me a couple days, I'll have more info on the 1972 murder of Tammy Lynn. We'll keep this to ourselves, right, Tango? Billy?"

"Of course," I nod.

CHAPTER 19

A ROSE AT JOE'S AND SHADOW MAN

It's always the same crowd in the mornings at Joe's Home-style Diner. Even my Russian mafia man whose disguise, I like to pretend, is being a dancer is tucked back in his booth. The restaurant opens at six and every day, Colt Lucero plops himself down at the counter by the register with all the other single guys with nobody to sit with at home for breakfast. He always gets a piece of the discounted apple pie from the day before and a cup of coffee. It's two bucks and I get a buck tip under his empty coffee cup. He never says anything to me other than a "good morning" before he shoves the morning newspaper in front of his face.

Today is different. I plop down a plate with two eggs, four links of sausage, two pancakes and hash browns. It's called the Big Joe Breakfast and he looks at it and then at me suspiciously.

"It's for helping Billy," I tell him with a yawn. "Big Joe said it's okay to share my free breakfast with you. I never eat it." That's not the whole truth. Gil told me last night that Colt only gets a stipend of fifty dollars a week for working at the mission, plus free room and board. He said the reason he was at the theatre was because he started working part time for the college as maintenance there because he couldn't even afford toilet paper. I think Gil might have been stressing the point, but I've had lots of times I've grabbed napkins from the restaurant because me and Mia are out of toilet paper and a paycheck is four days away.

He looks like he's going to say something. However,

he stops and just tells me thank you. There's a guy standing at the cash register waiting to check out. He's sandy hair, buff and smiling at me like a first time dad smiles at a baby. I wave a hand at Colt and step over, reach out my hand for his check. I'd waited on his table. He just got a coffee and a biscuit with sausage gravy dumped on top. But he's got a rose in his hand. I'm looking at the glass shelves under the register trying to find a price on them, see if Joe is maybe selling flowers for some holiday I missed. He sells single roses on Valentine's Day.

"Hang on, dude," I tell him, start to turn. "I'll get you a price on the rose."

"Huh? No, no, no." He reaches out, pats my shoulder. "I didn't buy it here. I'm Finn Winters. It's for you."

"Okay?" I give him my best uncertain gaze complete with furrowed brow and questioning twist of my eyes.

"Anna Baldwin talked to my mom. We're supposed to go on a blind date. I, um, thought I'd stop by and—"

"Check me out, see if I'm worthy?" I ask him a little snottily. Finn Winters. The name sounds a bit too dramatic like the name of someone from a sitcom made by a local TV station. But I remember Ruth Winters. She's a bit of a leftover hippy from the 1960s. I can imagine she'd name a kid Finn.

"No," he says quickly, holding out a hand palm up. "To break the ice so it wasn't so—awkward."

"Well, this is awkward now," I mumble beneath my breath. I feel like an idiot because the poor guy is smiling at me and nodding his head up and down like he agrees.

I hear laughter to my left. Both our eyes swoop down to Colt who was, only moments earlier, eyeing both of us. His head twists right quickly and he's stifling a round of laughter and trying to look like he's found something incredibly funny in the newspaper. He even takes a forefinger and pokes the paper like he's pointing out some comical editorial. I know better. I can even see it from here. It is an advertisement for nursing care at the local assisted living center.

"Disregard the idiot reading the newspaper." I roll my eyes, draw them up to the man in front of me. "I've been busy. I didn't hear anything from Anna." Just out of spite to Colt who is still stifling his laughter, I reach out and take the rose from Finn's fingers. "This is really nice. I mean, the whole thought process behind introducing yourself is— nice."

"So you passed the test," he tells me. "Barely." I look up a bit surprised and when he smiles at me, I realize he's kidding.

"Oh, I squeaked by, did I?" I return. There's a family behind him and I reach over his shoulders, wiggle my fingers for their check. "I have a kid. Did Anna tell you that?"

"Yes, actually, she did. So I have your number. I'll call you. You good with that?" I nod. He turns and walks away. I watch him go while I check out the family behind him, make a bump of my hip to close the cash register. He doesn't have as much swagger as Colt, but he does have a certain posture that shows he's confident. (oh-my-gosh, why am I comparing the two?) He's what Poppy would call suave like the men in the old black and white movies who know all the right moves, all the right words. He's not my type. I like a little more grunge and a lot less fake.

"So Alex and Delia told me you used to be part of Shane Delgado's program."

I turn to Colt who is swiping the napkin across his

mouth. "Yeah." That's all I say and start to turn to grab the washcloth to clean tables.

"They also said you quit."

I stop, shrug my shoulders hard. "Yeah, so what? Shane Delgado is a—" I want to say shit. I can't. I made a promise not to curse on Billy's behalf. "Turd. Turd isn't a cussword, is it?"

Colt waves my question away with a slight flick of his hand. "I don't know. I just figured you had a problem with authority. But there's only two reasons I know where a woman rakes her nails down a guy's back. It is either really passionate love or really passionate hate," he answers with a shrug. "After that strangely beautiful ménage à trois you performed up on the stage with Shane Delgado and Adrien Moreau that, by the way, everybody is whispering about—" he holds up one hand, snaps his fingers and thumbs to make the blah blah gesture. "—I think it is both the former and the latter." He leans forward, looks to the darker part of the diner where Russian Mafia is settled into the booth.

I disregard his insinuation with a roll of my eyes, then realize whose name he just mentioned. "Did—did you say Adrien Moreau?" I swallow hard, twist around to look at Colt.

"Hush." Colt pushes a finger on his lips. "He'll hear you." Adrien Moreau was like the child prodigy of ballet at fourteen. I read in a magazine that his only setback was how young he looked and they even tried dying his hair gray to make him appear older next to his ballerinas. They had a difficult time placing him in roles because of his youthful appearance and he turned down many because they wanted him to play children. Ten years later, he has continued to be one of the top modern ballet dancers. He's been in the leading role of nearly forty ballets and has moved on to master teacher. My face is losing color. "The Adrien

Moreau from the Conciergerie Ballet Company?" I lean in, look over his shoulder to the shadowy booth in the back of the restaurant. "I didn't know that was him."

"Well, maybe if you didn't live in a box, you would have recognized him and you wouldn't have used him as a vengeance dance," Colt tells me, leaning forward so I can hear him. I too, lean forward. "By the way, he called you a diva. I personally would have pegged you more as a drama queen. But coming from him, you must have cut him deep. *Les plus sombres*, The Dark Ones, that's what they called him and his partner in an article in Fine Arts Magazine of America. The article said they are strictly coded like robots to certain historic ballet moves and take out anybody in their path who try to compete against them." Colt takes a sip of his coffee, purses his lips. It is probably cold. I forgot to warm it up for him. "And the rumor flying is he is starting his own company. Says he is breaking away from the bad image. Conciergerie dancers are too rigid. His partner is a strictly historic ballet dancer named Svetlana who has her claws in him, won't let him leave. She's in her thirties and that's all she's ever done is dance. She tears people apart with her scathing reviews of them. She's known as *Sorcière Noire*, the Dark Witch, by her peers. He is called Homme de L'ombre, Shadow Man. Her shadow that follows her around to do her bidding. Hope she doesn't find out you danced with him, she might turn you into a frog."

"I don't care. I'm not afraid of some stupid dancer, God Squad. What's she going to do, come to Joe's Home-Style Diner and beat me up?" I gripe, start to walk away. "I've got a kid to think about."

"That you used as an excuse, Tango, like five minutes ago to get out of a date."

"Are you my therapist now? I hope to God Anna's not

paying you to fix me. I'm not that broke." I snatch up the wash cloth. "And what is he doing here standing with his toes on the threshold of hell in Hensley Grove of all places?"

"I asked him to come."

"You dance?" My back is to Colt so I roll my eyes at the back wall before I turn a little awkwardly.

He laughs and shakes his head. "No, I don't even club dance. I just know him from way back. Shane asked me to contact him so he'd come and let some of his dancers get a chance at trying out. He's young, a virtuoso. He isn't like the older dancers that are at the point they are so big-headed they don't want to be around newbies. Delia and Alexandra are really good. Shane doesn't want to see their talent go to waste. Adrien's a nice guy. He's been going to a lot of small colleges in New York and California that usually get overlooked and giving underprivileged dancers the chance to dance professionally."

"Well, all's I know is he ruined my private dancing refuge." I let my shoulders drop. "And my chances of finishing my degree." I can hear Joe and another cook slapping a couple plates at the window between the restaurant and kitchen for me to pick up.

"Tango, you've got an order!" Joe calls out and I give him a wave.

"He ruined them or you did, Tango?" Colt scrapes a long gaze at me. "We were all just worried about Delia and trying to find her before she climbed a water tower again. We were five minutes from calling the cops. Nobody set out to take anything away from you. If there's a victim here, it is either Shane or Adrien. You beat the crap out of Shane, scratched his sides and bruised him up. You used Adrien to get back at Shane. So quit pouting and get back to doing what you do best."

"And what's that, God Squad?"

"You light everything on fire around you. Then you watch it all burn up until nothing's left but charred remains."

"What are you talking about?" I ask him, creasing my forehead, my eyes going back and forth between the order waiting for me at the window and Colt's smug expression.

"Control Burn. You know what that is? It's when firemen go out and burn an area they know is high risk to reduce the damage if a natural fire starts." Colt takes another sip of his tepid coffee, almost gags. "You set your life up like a control burn. You go out and purposely screw things up so you don't have to deal with the damage somebody else causes. It's so you have control."

I hear his words. They sink in like that unregulated gulp of hot chocolate already past the tongue before you realize the drink is straight out of the boiling pot. I feel the blister all the way to my soul. "You have no clue who I am."

"Well, yes, I do." Colt rises, drops his napkin on his plate and doesn't bother to leave his usual dollar tip. "You're the one that gives up, never gets anywhere. Are you going to deny it? Where's your big stage?" He tosses his hands out to encompass the dining room. My eyes follow before I realize he is making fun of me.

"I don't dance anymore, Colt. I'm an artist. I just changed roads I'm travelling on."

"Yeah," he says and does that stupid gun imitation with his forefinger and thumb while he clucks his tongue. "I'm sorry. You're right. I had you pegged wrong. I just got confused because this also doesn't look like an art studio."

"Now I know the truth." I can't avoid the solemn man in the back—my Russian mafia man (aka Adrien

Moreau). I offer him more coffee. He nods toward the rose I stuck into a glass on the counter. "The American infiltrator has a secret lover."

"Oh, so you're ready to play with me?" I ask him, trying to appear surprised.

"Yes. And her lover is at this very moment boasting he has bested me by taking my lover even farther away to—" He stops, drops his shoulders. I think he is going to ruin the mood I've set so I shake my head, hold up a finger.

"You can do this, I know you can, Russian Mafia," I whisper like a stage hand throwing out the lines to an actor. "Say something romantic like Brazil."

"Brazil? Did you call me Russian Mafia?"

"I did," I say. "Ah, you have discovered the truth!" I toss my hand over my forehead. "But I am willing to deceive him for you and for your beautiful lover to save your lives. She cries for you at night. I have heard her weeping." I kneel down at the booth with my elbows resting on the table and my chin on my wrists. "Listen closely and heed my words. For a small tip of five dollars which will cover my gas to work for a couple days, I will find your lover and have her delivered to your arms. This," I sigh and toss back my head, "I vow I will do or die in the process!"

Joe ruins my fun again yelling from the kitchen. "The FBI calls." I reach up the forefinger of my right hand and swipe at my eyebrow. "This is our code that an enemy is near. Heed it." Russian Mafia nods, gives me a half smile.

He also gives me twenty bucks in tips. "Ah, you found your wallet," I point to the brown leather wallet in his hand.

"Yes, my partner had it." Not bad for six cups of coffee and another round of Anna's mamaw's stew I made for him again along with some fried chicken Mia and I made for supper last night.

CHAPTER 20

I STILL CAN'T GET THE SUITCASE OPEN

I'm sitting on Poppy's suitcase. I'm out of breath. I've tried a thousand different ways to open it. The last was simply tossing it against the bathroom sink. It seems impenetrable even for a girl who was taught at age four how to jimmy open a lock on a pair of handcuffs with a bobby pin, and start a car without a key.

I asked Poppy if he wanted me to bring it to his house. He tells me to simply store it at my place, maybe lock it in a closet. And oh, by the way, did I talk to Reverend Greene at Holy Trinity? He called Anna again. He really wants that back wall cleaned up behind the parsonage and the education building. He said he'd get some of his teen group to do it, but they just want to draw happy faces. I told him I'm not feeling inspired. I worked on a bland background and stopped last week. I didn't tell him about the run in with Shane Delgado and it really has me down in the dumps. Not even Poppy knows who Mia's daddy is. I couldn't tell anybody. Shane threatened to get me kicked out of school if I said anything.

"I don't think it is going to open, Tango." Billy is standing above me. A trickle of sweat weaves its way along my forehead and stops just short of the bridge of my nose. I peer up at him through my eyelashes, try not to get angry that he announces it like a revelation I couldn't figure out without the support of his high IQ.

Rocky is sitting on my couch drinking a soda pop, watching a ballgame, and digging into a bag of potato chips that Anna dropped off with six other bags of groceries this afternoon. He guffaws a laugh, swipes a fist across his beard. Billy doesn't realize why he laughs too, but he joins along with Rocky. I give them a great sigh and shake my head.

"Did your Poppy even want you to open it?" Rocky points a chubby finger at the suitcase. "I thought you said he just wanted you to store it for him. It had girlie magazines in it. It's driving you crazy wondering if your Poppy likes porn, isn't it?"

"You're sick, Rocky," I mumble. However, he's right. But my interest has changed to the tiny binder Billy has been hugging in his arms and suddenly thrusts at me. I take it in my fingers.

"It is what the cops wanted. They were mean. I didn't want to give it to them. So," Billy says smugly. "I didn't."

"Alright, dude!" Rocky gets up and walks across the room toward Billy. "Way to play the cops." Billy cowers while Rocky thrusts out his fist so he can bump it.

"Bump his fist, Billy," I mumble while I open up the binder, peer at the contents inside. "It's a thing. You know how to bump fists."

Billy does as I say, then he hovers over me and points a finger at the college bound notebook paper within. There is a list like chapters, each with a girl's name. It corresponds with the following pages. Each page has the name of the girl carefully written at the top, a picture, and information beneath.

"Those are the names and dates of all the dead girls," Billy tells me with the same bearing as Joe at the diner explained how to run the cash register when I first started. "In 1958, Susan James was found between the Baymont Hotel and the Welcome Viaduct. You've been there, I think."

"Chloe took me there."

"In 1963, Lisa Tatum was found behind the storage shed for the baseball equipment at the ballfields northwest of downtown. We went there the other day with Officer Chloe. But I have a few more with descriptions. In 1972, Tammy Lynn's body was discovered at the mill behind a dumpster. They think Cathy Schuler was murdered around 1982 when she came up missing in Michigan. Her body was found almost completely decayed in 1983 along Second Street going out of town. It was right in somebody's front yard. Then, you know, this year Hannah Lafferty was found down by the river under the High Street viaduct and the train trestle, and Tianna Mills was found by the highway."

"Tianna Mills," I repeat the name. I didn't recognize it.

"Lucinda Delray with the Tri-City News Station said they identified the body today. It was the only one I didn't know until the five o'clock news." He stops, sighs. "However, I designed an app a couple days ago that allows me to collate all the information and compare it to murders in other areas. There are two more cold case murders that compare to this one in a fifty mile radius. There are probably more."

"Do they have anything in common?" I ask him while I peruse his work. Billy even has their weight, height and newspaper clippings he's found online.

"They are all dead, that's what they have in common," Rocky says and he thinks he's funny and laughs. Billy and I look up at him not amused. I shake my head. "Rocky, if you don't have anything constructive to add to this conversation, just watch your stupid show." Rocky has a tendency to be more in tune with the TV than what is coming out of his mouth. He doesn't even bother to look away from the set and laughs at the next set of one-liner, stale jokes spouting out of the actors' mouths.

"I am watching a stupid show. You throwing a suitcase all around the apartment, it's a comedy."

I shake my head just as my cell phone tings a message. I almost jump thinking it might be Poppy. Maybe he's got some sixth sense and he knows I'm trying to break into his mysterious suitcase. I tug the phone from my back pocket where I stuffed it earlier and stare at the text.

I'm sorry I was in your face this morning. Bad start to the day. Gil gave me your number. Hope you don't mind. It was nice of you to share breakfast. GS

GS. God Squad? I stare at the text. I think about just shoving the phone back into my pocket. Enough said, right? He'll apologize, then he'll be crappy to me again as soon as he gets around his friends. I've got enough people in my life right now dumping on me. I don't need to drop Delia and Alexandra's friends into the mix.

"Who is that?" Billy asks.

"None of your business," I return and start to shove the phone back into my pocket. "Now back to our conversation. Do the girls have anything in common?"

"I knew you'd ask me that. I wrote it down, Tango." He shakes his head like he can't get that I don't read his mind. He reaches out, flips a couple pages and points at a page that states: Characteristics. "See?" he asks me while his forefinger rolls down the page. "They were all between the ages of seventeen and twenty-seven. There were three blondes, three girls with brown hair and one girl had black hair and one girl had red hair. Four had blue eyes and two had green eyes. They were from all over the place—Michigan, Indiana, you name it. I looked up identifying characteristics of a hundred serial killers to see what they might look for. Nothing matched any of these girls and—"

There is a message *ting* interrupting our conversation. I reach around, tug out my phone.

I'm trying to be a different person than I have always been. GS

I groan, tug the phone upward. I know if I answer, I'm opening up that door. My finger is in mid-poke and I stop.

"Do you have a new boyfriend?" Billy asks me, rocking back and forth on his heels. I see him smiling like he's got a secret. "Tango's in love," he says in a sing-song voice.

"No, it is God Squad. He yelled at me and he's apologizing."

"You like God Squad?" Rocky is suddenly back in the conversation even if his rendition of it is distorted because he only heard the parts he wanted to hear. "That's hilarious. You know he's got a girlfriend. He's going out with that beauty queen that brought the food pantry box. Stick with your own kind. If he's asking you out, he's just using you."

"That offends me," I grunt, shake my head. "And no, I don't like him. But how do you know he's dating Taylor Peirce?" I ask Rocky flatly.

"Because they were at Don's All-Nighter the other night. She and that white-haired girl—Alex, they were grinding on him pretty hard on the dance floor."

"He doesn't dance. I doubt he drinks either."

"I didn't get to finish," Billy interrupts. "Serial killers, they almost always keep trophies, something from the girls they murder."

"Yeah, I suppose." I say absently. I turn, poke in a return message:

Why do you want to be different? Everybody says you're nice.

Ha ha. You don't. And not always nice. At my worst point, I was sitting at a park in downtown NYC in the winter. I didn't have a coat. I was sitting on a bench and a homeless man came up and handed me his only blanket. It was his shelter, his bed, all he owned beside a pillowcase of junk. Here I was in a suit and tie and three-hundred dollar shoes and a guy who was dressed in a pair of jeans from 20 years ago and a torn and dirty t-shirt was trying to help me. I'd passed him by on my bike five days a week for an entire two years and rolled my eyes each time.

Well, I groan to myself, I opened it up for that one. I don't want to answer, don't want to get involved. I'm fine with Rocky and Billy as friends. They don't expect anything out of me.

Baby steps. I text him in return. *You know, you're a work in progress.*

Alex is at dance class. I'm bored. Want to hang out?

Probably shouldn't. Painting the town in black after last night. You know, going out for a five course meal, then going to my art studio. I'm not lying. I already have a couple projects mapped out. One is an old school bus abandoned in a field off the highway and another is a billboard that fell in a storm a couple weeks ago.

Art studio?

"Tango, I don't like it when you ignore me." Billy is tugging at his ear. I roll my eyes.

"Yeah, you were talking about trophies. Serial killers take something—"

"Yes, I think if you find out what they are missing and find that something, you will find the killer."

"Well, dude, that's a no-brainer," Rocky mutters. "How's she going to do that?"

"Look through her dad's stuff. If it isn't there—"

"I don't have his—" I start, but Billy, he's pointing at the suitcase. "Isn't that his?"

CHAPTER 21

INTRODUCING GOD SQUAD TO MY ART STUDIO

"So, God Squad, this is it." We're standing in an alleyway behind Holy Trinity Church. "You wanted to see it. It really exists." It's dark. Only the shine of the moon gives off a gentle white orange along the gritty and broken asphalt. It barely climbs along the brick wall I'm going to paint. I'm tossing my backpack on the ground and setting Mia down next to it. "This is my art studio, my gallery."

"And why didn't I expect this?" he asks me. "You're full of surprises tonight." I see his eyes roam from the top of my black hoodie to my dark tennis shoes. Then he lets those big dark blue eyes roll over to me lugging a plastic lantern out of the backpack.

I'm actually surprised he's made it this long into the evening without bucking. I enticed him with a full dinner which I'm supposing he thought was going to be at the country club. However, we ate chicken sandwiches in the kitchen of the Hensley Grove Gospel Church. On Friday nights, they offer a free meal to those who need it. I go down and volunteer for two hours each week, slapping chicken salad on day old bread they get donated from the Jenson's Grocery in town. There's always chips and soup and leftovers the college provides from their dining hall. Whoever volunteers there gets a meal before we all line up to dish out the supper.

"Hey, you got a free meal without having to have sex with me, God Squad," I tease him. I'm bundling my hair on top of my head with an elastic band.

"Oh, I should have known this was a date. And now I

get to break the law with you?" he asks me. Then he reaches out, nudges my hand away from my head. "Leave it down. It looks nice."

"You sound like Rocky. He says it looks trashy to tie it up," I tell him. "Regardless, we're not going to get caught." I wiggle the band out, let my hair fall, and then jab a thumb over to Chad Evans. "Chad's going to be our lookout. He'll tell us if anybody comes." He's rolling his wheelchair back and forth, back and forth before he spins it around in a circle. He's got his red hair cut short and he's freckles and all-American boy. I don't think he's turned twenty yet. He's got a huge crush on Hannah Lafferty and he was always asking if I saw her in school. Well, that was before she came up dead.

"She pays me ten bucks to be a watch out. I get another twenty if the cops come and I fall out of my wheelchair while she gets away."

"Nice," Colt says sarcastically, rolls his eyes at me. But he has a crooked smile. "He's kidding, right?"

"No. He did some sniper patrol in the military," I return a teasing grin. "What I pay him's tax free and doesn't take away from his government checks. Who is going to arrest a military vet who falls out of a wheelchair, right?"

Colt just shakes his head, gives a funny smile to Chad. "She didn't hold a gun to your head or anything to do this, did she?"

"No, sir," Chad shakes his head back and forth, laughs. He's always so dang happy, always has a sparkle in his green eyes.

I'd already gotten the outline drawn along with the background. It's another three dimensional painting, so it is a mixture of paints. I hadn't planned on getting help, but Rocky shows up along with three or four girls he knows from the bar. Billy is tagging along. Since being dragged off to jail, he's been glued to Rocky when he's not working. With all the help, it only takes us about six hours to get it finished.

At about three in the morning, the lights to the parking lot flicker on. I can see Colt stepping back. He's been holding up a lantern for Billy so he can paint some grass on the wall. Now, he's looking around like we better get ready to run.

I'm not sure if Colt sees the entire painting until he takes two steps back. He's squinting at it and then, looking at me. He's spent most of his time talking to one of Rocky's friends, a little redhead that keeps giggling into her palm and won't look him straight in the eyes while they paint side by side. Until this point, I don't think he even snuck a peek at the images.

"You inspired me," I tell him, turning with a brush in my fingers. "I said you'd make a great muse. And you are, willing or not." The image is clear enough in the moonlight and light sweeping up from the parking lot. It's a scene like the one he told me about, the homeless man who gave him a blanket. He is standing atop a sharply dressed man sitting on a park bench with his hands clasped like he is in prayer. The homeless man extends a raggedy blue blanket toward him.

I didn't use Colt's face, improvised with a middle aged man. But I think he sees it. Just as he's about to say something, though, a shadow shifts along the parking lot. Everybody eyes me like they aren't sure if they should run or not. I swear, I see Colt shift on his feet like he's going to bolt. It's Reverend Greene and he's still in his pajama pants and bathrobe. There's a coffee cup in his right hand, his newspaper in the cleft of his arm, and he gives me a wave.

"You didn't think I'd really do something to get you

in trouble, right?" I lean in, elbow Colt. "Reverend Greene told me to paint over the junk and cusswords that have been here for years. He wanted me to stick with a theme: Do unto others as you would have others do unto you. You know, from the book of Matthew in the bible? He says it is pretty universal to all religions and beliefs so nobody would be offended. I hit a snag, couldn't think of anything because I was having way too many bad days in a row. Then you told me about your worst day and I thought of the wall."

Colt, he doesn't say anything. He just stuffs his hands in his pockets, does this nodding thing to me. My heart drops. I try to read his expression, but I can't. I hate it when people don't get me. I can't shrug it off. It just lays there like a dead raccoon on the township roads when the highway department staff is laid off. His face is a bit pale while Reverend Greene walks up, tells us there's coffee and donuts for everybody inside. I opt to stick outside by the car where Mia is fast asleep in the back seat. Then Billy asks if I can take him home. He really, really needs to wash the paint off his fingers. Now. I don't get to say goodbye to anybody, just hop in my car and leave.

CHAPTER 22

A TINY CLUE

"Hey, you're Jessica, right?"

It is dead in Don's All-Nighter Tavern at two in the afternoon the next day. There's one old guy nursing a warm beer. He's half watching a baseball game and half staring at the bartender's butt while she scrubs her towel along the counter.

"Yeah, why?" Jessica stops, looks up at me. She's brown hair tied back in a ponytail and brown eyes. Rocky says she's been working at the bar for two years, started out going to college, then couldn't afford it anymore. She's a little annoyed at the college students that come in and flaunt they are almost ready to graduate. Rocky said not to point out I'm just two classes from my degree.

"Rocky Merino said you might be able to help me out," I tell her sliding into a sticky barstool. I've got Billy's binder in my arm and I slap it down on the counter between us. "I live next door—"

"So you're Tango," she says, pausing in her cleaning. "I've heard a lot about you. And before you ask if it is all good, you hope. It isn't. You'd think you two were an old married couple."

"Yeah, he's my ex-boyfriend's best friend," I mumble. "I think I'm kind of like the stepchild that got dropped in his lap when Kevin and I stopped dating."

"You think?" she laughs. "It's like this every day— Tango lit about a thousand candles in my apartment because she said it stank, then left and almost caught it on fire. Tango woke me up in the middle of the night because she had a bad dream. I got to stop on the way home and pick up a gallon of milk because Tango's out and her baby's crying for chocolate milk. Tango, Tango, Tango." She stops, takes a breath, and holds out her hand for me to shake. "I finally get to meet the wife."

I take her hand, give it a good shake. Then, I open the binder and flip it to the place I had a tiny Post-It note marking the image of Hannah Lafferty. I rotate it around so the binder is right side up for Jessica. I poke a finger at the woman's picture. "You ever see her?"

"The dead girl?"

"Yeah. Her name's Hannah Lafferty," I say, scratching my neck. "Did she ever come in here? And was she in here the night she died?"

"I don't know, Tango, it honestly gets so busy in here at night, I don't even look at the customers. Even if she was here, I wouldn't have known. The crowds on Friday nights are crazy."

"You were busy or —?" I ask her slowly, dropping my voice. My eyes barely wander to the old man who doesn't appear to be listening. However, Jessica's eyes make a quick dash toward him, then turn back.

"Really, I don't know."

I didn't understand. I mean, there was one person in the entire bar. Well, that is until seven that same night when I'm walking out the door and Rocky is taking the last step up the stairway toward his apartment next door.

"What are you all dressed up for?" He's juggling three plastic sacks of groceries and a case of beer. He's making a sloppy swing of his key fob so he can snatch his apartment door key on the end. His eyes roll from the top of my head, down the red dress and to my high heels.

"Anna fixed me up with some guy from her church," I reply.

"You usually duck and cover when she gets on a rampage about that kind of stuff, what gives?"

"I know, right?" I laugh. I walk over, snatch up his keys from his fumbling fingers and shove it into his door lock. I turn the knob, push the door open for him. "But she's been all up in my face about breaking up with Kevin and getting my life back together, as she calls it. I personally didn't think I was that bad off."

"Yeah, but you need to be careful," Rocky goes on. I'm juggling Mia while I follow him inside. She keeps snatching at my hair and making little meowing noises in my ear. Now she's banging the curls dangling on my shoulders. It took me an hour to straighten the frizz, then curl it in ringlets.

"Baby, stop, please."

"I'm a cat, meow."

I'm terrified her popsicle-sticky fingers are tearing up my hard work. I try to ignore it.

"I talked to Jess today at the bar," Rocky tells me. "She said you came in asking about Hannah. You freaked her out. There are cameras all over that bar."

"So?"

"So the cops can pull the cameras." Rocky reaches out and gently wags a finger at Mia. "Little girl, listen to your mama. You're going to ruin the hair thing she's got going there."

"Hair thing?" I roll my eyes, get back on subject while Mia wiggles her shoulders at Rocky with a cocky whip right to left.

"I won't tell you how wrong it is she can do that exactly like you and she's three." Rocky shakes his head.

I ignore him. "But I'm not doing anything wrong," I tell him, scrunch up my eyes for reinforcement. "Anybody can ask questions."

"Yeah, I suppose. But who does that kind of stuff, Tango? I don't know anybody but the cops who go around asking questions about a murder. It's kind of weird. And if you come around asking questions to people, it puts them on the cops' radar," Rocky replies, drops his groceries on the table in front of his TV. He stops, throws his arm out while I lean against the doorframe. "You know they are watching you to see if he's here in town."

"Who is watching me?"

"I don't know. But I've seen a white car sitting out in the parking lot and a black one on the highway. When I went past the diner the other day, a green car was sitting in that parking lot. It had two suits inside." Rocky sighs. "Okay, I'm thinking you're not an idiot, but let me lay it out for you." Rocky turns around, folds his arms on his chest. "There's been two bodies found dead in Hensley Grove in the last two weeks. There's a long line in front of them that the cops were trying real hard to erase because they've never solved the murders. Your dad is the number one suspect and the murders didn't happen when he was in jail. Now he's out and nobody knows where he is. But they're thinking that the most natural place for him to show up would be his kid's house. Because who else would cover his tracks for him?"

"What I'm trying to do, Rocky," I spat at him, "is show it wasn't him."

"Why are you trying to prove it wasn't him? Who cares?"

"I do," I grunt. "You know that. You know how hard it is for me to sleep at night knowing everybody looks at me like I'm some piece of trash, the daughter of a thief and—"

"I'm telling you as a friend—drop it. And stop pulling Billy into it. He's fixated and he's going to get himself in trouble." Then Rocky looks up toward the ceiling like he's thinking something out. "You don't know where your dad is, do you?"

"Of course not."

Now his eyes are going back and forth between my own like he's trying to dig out some lie settled in there. "Well, if you do, you better run straight to the cops. And you better watch who you blah-blah-blah to about this stuff—"

"Blah, blah, blah," Mia repeats and giggles. Rocky smiles softly.

"I wouldn't trust anybody right now," he says quietly, "including that God Squad dude that you were hanging around last night. You know where he came from?"

"No," I shrug. "I'm not hanging around him. He just kind of tagged along. He's one of Gil's buddies and he's dating Mean Alex and-slash-or Taylor."

"Yeah, that makes it even stranger he's wanting to hang with you. He could be cops. After you took off with Billy last night, he kept asking where you went. Your Anna might be talking to the feds. You don't know."

"You make me sound like I'm hiding something, like everybody thinks I'm hiding something."

So Rocky gives me this cold, hard stare like he might be one of those people thinking I'm hiding something. Anna used to give me the same gaze when she knew I took a couple dollars from her purse for one of daddy's friends, but I told her I didn't. It is unsettling. I don't have that many people left I can trust after Kevin and I broke up.

"You look nice tonight," Rocky suddenly says, drops the rigid glare. He smiles and it is genuine. He scrubs a hand across his forehead. "And yes, Hannah—the dead girl—as Jessica called her, she was at the bar the night she died. Jessica said she'll deny it if the cops ask. Because she already has. Jessica said these two young cops came in and questioned her at work. She said she didn't have time to think it out, just told them she didn't see them. Now she's freaking out because she lied to the cops, get it? You want to know why she lied to the cops?"

"Uh huh," I say slowly.

"Because Hannah was with that chief of police. He was talking to her at a side table. It was from about ten-thirty to 10:45 and then they both were gone. You didn't hear that from me."

"He came into Joe's the other day while I was working and told me I should *run*," I divulge to Rocky. "He said: *Here's a tip for you. Run.*"

I get the cold stare again from Rocky and he tugs on a bit of chin hair. "Oh, girl, I hope you're not in a whole lot of hurt soon. Just drop it. Stay away from cop stuff. Maybe quit doing your graffiti for a while until things cool off."

I don't know what that means. A whole lot of hurt? I tip my head to the side, furrow my brow, but Rocky doesn't divulge an explanation. I don't know if I want to understand his words, so I don't ask. "Hey, I'm sorry if I unload on you all the time," I finally say to him. "I never meant to ask too much from you."

"Ha ha," he laughs. "You did talk to Jess. She's right. You do ask a lot. And I don't mind, Tango," Rocky shrugs off our conversation, chucks me on the shoulder. "It's nice to feel married once in a while, but not married at the same time. No ball and chain, I can stay out as long as I want—"

"No fringe benefits," I add and wiggle my eyebrows.

"Yeah, well there are some disadvantages to our relationship, but we can work on that—"

CHAPTER 23

DATE FROM HELL AND A KISS FROM

ANOTHER GUY

I can't believe I'm nervous for a stupid date. My tummy is jumping and my back is sweating when I step in the door at Anna and Poppy's. I'm dropping off Mia and meeting Finn here. Anna didn't say it aloud, but I know she didn't want a nice boy picking me up at the subsidized housing apartments. I don't think I'm worried about the guy so much as I'm worried about Anna. I know I'm going to do something incredibly stupid and she'll hear it from Finn's mother. Rocky's right. I usually run like hell when Anna tries to play matchmaker. I'm wishing I could turn back time right now and make up an excuse.

To make matters worse, my date has made himself comfortable on Poppy's back deck with Gil and his little posse of middle class twenty-somethings, all of which are going through some sort of quarter-life crisis. He's got an empty beer bottle in his hand. It is another reason I won't let Anna fix me up with a guy. She tries to surround/smother me in Gil's friends when I meet the guy of her dreams as if this date actually believes I would fit into the confines of the bland, boxed characters here. Tonight, she's invited them over for a cookout.

There is buff Ryan Sanderson, age 25, who is the high school gym teacher. Rumor has it, he is dating the new social studies teacher and the vice principal. He is already married to Gale who runs Hensley Grove Insurance in town. There's beany-donning Andy Harrold whose dad owns three dollar stores in the county. He would rather be a radio announcer for the local station. However, how many radio stations are there here? One and the station manager is also the radio announcer. There are nine or ten more including Taylor Peirce and Alexandra Edward who are both fawning all over God Squad. All of Gil's friends have personalities as bland as a pen full of overbred designer dogs.

Finn's an in-your-face kind of guy. He's got his sandy hair freshly cut and, although he's not really pudgy, the cut makes his chipmunk jowls more prominent. He jumps up, gives me a kiss on the cheek as soon as I set Mia down. My daughter makes a mad dash toward Anna who is lighting little bug candles on the deck. My eyes are on her until I realize everyone's staring at me. I get the subtle feeling that Gil's pack of high end pet store pups have been talking about the little runt mixed breed pup, me, that just got scooped up from the local pound. There are forced smiles and Taylor, who had been leaning into Finn, swipes back her black hair with a cool flip of her fingers and makes a quick retreat to her right. It is awkward and quiet while my eyes make a self-conscious bob from face to face.

"So, the diva has entered the room," Gil chuckles and my eyes whip over to his. There's stifled laughter. He's lounging with a cocky air back on the little porch swing with his arm around Layla and his fingers tickling her bare shoulder. I don't say anything, but I see Anna's eyes veer over to him. Layla is jabbing Gil in the ribs with her elbow.

"Gil, mind your manners," Anna tells him. I can see everybody is hiding grins.

"I didn't call her that first. I was just quoting—what's his name?" Gil turns to Alexandra who smiles and eyes everyone. She enjoys being the center of attention.

"Adrien Moreau," Alexandra pipes up. "Do you know who that is, Anna?"

"I do. I saw the signs for the arts program he was doing with his troupe at the college. I remember when he was just a young thing and played in Nutcracker in New

York. I went to see the show twice—" Anna's eyes swerve upward steadily and cautiously toward me. "And what does that mean *he called her a diva*? Are you taking classes in dance again, Raeanna?"

"No, Anna." I wave her words away with a hand, glare at Gil. "I'm not dancing anymore. It was a misunderstanding."

"Well, you were dancing the other night." Taylor is giving me a roll of her eyes.

"I just stopped in at the old campus theatre for a few. It's nice and quiet. I can study there." I shrug at Anna, ignore Taylor's remark. "Shane came in with his class and started dancing with me—"

"From what I heard, she ripped him a new one," Gil utters, sniffs a laugh. He reaches up and feigns scratching his sides. More laughter and Anna's eyes suddenly turn troubled. I remember this expression. I'd seen it in sixth grade when I'd gotten caught drawing on the girl's bathroom door. Then whenever she'd hear daddy was getting out of jail, her eyes took on stormy uncertainty and she'd fold her arms over her chest defensively.

"Oh, dear, not this again." Anna steps over and folds her hands across her chest. "They're just kidding, right?" she asks me. "I mean, that whole fiasco wasn't his fault. You didn't bring that up, did you? He did everything in his power to keep you in the ballet—"

I'm standing there with my eyes getting wider and wider. I can see the direction this strange conversation is going and I'm sure my date wants to bolt. "I'm not going to discuss that idiot in front of everybody, Anna." And yes, the fiasco was his fault. I was fifteen when he started telling me to stay after the special classes I got to take at the college while I was still in high school. He flirted and toyed with me. I was skinny and freckled and awkward. I had no clue about men and what they'd do to get you in bed. I really thought he loved me. I certainly didn't know the extent they would go to save their reputations from being marred by a pregnant woman if they were married to someone else. However, Anna doesn't even know Mia is his.

"So just as a precautionary, as long as we don't dance, I'm alright?" Finn teases me with a hand on my shoulder.

I'm feeling a little overwhelmed at the moment. I look up at him unsure if he is jumping in with the wolf pack or trying to ease the tension. He's smiling, looking over my head. I see where his loyalty lies. Everybody's still staring at me.

"Can we go?" I just ask him. I jab a thumb toward the door. For just a moment, he hesitates like he is indecisive whether he wants to stay with his new pack of playful pups or leave with the snarling, little runt.

"Sure," he finally says, stands back up and gives my arm a little nudge to the back door.

The car ride is awkward at best. If he isn't fiddling with his phone answering texts and swerving all over the road, Finn talks about his workout schedule, his beautiful trainer, his sports car, and his job as a marketing specialist. He tells me about his five-hundred thousand dollar house up on Lake Erie and his last four trips to Cancun. By the time we are seated at the table at Pelican Cuisine, I know everything there is to know about Finn Winters straight down to the size of underwear he wears to how many miles he gets to a gallon in his fifty-thousand dollar car. While he downs three beers, I've seen fifty pictures of him on the beach and another twenty with his buddies. I'm thinking there could not possibly be anything more to know about him when our server comes to the table in a short black skirt and he nearly keels over watching her leave after she takes our order.

"Holy hell," he says a little too loudly. "You got to love a woman who even looks good in spandex skirts." She overhears and has the audacity to turn and whip up a huge, flirty grin with him. Okay, now I know one more thing—he's got to be the worst date anybody could ever have.

"She was cute, wasn't she?" Finn asks me. "I mean, not as cute as you." He eyes me up and down and wiggles his eyebrows. "But I'd *do* you both."

"Um, I suppose," I mutter, focusing on the menu. I'm not a huge fan of Chinese food. I don't have a clue how to answer that question. I smile. He just stares at me. I'm only wishing this night was over and it had hardly started. Then I hear the ting of my phone in my purse. I'm wondering if I should answer it considering Finn's phone has not left his left palm since we got into his car.

How's it going?

If my date wasn't going so horribly, I wouldn't have answered God Squad. *Fine. Chinese. Not a big fan. What should I order? I don't do meat.*

Vegetable fried rice. Veggie dumplings. Steamed vegetables.

Thanks.

Welcome. It's got to be better than revenge date with me, right? He's nice?

Dunno. I think he's drunk. After discussion at Pop's, he thinks he's on a date with a prima donna.

Drunk? I'm bored here. Poppy burns hot dogs. Alex/ Taylor talk talk talk dance. Yawn.

Could be worse. I know the kind of underwear Finn wears. And it isn't because I've seen it—

"Is this you?"

I'm resting my hand on my chin and look up from my phone. He's holding his phone out and I'm staring at three pictures of me naked on the hood of a black Porsche and one very old pic of me from five years ago doing a dance duet with a boy in one of Shane's classes.

"Um, yeah," I mumble.

"I looked you up online. You do porn?"

I blink, feel my face turning a hundred shades of red. "It's not porn. No, it was for an art project."

"Ha ha, it looks like porn to me," Finn laughs a little too loudly and pushes the phone up to his face for a closer look. "Damn, girl, you got nice tits."

I try to scrub the red from my cheeks. I realize I left Colt in mid-sentence. So I write one last text: *He just pulled up Tango porn. Date with God Squad just made it back into number one slot.* I cross my eyes, stick out my tongue and take a pic to send with the text.

Just laughed out loud. Everybody staring at me—

"So what does it take to get you in bed on the second date, huh? Obviously not a wedding band." We make it back to Poppy's at nine o'clock. Finn wanted to go get drinks. I mumbled out an excuse that Mia wasn't feeling good. So we get back to the house and stop in the living room. Everybody is out back still. I can hear their muffled chatter and laughter.

Finn stops me in the hallway, leans into me, kisses my forehead, and works to my neck. He's pressing on me hard. He has bad Chinese food breath. His eyes roam to the back porch. Mia's running up and down the stairway giggling.

"You are smoking hot, baby." He takes a step back and rolls his hand from my shoulder to my waist. "Damn, you're hot. I love dancers. I love their bodies. And I'm thinking tomorrow night, we just go straight to my place. I'm only in town for another week before I've got a business trip to South Carolina. Drop your little girl off at the sitters for an overnight. Hell, I'll pay for it if you don't have the money. We'll get to know each other—you know, better." He stops and swipes a hand across his lips like he is wiping away a grin. "You can bring a friend if you want—"

Okay, I'm still lounging on the first part of what Finn says. I'm insulted. The rest is just a blurry blah-blah-blah. Because I'm not that girl who jumps into bed with every guy she meets. It offends me he assumes I am.

"Well, Finn, I don't need a wedding band. I don't even need a man around to make me feel whole," I grunt. "However, I do need respect. And since you spent the entire evening gawking at every girl's ass passing by our table and flirting with the waitress, I'm thinking it isn't going to take anything at all for the reason you're not getting anything at all. Because there isn't going to be a second date or a third date. Or any more dates. You offend me."

His face suddenly changes from a smug smile to one that looks like Mia after she tasted her first pickle. "You've got to be kidding me," he snorts. "Like you're a prize? And I just paid a hundred and fifty bucks for a meal for you."

"I assumed you wanted to get to know me," I growl. "Are you suggesting I'm a whore that needs to be paid for services?"

"If the shoe fits, wear it."

I walk over to the table, snatch up my purse and dig out the one-hundred dollars I set aside for my partial rent. Oh, and a small piece of paper with Jenny written on it in ink and with a tiny, red heart. Then I stomp back so I'm an arms-length away and I toss the money right at him. The moment I do it, I am already grasping for straws on how I'm going to pay my rent. "Here, jerk. I am not a whore."

He just stands there, catches the money in the air. I know out of spite, he's going to keep it. He's got this haughty tip to his chin. "What'd you think was going to happen, Raeanna? They call you Whiskey Tango. Did you think we'd go around picking flowers and holding hands? That's how it works."

"Well, work it out with Jenny," I croak. I flip the little guest check receipt into the air our server handed me when Finn got up to use the restroom. "She says she'd love to go out with you." He makes a sloppy, desperate catch of it.

"Is everything alright? You're home early."

I hear Poppy's voice while I'm stuffing Mia's toys into her bag. He's standing just inside the doorway with a bag of marshmallows in his fist and smiling too widely like he caught the end of the conversation. I look up, don't want to disappoint him.

"Yeah, Poppy," I say, forcing a smile. "I just need to get Mia home. She gets tired."

"We were going to make s'mores," Mia whines behind Poppy. "I want to make s'mores."

"How about we make quick s'mores," Poppy says while my ex-date sidesteps me with puckered lips, gives Poppy a fake smile and ducks out the back door to the wolf pack. "Can we do that?"

I can't tell him no. I sneak to the upstairs bathroom to hide for a few. I just don't think I can face Gil's posse right now.

"Hey, how'd it go?"

I'm at the top of the stairs. I see Colt making the climb behind me. "Yeah, not so good. Mia wants to do s'mores and we're leaving."

"You're leaving your date out there by himself?" he asks me, stopping at the top step.

"Listen, he's just not my type. He's got you guys. He's a little—" I want to say *jerk*, but I don't know God Squad that well. He's probably friends with the guy. "I'm just not so into dating right now, I guess. Too soon after Kevin."

"You're not doing the control burn again, are you?" Colt asks. "Because that's what it looks like to me. Maybe you need to give the guy a chance."

"I'm assuming Anna sent you up here to talk me out of leaving?"

"Yes. It's just kind of—rude to leave him sitting there."

"Finn is the rude one. You know, you don't know me. Can you just let it rest, God Squad?" I say to him. "Just tell Anna I've got a stomachache."

"Okay." He shuffles at the stairway. "It's not Kevin, right?"

"No. Why would it be Kevin?"

"Because your Poppy said he drove past three times tonight."

"He did?" Crap, why do I sound excited?

"Yeah, and he called. The only reason I'm telling you is so you *don't* call him back. Come on, Tango, you're way too good for a guy like that. You got a nice guy down there waiting for you. And an idiot stalking you. I'm begging you for your family's sake, don't get mixed up with the idiot."

"You need to stop, God Squad. You have no idea what is good or bad for me. You have no right to get involved. And you have no clue what Kevin is like."

"You're kidding me, aren't you?" Colt takes three steps up the stairway. "I don't know what Kevin is like? I was sitting there in the police station less than two weeks ago with you because you caught him fooling around with another woman. And do I know you? Enough to see that you sabotage everything you're good at so you don't have to fail. You danced the heck out of that theatre the other night and you say you don't dance. What is up with that?"

"Listen, God Squad," I know my voice is getting loud. I lower it to a whisper and take the three steps down to meet him face to face. "Maybe I don't want to dance for people that's why I'm dancing by myself," I tell him six inches from his face. "You ever thought about that, Lucero? Maybe I don't like guys like Finn and I like guys like Kevin."

"So you like tough guys, like getting treated like a disposable lighter. When the flame's gone, he tosses you in the garbage?"

"It is my damn life, I'll frigging live it how I want to live it whether you or Anna or Poppy like it or not. Maybe Kevin's *my* lighter. You don't know that. Because out here in the real world, outside your churchy, all-male society, I can actually make decisions. I mean, let's be honest. What do you know about love in your uncluttered, sterile, holier-than-thou and holier than hell world? You religious zealots from Abraham Wesley Outreach Program probably don't even kiss, just stand around and stare at your wives and girlfriends and wonder how the heck babies are made. You let Alexandra and Delia and Taylor wear you like an eighties pop star displays his bling. So, instead of bothering me, be bling. It looks good on them. Let me —"

He reaches out, grabs my left shoulder, and pushes on me until I take two steps back and stop with a soft bang of my rear against the wall of the stairway. It makes a solid thump in the silence between us. His grip isn't hard, but it is firm and he steps right up, pushes his hand over my right shoulder so I'm locked in there eye to eye with him. He's a frigging giant to my five foot six inches while I try to maintain my calm staring   up at him. My breaths are pushing my chest up and down, my heart is suddenly pounding bowling balls in my chest. I know better than to blink. I know better than to look scared. However, the one character flaw I've always had when daddy used to bang me around was a damn irritation lip twitch that is settling on my mouth right now. "This is easy, Tango. This is easy for a man to do," he tells me beneath his breath. "What is difficult is holding back."

"I'm not an idiot," I growl. I'm trying to pull off not being terrified. However, right now I know my eyes are as big around as two violet Christmas tree balls. "I was brought up by a daddy who didn't hold back. What's your point?"

Oh, my gosh, I swear his already deep blue eyes turn so dark then with anger, they are like two shiny blue sapphires. "You choose the guys that don't hold back and you are going to get hurt."

"You aren't holding back."

He sniffs a laugh, barely throws his head back. "Yeah, Tango, I am."

"No, God Squad," I whisper. "You are not." I know I shouldn't say it, but I do. And I know when I do, I'm shaking because I'm basing all my instincts on two men. One was daddy and he never read my expressions, just slapped me and he'd do it hard. The other was Poppy and he listened to every word I've ever said. He'd never raise a hand to me. He listened to me. He rocked me in a rocking chair for two days straight when I came in like a wild child kicking and screaming to live at his house.

Now, Colt is reading me. I'm hoping he's a Poppy kind of guy, not my daddy kind of guy. His eyes are snapping back and forth between my own. They are reading my expressions. His hand on my shoulder responds to the flinch I make. He lets loose his harder clutch. I look up toward the ceiling. "Because I know this is as far as you'll go," I say. "You aren't holding back because you won't hurt me."

Well, then his lips slammed on mine. I wasn't expecting it. In fact, it was the last thing I saw coming and my gasp exposed that little secret I would have rather he not know. I feel the fingers of his left hand soften its grip. It wasn't hard in the first place, but now his fingers are trickling down my arm and to my utter dismay, goosebumps are bursting across my skin. And the kiss, yeah, it's pretty good. It leaves a thousand imaginary butterflies filling my belly, tickling it with their wings.

"Oh." My voice is hardly even a whisper when he pulls back. I didn't realize my hand was pressing on his chest. It is involuntary. However, I think he thought I was pushing him away. He's just blinking down at me like he's as confused as I am unnerved.

"Why'd you do that?"

"Crap, I don't know." And his own words sound almost like Gil griping at his dad when he used to ask him to put out the trash. "I'm—I'm sorry."

"Raeanna—"

I can hear Poppy's voice downstairs and I bolt. He meets me at the bottom of the stairs telling me he made a s'more for Mia to go. "Are you okay, hon?" he asks.

"I'm not feeling good."

He nods at me funny, looks over my shoulder just as Colt makes the last step down the stairway. I'm sure he heard my feet stomping descent down the stairs. Something in Poppy's eyes tell me he wants to ask me more. However, he doesn't right then. At least not until he walks me to my car.

CHAPTER 24

THE MYSTERIOUS SHOEBOX

A tiny flashlight with a corroded battery. An antique porcelain doll the size of my palm dressed in a piece of hand-sewn fabric that looks like a larger doll's skirt. A tangled mess of necklaces, a couple bland, gray stones and a silver lighter with a turquoise horse head. They are all in a shoebox Poppy gave to me last night when he walked me to my car.

"I need to give you this." Poppy had a raggedy cardboard shoebox cupped between his elbow and side that he pulled out when he closed the car door behind me. He held it between us, wavering like he didn't want to give it to me when I reached out my hands to accept it.

"When you came to us the first time, you were only three years old," he told me with a soft smile. "We figured you'd be here a couple days, then go back to wherever you came from—"

"I thought I was six."

"Um, that's when you came to live with us all the time," Poppy said. "We had you on and off since you were just a wee little thing, all big eyes and knobby knees and—bruises." He finally gave the shoebox to me. It was red and white and says OCEAN CITY SHOES on the top in big, bold letters. "When you came the first time, the police went to your daddy's house and got some of your little clothes and shoes and toys. They found this and figured it was yours."

"Is this like that stupid suitcase I'm hiding from Anna for you?" I asked him flatly. "Because I don't know what's in there, naughty magazines? It makes me nervous being a coconspirator to some crime."

"Just keep it safe, Raeanna," he told me softly. "Hide it as best you can."

"Hide it. That comforts me even more. What's inside the suitcase?"

"I don't know. Just trust me." Poppy had sighed deeply, leaned back and looked toward the tiny tea lights brightening the dark backyard. He had his color back but he needed a haircut, at least by my standards. He liked to keep his gray hair a bit scraggly, 1980s style. "I need you to keep another secret to yourself."

I was looking at him. Secrets. What was with the sudden rash of secrets? This was certainly not the norm for Poppy. "Yeah?"

"I'm concerned about Gil's friend, Colt, who volunteers at the outreach program. I'm worried he has an ulterior motive for being here in Hensley Grove." Poppy stepped back, patted the window sill of the car. "Now this isn't something you tell anyone else. Nobody knows that I'm aware of this, but Ralph Edward at the Wesley Outreach Program came by requesting a donation for the program. The six o'clock news had just done their Weekly News Update and it was about how senior citizens get taken advantage of all the time with fake requests for donations. They had a list of different ways you can check out a place requesting donations to make sure they are, well, legitimate."

"The Wesley Outreach is a fake?" My eyes went back and forth between his own.

"No, no not at all. They have a federal identification. But when I looked up Ralph Edward's name and Colt Lucero's name, I found some interesting information. Ralph Edward is Alexandra Edward's stepfather, were you aware of that?"

"I guess," I shrugged. "But I don't really keep tabs on those girls."

"And Colt Lucero's last name wasn't always Lucero, it was D'Angelo. Does that ring a bell to you?"

"Poppy, can you please quit holding up the pieces to your puzzle and just slap it down on the table and put it together?" I shook my head mildly back and forth. "I swear you like drama more than all of Gil's friends together."

"Don't get sassy with me, young lady." Poppy gave me a teasing glare.

"Yes, sir."

Now, I'm getting a real glower because he knows I'm not about the *yes, sirs* and *no, sirs*.

"Anthony D'Angelo was the pilot on the plane that crashed on the Black Street Bridge twenty-odd years ago, sweetie-pea." Poppy leaned hard into the window, drops his voice. "His last name was D'Angelo. His mother remarried. Colt D'Angelo is Colt Lucero. He's the pilot's son."

"You don't think it is coincidence that he's here?"

"I found where he worked for a supermarket tabloid called *Celebrated*. You know, those gossip magazines they have sitting at the front register at Jenson's Grocery with all the celebrity gossip and scandal, and weird alien stories."

"God Squad worked for a tabloid? Well, I wouldn't have thought that," I mused. "Mister Perfect. He doesn't seem like the type who'd—oh." The realization floods over me. "You think he's here for the story?"

"Raeanna, I just found the information this afternoon. I was stunned. I don't want to jump to conclusions and I haven't even told Anna," Poppy smiled softly. He always does that when he talks about his wife. "She likes the young man so much, I don't want to tell her he might be here with ulterior motives. And you, I am concerned he might try to wheedle out something you don't want everyone to know. Has he asked any questions of you?"

"I don't know." I thought about it a moment. "I mean, he might have in conversation, but I don't know anything about the plane wreck or my dad maybe stealing anything, you know that, right?"

"You would tell me if you remembered anything."

"Of course, Poppy. You know I was like two years old when it happened, right?" I asked. "Half the time I can't even remember Mia's date of birth when they ask me at the doctor's office. Remembering anything more than a vague memory of my mom that could quite possibly be nothing more than a magazine picture I saw at some point would be pretty slim."

"Well, keep your distance from him, will you?" Poppy said, leaned back and patted the door like it was a horse and he was shooing it away. "At least until we figure out what is going on. I'd confront him, but I don't know if he has information and he'll use it against us. I don't want to be melodramatic because he might have good intentions. Or he might just get mad and make up some big scandal with you and the family involved—"

I nodded, felt a bit queasy. "I only see him when he's hanging out with Gil. Have you said anything to him?"

Poppy lounged on my words. I'm wondering if he isn't afraid Gil will do something rash. So, I put up a hand. "Never mind. Just keep me posted. I'll keep a wide berth."

I'm contemplating the conversation while Mia and I sort through the contents of the box before I put her to bed.

"Mama, can I have the baby?" She likes the little doll and keeps picking it up and cupping it in the palm of her hand. I stare at it myself, tug it from her fingers and try to latch on any memories of it. Blank.

"If you are careful with it," I tell her. I push myself to my feet and find a tiny and empty plastic butter dish to make a bed for the doll. With a few white tissues under and one over, the doll has a new bed to sleep in next to Mia when I lay her down for the night.

The lighter, it is a different story. While I turn it around in my fingers, I keep getting the image of Mama's thumb flicking it over and over. Flick. Spark. Flame. Flick. Spark. Flame. The horse. I remember her showing it to me. I can't see her face. I'm not sure if the memories are real or maybe something I made up so I sigh and set it back down into the shoebox. They are muddy and just out of reach.

My cell phone rings. Gil. I groan thinking maybe Poppy told him about Colt.

"What the hell is going on between you and Colt Lucero?" He is yell-growling at me on the other end.

"Nothing," I bumble through the word nearly stuttering. Had Poppy seen something on the stairway?

"Well, there's something going on. Because a guy doesn't get up and pound another guy halfway across Kentucky because he said something about a girl unless he's drunk or got something going with her."

"I have no clue what you are talking about. And, Gil," I added smartly. "We've got nothing going, as you call it."

Gil didn't hesitate to fill me in regardless. It seems while they were finishing up with the s'mores, Finn had made himself comfortable in a seat by Alexandra and Taylor, flirting with both of them and getting louder by the minute. Everybody was just chatting and laughing and having a good time when Finn, all of a sudden, realized he wasn't the center of attention.

He reached into his pocket and pulled out a hundred dollar bill, waved it in the air. He started laughing and telling everybody the story of our conversation straight down to calling me a whore and me tossing the money at him. I guess he even had the balls to roll his eyes and laugh at me for being such a prude-slut.

"So your date says this: *I mean, what should she expect wearing a dress like that, you know? Don't get mad at me for thinking she's a bit slutty looking but doesn't follow through. And, gentlemen, I'm not paying a couple hundred bucks and not getting laid, am I right?* And that's a pretty close quote," Gil says. "And granted, we were all staring at him like he was high or something because mom and dad were in the kitchen putting stuff away in the refrigerator. I mean, did he not know I was your brother?"

"And you defended me?"

"No," Gil shrugs off my words. "I was just sitting there stunned. We all were. It was completely silent while we stared at him. Even Alexandra. Regardless of what she thinks of you, she wouldn't even call you a prude-slut aloud. I mean what does that even mean?"

"It's somebody who has a reputation for dating a lot of guys but never goes all the way."

"Well, I know that, Tango. I work at a high school. I'm just saying why would you say that in a group of people you don't know and aloud? But nobody had to say anything, Tango. Colt stood up, grabbed Finn by the shirt collar and just started waling on him. He punched him from the back porch, down the stairs and halfway through the back yard. Me and two others had to pull him off. Poppy came out and escorted both of them to their cars."

"Well, I guess thanks for giving me a heads-up," I mutter. "Poppy's not mad at me, is he? Finn was a jerk. I didn't want to tell your mom that."

"I just don't think mom understood why you were being so standoffish to him and everybody. Then she couldn't figure out why you couldn't just tell her that the dude was a screw-up. Why didn't you just tell them?"

There's a knock on the door. I look up at the clock on my living room wall. It's a pink cat with a tail that used to swing back and forth. It just makes a clicking sound now. It is ten-thirty, too late for Billy to come over to hang out and too early for Rocky to be home from work. I listen to Gil rambling on and give a couple uh huhs while I peer through the smudged peephole on the door.

Surprise, surprise. It is Colt standing in the yellow light of the balcony. I unlatch the door, open it enough so he can see me pushing a forefinger over my lips to shush him. I point to the phone, then wave a hand for him to come inside. Gil's getting ready to hang up, but has to summarize our conversation and then attach an addendum: "So, Tango, just do us all a favor, stay away from him, alright? You do something to people that makes them weird."

"If you're talking about Billy, he was born with autism," I say, eyeing Colt. He's got a really red eye and a puffy lip. "And Rocky, he's just jaded from bad jobs and too many girlfriends."

"Whatever. You're not lying, right? You're going to stay away from him."

"Yeah, yeah, you know I don't ever hang around your friends, Gil," I grunt while I walk to the kitchen. "They're creepy, churchy, and wear khaki all the time. I'm all about rainbows and deviant art. I'm telling you the truth."

I dig out a handful of ice cubes, stuff them in a clean baggy. Then I snatch up a clean wash cloth from under the sink and work my way back out to the living room with my phone still attached to my ear.

"Promise me," Gil is telling me on the other end of the phone. "Because dad's going to ask if I made you promise."

"I promise I will not be anywhere near Colt Lucero," I lie. Colt is kind of wavering near the door. His eyes make a snap upward to mine and I roll them. I point to the couch and he follows, sits down a little sullenly. "Geez, Gil, he makes me ill. You know that. He's such a prude."

Colt is just staring at me, expressionless. I extend my hand, wiggle the rag with ice cubes at him. He takes it in his fingers, then appears to wrestle with deciding whether to push it on his soon-to-be black eye or if he should tend to the fat lip. I point to his eye, then lean over and push his hand upward so it is just above his cheek. Gil is yawning into the phone and I take it as an excuse to tell him I'm going to bed.

"Goodnight, Gil," I grunt and he's used to this, me just hanging up the phone on him. Such, I do. Then I sit down on the couch with a plop at the opposite end.

"You know, you're the only one of them that didn't have on khakis tonight," I say, snatching up the remote and flipping through the channels until I find an old 1980s sitcom. I look over at him, wiggle my fingers at his clothes. He's wearing ripped blue jeans and a button up shirt.

"Tango, I really screwed up tonight."

"I heard the story," I say and I can see him trying to read my face. "My God, the drama. And I'm just glad it's somebody else screwing up other than me." I shrug. "Do you like sitcoms or old movies?"

"Sitcoms. But, no, this is getting to be the hundredth time in a couple weeks I screwed up. It was not even thinking Zane Hill was getting beat up by his dad. Then thinking you were trying to get me to break the law painting graffiti at the church. And then, listening to Anna and I just—I didn't think for a second you weren't sabotaging the date with that Finn dude."

"I always give people a certain amount of time to get to know me. Poppy says I have to do this because I can come off as being what he calls pugnacious and like a firecracker the moment it lights up. So enjoy the grace period." He doesn't look so convinced. "Listen, Anna will still believe that Finn was just a nice man. It was something I did to set him off. Poppy, he won't give a darn who caused the problem even if it was me. Gil is certain that something in my personality makes people act crazy. It's like a cold I'm passing around to everybody if I get too close."

He bobs his head up and down easily. "You do realize I'm trying to apologize for—tonight. I shouldn't have cornered you on the stairs. I didn't mean to kiss you. I shouldn't have punched Finn."

"I think Gil said it was more akin to *waling on* him," I tease with a slight smile. Then I roll my eyes. "The kiss. You caught me off-guard with that one. Never expected it coming for one second. It was kind of like jumping off the water tower with Delia—"

"It was that bad?"

"Sorry, maybe wrong analogy for you. But it was scary-fun for me." I shrug. He seems to absorb this while he sets his eyes on mine. Damn those blue eyes. He pulls the gaze away first, sits back on the couch. It probably isn't four minutes that we watch TV in silence when he shifts.

"So I've always thought I had a knack at figuring people out. You've sent me left of center. Now I'm doubting myself. Tell me about—you."

"Me," I say. And I'm thinking about what Poppy said. I need to be careful. "I get up in the morning, take Mia to the sitters and go to work. In the afternoon, if school is in session, I drop her off at Anna's and go to class—"

"You know that's not what I mean."

"Okay, that's fair," I sigh. "You're right. I like to dance."

"Why don't you?"

"I did," I tell him. "I got pregnant three years ago. I didn't terminate the pregnancy which was what everybody proposed would be the best way for me to handle the situation. So I had to stop. Shane Delgado has kind of held that over my head ever since. He really pushed me as a student and I did well. I let him down. After that, he wouldn't let me in his classes. When I sign up, he says he has too many students. When I confront him, he threatens to get me kicked out of Field's."

Okay, Colt is staring at me with a fixed gaze. "So the rumor is that Shane's Mia's—"

"That's funny. No," I interrupt. He's asking way too many questions for me to be comfortable. "Does it matter?" I stand up quickly, hold my hand out toward the door. "Listen, I've got an early morning tomorrow. You know, the same boring thing day after day and nothing to—" I stop myself before I say *add to your list of juicy gossip stories for your magazine when you write the story about the crazy serial killer's daughter.* "—help promote your status with Alexandra and Taylor because you've put together the final piece of the puzzle showing the downfall of Tango they've been trying to finish for years."

He pushes himself up and looks a bit bewildered. "I didn't mean to offend you, Tango. No, it doesn't matter. I didn't—" he sighs. "Yeah, I guess Alex did say it was a big rumor." He waves his hands over his face. "And the eyes. They look like his. But a thousand other men have eyes like that. I shouldn't have assumed." He extends his hand with the melted icepack, the condensation on the outside dribbling down his fingers. "It doesn't matter. Still, I just wanted to tell you I'd open the doors for you on Mondays, Wednesdays and Fridays when I work over at the building. Barney Greene said he wanted to lay low for a few weeks and make sure the dean of the college hadn't gotten wind of you sneaking in there. He said you didn't show up this week anyway."

"Why are you offering?" I ask him.

"What?" Colt gives me a questioning gaze.

"Why are you being so nice to me?" I ask him. "I mean, I guess I've got to be honest, God Squad, we aren't anything alike. You're all middle class and I'm—" I wave my hand around, encompassing my shabby apartment. "—subsidized housing units. Your girlfriends and by the way, I made it plural because I'm not sure if it is Alexandra or Taylor this week, are my nemeses. Your friends don't even care that I am still in the room when they talk trash about me. Is it just for your work like to help the poor? Because I'm not sure what you're even supposed to be doing at that mission. I'm not the kind of poor that wants or needs help."

"Well," Colt is looking to the ground like he's choosing his words carefully. He veers around the couch, heading for the door. "I just signed up for mission work. I'm not necessarily religious. I just wanted to make a difference, help people out. The agency placed me with the Wesley Outreach Program." He gets to the door and reaches out for the knob. Then his eyes come up, roam around the room. "I don't know so much about how much money you make. I suppose if you could afford better, you wouldn't be living here. The box of food was a stupid idea. I didn't think that one out. I guess you're figuring out if we're going to toss weaknesses out on the table here, mine is not looking at things from all angles, making stupid decisions." He sighs. I think he's going to end there while he starts to open the door, then stops. "Tango, you're just—well, I keep finding myself drawn to you, to all the stuff that is so different from Alexandra and Taylor. What the heck? Who jumps off water towers to save somebody else? But Delia and Alexandra and Taylor, they are just like those wind up ballet dancers on the music boxes going around and around. I feel like I've been running around my whole life with boring wind up ballet dancers. Your Anna told me she got you one of those when you were seven. She said you jerked the little dancer right out of the box and held it up high. She said you said: *I'm settin' her free, Anna. Ain't nobody gonna make her do circles for them.* You're like that. Free. You're like the one that was lucky enough to get ripped off the box and you jumped."

"That was deep."

He shrugs. "If you like those things, I'm sorry. You won't get them much from me. But I'm tossing it out there. Gil probably told you I got a job working for the college. I'm the new guy. I get the worst shift from seven until midnight and the wonderful job of sweeping the office staff's floors. I'll be waiting at the doors of the theatre on Monday at seven if you want to dance."

CHAPTER 25

DANCING WITH ADRIEN MOREAU

It is dark and Mia is clinging to my neck on Monday while we walk to the back door at Field's Community College. She's holding her little doll from the box Poppy gave me. I can see Colt's shadowed image in the window glass even before he opens the door wide to let us inside.

I'm surprised when Mia smiles shyly at him and wiggles her fingers. "Hey, Colt," she says softly. She holds her right hand out, gets a sly shift to her eyes. Then she makes like a biting dinosaur by clapping her thumb and fingers together. "Gonna, gonna, gonna—"

"—eat you," he finishes for her and does the same back to her, tickling her shoulder with his fingers. She giggles softly and they share a look that almost makes me jealous. I feel left out. He looks up at me, seems to recognize this. "She missed you when you were out to dinner the other night with—"

"Satan," I finish for him. Then I reach into my open duffel bag on my shoulder and pull out a paper sack. "Supper for you." Inside is leftover chicken from my supper, mashed potatoes, and apple sauce. Oh, and a brownie from Joe's Home-style Diner.

Colt looks into the bag. "Yeah, well he evens out the bar with stupidity for us guys too poor to ask a woman out, so I'm not complaining." Colt looks a little discomfited at the memory. "But Mia was standing at the front window in the dark watching for you and crying. I asked her what was wrong and she just said she was waiting on her mama. Anna was busy getting the potato salad so we hung out." He pauses, takes a breath. "Man, this smells good."

What he doesn't know about Satan is that he showed

up after Sunday dinner at Anna's with two dozen red roses, a pink teddy bear, and his mother, Ruth, in tow. It seems Anna and Ruth got together after the choir sang and decided to play matchmaker again. Neither had heard the correct way the night had played out. They received an altered, watered-down version where Finn had just been nervous about going out with such a pretty woman and said some stupid things.

I realized a quarter of the way into Finn apologizing to me with doleful eyes, Anna didn't know the fight had to do with Finn trying to mar my reputation. I could see it, though, through her eyes. Me having Mia was a real gut-punch for her and Ruth seems to think her son is as righteous and handsome and decent as the good guys in the bible she was toting against her chest. So with Anna standing there with pleading eyes and imagining me wearing a white dress and walking down the aisle with a bible superhero, I couldn't say no to going to a movie with him, could I? Of course, Gil and Layla could tag along.

"Hey," Colt says while he walks with me through the back foyer to the theatre. He's got a broom in tow and it bangs against the theatre door frame when he follows me inside. "Adrien Moreau came by."

"What?"

He points up to the front rows of the theatre chairs. "The dancer, Adrien, came by. He wanted to talk to you."

I know he sees the wild pony in me wanting to buck out that door when my feet brake. I swear right then, Colt takes a sidestep and blocks me as I see Adrien's head turn, recognize I am here. I narrow my eyes at Colt.

"He's been coming in every night looking for you, Tango," Colt tells me in hardly a whisper. "He's been sticking his head in the door three or four times waiting for you to show up. You haven't and he didn't want to ask about you because of, well, Shane. I knew you wouldn't come if I told you."

"And you're right."

"Just talk to him."

I settle Mia into her usual seat, pop open my phone with a movie. Adrien's a double cheek kisser and an arm holder. He latches on to my upper arm, albeit gently, and is looking at me up and down. "Hello, Tango, that is what they call you, right? Like the dance?"

"Well, not the dance, the attitude."

"Sensual and spicy and nostalgic," he offers and nods. I just let him go with it, right or wrong. "Like your saucy dance between Shane Delgado and myself, that—I think the girls in his class called it your very own *Whiskey Tango Ménage à trois*?" His accent is deep, but he is not too difficult to understand. "Will you dance with me—a pas de deux, a dance for two? I promise it won't be but a half hour. I want to see more of what you can do. We can start with your tango, no?"

I do not get to say yes or no. He's so young to know so much about dance, so gifted. I don't feel like I can say no to him. I feel like I shouldn't say no to him in the same way if someone offered me a beautiful bracelet, it would be a loss to not place it around my wrist.

He takes up the better part of five hours pushing me just like he did the last time we danced, even going as far as getting me to do a one-armed handstand while he holds me up. This time, I know he is getting to know me.

"So, are you courting me, my Russian Mafia spy?" I ask him during the same kind of banter we had last time. The exercises we do together, the warmups and the basic routines are all the drills new partners do to get to know each other. It's like the kissing and touching and the feeling up of each other on the first few dates before the big one comes along where you go all the way. "Or am I just another secret lover you expect to chase from country to country until you murder me for secrets in an old theatre in the backwoods of Kentucky?"

"The latter sounds enticing."

"Murdering me?" I ask him with a yawn and haughty airs while he holds me above his head. "You'll never catch me. I have more lovers than I care to deal with. They are all like you. I tire of them, toss them away." He has the guts to free one hand, reach up, and tickle my belly. He thinks it is funny that I sometimes snort when I cackle-laugh.

We stop just two times. Once, so I can give a drowsy Mia her snack.

"This is your little girl?" he asks me from afar. I nod. He looks from me to her and then back again. "I'm not around ones that little often. She looks like you."

"My old boyfriend used to call her Mini-Tango." I wait for the impatience telling me he thinks kids are a pain in the ass.

"Mini-Tango," he repeats to himself and Mia looks up like he's called her name and smiles. Then Adrien just watches me open her little clear plastic baggie of animal crackers and a tiny carton of milk.

The second time he calls out for Colt when he is taking a break and leaning into the doorway watching with a bottled water in hand. "Hey, concierge—?" he turns to me. "What is the name for the man who cleans?"

"His name is Colt."

"Isn't that a baby horse?"

"That's his given name."

"Oh." He looks discombobulated, nods and his face

goes beet red before he turns his attention to Colt making his way up an aisle. "Colt can you spot for us, make sure she doesn't fall?"

He wants me to perform a grand jeté before I jump into his arms. With one snap of his wrists, he lifts me into the air so I am facing him. Then while I work my legs around, he constantly works his own hands around my waist so I am twisting and spinning in the air, belly to floor, belly to ceiling. When I have finally made full turn, Adrien then gives me one last spin and I am to slowly descend behind him and perform a pirouette. Behind him. Yeah, that didn't work the first three times. I end up taking out Colt like a comet free-falling to earth and both of us slapping the floor so hard, it takes away our breath.

Adrien doesn't scold me like Shane used to lash out at me, screeching and screaming with hands in the air. "Again," he just tells me firmly and so many times I am sore and bruised and panting.

"I like the way you look me in the eyes. You listen with them. The other girls, they are all blinky and scared. You are a perfectionist, I see that. Now, I am going to make you mad," he tells me and he says my hair is ugly brown. "Yes, that is the passion I am looking for. You see?" I did see. It makes me angry and he gets the response in the next dance while I grit my teeth at him and gave him stink eye. "Now look down, then look up as if I am your favorite love and you wish I would never, never leave. But you know I am." I do and he is gleeful like a child when I do it. "Yes, yes, that is it!" It was not until a quarter after eleven that he suddenly stops, looks up at the clock on the wall at the far end of the theatre.

"Arrh, it is eleven? I missed my flight." He just stops there, picks up his phone from a pile near the front of the stage. "I've got to go. Wednesday? You'll be here, good?"

I sit down on the stage and watch him leave. I shake my head like I'm trying to make sense of this peculiar relationship I have with this stranger.

"What the heck was that?" I ask Colt who is dangling his keys in his hand and looking at the clock himself. "I can't tell if I feel like a spurned lover or—just a person walking down the street that got a flirty gaze from a stranger," I ponder aloud. "No, maybe a whirlwind romance with somebody else's husband. Honestly, he's probably trying new things out and doesn't want to break his real partner, what did you call her? Sorcière Noire. I'm kind of his stunt trial. I'm going to be sore tomorrow. Can you help me stretch down?"

"Tango, I've got sixteen offices to vacuum before I go home," he tells me with pleading eyes.

"I'll help," I nod, look at Mia sleeping soundly on the red velvet seat in the front row. "We'll sweep and then we'll stretch, deal?"

Two hours later, my legs feel like concrete after we finish the last two rooms. I feel one-hundred and ten years old when I show Colt a few partner stretches and have him push and pull my legs. He is quiet, doesn't say much while he mildly tugs and bends my legs back and forth. "Okay, harder, harder," I tell him seriously and twice he stifles a laugh and rolls his eyes at me. Oh, yes, it does sound suggestive—me under him and grunting with the pressure.

"So, do ballet people do this all the time, court other dancers? Because that is what it was like with you and Adrien. It is like you are two lovers meeting each other." The ache in my thighs and arms is excruciating while he presses me down into the splits. "He told me earlier he flew in last week twice to find you. And he acts like you're being coy about it all, playing hard to get."

"I don't know. I'm not being coy. I like to dance. I

really don't know where to go with it. You see how he is, right?" I poke Colt in the shoulder. "Arrogant, condescending. I hate that. I hate conceited people."

"Really, that's a surprise," Colt laughs. "Because I see how well you get along with Shane's Diva Dream Team."

"Yeah, I jump off a building for Diva Delia and she stabs me in the back every time I turn around still," I huff. "I don't know how you handle being with them. But you see what I mean, right? Adrien acted like he didn't know you."

"In his defense, Tango, I'm not sure he did recognize me even when I talked to him the other day. I was standing just inside the door. He's not used to seeing me dragging a sweeper. He tipped his head to the side tonight and I think it occurred to him. Maybe he was too embarrassed to ask."

"Too embarrassed to ask if he remembered you, but not too shy to frigging nearly grab my crotch." I hold out an arm, squeeze it with my fingers just above the elbow. I know he was trying to get a feel of my weight, my balance and my strength, but Adrien poked and prodded me everywhere he shouldn't have poked and prodded. "You saw him, didn't you? I don't mind guys feeling me up, but he went a little overboard for the first date."

Colt muffles a chuckle and shakes his head. "Yeah, I felt like I was watching soft porn for a second there. He was so strangely systematic and efficient, it was weird." We shift so we are sitting with our feet touching.

"Well, I'll just say this. He surpassed my stranger-touching-me comfort zone." It is quiet a moment. He is pulling me forward until I lay flat, then I pull him forward. He doesn't go so far to the floor. "Hey," I say to catch Colt's attention while we're halfway. He looks up. "I don't know if I want to do it again, Colt." I look up and he recognizes I am serious, calling him by name. "I let everybody down when I got pregnant. I lost it all. I'm sure you've heard Delia and her pack talk about me."

"They do."

"Now, what if I fail again?" I ask him to lay across my back on his belly while I sit with my legs crossed. He is to gently push on my knees.

"You really didn't fail the first time. You just made bad choices."

"I really didn't think I had a choice with Mia's father," I divulge softly. "I was scared if I didn't sleep with him, I wouldn't be able to dance, God Squad. I was so young and naïve. Poppy and Anna were so overprotective. I was afraid if I denied the man, he would kick me out. I would let Anna down. It started when I was in high school and I didn't know how to make it stop later. Promise me you won't tell Anna this."

"I won't." Colt gives me a pat on my arm. "I feel your pain. Maybe it is different, but everybody wrestles with trying to please parents. I'm trying hard not to be like my parents. Well, my step-dad. He's a jerk. I still want my mom to be proud of me. To please her, I have to please him." It is nearly silent in the theatre for a moment. Then Colt huffs a laugh. "I'm trying to be cool about this, Tango, but you are killing me."

"It hurts?" I ask him and he laughs softly.

"You're kidding me, right?" He jabs me with his chin. I realize what he is implying and I look up, catch his gaze. What the hell? Is he actually looking at me shyly?

"They are sexy, sorry," I say. "It's nice to have somebody to do them with instead of being alone. After a while you learn how to turn that part off."

"Really? How?"

"You think of other stuff, God Squad, just like any time you're talking to somebody that's married or you work with them and you feel attracted or horny—" I stop, sigh and drop my head. "Okay, no," I answer truthfully. I can't tell you how difficult it is for me to feel him pressing down. He's strong and incredibly well built, slim. He smells like a sporty aftershave. I can feel his belly muscles working against my back. I can see his lean, muscled arms on either side of me. His hands on my knees are gentle and strong like a lover. "With some people, it is just hard. With you, it is—not so easy for me either."

"You feel the same then. At least that makes it more or less awkward."

"What should I think, God Squad?" I muster feeling a little rejected. "You kissed me like we were making love for the last time—"

"We should probably stop." He finally pats my knee and sits up. "I can't do this with you, you understand?" He reaches out a hand, helps me to my feet. "It isn't that I can't have any, um, relationships with people in my work district. It wouldn't be appropriate and Taylor and I have been kind of seeing each other. I don't want to hurt you or her."

I suppose I understand. It doesn't make it any easier, suddenly wrestling with this crazy tickle-jumping in my belly. He's way too attractive for a brown-haired, awkward woman like me. I'm almost embarrassed right then opening up to him. He probably gets women doing that all the time.

"No, I get it," I lie. "Anna's concocted another date with me and Finn. This time, Gil is going to referee."

"You're kidding me, right?" Colt steps back. He almost looks angry, blue eyes looking back and forth between my own.

"No."

He doesn't say anything else to me, not a single word when he walks me and Mia to my car and helps me get her seated. Not even a goodnight.

CHAPTER 26

DON'T

Don't. That's the text I get from Colt two days later while I'm sitting at a table at the country club restaurant. I am zoned out from the conversation Gil and Finn are having about a recent Hensley Grove High School varsity football game. Layla is two glasses of wine into the conversation and is giggling into her palm every time one of the men says something. Even her eyes are glassy. The last I remember hearing is Finn dead-set on convincing Gil that if they changed around the player order, they might win a game sometime. I yawn, hear the ting, and check to make sure it isn't an emergency with Mia.

Don't what? I text back. *Don't get the fish? Don't forget my deodorant?* I wait for an answer. Nothing. So I sigh and write back. *Here's a don't for you. Don't be my conscience and tell me what to do.*

Ten minutes later, another text tings on my phone. Gil and Finn are still discussing football. Layla is nursing another glass of wine. Finn leans in, pushes an arm around my shoulders right in mid-sentence. "Thanks for giving me a second chance. I get stupid when I drink." I look down and I know he follows my eyes to the second bottle of beer at his wrist. He laughs, gives me a smile. "It won't happen again." And yet, even Layla's gaze follows his while it wanders across the room to a pretty woman in a blue dress getting seated. She turns quickly, forces a smile at me.

I reach for my phone after Finn gets back into his conversation with Gil.

Sorry. It's none of my business.

Are you trying to guilt me? Because that's what got

me going on this stupid date, Anna guilting me.

Yes.

Why are you doing it? I text that back to Colt and look up to see Finn, Gil and Layla staring at me.

"You've got to be somewhere else?" Finn says that while I let my phone drop to my lap. I know he wanted to come off as just teasing, but his voice isn't convincing. Nor is his flat-line expression displaying anything but spite.

"Mia isn't feeling good." Alright that was a knee-jerk reply and not thought out well considering she was fine and at Anna's. "I'm just a little worried."

Gil snatches up his phone. "I can call mom and see what's up. Tango, Mia's fine. Mom's raised more kids than I can count on my fingers and toes."

"No, no," I jump up from my seat, about spill my water. "I'll go call her."

Three minutes later, I'm leaning into Uncle Lion's office. I can tell he's on the phone, the top of his gray pile of hair on his head bobbing up and down each time he answers. Still, he waves me into the room. "Hey, my niece just stopped in. Let me call you back," he says in the phone while he pokes his finger at a chair across from his desk.

"You're here again?" he banters with me when he sets his cell phone down. "Another date?"

"Anna fixed me up."

"Oh." It's like he knows. I can tell by the way he dumps the word. "Doesn't sound good. Churchy boy?"

"Well, she thinks so. He's more a jerk."

"Well, you can hide out here as long as you want, lock the door when you leave. I'm getting ready to head home for the night." Uncle Lion stops and smiles.

"Eventually he's going to track you down." He pauses, seems to reflect on something before he looks up and locks eyes with mine. "Unless you want a ride home?"

"No, that's okay. I hate to bail on a date."

"Okay." Uncle Lion rises. He leans over and opens a drawer in his desk. "I keep forgetting to do this. The young woman that was here the last time you came for dinner, she left me her number for you to call. I've been meaning to get it to you. I completely forgot. Her name's Bella. Bella Price. Nice girl. I know her father well. We vacation together down south every January. Not sure what she wanted, but maybe if you two get along, you can come along on a trip sometime."

I doubted Colt Lucero's ex-wife would make a good friend pairing with me. If she wanted to talk to me, I am sure it was to give me hell for going on a date with her ex-husband. I didn't tell Uncle Lion that. I stand up and snatch up my phone to check the texts before I leave.

Don't. Because I like you.

That's what it says. Because he likes me? What does that mean? He likes me as a friend because Anna asked him to be nice to me? He wants to be my boyfriend? I groan. "Uncle Lion, can I take you up on that ride home?"

"Why'd you pull that shit? And yes, I said shit. Shit, shit, shit." I note when I'm saying it to Colt, he's wincing each time the word comes out of my mouth. He's standing at my door two hours later and after I stutter an excuse to Finn at the table. Gil could tell I was lying. He always knows when I'm lying because I tug on my bottom lip. I spend a half hour begging Anna to go along with my lie that Mia got sick. Now I'm home and in my old sleeping get-up—black tank top, raggedy shorts, and my hair bundled on top of my head. "And now you've got the guts to show up at my door. He keeps adjusting the neckline of his t-shirt like it has a collar. "*Don't* what? And you *like* me? What does that mean?" I jab a thumb behind me and open the door for Colt to come in. He's holding a brown paper bag in his hand and stretches it out toward me while he does his nervous hand through his hair ten times. "What's that?"

"Chocolate ice cream and chocolate syrup. There's a chocolate fudge brownie at the bottom. Triple chocolate. I thought I screwed up your date, gave you a triple chocolate day. You said you called the really bad days triple chocolate days because your Poppy gave you ice cream when things were tough. You told me that in the police station."

"Oh." I'm opening the bag, peering inside. Sure enough, there's a half gallon of Murphy's Best Ice Cream inside. It's a sweet peace offering. He actually listened to what I'd said. Kevin never did stuff like this for me.

"You didn't have to do this," I tell him. "Just tell Anna I'm not fixable. I don't care. She knows it."

"You're not broke. Maybe cracked a bit," Colt reaches up and knocks my head with his knuckles gently. He gives me a half-grin. "Do you like this guy?"

My tummy jumps. I realize right then, I want Colt to like me in the way boys like girls. "No. He's a jerk. You know that."

He just stands there, rocks back and forth on his feet. "Do you like—me?" He looks over my shoulder, at the floor, then finally shyly back at me. He's smiling timidly like a second grade schoolboy asking a fifth grade girl to dance. By the time his eyes come up, I'm already taking a step forward. I'm so close, I can feel the heat from his body when I reach out and grab a swatch of his t-shirt. It is soft in my fingers and I tug it hard toward me. He's tall so I just stare up at him, give him an angry glare.

"Yeah, God Squad. I like you. I don't know why. But I do. So I'd take advantage of the moment—"

"Put your hair down," he says it gruffly, softly. He doesn't wait for me to grab the hair tie holding up the twist on top of my head. Colt just reaches up and wiggles it free so my hair falls in rivulets down my shoulders, down my back. His hand falls with it. He's just staring at me, staring at my eyes. Blue. Blue. His eyes are so deep blue and making my stomach bang, bang, bang beneath my ribs. Then something shifts in his gaze. Something wary and terrified and I can almost see the wall he's building to shut me out.

"Stop," I say it softly. He's going to bolt. And everybody thinks I'm the wildcard, the pony that wants to break past the pasture gates all the time. Nope. I finally found my match. I release my grasp on his shirt in slow motion. He still hasn't taken his eyes off me. "So it just has to start with a kiss. And maybe it ends there. We don't know, right?" I say. "No harm done either way."

He nods. I think. So I start to push my hand back out, hesitate, then let my fingers settle on his chest. I want to touch him. I want to run my hands down his chest, feel the muscles. I don't. I just let it rest there.

"You're okay?" I ask.

"You act like I'm a stray kitten you're trying to tame."

"You've got the stray kitten look in your eyes," I tell him. "You look like you're going to climb the nearest tree." I want to slip my fingers past those ripped jeans and find out what makes Colt Lucero so crazy with passion, he's begging me not to stop. What the heck? Where did this come from? I hate doubting myself. But I'm wondering if I haven't gotten so used to just turning it off dancing with different partners, I just don't let myself feel anymore. I've never really wanted to do this before, let my own wall down. For the first time, I realize I'd been looking at relationships in all the wrong ways.

"I want to run. I don't want to run. I can't. I don't think I can do this. It isn't just the church stuff—"

"I know who you are, Colt," I mutter. "Is that what's stopping you? Or is it Taylor?" I snap my eyes upward. I don't pull my hand away. It is resting gently just above his belly button.

"What do you mean, you know who I am?"

"I know your dad was the pilot on that plane that crashed at the old bridge that used to be on Black Street. I know you work for that tabloid magazine that sits up by the counter at Jenson's Grocery." I take in a deep breath. I'm standing there wondering why I feel like I'd do just about anything to feel another kiss from him. Like tell him something Poppy told me not to tell.

"How'd you find out?" he asks, then shrugs it off. "I figured everybody would know. I mean, it isn't hard to dig stuff up on the internet. I suppose everybody knows."

"I don't know so much about that, God Squad. Maybe just me and Poppy."

"So maybe I should go. You understand why this isn't such a good thing, right?"

Oh, yeah, I do. Because his dad stole the money and took off for Mexico and my dad got blamed for it. But he's not his dad. I'm not my dad. "You've known up to this point. I've known for a long enough time to absorb it." I look up at Colt. He's still staring at me. We're close. We're so close and he's got that wild sway to his eyes that I know whatever I say and however I say it might break whatever we've got here, even if it is the tiniest of connections. "It's just a kiss," I tell him again. He laughs gently, deeply. So I'm thinking he's going to step back because there is this long, awkward silence between us. I think he's going to walk out the door.

"Tango, it's never just a kiss with you. Or a dance. That's what has driven Adrien Moreau to banging on the theatre doors every night. You know Kevin sits out in the parking lot still. It's what left me pacing around my house tonight and stupid-texting you home from the date." He looks away for a second. "It's what leaves Shane Delgado hate-loving you so badly, he can't be around you."

"He told you—something?" I hiss, feel my heart drop.

"He didn't need to tell me, Tango," Colt muttered. "You could feel it in the theatre that night. You could *feel* his anger and his pain and it was all aimed at you. It was like two thunderstorms getting ready to crash over everybody's head, thunder and lightning and all hell breaking loose. It doesn't take a genius to figure that one out. You make people—feel things. Sometimes, it isn't the type of sensations they want to feel. Maybe I don't want that. Who wants to be in a long line of—?"

"A long line?" I sniff hotly. "Nice, Lucero, you make me sound like I'm a—" And I stop there because he's giving me that stupid look like he knows what I'm going to say and he doesn't like that particular word.

Still, maybe he wants to be there, though. Because I toss up my hands, step back. "Fine, then don't *feel* whatever it is you say people feel around me. But maybe I want to—" And Colt Lucero simply slides his arms around me, jerks me toward him. It is so natural to wrap my legs around him when he pushes me upward with his hand supporting my rear. It isn't awkward. I latch on to his neck while he shifts one arm along my back and to my shoulder, tugging my head toward him.

I wasn't expecting it. I think I thought we were playing a game, a toss of a ball back and forth between rivals. I throw the ball hard, he catches it and meets my speed. He throws it soft, I catch it and return it with the same pace. Then eventually, we tire and walk away.

I realize this while he softly kisses my forehead and my cheeks and then, finally gets to my lips. I figure, well, it's going to stop here. He'll just release me, let me slide back down to my feet again. Colt pauses. He gets this funny smirk to his face like maybe I tossed the ball a little hard and okay, he gives up. He's got these perfect lips that curve heart-shape. I guess I didn't really notice them until now while he's hovering there kind of laughing with his eyes in defeat.

"What?" I ask because he's not putting me down and he gives this little chuckle.

"I feel like I'm standing on the ladder of that water tower again," he tells me. "My stomach's jumping. My head is dizzy. It's that moment I realize you're completely bat-crap crazy and oh-my-God you're going to jump. You're really, really going to take that jump. And I'm like—scared as I've ever been and that's saying a lot. Because, Tango, I've been in some pretty terrifying places. But I know deep inside, it's the stupidest thing I've ever done and I really don't care because I'm taking a dive off a hundred foot tower with you."

Oh, holy hell. His words were so powerful, so deep. I think I was starting to giggle. I don't know. Now, I'm holding my breath. "Jump," I say in a whisper so softly, I can't believe he heard me. I'm just staring at Colt Lucero and not caring about Poppy's warning, just drinking in his words and then, tasting his kiss on my lips. He's like two soft kisses, then one long one. It's like a dance pattern, but so sensual I don't even notice at first, he's upping the steps, kissing me harder and turning so I'm against the wall.

He's kissing my neck and my arms are covered in goose pimples and he's making me laugh softly because I'm terribly ticklish just beneath my ears where he has worked his way around. And this is where it gets awkward, those moments where you're tucked into somebody's arms and you've kissed until there's no place left to kiss that's rated G. And we're both realizing this is the line we can cross or not cross. My heart is pounding. I know his is pounding too because I can feel it against my chest, feel it against my hand resting lightly on his t-shirt.

"Are we still—jumping?" he asks me and his voice is shaky and I realize my right hand is trembling when it slides down along his ribs and stops just short of where my thigh is pressed against the waist of his pants. It occurs to me I am just as terrified of him as he must be of me. Because there's something here, something between us I can't quite put my finger on that's just one step farther than I've ever felt for a man, even Kevin.

So we're bumbling there and I can feel his hand slip up my t-shirt and stop just short of my right breast. I lean into him, nudge his forearm toward me with my elbow.

"Yeah."

We end up on my bed with the covers still on afterwards. I think I hear Mia waking up. I sit up, slip on his t-shirt that's resting half on and half off the headstand. I'm always so careful, so self-conscious of the scar Daddy left on my back. Big rule. Nobody sees it. I've learned to turn just the right way, swing a towel over it, whatever it takes like grabbing the first thing I see like the t-shirt. "Stay, I'll be right back." I snatch up my underwear on the floor near the door and slip them on. I turn just in time to see Colt staring at me hard, his face then turning red.

"Sorry."

I can see down the hallway into Mia's room. She's sound asleep, just tossing with a dream. I tuck her in, make my way back to the room. "You want me to stay a while? Leave?" Colt asks me. "I honestly didn't see this thing coming. I mean, this quick. I'm a bit blindsided, not sure—"

"I'd like you to stay. You want to stay?" I just toss it out there. I'm tired of the game we play.

"Yeah, I do."

It's not something I can usually do, can really ever do —sidle up to a guy who is kind of a stranger and lay down next to him. Casual sex just isn't my thing. I'm standing next to the bed, knocking my knees against the mattress. "This is awkward," I say. "I don't know what to do."

"I was hoping you had an answer for that," Colt laughs and sits up in the bed.

"Because I've got a long line?" I toss at him. Crap, I'm back to playing the game. So I hold up a hand before he can answer. I see him cringe. "Just so you know, I don't have a long line. Just Kevin. Just Shane. And now, you." I think it out a moment, hope he doesn't think I'm clingy with guys because I stick to one or two. "Not saying it is a relationship or—"

"Girl, you are good at painting. And you are great at ballet. You just blew me away from the front door and all the way back to the bedroom. But you're not so good with this," he waves a hand back and forth between us. "Now."

"Oh, great, so you noticed that, huh?" I ask, scoot my knee up on the bed. He waves an arm at me and I do a crawl -slide across the mattress until I'm reclining next to him. My head's on his bare shoulder. My bare leg is slipping along his thigh.

"So this part is easier for me," Colt says. He reaches

up with his free hand and rubs his dark hair. It is sticking up and I smile while he tries to brush it down. "Are you a cat or a dog person?"

"Um," I furrow my brow, give him a questioning gaze. "I can't have pets here."

"It's just small talk."

"Oh, I like dogs."

"Me too," Colt adds. "I always wanted a German shepherd. When I was ten, I dreamed about having one that would walk me to school. My mom always bought these silly little shih tzus. They peed everywhere and tried to bite me all the time."

"Anna had a beagle. It stunk," I told him. "Poppy feeds about ten cats off his back porch. He picks up cats like he does kids."

"They had a lot of foster kids, huh?" he asks me. "Your Poppy said one was special enough to him that he fought tooth and nail to adopt her."

"Yeah, that would be me. Sometimes I feel bad for them for all the work they had to put into me. I was a handful."

"That's what parents do."

"Yeah, but most kids don't screw up like I did. I came pretty close to making Anna proud. I blew it." I turn and roll my eyes. "Enough about me. How have you screwed with your parents' heads?"

"Oh, that's a book in itself, Tango." Colt laughs gruffly. Then he tickles me on the neck so I can't help but snicker. "You're really ticklish."

"And you are avoiding my question."

"Well, for one," Colt stifles a yawn and I see him looking up at the little clock on my bed stand. "I quit my job at *Celebrity Magazine*. It wasn't an easy thing to do because my stepdad owns the company. Then, my mom pretty much summed it up on the phone when I was finally on a flight to Cincinnati and I told her what I was doing. She said my obsession was going to end up getting me killed."

"Your obsession?"

"Since I was eight." He sighs and rolls his eyes. "You'll laugh, Tango." He comes to a lull there and I look up, realize he is divulging something to me that he may not have said out loud before. "When I was about seven and a half, I got a bunch of books and stacked them up so I could look at the stuff my mom always hid on the top shelf of her closet. I remember Mom always getting stuff out of there after she thought I was asleep in bed. She'd sit on the bed and cry and look at something she had in a box. Rummaging around, I found a box with pictures of my real dad, stuff he had on the plane they gave to mom and newspaper clippings from the wreck. Some of the stuff the cops said was really harsh about him bailing out of the plane with like a million bucks in a duffel bag. I've got to be honest, I really think that deep down, my mom doubted he died in that crash."

"They never found his body."

"Nope." Colt hugs me with his arm. "I should let it go, right? I can't. For years, I'd get into the box, obsess about figuring out what happened to my dad, dreaming I'd clear his name."

"So you came back here to figure it out?"

"Oh, man," Colt laughs softly. "Please don't think I'm crazy. I've been fixated on clearing my dad's name, acting out some sort of revenge on Dell Smythe. I'm sure you know who that is. I wanted to make him feel how I felt, how my mom has felt for twenty years. So I started coming up with this idea, that I'd go Hensley Grove, take from Smythe what he took from me and my mom, the thing we loved most. I'd rip it right from his arms. And that would be Dell Smythe's daughter. I knew he had one. I know she grew up here— I figured I could do it, I really did. I mean, I'm the good guy, right? They're the evil villains—"

I'm floored. I can actually feel the blood running from my cheeks, feel a woozy-dizzy I have never felt before. I guess it never came up. I just assumed Colt knew who I was since, at this point, he had been friends with Gil, friends with my enemies who talk trash about me all the time. But, I suppose, in a small town, they protect their own.

I sit straight up in bed, swing my legs around so my back is to Colt. I hear him shift, lean up on his elbow. "Oh, no, I said something wrong. You're pale—I know, it's crazy. I—"

I can't even speak. My throat is tight and I'm woozy while I reach over and unlatch the kid safety locking mechanism on the drawer in the stand by my bed. I've got a tiny pocket pistol tucked beneath some tissues. Kevin bought it for me to carry to classes at night. I was afraid of the stupid thing, figured I'd shoot myself accidently instead of the pervert that might be following me so I kept it in the drawer. It is a pretty pink and it doesn't have any bullets inside. The bullets are under my mattress so Mia can't load it up. Still, I snatch it out of the drawer and I stand up, turn to face Colt.

"Here," I say, dropping the pistol on the mattress between us. It sinks slightly in the flowered comforter. "Here's your chance. The bullets are under your side of the mattress." I can see Colt staring at it confused, unsure. "Shoot. Get your payback. Live your stupid dream." He glances up at me.

"I don't understand."

"Colt, I'm Starr Smythe. Dell Smythe was my dad. I changed my name to Raeanna Baldwin when I got adopted. Ray is Poppy's name. And I added Anna on to the end. I thought you knew that. How can you possibly not know that? We talked about it while we ate ice cream after dropping off Zane." I actually think I'm going to cry at this point.

"You said your dad was a drunk, not a serial killer. There's a big difference. I thought he was just some dumb drunk who hit his kid. How would I assume that he was Dell Smythe? All your adoption papers are restricted."

I'm pinching my fingers on the upper bridge of my nose. "Nobody ever told you? Not Gil, not Taylor or Alex?"

"No—why would they?"

"Get out," I tell him, wiggling the fingers of my hand toward the door behind me. It almost sounds like a growl. He's right. I suppose it isn't something that Gil would blast around that his foster sister's got serial killer blood in her. I think he's in shock because he's just staring at me, blinking, blinking, blinking. "Get out of my house! Get away from me. Now!"

I turn around because for some stupid reason, modesty seems important right now again while he starts to stand because we're strangers again. And enemies, I would assume. I'm thinking that it might be a stupid move because he could, in all reality, be crazy and shoot me in the back.

"I don't want your frigging gun," he says sharply. I can hear him slipping on his pants. There is a stifling long silence while I'm waiting for him to finish.

"Yeah, that'd be dumb, wouldn't it?" I mutter, staring at the wall with my arms crossed wondering why he can't just quicken it up and leave. "They'd trace it back to you."

"Yeah, you're right."

"Well, in my story, you aren't the damn superhero and I'm not the evil supervillain. It's just the opposite," I grunt at him. "My dad was an innocent bystander. Your dad took the money."

He huffs a sarcastic laugh. "My dad never stole a dime in his life, Tango. He was a scout through high school. He was an honest, hardworking man. What can you say about your family?"

"Go to hell. Get out of here, God Squad."

"I need my t-shirt."

I bit down hard on my bottom lip. I almost draw blood. I suppose I'm so mad, I don't even think about the stupid scar below my left shoulder blade and I stomp across the room, dig out a shirt from my drawer. I don't want to face him. I just want him out and I rip off his t-shirt and toss my own on. Then I fling Colt's shirt over my shoulder to him.

Bang. Bang. The timing is awful, Billy's sign he's going to bed. I have to pass Colt to get to the wall and I bang back at him. "Goodnight, Billy." I realize even before looking at the clock, it isn't time for him to go to sleep yet. He must have heard us fighting. Billy is just checking up on me. "I'm fine."

I hear my front door close. I don't grasp until the quiet surrounds me the incredible mass of emotions Colt seems to leave me with whenever he has been around. I do pick out a few and recognize them for what they are—right now, rage while I stare at the bag the chocolate ice cream was in when I set it down on the table. It is running brown streaks across the floor. Twenty minutes ago, passion and desire. Yesterday, he irritated me mostly. Now, right this moment, it is an incredible thirst I can't quench. It's a yearning. It's a loss. It's love, bittersweet and screwed up.

CHAPTER 24

THE FOUR HORSES OF THE APOCALYPSE AND MARK LAFFERTY

"Maybe another time, Tango. I'm supposed to be at practice in five minutes."

I'm trying to keep Chloe Murphy's attention. She is in mid-step on the second step of three leading into Holy Trinity and looking at the watch on her wrist. It is Thursday night and she has choir practice with Anna, so I knew she'd be here. I had tried to call her at the police station sixteen times this week. She hasn't been returning my calls. I pulled my car up as close as I could to the steps and waited for her while Mia sat in her car seat and dug out the last of the cereal in the little plastic baggie I gave her.

"I was hoping you were able to work on another one of the murders with me," I say to her. She keeps rubbing her palm across her hair and giving me the same look Gil used to give me when his friends came over and I would get in the way. "You know, I take Billy to his acapella get-together and you give me info about Tammy Lynn? Remember? We talked about it."

"Yeah, sure. That was the plan. Things have changed a little. The files on the murders are unavailable now. I can't share any more information," she tells me. Her face is expressionless and she gives an impatient glimpse toward the church door. "Chief Peirce has all information restricted to only police personnel. Everything is locked in the evidence room. Just drop it. The police will take care of it. Sorry."

I watch her turn towards the church and take the last step. "Hey, what happened? Why the cold shoulder?" I know I shouldn't even bother to ask her another question. She's ignoring me just like everybody else has been doing over the last week since Colt came to my apartment. I know the answer just like I knew when Mia and I stood outside the theatre doors on Monday in the dark and then again on Wednesday. Colt wasn't there to open the door. I saw his shadow, I think, upstairs in one of the offices. I drop his bag of supper at the doors, leave it in the light so he finds it. Then I harass myself all the way out of the parking lot for worrying he's getting enough to eat. He's more than he said he was and I should have listened to Poppy. Even he's strangely subdued around me.

"I don't know." Chloe gives me a bored stare. "We're like on lockdown. Somebody must have said something about me working with you."

"Who knew? Who cares? What could I possibly do to hurt the case?"

"I don't know, maybe because you're the prime suspect's daughter?" Chloe is forthright and although it is like a knife in my gut, at least I know the truth.

"Nobody has seen my dad in three years, Chloe."

"Yes, listen carefully. It isn't our usual office protocol to bring in family members of suspected murderers to aid in a case even if it is cold."

"Cold? That makes no sense. Hannah Lafferty was just murdered this month."

"Just leave it alone, Tango." She gives me this long, deep look. "I'll spell it out for you. They believe that Hannah Lafferty's death may have been a suicide. You'll hear it on the news probably tomorrow. The coroner hasn't made an official statement. However, it is what was announced in our office informally and to the family today. She stood on the High Street viaduct until a train came along the tracks below, then jumped to the trestle underneath. Nobody even knew her body was there for three days and it was crushed to a pulp. The family asked for a DNA sample to be sent to make sure it was her body. However, Chief Peirce talked them out of it. It was her."

"What about the other girl, the second—?"

Chloe rubs her hands across her cheeks. "Okay, the Mill's girl, Tianna, that was found on the highway was from Columbus, Ohio. They believe her death was drug-related. She was a known heroin user and a prostitute. That's not confidential. It was in the newspaper today."

"You don't think that's true," I call out to her back. A suicide and a drug hit. I don't believe it. "Somebody murdered Hannah."

"Well, if you see your dad back in town, give me a call. Maybe we can talk."

Ouch. I'm staring at Chloe's back after she smacks those words at my face. I know her attitude change occurred after Colt Lucero found out I was Dell Smythe's daughter. It couldn't be coincidence. It is he who has shut everybody out from me. Regardless, now I've got no place to dance, no way to get any more information to prove my dad's innocence. I figure, screw them. I really didn't need their help anyway.

I dig out the last three dollars in quarters, nickels and dimes and take Mia to Joe's Home-style Diner. It is eight o'clock and almost closing time. Joe Timberline, the owner, comes out and sits with us in a booth in the back.

"Why the grumpy face?" he asks me, scratching the top of his bald head. He's one of those guys that are difficult to age. He's got no wrinkles on his pink, puffy face. "You're off today. You should be happy." He's got his chubby elbows on the table and his hands folded near his chin. I am leaning over to scrub Mia's chin with a napkin.

"Can I eat like a piggy, Mommy?" I know what she

wants to do and that's just abandon the spoon so she can stick her face into the bowl. She already has whipped cream smeared all over.

"No, baby. Not in a restaurant." She is licking the spoon with the tip of her tongue and crossing her eyes at me. Joe thinks it is funny and keeps chuckling. It only makes her smack her spoon on her lips harder.

"Aw, Mama, let her eat like a piggy." Joe reaches out like he's going to snatch her spoon. "You're churlish today." I slap his fingers away.

"Joe, you're not helping," I scold him lightly. "And what is churlish?" Joe is a closet contemporary romance reader. He doesn't think I know this. However, I am always finding soft porn romance with feisty, big-titted heroines showing a bit of cleavage on the covers in his desk drawers. I would think he's just keeping the books around for the covers, except he uses his reading glasses to mark the place he stopped. I note they work back day by day. And I also know when he's diving into a new one. He tends to take on the personality of the leading male. The book stuffed into his desk yesterday was about a college professor.

"Churlish. Surly—impolite."

"Ah," I nod. "And no, I'm not. But listen to me. I'm just trying to do some research on the murders that have happened in Hensley Grove," I tell him. "And I just keep hitting dead ends. Nobody wants to touch it with a ten foot pole when I'm around."

"For good reason," Joe shifts his shoulder, turns his attention from my kid to me. He crosses his legs, leans back as if to analyze me. Ah, the professor again. "They're afraid they'll say something wrong to you, offend you—"

"Bull," I grunt and poke a finger in the air. "They are afraid I will be able to prove they are wrong. They think they've got this stupid murder thing pegged on my dad, stuffed in a box and tied with a bow. They don't want to look like idiots."

"Well, maybe that's so." Joe leans back. "You aren't your dad. I think you worry about it too much."

"Yeah, walk in my shoes for a day," I mumble to him. "My pimpled junior prom date called me two days before the dance and cancelled because his mom found out it was me he was taking. Every friend I met in elementary school's parents called Anna and Poppy to make sure I wasn't going to go crazy and pull out a knife on their kids if I came to spend the night. The few friends I have now, I worked hard to get. I could go on. I don't want to."

"So write a book and call it *My Dad's a Serial Killer*. Maybe you'll make a million bucks. People like to stick their noses in other people's crap. They like to know somebody else is worse off than them." Joe's got a poker-face, but I know he's teasing me. "And, people will use a dry erase board eraser on your past if you're holding out a hundred dollar bill at them."

"How bad do you think my life is?" I sniff back at him. "I'm not at the bottom yet."

"I know for a fact that Sophie came in and asked to work opposite hours than you because she's dating your ex and she was the cause of the breakup. I know your buddy who shares—" he holds up the index and middle fingers of both hands in quotation marks, "—your breakfast with you every single day and gazes at you from afar like he can't get enough of you hasn't been here for a week and a half. You borrowed a hundred dollars from me to help pay your rent. Your car is barely working—"

"Enough!" I mutter.

"Just saying." Joe shrugs my words off. "So not to

change this awkward conversation, but was it you who painted the four horsemen of the apocalypse on the train cars at the old depot in town?"

"Wh—at? Me?" I ask, drawing the word out. "No." I'm obviously not that convincing because Joe eyes me warily.

"Yeah, well somebody did. It was all four, one for each car. Conquest, War, Famine, and Death. When the police stopped in here to see if you had worked that night, I told them you were scrubbing the grease vats until two in the morning and couldn't have possibly done it. It was brilliant except for the tiny factor that the Horseman of War looked a bit like your buddy that used to sit at the counter and the Horseman of Death looked like the Hensley Grove chief of police. I had this horrible bit of anxiety you were going to put me down as Famine. I didn't recognize that guy. Conquest was a woman with brown hair." He reaches across the table and wiggles a strand of my frizzy hair. "Maybe, Tango, you need to step away from this murder thing. You're getting a dark twist to your graffiti."

Mia is wiggling back and forth in her chair by the time I roll my eyes at him. "Gotta pee," she keeps telling me and I pick her up, take her back to the restrooms. When I come back out, Joe has gone back to the kitchen.

"Hey, lock the doors behind you when you go, would you?" he yells out. I wave at him and slap down three dollars in assorted change for Mia's sundae on the counter by the register. While I'm lugging Mia back up to my hip, Joe yowls out that he didn't want the three dollars. He'd already cashed out the register. I know better. But I scoop them up and pour them into my pocket. I am tediously close to empty on gas. And if I hadn't stopped in at the Hensley Grove Speedy Gas and plopped the change down again in front of a guy in a beanie hat and gray hipster glasses, I think I would have listened to Joe. I would have probably stepped away from the murders.

"I need two dollars and ninety-five cents in gas," I tell the guy while Mia squats down and pokes the candy bars with her stubby forefinger. He looks vaguely familiar. I can't quite pinpoint where I've seen him before. He's got black hair and it is long enough it drips out of the hat. He's quiet and deadpan. His cheeks are covered with a scrubby fuzz of dark hair. He reaches out, lays his hand on the coins. He doesn't bother to count it, just sorts it slowly into the register. It is so slow, it is almost like he is drawing out the act to make me wait.

"Do I know you?" I finally ask.

"Yeah, I'm Mark Lafferty."

"Oh." I nod.

"You used to take dance classes with my sister."

"Hannah." I stand there to the count of ten, wait for him to say more. "Yeah, I did."

"Mama," Mia interrupts when she turns on her little legs. "I want a candy bar."

"Not right now. I left my purse at home." I fib to her so I don't have to disclose my financial status aloud.

"It's in the car. In the seat. Go get it. I want—"

Mark doesn't say anything else, so I reach down and pick up Mia and mutter a feeble: "I'm sorry about your sister."

I pivot on my feet, anchor my eyes to the door while Mia gets ready to let out a squall of tears. Her back is starting to arch, her legs are kicking into my thigh.

"She didn't commit suicide. The cops came to the house today, told us she jumped off the bridge in front of the train. That's bullshit."

I come to a dead standstill. Mia's in mid-temper

tantrum and banging her head off my shoulder.

"I know you two didn't get along," he says. "I'm just saying."

"We were both competitive." I turn, try to press Mia's head to my chest to quiet her yowls. "Out of all of Shane's dream team, Hannah was the nicest to me."

"That's not saying much." He chuckles softly and sarcastically after he says those words. "She could be a witch."

My head tips to the side and I see him looking up at the ceiling and I know he is trying desperately to hold back tears. "Should you be working tonight?" I ask him. I don't know what else to say. The guy looks numb and I think he's held it in so long, he's going to burst.

"What else am I going to do? Go home and stare at the walls and think about her? Go to my parent's house and watch them—"

"No," I mumble. There is a ting at the counter and he looks up. Somebody is getting gas. He silently processes the request, turns and looks at the clock.

"I'm sorry, I—I'm weirding out tonight. It's kind of coming to a head. I thought work would keep me from thinking about it because I'd be busy." He waves a hand to the empty parking lot. "Not busy."

"Do you want us to sit with you a while?" I can only assume he is going to say no. I'm almost yelling over Mia's screams and her huffing breaths. "Who could ask for better company?" I tease him lightly.

"You'd do that?"

No. "Of course."

CHAPTER 28

MARK LAFFERTY STABS ME IN THE BACK

Mark Lafferty is one of the quietest guys I've met. But it isn't an uncomfortable quiet. He and Hannah were twins. He reminds me of Hannah personality-wise because he sits back and seems to take in the scenery around him rather than talking much. However, he went to the state college and got a degree in business management. He tells me she must have sucked out all the creative and artistic aspirations in embryo because he's all scientific and math oriented.

You would have thought since the two were so different, they wouldn't have the same unquenchable desire to stab me in the back. Hannah always intentionally cut me with her whetted tongue, finding the most hurtful things to say about me. Maybe Mark's lashing out was unplanned. It didn't matter, nor was it expected. What he did was far more damaging than anything his sister had ever done to me. And it all started with me stupidly trying to be kind to him and not thinking for one minute he was just like all the others like him.

"I could have choreographed all her dances, managed them down to the step," he tells me. "But if you asked me to do the waltz, I would have tripped over your feet at each step." Mia and I sat with him until his three to eleven shift was over. He bought her a candy bar and she fell to sleep in his lap. Then I dragged him back to my apartment to watch some old 1990s comedies on TV.

"You're really nice," he tells me while he sits on the couch with his arms crossed next to Billy who is staring him down like the old dog who thinks he might be getting replaced by the new stray I dragged home. "Do you want me to leave?"

"I don't want you to leave," I tell him, yawning out loud. I take the bag of microwave popcorn in my hand and pass it down to him. "You are good company, just quiet like my teddy bear. Maybe that's better that you're quiet. I just broke up with my boyfriend. I'm tired of sitting here and laughing out loud and by myself."

"Hello, I sit with you," Billy gruffs. I roll my eyes. "Rocky sits with you."

"Yes, Billy, you do. I appreciate that. You're my best friend ever. I told you that. BFE."

"My therapist tells me I'm quiet because I've lived in the limelight of a gifted sister," Mark divulges suddenly. "It was always Hannah's dance classes mom was dragging me to or Hannah's gymnastic classes we'd drive to forty minutes away and three times a week. I spent most of my life hanging out with moms in the waiting rooms."

It makes me wonder what Gil thinks of me. I'd never thought about all the times he sat in the waiting room with Anna at Denise Beller's Uptown Dance Studio while I took classes. Or how many times he got stuck with Poppy at Showtimes Gymnastics.

"Um," I finally say what has been gnawing at my soul for the last three hours. "You know the cops have questioned me about my dad being involved—"

"Yeah, don't worry about it," he answers, doesn't even bother to look at me. "They even dragged my poor dad down to the station to question him. That was rough." We stayed up until four in the morning and Billy mumbled an excuse to leave. Then I got us a couple blankets and I curled up on one end of the couch. Mark laid down on Kevin's recliner.

The next day is the first day I haven't worked or been to classes in two months. I drive Mark back to his car and I look into the rearview mirror. I see something sitting on the flat area below the back window and just behind Mia's head. It is a tan manila envelope. I get out, open her door and snatch it up in my hands. I wonder why I hadn't seen it when I set Mia into her car seat.

"You need help?" Mark asks. He's just getting out of the passenger side. I don't answer, just open the envelope and peer inside. Then I tug out the thick wad of papers and stare hard at them.

"Oh, crap," I say. Mark has worked his way over and is peering over my shoulder.

"What?"

I pause, turn my head slightly to the right and look up at him. "You may not want to see this, Mark." I start to tug it down. He reaches out, stops me with his hand on the paper. My eyes veer upward, try to read his own while he absorbs the eight and a half by eleven sheet of paper within. It is a copy of the image of a view from the stone viaduct and looking downward past the small section of train trestle running beside the river. Beneath and barely discernable are several blurry splotches of what I can imagine are the jumbled remains of his sister.

Just as I hone in on the image, I tug it away from Mark. Too late. He has his palm shock-cupping his mouth. He's blinking at me, his eyes guarded beneath a furrowed brow.

"How—why do you have this?"

I'm wondering too. It is the entire packet Chloe was withholding from me. "Well," I start. "I don't know. I was working with somebody. I asked for it. They told me they sealed all the information off so nobody could see it but the cops. I'm not sure how it got here or who left it."

The moment he saw the information in the packet, I knew it was a mistake. Mark mumbled a thank you to me, then left looking dazed. I wished I could step back four minutes and just restart the moment and instead of peering inside, tossing the folder on my passenger side seat and driving off without Mark knowing. It would have saved me a whole lot of grief.

At three-fifteen, Gabe Reynolds knocks at my door. He is fully attired in his Hensley Grove police uniform complete with gun and baton. Mia has fallen asleep on the couch watching TV and I am kicking myself, knowing if she slept now, she wouldn't go back to sleep again until eleven tonight.

"Hey," I greet him in the crack of the door. I note his straight-faced expression. I look out the door, see Missus Finch standing with her hands folded at her chest staring down the hall at me. "If it is the noise, it isn't me."

"No, it isn't the noise. Raeanna, the police have been informed that you were given classified information. I'm here to confiscate the material."

"What?"

"It appears Officer Murphy gave you information that is not considered public information as it is part of an ongoing investigation. She is now on administrative leave for her misconduct. Chief Peirce sent me here to obtain the packet that was given to you." He sighs. "You can either give it to me or I can obtain a warrant and have your car impounded and your house searched."

"You're kidding me right?" I ask him. "Who told you I had something like that?"

"I'm advised to keep all contacts confidential."

My heart is pounding in my chest. "I don't know what you're talking about," I tell him.

"Listen, Tango," Gabe leans into the doorway, looks right to left. His stoic behavior fades away and he just looks tired. "Just please give me the packet. If Chloe gave it to you, she shouldn't have. I don't think she would. She's been my partner for two years. I don't want her to get fired for this. She's out for three days without pay. I heard the chief say that if we don't come up with the packet, she's going to be fired. Mark Lafferty freaked out when he saw whatever you had. He went and told his friends including Taylor, the chief's daughter. She hadn't heard it five minutes before she was blabbing to her dad. Just let me have the packet. Stop whatever you're doing. Let us figure out what's going on with the crimes, alright? That's what the city pays us to do. It is our job."

"Okay."

"Thanks, Tango." The stress wipes from his face. "Listen, I'm telling you this because I like Ray. He's a good guy. The kind of guy that let a short, fat boy play on his baseball team when none of the other coaches picked me. You really ticked the chief off with that drawing of him. Then you show up with a packet that nobody else could have gotten their hands on." He stops, looks over his shoulder. "I know Chloe is covering for you. I don't know why. But, there are eyes on you and I'd be careful what you do and how you do it."

My mouth opens to tell him that Chloe was the one who showed me the folder in the first place. Most likely it was she who put it in my car. I don't and instead, push up a hand, ask him to wait outside the door. I'd put it somewhere and had to dig it out. What he didn't know was that I got out my phone and spent fourteen excruciatingly long minutes taking pictures of each page, all one hundred and fifty-two of them. Then I carefully place the information back into the packet and handed them to Gabe.

"This stuff creeps me out anyway," I tell him, tugging on my bottom lip. "I'll stick to dancing."

Then, after he leaves, I load the pages on to my laptop. They are slightly blurry, but decipherable. I feel so emotionally scarred right this moment, like my heart has fallen so hard, it is skinned. I swear not to let anybody else like Kevin Wilson, Colt Lucero, or Mark Lafferty crap on me again.

CHAPTER 29

DANCING ~~WITH~~ FOR ROCKY

"Rocky, take me dancing."

That's all it took for me to drag Rocky down to the dance club in town. He used to take me all the time for Kevin. Kevin hated going to the clubs. Well, club. There's only one in Hensley Grove and it really isn't much of a club at all, mostly just a bar with lots of tables and an old wooden floor that is usually too packed to do anything but bounce up and down with arms in the air. It's Gamble's Bar and Backroom and probably wouldn't exist at all if Hensley Grove didn't have a college and one with a dance program.

Kevin never danced, just sat there and complained about how boring it was, then downed so many beers he started flirting with all the girls. And yet, he didn't want me to go by myself figuring I'd find something better than him that would actually get up on the floor. So after a few fights, we finally worked it out that Rocky would take me once in a while. Rocky didn't mind sitting there while I got on the dance floor. He'd go and plop down on one of the couches along the wall, sip his beer like the rich ladies at Uncle Lion's country club, and shove his sunglasses over his eyes. Then he would fall into a blissful sleep to the beat of the music surrounding him. And I'd dance on the floor, or if there was a particular guy that wouldn't leave me alone, I'd go over and dance in front of Rocky like I was dancing for him.

"I don't care as long as I can sleep," he tells me while he's downing six ibuprofen with a glass of orange juice. "And—you pay the cover charge and make me supper three times this week. I'll buy the food. You cook. I'm not going to sit around with your friends and gab tonight. I'm not going to listen to the *please, please, please, Rocky five more minutes*. Three beers or ten o'clock whatever comes first. Then we're out of there. I've got to be into work at five in the morning."

Like I have time for friends. No, but I do have two and a half hours of heavenly me-time while Poppy and Anna take Mia to the movies. I'm kind of dangling between the low of getting turned in by Mark Lafferty and a strange high I'm sneak-looking into these murders.

I drove by the subdivision where Cathy Schuler's body was found in 1983. I couldn't stop. There was a middle -aged lady working in her garden and a couple kids running through a sprinkler in the yard. She'd been dumped after her body had been decomposing for what was estimated to be a year. It was almost a skeleton with just fibers from her clothing and bits of dried skin still clinging to her bones. Investigators believed she had been initially laid out in a remote area, then brought to the yard on Second Street, perhaps to be detected.

Cathy was a blonde-haired, blue eyed nursing student at Carlson Junior College in Detroit, Michigan. She liked to get out of the city and ride her bicycle along the northern Ohio and southern Michigan backroads. Most of the time, she was by herself. On the afternoon of August 3, 1982, she called her mom who lived in Cincinnati and told her she was going to her math class, then heading off for a bike ride. To save on long distance calls, Cathy usually only called home once a week to check in. When the week passed and her mom hadn't heard from Cathy, she tried her apartment roommate. The roommate had stated she had been out of town herself, visiting home, and had not seen Cathy for at least two weeks. After contacting campus security and then the local police, her mom was told Cathy was an adult and she should wait to file a missing person report. Cathy was a busy person. Maybe she was just at the library or riding her bike or had simply met a guy and was staying with him.

It would be two months before a jogger running along an old state route near Adrian, Michigan found her bike tossed over the side of the road. It was another three weeks before he decided to call the police about it, thinking it was just stolen. The only sign of Cathy where her bike was found was her watch and a water bottle. Then, her body showed up in Hensley Grove nearly a year and a half later. She had been carefully laid on her back with her knees bent and her hands clasped at her chest. A cigarette was found in the chest cavity where they believe it had fallen from its place between her fingers.

There was a scrawled note at the bottom of the report that appeared to be written in some time after. It suggested Cathy may have been kept alive for six to eight weeks before her murder, then her body discarded somewhere quickly where she sat for ten to twelve months before being dumped again. Another note scrawled on a following page stated that a Timothy Collins, a former boyfriend, had been arrested for the murder. He was acquitted ten months later and released. Then there was a note that had a date written next to it that I assume was written some time after. *1986— Sister called. Said they got Cathy's effects. Always wore a Saint Agatha Catholic pendant (protector of nurses) on a necklace. It was not among her things. If found, please send.*

I had pulled up the picture of the crime scene on my phone and engraved it in my mind so when I passed, I knew to look for a maple tree that was small in the picture and way over thirty years of growth bigger now. Sure enough, there was the tree about five feet from the sprinkler and one little girl's right foot while she tip-toed across the water that was arcing low for the moment. The only thing missing was a concrete front porch and the sidewalk was more grass than concrete now. I slowed and took in the area. They were all cute white wood houses with well-kept front yards. On the left, it was all the same. It reminded me of Poppy's subdivision and I felt a melancholy ache. Home. I wished my apartment had that feeling.

There seemed to be very little similar in the abduction and murders. The places where these women were seen last, the color of their hair and eyes, and even finding out who killed them was like trying to find a toothpick dropped in a brown-grassed lawn. The only thing they had in common was they were dumped in Hensley Grove and each held a cigarette. However, I just knew that there had to be something missing, something everyone else didn't bother to see, but I could discover it. I think I was becoming more fascinated, more obsessed with figuring it out than Gil had been in tenth grade when he spent three days straight one summer trying to win a stupid war on a video game.

But I'm not thinking about Cathy Schuler an hour and a half into dancing until my stiletto-heeled feet feel like they are going numb and falling off. There's some sort of an orientation at the college so it is crowded and loud. The dancers have spilled out from the small dance floor and they've moved tables around to accommodate them.

I've stuck close to Rocky because I don't recognize a whole lot of people here tonight. He's three beers in and sleeping soundly on the couch and looking wide awake sitting up with his sunglasses on. I figured I could get another fifteen minutes of ear-aching, dirty dancing music before I have to wake him. But when the song comes to a lull, I feel a quick tap on my shoulder.

It is Delia who did the tapping. She's got her little

posse of Taylor Peirce and Alexandra Edwards. Colt Lucero is not far behind, always being dragged like a leash by one of their hands. Oh, crap. And Adrien Moreau. I see him. I turn away quickly in—what? Panic? My heart makes this crazy jump. It's the kind of jump I used to get when I started getting attached to Poppy and his car pulled into the driveway after work. I mean, how do you stop that? I just take a breath, shut it out.

Then I focus on the three stopping in front of me. It's weird not seeing Hannah with them and a flash of an image of Colt replacing her makes me a bit queasy. We're back to the pretty four again. I eye Delia cautiously, thinking maybe she is playing cat and mouse waiting for me to bolt so she can toy with me.

"Yeah?" I ask her. "What do you need?" I'm neither smiling nor frowning, just staring at her and refusing to look at Adrien. I suppose I'm going to lose him to the pretty people now. I scoot down my dress where it has ridden up while I was dancing. I see Delia's eyes slip from mine to Taylor's and Taylor is peeling her eyes from Colt and then staring fire-hot darts at me.

"Mister Moreau is looking for you," she is yelling over the music and jabbing a thumb behind her. "He asked us if we knew where you were. We figured it was either here or the strip club out on the highway." She laughs like what she's saying is funny. I don't laugh along. It is blaring and the lights are flashing. She's like baby blue sparkles and sunshine to my black dress and black heels right this moment. I overdid my eyeshadow in gray and my eyeliner's thick. It makes my eyes look a little too cat-like.

Adrien gives a wide berth, goes around Colt and holds out a plain white envelope. "This is for you."

I take it from him, lock eyes for a moment. They are dull and bored. It is the same look I got from Billy yesterday when he told me Malinda was making him ask me to teach the acapella club some dances for the competition. He handed me an envelope too. Inside was thirty bucks they collected to pay me to do it. Thirty bucks. It could be my gas for three days.

"What is it?" Taylor is leaning over and I see Colt tug her back by her hand. I open up the envelope and peer inside, bring out a sheet of paper that has the reservations for a flight and an audition application for the Jade Carew National Ballet Competition. It is for entrance into their summer conservatory. Then, there is a ticket.

"Think about it," Adrien says. I close up the envelope. My stomach is feeling a bit jumpy right now.

"So I've got to know. How much is the dude paying you to dance for him?" I look up and blink at Alexandra who is pushing back her perfect white-blonde hair. She's worked her way up beside Adrien and is shoving her shoulder into his. She is almost as tall as him. It bothers me looking up at both. I feel like an elf. And I don't want to admit it, but seeing Colt with Taylor is just leaving me feeling used. Seeing Alexandra sidling up to Adrien is making me feel protective of him, bitter—okay, jealous. She is staring at Rocky's sunglasses and looking like she's afraid he might big bad wolf her and jump out of his chair, eat her. "I just want to know, Tango," she says leaning in hard at me and wiggling her fingers together. "Just in case I need to add pole dancing as the last thing in the world I would do if I had to choose between prostitution and—this."

I lean forward. Then I give her a little push with my hand so she is forced to step back from Adrien. I cringe, know it is noticeable that I am between the two. I used to do that to Gil when he'd get to Poppy before me and jump on his lap. "Go away. I was having fun until you showed up."

None of them move. They are just looking around like they'd never seen the inside of a dance club before. I know it is because Adrien is here. They are trying to pretend their crap doesn't stink. So I decide it is time for me to leave. I awkwardly turn and bump my knees to Rocky's knees to wake him up. "Come on, big dude, it's time to wake up and go home." He's not so quick, so I lean over and give his shoulder a wiggle. "Rocky, please-please-please get up!"

I don't quite expect his reaction. Rocky shoots up out of the lounge chair and almost knocks me over in the process. I take three tippy-toe steps back, no mere feat in six inch heels. I can't see his eyes and wonder if he is still sound asleep. He stands straight up and looks me up and down. "Baby, you alright?" Baby? He never calls me *baby*. "Which one is it?" Then and only because he's the only man in a five foot radius, Rocky starts jabbing a finger over my shoulder and right at Adrien. "You. Did you touch her? Because I will so kill you right here and right now if you—"

"Rocky!" He is so big, I almost feel like I have to jump up and down to get his attention. "It isn't him. Home. I want to go home." My hand is patting at his belly and Adrien has this strangely fascinated pinch to his lips like he's either trying to figure out why the big dude is getting ready to kill him or he's wondering how he'll look laying in the hospital bed after.

"Oh, home." Just like that Rocky just stops dead still and snatches off his sunglasses, swipes a hand over his half-asleep eyes. "Sorry, dude." He reaches out a bear paw and pats Adrien's shoulder. I wince thinking this could have really turned out badly. Adrien isn't that much smaller than Rocky and he works out. "Yeah, okay, just point me in the direction."

Delia, Colt, Taylor and Alexandra all step back and away like slaves falling away for a pharaoh. Adrien is just looking from Rocky's back to me.

"Is that your boyfriend?" he asks me when I pass.

"Bodyguard." I guess I don't realize how big ol' Rocky is until he lumbers through them, looking down at each with a slight furrow to his brow.

"Think about it, alright?" he asks me again. His hand is on my arm and I look down before he pulls it away. I nod, find myself swept into the dim room and the crowd.

"Who the hell were they?" Rocky asked me when we are settling down on his motorcycle. They aren't far behind. I see them pouring out of the bar while I adjust my dress so it isn't up to my hips. I hope he's slept off his three drinks while he starts the engine and I latch on hard to his waist.

"That's Shane Delgado's dream team," I tell him. "Except for God Squad. He was the pup on the leash. The guy you were going to kill, that's Adrien Moreau."

"The famous guy?"

"Yeah, the famous guy," I agree over the engine. "*Baby*? Where did that come from?"

"I don't know, Tango, you gotta quit doing those dances three feet from me, shaking your tits, shaking that little ass of yours all over the place. That kind of dancing, it does stuff to a man."

"You were awake?" I huff, stuffing the envelope down into the front of my dress so it didn't blow away.

"Hell, yeah, I wouldn't miss—all that for a million bucks."

CHAPTER 30

BLACK STREET SHACKS

Albert Tatum is still alive and living on Ridgefield Drive. His house is a brick ranch. His yard is uncluttered and he's planted wildflowers in a huge garden. There are daisies and Black-eyed Susans poking out all over.

"I know this might be awkward, Mister Tatum, but I was wondering if I could ask you a few questions. He is kneeling over the flower bed, a trowel in one hand. He's ninety-something and gray haired. His eyes glint angry.

"Do I know you?"

"Nope, well maybe." I sigh. Here's the hard part. "I'm Raeanna Baldwin. My dad, he's the one they say—"

"Yeah, I do know who you are. You're that Delbert Smythe's kid. The one that used to help him break into houses."

"And the man they say may have murdered your daughter in 1963."

"It isn't a *may*. Dell Smythe murdered her. I don't care what the cops said. The judge that let him go was bribed."

"Well, I'm trying to find out if he did or didn't do it. I—I'd like to think he didn't."

He laughs, shakes his head. "Well, good luck with that. You got a suitcase full of dreams you're passing out today? Because when I was down at the station three weeks ago asking if they were ever going to reopen the case because it was my last wish before I die to solve it, they said absolutely not. So—go on and get. I got a garden to work."

"Do you know who she was meeting the night she

disappeared?" I ask quickly. "They said she was at the Fourth of July picnic and someone saw her leaving."

He pushes a hand on his leg, shakes his head back and forth like a bull getting ready to lunge. "No, darlin', I don't. She was a good girl. I don't want nobody to think any different, you understand? She wasn't meeting nobody, just going to the picnic and coming home. Back then, we thought the streets were safe from stuff like what happened to Lisa. We didn't think twice about letting her walk home."

"The notes I read said she was all dressed up."

"She was," he tells me. "Lisa always dressed up even when she was in school. I can see you're like her." He nods at my dress. "Some girls, they dress up. Some girls don't. And her mama liked to buy her pretty clothes. I remember like it was yesterday the red dress she was wearing that night. It was brand new. She was excited about wearing it, kept going around in circles to show it off before we went to the picnic. It made me so mad when the cops said she was asking for it wearing that dress."

"You're kidding me."

"No, they assumed she was sneaking around seeing a boy or maybe she was just walking home and because she was dressed up, she was looking for trouble."

I sigh. "What direction would she walk from the park to here?"

He lifts up a hand, points toward the street. "Only way you used to be able to go. Ridgefield Drive up two blocks to Black Street, across the bridge, and straight over to the park. There's no bridge there since the plane wreck."

I bob my head up and down. He just stares at me a few seconds and doesn't say anything. "Sorry I don't have that suitcase full of dreams, Mister Tatum," I say. "If you think of anything, I work at Joe's Diner."

I walk the tree-lined streets. It is an older section of town, but well-kept all the way to where the Black Street Bridge is nothing but concrete pillars sticking up along the edge of Rocky Fork Creek. I remember walking here with my daddy once in a while. He liked to fish off the shore. It makes my tummy ache while I clamber down the dirt-grass incline and stop at the muddy edge of the water.

It is strewn with old cans and glass and dead trees. There's a couple white buckets folks have sat on to fish. *Daddy, where's my mommy?* I can almost hear my voice asking him that. I look up, see his rugged face and the thick dark hair on his head. *Probably to the Cumberland by now. She got a new man and left you in her place. You stay close, now. You remember when you fell into the creek that one time. I almost didn't get you out.* I kind of remembered. Maybe it was just what I made up in my mind.

"Arrr," I growl and feel a shiver. Why do my memories of my daddy have to hurt so much?

I can't get out of there quickly enough. I stop at the top of the hill, look out over where the bridge was and to where the park still is today, little more than old ballfields and a broken down playground. It isn't that far. How could it not be safe at dusk with the cicadas calling and the sound of people at the ballfields having fun? I try to imagine it, Lisa walking home, passing houses and probably people coming and going from the picnic. At no point can I see her being out of sight from someone. How does someone completely vanish from sight and end up dead at the ballfields six blocks from start to finish?

Just one day later, I get a little scratched note at Joe's to call Mister Tatum, he stopped into the diner. Such, I do. He tells me that there was always one thing that bugged him. The Black Street Bridge used to have a couple dark crevices where the bridge abutted the roadway. He thought maybe she might have been taken there. He'd gone down himself, looked for any sign of Lisa right after she vanished. Nothing. The cops, they checked it out, then told him nothing turned up along the creek bank.

After her body was discovered, the one item that she had been wearing that wasn't with Lisa was a gold-toned chain necklace with a pearl given to her by her grandmother. Her dad passed the bathroom and saw Lisa putting it on before she left that hot July night. The night her body was discovered, he noted the necklace was gone. He thought it might be trivial, but decided to check out the shacks again. However, a couple heavy rainfalls had passed through and the area was knee deep in creek water. He thought if he found the necklace, maybe they could figure out who it was that killed her because someone might have seen Lisa or her murderer along the creek bank.

1962. It seems that year unemployment in our part of Kentucky was high. The Cannon Bread Mill was having a difficult time making a profit and laid nearly a quarter of their employees off. It was that year, I found newspaper clippings at the library of the mill taken from the Black Street Bridge. EMPLOYEES PROTEST LAYOFFS—ENTIRE FAMILIES LIVING IN SHACKS ON RIVER.

It appeared that year, the employees didn't have a union. The mill would lay folks off, then bring in cheap help from Tennessee. In protest, about twenty families moved into tiny white-board shacks along the Rocky Fork Creek, spending an entire summer and fall there until high water forced them out. In the articles, they showed the shacks beneath the bridge and the families they interviewed standing outside.

I make a copy of one picture and take it to Poppy's.

"Poppy," I shoved it under his nose at the dinner table after Anna goes into the kitchen. I can hear her talking to Mia, hear Mia giggling. "Do you know when they took down the shacks on Black Street Bridge?"

"What? Why's that?"

"I dunno." Actually, I do. I am wondering if Lisa Tatum was dragged down to the shacks and killed or left there long enough until it got dark. Because daddy loved hanging around that river. But I don't tell Poppy that. "I was just bored and went to the library and found some history stuff. In the 1960s, they put up shacks in a protest because of mill layoffs."

"Um, yeah, I remember that. I worked at the mill, didn't get laid off though. I've always been lucky about that." He takes in the picture, narrows his eyes. He's got his color back in his face and he looks like the same old guy I remember. "I love you, Poppy," I tell him and he snaps his eyes away, gives me a big smile and tweaks my cheek like I'm two years old.

"I love you, sweetie," he returns. "I can tell you I remember most of the shacks got taken out by the floods that year. We got a lot of rain. Some probably stayed. They made everybody move out of them, the cops came and knocked a lot of them down. It was a big deal and they had to stop. The news people came from as far away as Cincinnati about it. I think I remember going over the bridge and seeing some buildings left for maybe a couple years. We tried to ignore them, I guess. They just brought up bad memories of the strike. They were falling down, covered in weeds. They looked awful. But nobody wanted to touch them and stir up trouble." He stops, eyes me carefully. "What's up? It's not the picture you came about, is it?"

"No, not really." I lean back in the dining room chair. "Do you think I'm silly wanting to dance? I mean, don't think like a daddy, think like a stranger or something."

"I think life's too short and you should do what you want to do."

"Are you a politician? Because you're not answering me," I huff, then shrug. "Well, there's this guy, Adrien Moreau. He's like a really big ballet dancer. He was working with Shane's classes and we kind of ran into each other—"

"Oh, romance—"

"No," I groan. "He's been teaching me stuff and he hasn't asked for money. Then he gives me airplane tickets and an application to try out for a dance program in New York. It's just a summer intern kind of thing, working with professionals. But his partner is the one responsible for the tryouts."

The kitchen is quiet. I notice it immediately and I know Anna must have stopped what she was doing to listen. Poppy disregards this and looks at me. "Second chances aren't a bad thing, Rae. If you want to go, I can give you a little money for food and you can take a taxi from the airport."

"What about Mia?" I ask him. "I can't just stop being her mama every time something comes up. I can't drop her at sitters for ten hour days for practice—"

"Why don't you cross that bridge when it comes," he tells me. "We're here for you."

I think about the Black Street Bridge and how it stops on either side of the road now so you can't cross it. I wonder if I'm going to be like that, standing on one side and always looking over to the other, wishing I was there. "Yeah, okay." I nod.

Poppy leans in. "You still have that suitcase, right?"

His voice is soft, his eyes wavering to the kitchen where Mia and Anna are talking again.

"The suitcase full of dreams?" I kid him, remembering what Lisa Tatum's dad said.

"I don't think it has dreams in it," he says. "Just old clothes maybe. Wish I knew where the key was."

"I thought it was old pictures and stuff."

"I don't know. I thought I could dig up some keys down in the basement, but Gil follows me around talking while I'm puttering around down there and I don't want him asking questions."

"There's no way to open it?"

"I've never been able to do it."

"It is supposed to have an interlocking twin, you know that right?"

"I do."

"Where is the other half?"

"I don't know."

"Why am I hiding it?"

"Shhh," Poppy hushes me with a finger to his lips. "Later. We'll talk another time."

"One more question, Poppy." I squirm in my seat. "Do you know where my daddy lived at any time?"

"Just the last time. Because we went with the police to get you. Up on the Rocky Fork Creek in a little cabin. I don't think it's there anymore. Wasn't more than a shack. There are so many floods going through there."

"You went with the police?" I ask him. "Why?"

"It was kind of the final straw. They kept sending you back to him over and over. When the police came to get you, you ran away into the woods to hide. So they came and got Anna and me to see if you'd come to us. You were always like a little wild doe. That was when you got sick, you remember?"

"No."

Poppy smiles sadly at me. "You were really sick. Your dad, he had that star tattooed on your back. You were five and a half and he had one of his buddy's draw it. It got infected or nobody would have known. He didn't take you to the hospital. The children's services agency visited the house and saw it."

Oh, yeah. I rub my shoulder. They used a pen and a needle. They were drunk and laughing so hard, my daddy kept falling over. I can still remember how bad it hurt and daddy telling me not to cry. I didn't, of course.

"Before that, he lived right along Black Street in one of those old mill row houses, a little white one. It's gone now. They took them out because of the flooding there."

Black Street. I feel my face flush like I should know something, like it should have some meaning other than the plane wreck there. It doesn't. Anna swoops in with pie for us and I rip my eyes from Poppy. He's smiling at Anna and me, I'm basking in old memories better left forgotten.

CHAPTER 31

DEAD GIRL: TAMMY LYNN

"Hey, I just wanted to tell you that me and Sophie are going out." Okay, my vow to keep an emotional guard up only lasted twenty hours. That's Kevin. I'm slightly amused he has found me. I'm in Taggert's Art Supply in downtown Hensley Grove kneeling in front of a display of art paint. He has never shown any interest in my art. He has never supported my desire to paint or draw. I listen to him while I am staring at a set of tubed acrylic paints that is on clearance at half price and I still can't afford to buy. Forty-two dollars. I'm in that horrible place where I feel artistic and angry. And mind-muddied because I don't understand why Adrien gave me the plane tickets and the application for tryouts without an explanation. I mean, who does that kind of stuff?

I can't express myself in dance because I don't have any place to go considering the current nighttime janitor's main goal in life since he was eight has been to murder me. I only have a few cans of yellow, baby blue, and gold spray paint left for graffiti. They aren't the colors that express my current cruddy disposition. I tend to use a lot of golds, reds and blacks when I'm in this dank and irritated mood. I have less than forty-eight dollars to my name and it has been raining for three days straight so I can't even find a wall that isn't dry enough to get a good stick.

"You're telling me this now?" I hardly turn my head upward to see him. I still feel something for Kevin. "I mean, why not let me know seven months ago when you were screwing her on the side and telling me I was the only woman for you."

"Don't, Tango, you know I didn't plan it. But I didn't want you to find out from somebody else."

"Well, I don't know what to say." I poke the paint with my index finger. "Good luck?"

"Stop. I made a mistake. And there isn't a second that doesn't go by that I don't regret it. If you told me right now that you'd get back with me, I'd drop her like a plate full of hot pizza."

"You like pizza, Kevin. It wasn't just one time. It was an entire season of your football, an entire season of basketball and half a season of baseball. I'm not getting back with you."

"I know. How's the mini-Tango? I kind of miss the half-pint."

"Fine. Anna's watching her for a while tonight. She asks about you. Maybe you can take her to the park sometime."

"Maybe." He nods and starts to turn. I know better. He always thought Mia got in the way between us, always gave a grand, annoyed sigh when she slid into bed between us at night. I see him give a fist to his palm a few times before he leans down toward me. "Hey, I was wondering. Can I borrow twenty bucks? Sophie quit her job at the diner. We're kind of having a hard time coming up with gas money."

I stand up and pivot on my feet. I want to hold up my middle finger and tell him to go to hell. But he is looking at me with sad eyes. Did I say I still feel something for him?

"Yeah, sure, Kevin." I reach into my purse and pull out my obsessed-with-daddy-coming-back twenty dollar bill and hand it over to him. I suppose it is now an obsessed-with-Kevin-coming-back twenty. He doesn't even thank me when he turns to leave and I wonder if he'll use the money for gas or groceries or weed. Knowing Kevin, he's using it to buy Sophie a new pair of black, lace thongs.

Later, I can't remember if I have fourteen or fifteen dollars left in my bank account. I need gas too, so I start to pull up my online banking and pause on the pictures I took of the packet Gabe confiscated. I know I should leave it alone. I don't think anybody thinks it is sane that I'm actually trying to clear my dad's name considering he was so mean to me. But I know his blood is my blood. Maybe the stuff he does wrong rubbed off on me. It terrifies me. Maybe, I suppose, it could be that I just want to know I'm not going to suddenly go batshit crazy and turn out like him.

Tammy Anise Lynn. I sit in my car and pull up the file on the girl found behind the Cannon Bread Mill. The rain is making a tap-tap-tap on the windshield. She was only seventeen when she died. The notes say she had black hair and green eyes and was wearing a white cotton shirt, a pair of blue jeans and a black velvet choker necklace with a turquoise heart when last seen. She was from Bethel, Ohio.

Tammy had cut school somewhere around noon on Thursday, March 23, 1972, right at the beginning of her lunch period. She had plans to go with two high school friends, Janie Dickson and Linda Moffat, to a rock concert in Cincinnati later in the evening.

They met three blocks from the high school. Eddy James, an unemployed mechanic, was the twenty-four year old driver who took them to the concert. He was dating Janie Dickson. The concert didn't start until eight that night and they spent most of the day hanging out at Eddy's house. Sometime during the afternoon, Janie stated she walked into the kitchen and believed Tammy and Eddy had been kissing at the sink. The two denied it. However, for the rest of the afternoon and at the concert, Linda Moffat claimed her two girlfriends were yelling at each other angrily off and on. When the concert ended around ten-thirty. Janie refused to get into the car with Tammy and walked off. Linda claimed that she set off in one direction to find Janie, and Eddy and Tammy went a different direction. When they returned to the car, Eddy was alone and stated only two minutes after he and Tammy began walking, she turned around and said she didn't think Linda should be walking around by herself. Tammy turned and headed up the street outside the building and he had not seen her. It was the last time any of them saw her alive.

"Her body was discovered behind the Cannon Bread Mill Building C and the railroad tracks six and a half weeks after her abduction." I'm pinching my screen, trying to read the information in the dim light. I scroll down, eye the image. It's the same kind of image as the others. There are five to six suited men standing around, posing like an old western posse with their dead bad guy centrally located between them. Tammy's body was discovered by one of the night watchmen for the mill, Benny Adams. He heard the sound of raccoons fighting while he was traversing the tracks along his usual guard rounds. He saw what he thought was a post leaning against the brick wall of the building. Upon closer inspection, he found Tammy standing fully erect like she was leaning against the building. Her body had been taped to two by four pieces of wood in a standing position. There was a cigarette in her fingers dangling by her knees.

"Freaking creepy," I mumble, pushing the phone up for a better view. I check the clock on my phone. I've got an hour before Anna's expecting me home. I always tell her I get off an hour later from work than I actually do. It gives me fifteen or twenty minutes to relax, or tonight, to go check out the area where Tammy's body was found.

I think she knows I give myself some leeway. Anna doesn't complain, nor does she ever question me. So I start my car and drive out on to the wet pavement.

In hindsight, I should have used the flood level of the Rocky Fork Creek as a sign to turn around. Every spring, the waters overflow the banks downstream in my cruddy section of town. Most of the time, it just laps at the front porches. Last night, there was a torrential downpour and a quarter of the town is flooded. I have to go around six detours on flooded streets to get to the mill. And I am a half hour into the drive before I wished I'd never gone at all. The rubber on my driver's side wiper blade is dangling low and slapping hard against my rearview mirror when it rolls to the left. The metal blade, then, scrapes along the glass with a sound faintly resembling fingernails on a metal rooftop.

I drive along an old service road on the far side of the railroad tracks until I can see the building that was visible on the crime scene photo. The road is rutted and pocked with old lumber and bricks. Some of the puddles are so deep, when my tires dip down into them, the water comes up to the center of the rims.

I stop just short of an old shack and get out, blink against the raindrops tumbling from the clouds. I let me eyes veer toward the darkness where I can hear the river rolling hard. The mill stands up high on a hilltop. I'm not sure, though, if it has ever peaked and come to the buildings. I remember coming here with daddy and watching the flood waters in the spring. *Starr, watch for the big logs coming down.* I shiver. The air smells like the bitter-scented black creosote soaked into the railroad ties and dead fish from the river a stone's throw away. I look at the building and there is actually an old cross leaning up to the place where Tammy's body had been found. When I jump across the tracks and make my way to the building, I can see plastic flowers strewn across the ground, remnants of an old wreath dangling near the top of the cross.

I'm not sure what makes me decide to retrieve the last of my spray paints out of the trunk of my car. I know I've got less than fifteen minutes to get to Anna's. I wrestle with the urge to take out my anger on old brick even if it is in yellow, baby blue, and shiny gold that's sitting in my backpack in my trunk. There is a vacant building and my almost compulsive desire to draw a few letters and curves and leave a bit of my soul in paint on its wall.

In less than four minutes, my backpack is hoisted over my shoulder and I'm using the leverage of my right knee to push open a thick wooden door with white-peeling paint. It is only three feet from the cross and I shudder to think this would be the perfect place for a ghostly murder. I suppose the image of the skeletal remains of Tammy Lynn chasing me down the road is what gave me the strength to shove open the door in one huge grating bang. My feet are dancing through while I try to keep balance and I stop just within the bounds of a huge, room.

When I was ten, Poppy let me and Gil go trick or treating by ourselves up and down the quiet streets around his house. It was a mistake. However, in his defense, he did follow us in the shadows for the first few streets. When he saw we were using our please and thankyous, he threw caution to the wind and left to help Anna pass out the candy at their own front door.

It was one picket fenced home after another, a safe and cozy place to knock on doors and politely ask for candy. Except for one house that Poppy told us to steer clear. It was owned by Bob Winkleman who lived in an old beat-up house on the corner of Berry Lane and Beekman. He was thin, wiry, crazy and hated kids. If some unsuspecting kid came near his house walking to school, he would chase them down the street with a broom. It was always rumored he killed kids and buried them in his basement.

Well, Gil bet me all the candy in his bag that I wouldn't go knock on his door and ask Bob Winkleman for candy. I remember standing there and staring up at him, trying to weigh the consequences. I knew Gil had three full size chocolate bars in his bag. I figured nobody could be as scary as my dad. Consequently, my love for chocolate far outshone my need for common sense. While Gil stood at the end of the broken concrete sidewalk and slightly in the shadows. I clambered over a chest-high stone fence he built to keep people out and marched right up to the door. Then, I rapped my skinny knuckles. I stared at the door waiting for it to open wide. "Nobody is going to answer it because I am outside!" Old Mister Winkleman was hiding in the bushes that night just waiting for some dumb kid to toilet paper his bushes or paint his dirty windows with soap. I recall opening my mouth wide and the sound of my own cat yowl and simply turning, flying as fast as my scrawny legs could carry me. Unfortunately, I forgot about the stone wall and I smacked head first right into it at a dead run and screaming holy hell. Then there was nothing but black.

I get to relive that very sensation fifteen years later while I stumble through the door and come face to face with the hugest man I have ever seen. I see him reaching out for me and I back pedal my two suddenly awkward feet. My heart's pitter-pattering in my chest full throttle and I swing my backpack clumsily at air. I scream, turn and run smack into the partially open door I just came in.

"You killed her."

I am blinking up into the oozy spray of flashlight and laying flat and sprawled on the gritty concrete floor. I think

I feel some kind of bug wiggling at my neck. There are faces everywhere, two in particular are within an arm's length of my own.

"No, she ain't dead," an old face says, round and wrinkled and with two blue eyes. "Them's her eyes and they open."

"Shit," my own voice mumbles while I sit up slowly. "Are you trying to kill me? I've got seventy-five cents to my name. It's in my car's ashtray under the radio."

"Looked more like you was trying to kill yourself."

I groan at the woman staring at me. I think I might be in a drug den or something. She is leaning over with hands on her knees. Now she has pushed herself upright. She's forty-something and wearing old jeans and a red t-shirt smudged with gray grime. She's got one of the dollar store plastic lanterns in her fist and is waving it back and forth.

I push up on my elbow, let my eyes roam around the dirty room. More lanterns light the floor. An old conveyer belt is laying in one corner. There are boxes and machinery parts settled on the far wall. Between, there are mattresses and blankets, black plastic garbage bags and a few stuffed animals.

"You live here," I mutter, pushing myself to my feet.

"Are you the police?" a man asks me and I huff a laugh.

"Probably the farthest thing from the police right now." I jab my thumb to my backpack I'm lugging up over my shoulder again and give him a half-cocked smile. "I was getting ready to paint the walls. You know, graffiti."

"Oh, I thought you might have been looking for a place to stay," the old man says. "The river's flooding. Everybody who lives along the river knows to come here.

Figured you'd just heard about it."

"Are you hungry?" There's a little girl near my elbow. She's got on worn blue jean shorts and a t-shirt. She's Mia's age and trying to stuff a piece of half-eaten, soggy bread into my hand.

"No, baby." I kneel down next to her. "I do have a headache from running into the door."

"Yeah, boom!" she says.

"Yeah, boom," I agree. I look up and catch a woman's eyes hovering over the little girl. It must be her mama.

"You got food?" I ask her.

I expect her to tell me they do even if it is out of politeness. It just gets quiet.

"We've got nothing, sweetheart. Those of us that got houses under water got what we could and got out. That meant the kids and clothes. The rest are homeless—"

"Misplaced," the huge man holds up a finger and corrects her. "Homeless makes us sound poor. I like to call us *misplaced*. They call me Big Bob." He holds out his huge paw of a hand and drags me over into a big bear hug. I wince. "And this is Katie." It's the lady with the little girl. She gives me a little wave.

"They call me Tango," I grunt. "You know, Whiskey Tango."

"Oh, the star with the WT. You're the one that does the art on the bridges," Katie says. "I've seen your stuff."

"Yeah, that's me." I shrug. "Don't tell the cops, please." Then I sigh, look at my phone clock. "I don't have time to paint tonight. But I got fifteen bucks on my debit card. I'll run downtown to the grocery store and get some bread and sandwich stuff."

CHAPTER 32

ALWAYS SCREWING UP

"I can see where that can be misconstrued for dealing drugs." I'm saying this to Gil at twelve-ten and in Poppy's driveway. It is the most sarcastic tone I can work up over Mia screaming in my arms. I am narrowing my gaze over Gil's shoulder. I can see God Squad about ten feet back with his hands in his pockets like he is there for support, but staying back.

Of course, the grocery store closes at ten o'clock so I had to go to Hensley Grove Speedy Gas for groceries. That, in itself, was a humbling experience. Mark Lafferty was the only one working again and he had to spend the most excruciatingly longest seven minutes of my life cutting up deli meats for me in complete silence. He didn't even look at me. I didn't look at him until he had checked me out at the register. I was thirty-six cents short and had to snatch the extra change from the little penny bowl on the counter.

"You know, you could have just dropped it. You didn't have to go to the cops," I said right before I turned. "They came to my house and acted like I was some kind of a criminal," I went on with my hand on my chest and a little loudly. "I didn't do anything. The cop that I was working with didn't do anything. Now she's on administrative leave."

"You don't think it's strange that you've got pictures of my dead sister?"

I didn't say anything, felt my cheeks burn. But it angered me. Right as I pushed through the door, I looked back at him. "You're the one that said the cops were wrong. Your sister wouldn't commit suicide. Maybe if you would have stopped and asked, you would see we had a common goal. We were working on it, trying to find out who killed your sister. But it's no big deal, asshole. Let them close the case, shut it tight with packing tape. Everything will be just fine until the next girl walking down the street gets murdered."

Okay, I was a little harsh. But ten minutes earlier while I was shaking the locked door of Jenson's Grocery, irritated and knowing it is closed because of the dark parking lot, a shadow slips up about five feet away against one wall. It's a younger guy, maybe in his late teens and wearing a hoodie.

"Hey, you're Tango, right? Kevin's girlfriend?" It sounds like he's trying to disguise his voice.

"No, I'm not going out with him anymore. If you're looking for Kevin's girlfriend from October of last year until today, it would be Sophie Wells. Give him another week and I'm thinking he'll piss her off enough you'll be looking for his next girl." I stare into the darkness, feel my fingers slip into my purse and around the DEAD STOP ASSAULT BEAR DETERRENT in the side pocket. "And didn't anybody ever tell you to never sneak up on a woman in a dark parking lot?"

"Well, it's not him I'm looking for. They just told me that you were going out with him. I'm looking for you." He appears really antsy, kind of does jerky steps over to me. He's making it clear he wants to hide in the shadows. He holds out his hand and I swear my own hand is clutching the bear spray so tightly, I'm surprised the can doesn't burst. "There's a guy named Body who wants to talk to you about the dead girls." A tattoo. I can see the image of a thin chain running around his wrist. It is deep green. And a bit of rainbow snap bracelet.

"The dead girls?" I reach out, unsure, and take the

small paper he is handing me. It looks like one of the red
and white envelopes the Hensley Grove National Bank puts
my money in when I take out cash at their counter.

"Tianna's one of them. I think her last name was
Mills. They found her down at the highway, the dead girl.
He said not to tell anybody you're meeting or he won't
show," he says leaning into me. I can smell pot on his
breath. "I would show. Body isn't somebody to mess with."

So now, I'm lying my way out of two incidents that
occurred tonight that I simply would have avoided if I
could.

"It was just some dude looking for Kevin," I lie to Gil.
"And I don't know where Kevin is."

"Tango, you were in the parking lot of Jenson's
Grocery an hour and a half ago. Something passed between
hands." Gil lets his head swing toward the bottom of
Poppy's steps. "Colt was running with some friends and saw
you."

"Saw me what?" my voice is getting louder. "What
the hell, God Squad?" I hold out my arms. "Are you the cops
now? Back off. Leave me alone. You assume because my
dad's a crap, I am too. Well, I'm not. And if you also think it
was going through my mind that I was going to rob the
grocery because my dad would rob a grocery, you are
wrong."

"Tango, we all saw you shuffling stuff between hands.
You can ask Taylor and Delia. They were with me," Colt says
a little too flippantly. "I'm sorry. If you've got a drug
problem, your family can help. If not, I'm sorry. Hope you'll
forgive me someday."

"Gil, I don't have a drug problem," I laugh with a bit
of acid in my tone. "Colt's an ass. Don't listen to him. Gil,

you know me. I don't—"

"Then why are you acting so weird, Raeanna?" Gil leans back against his car, folds his arms. Oh, he's being serious using my real name. "I mean, where were you tonight? You were supposed to pick up Mia three hours ago. Mom says you've been coming in late, leaving early. You aren't dancing anymore. You didn't show up for the janitor interviews and Anna had to drop your application off at the school. You didn't sign up for summer classes like you said you were to finish your degree—"

"For one, the classes aren't my fault, Gil. Two, I don't want to sweep floors for a living. I want to be an artist." I try to adjust Mia who now has snot running down her nose and I am hoping it is rain from the big trees in Poppy's yard dribbling on my shoulder and not the stuff from her nose. "And three, Shane told me if I stepped foot in his class, he would have me kicked out of the school."

"Again, from what I heard, you were the one that provoked him. I mean, come on, Tango. Mom says Shane Delgado is the number one instructor of ballet in the Midwest. Maybe he's a bit dramatic, but he's professional and he has to maintain a certain amount of respect." Gil sighs. "Rae, these are all signs that point to something that isn't good. Anger problems, sneaking off, and when I stopped at your apartment the other day, Rocky Merino answered the door. Why are you hanging out with that loser?"

He answered my door? I know I paused just a little too long. Gil must have seen my sudden apprehension.

"You didn't know he was in there."

"He's my friend," I say, dismissing it with a shake of my head. "He can come and go when he wants." Why was Rocky in my apartment? How did he get a key?

"I'm not discussing this anymore with you, Gil." I turn and aim myself toward my car. He doesn't follow.

"Well, better me than the cops, Tango," he calls out. "Because they are the ones that will take Mia away, not me if they think she's not safe. Mom's really worried and dad, he's talking about pulling down your old baby bed for Mia. Do you see where I'm going? You say you aren't going to be like your dad, like your mom. But you sure are acting like you are."

I had swung around the front of my car and pause with my hand on the passenger side door, ready to set Mia inside. "Is that a threat, Gil?" I ask him. My heart is making a pounding thud in my chest. My family has never turned on me. They have always been there to support me even when I painfully screw up.

"Just don't screw up again," he answers. "It's as easy as that."

CHAPTER 33

MY BREAKFAST BUDDY

Screwing up may not be easy for my foster brother. However, my blood runs deep with a long line of relatives that must have been as good as my dad at not being able to get from Point A to Point B without stumbling, tripping, or falling flat on their faces. Because I can't make it one entire day before I'm one inch from standing in front of a firing squad again.

"Hey, Joe, I was wondering if I could borrow fifty bucks until payday."

Joe is sitting in his office hiding behind the newspaper when I round the corner. He hates Monday mornings and specifically hired a cook to cover for that day. He barely peers out the side of the Hensley Grove Tribune. "You already owe me a hundred and ten from your paycheck. If you flirted a little more and stuffed your bra with some of the toilet paper in the bathroom back there, you'd probably get fifty bucks in tips instead of the ten you got yesterday because you mouthed off to everybody."

Everybody was one old lady who sat there and talked to all the other old witch friends for a half hour before she took a sip of her soup. Of course, by the time she'd gabbed about every woman in her book club and her bible study group, it was cold. And I told her that in not so many words.

"She told me I was a shame to my generation by wearing this skimpy dress after her generation burned their bras in protest for women's rights," I retort.

"And when I was tossing her guest check in the trash because I gave her a free meal, she told me you said that women never burned their bras. It was a myth," Joe mumbles a little hotly before he raises his voice higher mimicking my own: "*And besides my generation doesn't want to see a bunch of old lady tatas bouncing around like rotten grapefruit just to prove a point.*"

I had automatically dropped my head to look at my boobs after his remark. Sure, they are small. But Kevin told me small tits are just fine. As an afterthought, and as I tug my chin back up I realize he was always staring at Sophie's chest. "I'm not going to stuff my bra for tips, Joe."

I hear laughter out in the dining area. I cringe. Surely our conversation hadn't wafted out there. However, that's where Joe's eyes walk, right over my left elbow and to the dining room. It was probably just coincidental. Joe rolls his eyes and turns his attention back to me. "I see he's back."

"Who is back?"

"Your breakfast buddy."

I'm not turning. I'm sure if I did, straight down the hallway, and out the open kitchen door, I would see Colt Lucero sitting at the counter.

"Is that who just laughed?"

Joe bobs his head up and down. "I'm not his buddy anymore," I divulge. "He told my brother and my Poppy I was dealing drugs in the parking lot of Jenson's last night after it closed. Can I borrow the fifty bucks or not?"

Now Joe is giving me the stare. "For drugs?" When I glare at him, he shrugs. "You do realize how detrimental it was for your defense when you said those last two sentences side by side, don't you?"

"Never mind." I groan and let my head fall back. I am dead broke after spending my last fifteen dollars on food. Then I borrowed forty from Poppy two days ago so I could take up some more food. I told him I couldn't afford my phone bill. Anna gave me ten yesterday, just stuck it in my hand and gave me sad eyes.

I'm not going to tell Joe I need it to buy groceries for forty plus people taking up residence in an abandoned mill. I'm not telling anybody anything anymore. It only comes back to haunt me. "It's for a friend, a family, that needs food, not drugs. I'll go stuff my bra and flirt. I'll take my own generation back sixty years."

"No, dang it, Tango." Now it is Joe groaning at me. He is leaning sideways so he can tug out his worn, brown wallet. "You'll do no such thing. It brings down the wholesome atmosphere here."

"I wasn't going to climb on a pole, Joe." Again, laughter. It is the kind that is loud and trickles down. Joe stifles his own smile and leans in. "I'm thinking he'd like that."

"Oh, shut up!" I take the fifty he's handing me and already doling it out in bread and meats in my mind and trying not to let Joe see the two big balls of red embarrassment on my cheeks.

"And if you come in after closing, you can take all the day old breads and stuff. For your *friend*, right?" he says softly like it is a secret just for me. "I'll put them in a black plastic garbage bag on the table. Don't wait too long, the neighborhood cats will get into them."

Cassie Jones is the new waitress Joe hired. She is pudgy and sweet and a little dingy. She fits the usual mold of what he tends to hire. He has one girl that is voluptuous and cute and can't seem to get her job done, and me who follows the pretty girl around and cleans up her mess.

However, I figure I've got seniority since I've been here longer. I tell her she's got the counter because all the new girls cover that area. I don't tell her it is actually so I don't have to deal with Colt. It's a mistake. Cassie takes one look at Colt's cute face and she trips over her feet, then spills coffee on three of the four customers sitting at the counter. I know he knows I shifted the tables I cover because I see him following me with his eyes. At first, they are wary. Then I see him turn back to his coffee after Cassie brings him ice for the fingers she burned when she overshot his cup. The next thing I know, he's got this really sad twist to his lips when I look up, a miserable set to his eyes. He turns away, plays like he's on his phone.

"Why do you have to do that?" I say with my hands out to my sides. I lean in, see Joe peering from his desk.

"I'm sorry. I don't know what you're talking about."

"Yeah, you do, God Squad." I push both my hands on the counter, lean into it so I'm maybe a foot away from his face. Then I give him the most doleful gaze I can muster. "You're doing this." I lean back, bring up a hand and wiggle it around my eyes. "You're looking at me like a kicked puppy, giving me sad eyes. What the hell? You turned your back on me, told my family I was doing drugs, asshole."

"You said you wouldn't cuss if—"

"And I'll tell you I'll jump to the moon if it saves one of my friend's ass."

He grimaces. "Then it won't happen again. No more saving your friends' butts. And I do it a lot."

"You did it once."

"I saved your butt just a few days ago," he tells me. "Taylor saw you taking money and she wanted to call her dad. She rounded that corner, had her phone out and was just getting ready to press her dad's number. I talked her out of it. I told her I'd go talk to your dad first if she wouldn't call. Better your family than the cops."

"No," I say with a finger waggle at his face. "It is not better and I'm not dealing drugs."

"Well, I hope you're telling the truth. Because it cost me a date with her."

"Oh, yucky?" I question him with my hands out. "Get real, Lucero. Am I supposed to feel sorry for you because you have a date with Taylor Peirce who leaves ninety percent of the guys at Fields drooling like little babies?"

"She'd be fine if she didn't open her mouth," he says. "And ninety percent of the men who go to Fields wouldn't be asking her out so they could talk to her, would they, Tango?"

"And you are in the ten percent that want to talk to her?"

Colt opens his mouth to reply. He doesn't. He gets a silly smile and wipes it away.

I roll my eyes. "Yeah, that's what I thought." I push away from the counter and give him a sour face. "Have you been getting your suppers I leave you at night or are the neighborhood cats eating them?"

"When did that become a *thing*?" he asks me with a smile. "Yeah, I have. Every night. Seven o'clock. I've gained two pounds, thanks."

"Are you complaining?" I start to leave.

"No, no, don't leave mad," he says. "I was just trying to decide if I wanted a pole dance or a piece of apple pie."

Crap. He must have heard the entire conversation with Joe. I watch while he gets his wallet out, pulls out a five dollar bill, and slides it over to me. "What can I get for five bucks?"

I just stare at him. "Why did you talk Taylor out of calling the cops if you want to ruin my life?" I ask him bluntly. "Because the last time we talked, that seems to have been your motivation to get up out of bed since you were what, eight? I think you compared me to the evil villain in every story that gets killed off in the end."

"Yeah, that kept me up for a lot of nights between then and now." He drops the smile, doesn't give me any eye contact. He doesn't apologize. It is almost like he thinks it is alright to pin me as the villain.

"Yeah, that's what I thought."

"Did you ever find another place to dance?" Colt taps his finger on the counter. Between the two of us, we've shifted the subject away from every awkward answer we would have to make. "Adrien stopped by last week twice. Wasn't sure if he caught up with you."

"Nope." I am not quite telling the truth. Three days ago while I was dropping off some blankets at the old mill for Big Bob, I pushed open the door of one of the rooms and peered inside. It was vacant and dusty and full of rat poop. There were moldy cardboard boxes nearly glued to the floor and glass. I found an old broom in a closet and swept what I could of the floor. Katie came in with her daughter because I had Mia with me. She asked me what I was doing. I told her I was cleaning the floor. It was probably stupid. I told her about my dancing and how I was sneaking into the theatre until last week. And not being able to do it anymore. When I came back two days ago, they had cleaned up the room, washed and swept the floor. There was gold Christmas tinsel decorating the walls and the kids all put up pieces of cardboard they pulled from boxes and drew pretty pictures on them.

"I couldn't unlock the doors for you," Colt says. "I would have. It just wasn't a good idea. You know that cop, Gabe, is following you around, don't you?"

I narrow my eyes. It wouldn't surprise me. It was difficult to tell in town when there are so many cars. But a couple times, I'd seen car lights come on when I pulled out of the parking lot of the apartments. I thought I was being paranoid. And I was careful to make sure nobody was around when I drove to the mill. Now, I'm glad I was cautious.

"I'm not doing anything wrong so it doesn't matter."

Colt wipes his mouth with his napkin. "Okay, I get it. I'm just telling you. Be careful. You know Chloe Murphy?"

"Um, yeah, she goes to church with Anna."

"You know she's investigating the rumors about my dad and your dad and everybody that could have been involved. I don't trust her. Taylor says that she is working with her dad in the investigation—" He suddenly jerks around. It is about the same time I remember sitting in the hospital with Poppy and reading the newspaper article about Chloe trying to solve the murders. But Colt had been talking right to me, then his eyes veer up over my right shoulder. I slip a quick peek to my right while I snatch up the washcloth on the counter. I can see a man coming through the doorway.

"You hate me—" I start to say.

"Tango, go." That's all Colt says. I recognize the man. It is Ralph Edward, Alexandra's stepfather and the man who runs the Wesley Outreach. He is smiling a bit too widely at Colt while he jerks open the door to Joe's diner. I make a quick snatch of the five dollar bill he'd left near his coffee cup and pivot on my feet.

I know Colt is watching me while he makes a quick jump up like he's finishing his coffee. Ralph Edward gives me a quick snap of eyes. His smile turns to a frown while I slip along the tables and snatch a bit of Cassie's sleeve. I can see Colt staring at Ralph, then turning his own gaze to me.

Cassie is wearing the same dress as me. However, where mine looks like a costume a preteen would don for

Halloween, hers looks like the dream of every guy who fantasizes about being a pirate and taking the bar wench over the closest keg of rum. Her chubby legs are muscled and she's got a good three inches of cleavage between lace bodice and black choker. "Hey, the guy at the counter, he left you this," I tell her. "Said to make sure you got it."

I didn't understand the wide-eyed snap of eyes I got from Colt before he turned his attention to Ralph, jumped up and grabbed his hand in a shake. That is, until Cassie giggles into her hand.

"What?" I ask her. I'm thinking maybe my stupid skirt is riding up again. I can usually tell by the number of eyes riding up my calves, past my knees and then stopping short at my thighs.

"Oh." She leans in and she's got a sly and almost lusty gaze past my shoulder. "He wrote this on it: *I'm not in to one night stands. Call me.* And he put his number."

CHAPTER 34

RUNNING SCARED

It is dark, but not so black out that I can't see shadows on the grass. The skylight's not just because of the moon making an appearance every time the puffy getting-ready-to–storm clouds lapse for a few. It is the inferno burning steadily skyward a quarter mile away. It is only an orange glow, though, that is hidden when I move to the shadows of the trees. The moonshine, however, is stalking me, tormenting with every step. I can only hide when the thick clouds sweep between its shine and the embankment of the road where I am stepping. I hunker down as low as I can with my eyes peeled to the sky until the puffy black clouds hide the moon and leave my steps in darkness. Then I make a mad dash until I am exposed again.

Right now, I'm hovering in a ditch near a concrete pipe jutting out beneath Old Hensley Grove/Petersburg Road. The fire burning behind me is starting to catch up, the smoke is burning my nostrils and my eyes. It isn't the wildfire that scares me. I'm wondering if I can fit in the pipe, slide in feet first because I see car lights coming slowly and steadily along the roadway a quarter mile away. I'm not sure if I should keep running or stop. It makes it more difficult because it could mean life or it could mean death, my decision. "Crud, crud, crud." I'm freaking out of breath. Sweat keeps popping up on my forehead and along with it, little stinging bugs that are biting the crap out of my neck, back, and ankles. They are edging closer. I'm shaking so badly that my hands feel like they are falling to sleep. Now I can hear the gravel from the road popping underneath the tires. I think they are going to kill me. No, I *know* they are going to kill me if they find me here.

They. It started with that stupid red and white bank envelope the boy in the hoodie gave me in the parking lot of Jenson's Grocery. Zane, that is. I know it was him. There was nothing inside it. I opened it, peered inside. But there was a little flap tucked into the envelope used to hold the cash safe inside. I saw writing on it and tugged it free. It said: 54889 Vigo Mill Road. That was it. There was no way I was going to this place. It was twenty miles out of town and up and down old gravel roads. Well, that is, until I get a strange call from Mark Lafferty this afternoon. *Tango, there was a boy in here about two. He kept looking around the store, poking stuff and then opening the pop coolers. I figured, he was waiting for me to turn my attention someplace else. Then he was going to steal something. About twenty minutes in, he finally walks up and asks for you. Said somebody told him you worked here. I told him I knew who you were. But you didn't work here. Then I see a green car pull in to the gas pumps and he looked terrified. I mean, I watched his face turn white. He did everything but knock over the candy rack trying to get out of there. He left something. Maybe you ought to pick it up.*

Against my better judgment, I drive over to the Hensley Grove Speedy Gas on my way back to Anna's after working at the diner my seven a.m. to three p.m. shift. It's like Mark is waiting for me at the counter, his hand doing a nervous tap-tap-tap with his nails by the register. "It's back here." He flaps his hand at me like he wants me to follow when he slips around the counter. I hesitate. He turns, shakes his head like he knows I don't feel comfortable walking back there with him. "It's alright, Tango." So I follow him across the room and to a little hallway that leads to the customer restrooms, the storage area, and a room that says: SPEEDY GAS EMPLOYEES ONLY.

Mark pushes open the two aluminum doors to the storage area and takes me around a metal desk and a freezer section. He stops just short of a small alcove and offers up his hand toward it. I blink. There's a boy standing there. He looks like he's been dragged through the brush a couple times. His maroon t-shirt is grimy and pocked with holes and the hoodie jacket he's got over it is dirty. His jeans are smudged brown. And his dark hair is askew on his head like he's been rolling his hand through it over and over.

"Hi, Tango."

"Zane?" I move a little closer. I can see him in the dim light. "What are you doing here?" I ask him, moving up so I am close enough to recognize the hoodie from Jenson's Grocery. "What were you doing at Jenson's the other night?"

"It's all screwed up, Tango," he whispers almost like he is going to break out in a sob. I reach out, snatch up his fingers, and pull up his arm so I can see the chain tattoo, then the snap bracelet. "I don't know what to do." He sees me looking at his wrist and gets a wild jerk to his chin like he's going to bolt.

"It's okay," I start to tell him, start to push a hand up to pat his shoulder. He just folds himself on the floor and starts sobbing into his hands. I can't do anything more than drop to my knees and push my hands around his neck, pat his back like I did to Mia yesterday when she was inconsolable over a lost chocolate chip cookie in the heater vent.

"Everything." Zane huffs. "My dad. Troy's dad. I thought it was going to be safe, but Ralph Edward came and got me. He made me come home. So I ran off again because I didn't even get through the door before my dad was shoving me around the living room. And mom just stood there like it was okay."

"Well, it isn't okay."

"And I went to the Matteson's house because I'm thinking Troy would help me. Troy's dad told me to get the hell out of his house, out of this town. The cops keep stopping by his place because of me."

"It was you who gave me the note at Jenson's, right?"

"Yeah, that girl that works at Don's All-Nighter Tavern gave me a hamburger when I tried to get in the bar. Her name's Jessica. I was starving. She gave it to me out back. Then she said somebody dropped that paper off at the bar and she asked if I'd get it to you. She'd give me a hamburger and ten bucks."

"Do you know who that was that scared you so bad?"

I forgot Mark was standing behind us. I crane my neck to look up at him. He's just standing there with his arms dangling to his sides and staring at us both.

"No, I really don't." Zane is shaking in my arms, wiping away snot from his nose with his sweatshirt sleeve. He leans back and his already blue eyes are the color of a clear winter sky while they swim in his tears. "I just know that it was a man because I heard his voice in the back seat. He had a gun and he shot at me outside town like he was going to kill me. He tried to run me over when I ran. I've been hiding under the stands in the ballfield for three days."

"They pulled into the pumps and left," Mark tells me. "I watched them cruise along the street really slow like they were looking for him until they disappeared around the corner. It was an old light green sedan. I didn't see any plates. They were too fuzzy from this far. And I didn't want to run out and look like I was trying to see their plates if you know what I mean."

"You don't know why somebody would be trying to hurt you." I push back a little while Zane smudges his eyes with his sleeve.

"No. My dad is a mean, but he wouldn't shoot me. It has to be the note." He scrambles for his hoodie pocket, brings out another bank envelope. "This. It's another one."

"How'd you get the second one?" I ask him, let him slip it in my hand. I hold it up, open the flap where the last writing had been. Sure enough, it is the same strange scrawl: *Please hurry. Don't have much time left. 54889 Vigo Mill Road. Park at the National Forest backpack lot and walk up the road to the drive. Come on Wednesday.*

Wednesday. That's today.

"I went back to get my ten bucks from Jessica at the bar."

"This doesn't have to do with my sister's death," Mark asks slowly, "does it?"

"No," I lie. Because I think it does. I don't have a clue how the pieces to this little puzzle are going to come together, but I really think there's something big going on in Hensley Grove.

"Yeah, you can lie to me all you want. I get it," Mark shuffles his feet behind me. "I realize now I shouldn't have said anything to Taylor about the crime stuff you had. But I asked her about you and she said you were—you were kind of—" He stops there. I know what she says about me, calls me a slut and poor white trash. "I guess I just assumed that if you lived at the apartments, you were—what she said you were. I didn't know you. I—I don't know you."

"I'm not what Taylor tells everyone I am."

"I just figured you were going to put it online, blast out pictures of Hannah's dead body everywhere."

"I wasn't going to do that." I rise and so does Zane. I

wave Mark away with my hand, then swipe the dirt from my knees. I can see Zane standing. "Tango, I don't know where to go."

"You're coming home with me," I tell him. He looks over my shoulder to Mark apprehensively. I know what he's thinking. But somebody is trying to get gas and the register is tinging over and over.

"I won't say anything. I swear," Mark states softly. "Go out the front door and come around back to pick him up." He starts to turn, pivots back around. "Listen, Hannah didn't commit suicide. I don't give a rat's ass what the cops say. I know they've convinced my mom and dad. I know they've persuaded Delia. I talked to Hannah two hours before she left that night. She was all excited for Adrien Moreau coming to town. Said she might get picked to dance with him in class. She had an old ballet recital program she wanted him to autograph. There was some kind—" he stops and shakes his head at another car pulling into the gas pumps. "—some kind of competition they were doing and she wanted to be the lead. I guess they win each year and the lead always gets into some big dance company."

"It's the Edna Fields Performing Arts Contest," I sigh. I scratch my head.

"I want to help. I want to find out who did it."

"Well, earn my trust. Don't tell anybody Zane's staying with me."

CHAPTER 35

BOGIE

That was seven hours ago. What happened between occurred so fast, I keep thinking I lost track of time somewhere along the line. In the long stream of lies I've been telling, I call Layla and ask her if she and Gil can watch Mia for me tonight so I can earn some extra money cleaning the grease vats for Joe. Layla hesitates, then tells me she'll watch Mia to get out of going to the alumni baseball game at the high school. Then I get Zane comfy at my apartment with a pizza and TV.

Between, Billy Thompson stalks me all the way to my car. "What do you want, Billy?"

"Nothing."

"Billy, what do you—" We do this five or six times until he just stops at the bottom of the steps. "Alma Bean, the girl with the eyes that make her look like an ant, wants you to put together a dance to go with the songs we're singing for the competition. She said to tell you that you have to be in the competition because you have to do it each year for credits. She says if you don't—"

"I did Neil Wright's art show. The visual art students are allowed to do that as an alternative to the competition since we don't perform."

He seems to ponder this while he snatches his chin and narrows his eyes. "Well, good, I'll tell her that. I didn't want to go to the acapella club stuff anyway. All the girls are either too fat or too skinny."

I stop and turn. "Is that a threat, Billy? Because it sounds like if I don't do what you say, you won't go to the only thing you ever do barring stalking girls in the parking lot and looking up porn online. It is, quite possibly, the only normal thing you do."

"Your boyfriend told me the acapella club isn't normal. It's for dweebs and dorks."

"Kevin said that, huh?" I ask. He bobs his head up and down. "Well, that's one of the reason's he's my ex-boyfriend, Billy. He does not appreciate art." I stop, drop my shoulders and stare at the ground. "You know, other than Poppy, you are the only one that tells me my art is good?" I tell him. He bobs his head again. "Here's the deal. I'll create a dance for your team if you make up a map and plot out all the places that they found the bodies of the dead girls."

So Billy agrees and I drive up the shabby asphalt roads until they turn to the gravel roads the county provides. Then, they started getting smaller the closer I got to where the old Vigo Mill used to be and turned to mostly dirt. In 1979, the state and the Rocky Fork Creek Preservation Group purchased the land here and put in trails and planted trees. There's a gravel parking lot near the creek that has backpack trails and all night fishing. Already, there are three or four cars parked there when I pull in, ease my own between.

It is remote and now, it is getting dark. I can't get cell phone service while I walk Rocky Valley Road until it stops at the old Vigo Mill Road. I have to shine my cell phone flashlight at the road sign to see which direction Vigo Mill goes. There's a bridge that leads into a driveway and I walk it across. The gravel road is surrounded by trees and it is eerily quiet while I walk about a quarter mile. The road is rutted here, deep ruts like people with ATVs have gotten stuck.

"Oh, crap." The muddy road keeps going. I turn my

head sideways to read one of the green reflective signs the township puts up to display the street address. It is attached to a wooden mailbox post.

"54889 Vigo Mill Road. Bingo," I say flatly and with a bit of regret. I see a part blue and part canary yellow mobile home seated haphazardly on a dirt hillside. There's no metal skirting on the bottom and four or five cats running underneath when they see me stepping up the hillside. Three hound dogs are barking wildly and chained to makeshift doghouses. And there's a handful of blue plastic drum barrels with roosters tied to them.

I rap my knuckles about five times. Nobody answers the door. I'm just about to turn when I hear a rapping on the inside window about five feet from the warped-board porch where I'm standing. My squinting eyes make out the features of an old man pushing back the curtains. He's balding with a swatch of black hair flapping over his head. He's pointing toward the door and I understand why when I push open the door against dingy swag carpet. He's sitting at a table with a portable oxygen tank and tubing connected to his nose.

"You are Tango." He has to breathe between each word, long drawn out and raggedy breaths. He is gaunt and so much so, he looks like nothing more than a skeleton with skin wrapped over.

"Yes." I stand at the door until he waves me over to the little chair across from the couch where he is seated. I can barely see in the dingy light. He is extinguishing one cigarette in a full ash tray and lighting another with his free hand. It smells like cigarette smoke and cat pee and I hold back a gag at the liter pop bottle that I know must be filled with his pee. There are three more in a line with lids on behind it.

"I hoped you'd come." The TV is blaring and he doesn't seem to notice this. He's gasping so hard I almost feel like I have to breathe for him. He smiles and it is a toothless grin. I try to smile back. My gut tells me I should just get up and leave. But I've gotten this far and if I bolted, I'd never know if he had some insight into Hannah's death.

"The notes—" I reach in my pocket, pull out the bank envelope, watch a cockroach weave its way across the floor. "The person that delivered the notes said I needed to talk to you about Tianna. Did you know her?"

"Tianna?" he says and shakes his head, scrunches up his face like he has no clue what I am talking about. "I don't know who Tianna is."

My heart makes a little jerk. I'm wondering if this isn't some kind of a trap. It is dark in the trailer except for the shine of light from the TV. I feel goosebumps wriggle up my arms. The dogs are still barking outside and I know I'm going to have a hard time finding my way back down the road again.

"I was the one that used to run the old Vigo airport before it closed down so they could build the county airport. They called me Bogie back then. Flew in Vietnam. I could sneak up on the hostiles, blew a lot to smithereens. I was the bogie, get it?" He asks me. I shake my head a little back and forth.

"I'm not sure."

"A bogie's an echo on the radar that might mean another aircraft is around. When I flew, you'd see them all the time. Didn't always know— but that don't matter." He stops. I can see his face getting paler. "I ran the old Vigo Airport for thirty years. Saw more than a few planes come in there." He must have noticed I wasn't registering any importance in his job because he held up a forefinger, then turned and snatched up a light tan folder. "November 5th. That ring a bell to you? The plane wreck in downtown Hensley Grove."

It registers. "They called you *Body*. Now I get it." I lean forward in my chair while he slaps the folder on his lap, opens it wide. "I made copies. I was supposed to do it, one for the county and one for the town of Vigo. I just took the files home with me because Vigo, it was so small, it didn't have no city offices. And Vigo, it don't exist no more. I had no idea what to do with the dang things, so I kept 'em in my spare bathroom."

He opens the folder, sifts around inside and tugs out a paper. "We had to keep tabs on all the incoming and outgoing flights." Then he pokes a finger at a paper he slaps down on one knee. "The newspaper in Hensley Grove, it said there was four men on a private plane. There weren't no four men on that flight. I know I got the call, talked to them in person. And it weren't no private plane. It was military. Look here."

I lean forward. It is a standard form with VIGO AIRPORT written on the top. It has the times the planes are due, the type of aircraft, the starting point and the final destination.

"It came from Dayton, Ohio. Wright Patterson Air Force Base," Bogie tells me. "It was heading to Eglin Airport in Florida. I got a call. They radioed, was having engine problems and needed a place to land. I came out and turned on the lights so they could come down. They never made it here." He stops, pokes a finger at the paper. "But look. Here's what's important. There was six people on that flight, not four. I was told it was high priority security and nobody could come to the airport because there was a large amount of currency on board and important passengers that needed safeguarding. I had to call the local police, let them know. They was supposed to set up roadblocks around the airport, set up some kind of security." Bogie laughs lightly. "Like anybody around these parts were going to do anything more on a November night than sit in front of the TV."

I take the paper from his fingers. "Can I take a picture of this?" I ask him.

He shrugs. "Sure."

"So who do you think the extra people were, Bogie?" I ask him. "And why weren't any bodies found?"

"Well, you know what? They was right. You're the only one that asked that."

"Who was right?"

He doesn't answer me, just stares at my eyes long and hard. "It don't matter. It's what I been trying to tell everybody, tried to tell the police over and over. I was told to be quiet. When I tried to call the feds about it, I got a call on my phone. The voice on the other end said they'd kill me if I said anything more. The bodies they started digging up along the river, they was them. I just know it. I called the cops, they told me to call the historic society about it. I did and they told me the cops said they was old and from an Indian burial mound and they covered them back up."

"But if it is military and they knew about it, why aren't they investigating? Surely, they've got the tools."

"I don't know. It was covered up quicker than the way I shove dirt under my carpet with a broom. I only know they must have been important to somebody at least until they died. Or maybe they were important for some reason and had to die. I couldn't find any reference to any political heads that came up missing after the wreck. Nothing. It was like it never happened. Maybe they was just important military personnel on a secret mission. They said it was classified. I don't know." He reaches down, wiggles the paper before I take a picture. "I just know the stupid cops didn't show up at the airport. I told them. That Chief Peirce, he repeated it back to me three times. But they was in town when the wreck happened like they know'd it was coming. Then they lied that there was four people on board when there was really six."

"Six?"

"Uh huh. They told me there was six."

I think about Anna then. She likes to do the crossword puzzles from the Sunday morning Tribune. She skims down through the clues and finds the words she knows and places the answer in the appropriate vertical or horizontal box. She's always left with a ton of clues she can't figure out, boxes that are incomplete. First, she asks Poppy if he knows the answer while she paces around from room to room. If he doesn't, she'll go until about Tuesday banging her head and trying to figure it out. By Wednesday, she's so frustrated she looks up a few answers on her little tablet. It is usually one or two words vertically that expose letters for the horizontal answers.

While I'm sitting there staring at Bogie, I'm wishing I had some sort of tablet to look up the answers to this puzzle that's getting set out in front of me. I've got the names of the dead girls and the places they were planted after they died. I mean, is it like Anna's crosswords? If I figure out who is murdering the girls, will it give me answers to this plane wreck? Or are they two different crossword puzzles? Or maybe it was just a stupid plane wreck and Hensley Grove is just the dumping ground capital of the United States for murders.

"It's like this, darlin', there's one thing I didn't tell

nobody. I think it's probably too late." Bogie presses his palm to his lips. He's got tears in his eyes when he looks up at his ceiling. "I swore I'd do it before I died. But I was just too chicken to do it back then when I thought they was gonna kill me." He takes two breaths. "I talked to that pilot on the radio that night. I sat in that airport waiting on that plane to land whether they wanted it there or not. They was all talking around him. It was loud. But he said to me—he said tell my Rita and my horsie boy I love them—" He huffs a breath. "Then I didn't hear nothing else but maybe thirty seconds passed and there was the explosion way off."

I'm sitting there staring at him. "You—you talked to the pilot?"

"I did."

"Then why did they—" Say he jumped? I don't get to ask the question nor a hundred others popping into my head right then. Bogie's hand goes up quickly in the air. His eyes are wide. "Somebody is pulling up the lane. Ain't nobody ever come up here, girl."

I could hear the crackle of tires on the roadway. He was right. He reaches over, flips off the little lamp next to the couch. I'm not sure what to do.

"You don't think the pilot jumped?" I ask Bogie quickly.

"Nuh huh, not a chance."

My heart makes a huge jump because I see, in the moonlight coming through the curtains behind us, Bogie's wide eyes. He shifts somewhat and he jabs his thumb toward the kitchen of the mobile home. "Go out the back door."

"O—okay," I stand up instantly. I hear the sound of car doors slam. One. Then a second. My eyes work wildly to where he is pointing and I snap to attention head toward the shiny gold knob. Bogie is taking the papers and folder and shoving them beneath his couch. "Up the hill, now, run!"

I hit the door running. The dogs are going crazy barking at the road. His little mobile home runs right into a hillside and I head up the hill my legs churning and banging on the ground. I feel the tiny wild rose thorns digging into my shins, hear the sound of my body slapping the leaves of tiny saplings and bigger trees. I hear gunshots, two of them and my body jerks in shocked reaction. I've got no clue if they are aimed at me. I fall to the ground, my breaths in huffs. I can't run anymore. I don't know if they can see me. There is a moment in my panic that I simply lie flat on my face and push my hands over my ears. I used to do this when I was little when I'd hear people fighting. Because sometimes my daddy would just go crazy and tear up wherever we were living. My safest place was under the bed, flat on my belly, and hands over ears.

I suppose it was and will always be a knee-jerk reaction to trauma for me. It also probably saved me from getting killed right then and losing my hearing. There was a moment of silence after the gunshots. The grass was tickling my nose and I smelled the wet dirt beneath my chin. BOOM! Then, came the explosion. I could feel the wave wash over my body, heard the crackle of pieces of aluminum siding blowing past me and hitting the trunks of trees. Fist size balls of burning wood and plaster were falling like snow around me. I freaked and I ran.

It was the road I ended up taking at the bottom of the hill and forty minutes of ducking and hiding while the moon stalked me like a crazy killer with a lantern. I come out in blackness at the forestry pull-off. I think I'm home free. I see my car still sitting in the parking area. It's all alone and relief washes over me. I'm grappling with my keys in the dark and the moon basks me in its brilliant glow. I blink while my keys dangle in my hand, see little flecks of light shimmering in the moon on the asphalt at my feet.

They are beautiful little jewels all around me. Then it hits me. It is glass from my windshield. It is glass from my side windows and it is glass from my rear window. Shattered, they are, from the explosion.

I hear the car before I see it weaving up and down the road, see the light flashing out. It is a small car, black with tinted windows. There's a dent in the passenger side door. That's when I take off again, shove myself through the woods to the roadway. And that's where I am trying to duck beneath a concrete pipe. And I'm sure when they pause, they can see my shadow dipping low because I just can't crawl into the pipe. I just can't push myself to do it. I'm scared and I'm in big trouble. And the only person I think I can trust right now is Kevin. It always seems like he's my go -to guy when I've screwed up.

"Hey, Kev, it's Tango," I whisper after the car passes. "Yeah, I know it's late. But I need you. Bad. The cell service is bad here and there's a good possibility somebody's trying to kill me—"

CHAPTER 36

GETTING JUDGED WALKING OUT OF
THE GRAND PLAZA HOTEL WITH MY SHOES IN MY
HAND

"Don't judge me."

I'm standing on the curb of the Grand Plaza Hotel with my sandals dangling in my fingers and bending low enough to see Colt Lucero leaning over from the driver's seat so he can see me through the passenger window. The name implies it is a luxury stay. It is far, far from it. It isn't just the location where it has been a shabby stable fixture for the last fifty-eight years where High Street turns into a four lane highway and the railroad runs beside it. The two story brick building is shoved into a parking lot and surrounded by fast food restaurants already crammed too closely together. There is a bowling alley to its right and an abandoned used car lot to the left.

The swimming pool out front is avocado green and I can even see the deep color beneath the parking lot lights. However, Kevin told me when we pulled in twenty minutes ago that people still swim in it. It just smells gross. Grand Plaza Hotel is where he and Sophie live now for a hundred and forty bucks a week. There isn't a place for my car. Kevin towed me to Rocky's shop and we pulled it around back. Sophie gets off work from her job at Big G's Pizza at ten-thirty, so my tour was short and to the point.

"There are so many things I could say right now, Tango," Colt says blatantly. "But by the look of regret in your eyes, you've already kicked yourself enough."

Arrr, I just want to punch him. "Are you going to give me a ride or not?"

"I am here, aren't I?" he asks me. "Unless you want to fix me up with another one of your coworkers, of course. Cassie has texted me forty times in the last hour alone after that goofy stunt you pulled. She's talking marriage. Jealous?"

"I'm not the jealous type." I sigh deeply, grab the latch to his door, and plop down hard on the leather seats.

"Where to, princess?" he asks me waving his hand wide. He's obviously in a strange mood tonight. "Going to the ball or just coming home from it?"

"Please, God Squad, don't—don't make me feel any smaller than I feel right now," I tell him. My head hurts, my ears are still ringing.

"Smaller?" he grunts a laugh. "So here is the story I heard tonight from Officer Gabe Reynolds. Because he called me to check your story that you worked your shift today and you weren't out making a bomb in the back of your Poppy's shed. And yes, he really did call me before you ask. And yes, this is the same Officer Reynolds who pulled you and Kevin over on High Street an hour ago because you were illegally towing your vehicle with windows busted out from Kevin's baseball bat again. He said there had been a bit of a domestic dispute. By the way, I told him Kevin was notorious for busting up your car when you were heading out of the relationship again. Or maybe back into it. I'll quote your brother on the last one. Because Officer Reynolds said when he pulled you over—"

"Don't God Squad." I didn't want to hear it. I'd lived it an hour ago in front of about thirty cars who had stopped to ogle the situation. I started to tell Kevin what happened with the explosion because he picked me up in the middle of a forest fire and tied our bumpers together with an old chain he had in the trunk of his car. He waved me away with a hand and told me to save it for somebody else. Then, it came over the radio that a trailer on Vigo Mill Road had burst into flames and about thirty acres of surrounding forestland were on fire so I think he was starting to get the gist of the situation. I honestly believe he thought, for a moment, I was the one who blew up the trailer. And he still towed me to town. We passed the fire trucks and the ambulance and the police cars. And Officer Reynolds who was quite concerned about how my car had gotten the windows blown out.

"When he pulled you over, got Kevin out of the car and questioned him. Kevin piped right up and told him he'd smashed your windows again. He told Officer Reynolds how much he loved that—I won't use the word he used, but it starts with the letter *b*. Then when they were dragging Kevin off to the cruiser, you did everything straight down to jumping right into Kevin's arms and knocking him to the ground to kiss him. And while you're straddling his chest, you're telling him how much you loved him and you didn't care if he did it to your apartment windows too—"

"And Gabe let him loose."

"He did."

I rub my temples between forefinger and thumb. "Listen, Kevin said I need to start trusting people."

"It looks like you trusted him."

"Can you shut up for a minute, God Squad?" I ask him. "I think I'm having a—"

"Therapy moment?" He must see I'm not kidding. I'm about to have a mental breakdown, I think. He shuts up and I watch as he reaches into the pocket of his button up shirt and pulls out one of those tiny, palm-size dollar store journals with lined paper inside. There is a pencil attached.

"Here. I'm packing Tango treatment."

I'm staring at it while I take it in my hands. It actually says: TANGO THERAPY BOOK on the front. Then I look up at him. I think I smile. I'm not sure while I take in the moment, realize he'd been thinking about me when he went to the store, picked out the paper and the pencil just waiting for the time I'd have to use it. And now, I guess, that I would have to use it.

"Okay, this makes it easier," I say opening it and holding the pencil in my hand. I can't tell you how close I am to tears when I cradle this little journal in my hands. I don't know if he can tell. He looks over at me twice and I can tell Colt is fidgety before he stares out the window to the bit of sprinkles hitting the windshield.

"Kevin told me that maybe I'm kind of difficult to have a relationship with because I give people one chance and if they screw it up, I'm out," I tell him. "Not just boyfriends, but friends, and maybe family. He knows why I do it. I know why I do it. Maybe you know why I do it too. It's because I loved my daddy and I didn't know why he hit me. And I had to push him away so it didn't hurt me so much when he hit me." I look up and God Squad is just driving. He's not looking at me. "Kevin says I screw up all the time and look how long he stuck around. I should give other people a chance to have a relationship with me." He's just staring out the window expressionless. "Are you listening or just driving? Can you pull the car over a minute, God Squad? I need you to look at me. I need to see your expression because I have a hard time reading what people are thinking because, well, my daddy used to smile when he'd get mad."

Colt pulls off so quickly on the two lane highway, the driver of the car behind us lays on the horn far after it passes. He pushes the car in park, then flips on the inside light and turns to me. "Better?"

I nod, know he isn't making fun of me for the moment. He's so damn pretty, though, it is difficult for me to adjust to a friendship level sometimes. "Right now, I need somebody I can trust, Colt. I mean, you're not going to run to the cops or you're not going to tell anybody else anything I tell you. Can I trust you because—" I stop and let my eyes roam to the ceiling of the car. It is tan and perfect and not ripped like the roof of my car. "If you blow it, if you betray my trust, you will destroy every bit of faith I have in people. Because Kevin, he is the only one that has ever had my back. Even when he's screwing somebody behind it, of course—"

"Tango, you can trust me."

"Even if I tell you stuff that you could take right to the cops?"

He doesn't say anything, turns his head toward the window. "You know what I do, right?" he says softly. "I'm not here to convert people to Ralph's church, right? I think he'd like me to do that, but I don't. And he knew that from the start. I made it clear I wasn't coming for religious reasons. I just wanted to help people, to reach out to people who needed it and there just aren't that many places that provide room and board like Ralph's mission does."

"Okay, what's that have to do with you trusting me?"

"Because you sound like you're going to tell me you've broken the law. If I don't go to the police and you've done something to hurt somebody else, then I lose my credibility. I just want to help people like—"

"Me?"

"Well, yeah, people who are low income make a better life for themselves. I want to—"

"Save the world?"

"Yeah, kind of." He sighs, then laughs wanly. "It

would be hard if I'm caught breaking the law. That's all I'm trying to say. I don't want to take a chance and lose what little trust I've built up with people in Hensley Grove because I broke the law."

I think I take him in for a full thirty seconds before I drop my gaze to my hands. "Okay, here's how it goes, then. If you think I've done something wrong, stop me from talking. I won't tell you more. If I do tell you something more and you feel the need to turn me in to—the cops, whoever, then do it. You can make the decision. I won't lose my trust in you if you tell me you're going to the cops about it. But if I didn't break the laws, then you don't tell anybody. I think that's fair."

"Okay."

"I got a couple messages to meet with somebody about the murders."

"Somebody I know?"

I hold up a hand to pause his words. "I'm not hiding anything from you so just give me a sec, okay?"

"Okay."

"I kind of ignored the messages because I thought they were from some creep, right?" I tell him. "They were cryptic and he wanted to meet me way back in a remote area—"

"Please tell me you didn't."

"I did," I tell Colt and he's rubbing his forehead with one hand, shaking his head. "It was so remote, I had to walk. And when I got there it's this old guy on oxygen and he's telling me he ran the airport back in the 1980s." I see the spark in Colt's eyes. He snaps his gaze right into my own. "He was the one that got the message to land the plane at the airport in Vigo which is about fifteen miles outside town. It was the only airport near Hensley Grove until maybe twenty years ago. They didn't tell him the reason. He only knew he had a call telling him they needed to land there. And it was a military aircraft from an air force base."

"My dad wasn't—" he paused. "My dad wasn't in the military. Who told you this?"

"His name was Bogie."

"*Was*? What do you mean by that? I want to talk to Bogie. He's pulling your leg, Tango. Who is—?"

"I think he might be dead," I whisper in the silent car. "That's why my windows were blown out in my car. I met with Bogie and a car came to the trailer. I had to run out the back door and then it just—blew up. It just exploded and then whoever was in the car went up and down the road like they were looking for somebody, like me—to—to make sure nobody made it out of the trailer alive."

"Holy crap."

"Somebody knew Bogie had information. He told me for a while, he tried to tell the cops about it. They told him to hush up about it." I push my hand out, let it rest on Colt's arm. "Listen, here's where it gets strange and a little scarier." He looks from my fingers and then back to me.

"Stranger and more scary?"

"Well, for you, this might be something you've been wanting to hear." Colt looks like he's going to speak, I push up a hand to stop him. "Bogie had the records from the airport that night. He said he was threatened by the local police to keep his mouth shut about a plane that was going to land. The initial call that it was going to land came from Dayton, Ohio. It was from some federal officer—classified, like he had to keep it secret. Then after it wrecked, he couldn't disclose anything to anybody from the feds. Then the local police told him that too when he tried to figure out what happened. And Bogie, he said he had radio contact with the pilot that night. He actually talked to him."

"With my dad?"

"Yeah, Colt, look at me," I tell him because his eyes have this wild look to them. "Bogie said he tried to find information about you and your mom. When he contacted the police, they threatened him."

"The cops threatened to kill this Bogie dude?" Colt looks at me. "I don't know, Tango. What did he say my dad said?"

"Bogie said that the pilot, your dad, he told him over the radio to tell Rita and my horsie boy I love them."

CHAPTER 34

KEVIN'S WARNING

"Hey, I need to talk to you."

It surprises me to see Kevin drive up in his truck behind Joe's restaurant during my break. I'm sitting on the top of the picnic table with my feet resting on the seat. I've got a pencil in my hand and a pad of paper in the other. I'm using the nubby end of the eraser I've been chewing on to tap on the pad while I try to come up with a simple dance routine to go along with the eight songs Billy's group is going to sing at the college competition.

Billy gave me a list of the songs. He also gave me a list of the things people in his group can and cannot do. Suzette Reese can't move while she's singing, Billy can't face the audience, and Matt King doesn't want to be anywhere near Alma Bean because they just broke up from a six week relationship, just to name a few. I had stopped in at the tiny basement room they used this morning and recorded the songs in order. Then I showed them a couple simple dance steps to practice while I put together some sort of program for them. I can't sing. They can't dance. The thought we're working together on this is ludicrous. That the project could, quite possibly, make us the school laughingstock for the next year sends chills up my spine.

The sun's hitting my face just right, warming my cheeks when I see Kevin. I push off, take a few steps over to the driver's side window. He's alone. "You told me the other night that some kid brought you the note that told you to go up to that old dude's house, right?" Kevin's patting his fingers on the steering wheel, then he pokes at a picture of Jesus dangling from his rearview mirror.

"Yeah," I answer cautiously.

"That kid, it wasn't Zane Hill, was it?"

"Why do you ask that?"

"Because he's selling drugs, you know that right? For a dealer in town." Kevin is reading my face. He sees me looking away, tugging my lip. "Dammit, I thought so." He bangs his fist on the steering wheel. "You're not dealing or doing are you, Tango? Tell me the truth."

"No, I'm not."

He reaches out the window, snatches up one of my arms and looks for tracks on the inside. I still don't think he believes I'm clean. "You better not. Everybody knows I'll beat the shit out of them if they go near you with anything." He drops my arm, eyes me suspiciously. "You ever met Jessica Pelletier who works at Don's All-Nighter."

Yeah, I have. And I'm getting an idea that it isn't helping my case. "I don't know, I might have."

"Because she's the dealer and she ain't little. I know because Sophie used to work with her dancing poles at the strip club off the highway. You buying weed from her?"

"No!" I say and it sounds like *no-wah*. "Why are you asking me this stuff?"

"Because Zane was working for her and now he's not. And she's wondering where he is, asking around town where he might have gone. I think you might know."

"Shouldn't you be more worried that his parents might be looking for him?" I ask, trying to brush it off. Damn, I'm tugging on my lip.

"Babe, he's eighteen. He can do what he wants."

"Eighteen? I thought he was younger than that."

"Aw damn, Tango, you've got him, don't you?"

"I don't know."

"You don't know." Kevin grunts. "Well, there is something I do know. It's that you need a friggin' babysitter to follow you around all day like I used to, that's what I know. What has it been, four weeks since we broke up? How the hell can somebody get into so much shit in three weeks? It isn't enough you've got some crazy person coming after you, trying to blow you up in a trailer. It isn't enough the cops are following you around because they think you've got something to do with these murders. That's not enough, right? You've got to stir up shit with the local drug mafia."

"Drug mafia," I laugh out loud, roll my eyes. Kevin doesn't laugh with me. "Aw, c'mon Kevie, I go to work, I come home. I'd be going to classes if Shane Delgado wasn't mad at me. And I'd still be playing hide and seek with you in the apartment at night if you hadn't screwed me and screwed Sophie at the same time. So do what you do best. Screw *off*."

"Listen, I'm just giving you a little advice," Kevin says dully. He takes out his phone, taps it, and then holds it up for me to see. I can see a girl walking into the police station. He flips through the pictures. I can see it is Jessica Pelletier and she is talking to a cop. But as he scrolls, there aren't just a few, there are fifty or sixty. "She wants to be the queen of the drug world in Kentucky. And there are plenty of cops that will cover her butt to get information to put the bigger guys out of business, her supplier a guy named Cody, for one. You can take it or not. But I can tell you right now, Jessica talks to the cops all the time, gives them information. You didn't hear that from me. So if she is the one that sent Zane with the note to meet that dude whose trailer got blown up, I'd watch my steps. I'm thinking she might be trying to get you dead for some reason. Just saying." He leans over and snatches up something from the passenger seat, then leans out the window wiggles his fingers at me. I hold out my hand. "It's two hundred bucks. Tell Rocky to sell you his old truck out back of the shop. He will. He's been trying to get me to buy it for two years, doesn't want to see it go to waste."

"Where'd you get two-hundred bucks?" I ask him.

"Don't ask questions." Kevin drives off then. He hits the gas and leaves me standing there in the stink of the dumpster with flies buzzing around my arms. It leaves me with an empty feeling when he goes. I feel like a little bit of me gets ripped from my body when we're not together.

"Hey, you okay?"

I turn and Colt is looking out of the back door. I wonder how long he's been there watching me stare off at the nothingness Kevin left behind and scratching my arm thinking maybe I'd made another stupid mistake letting him go. He's got the sweetest ass in Hensley Grove.

"What are you doing there?" I ask him. I see him eyeing my hand with the money. I shove it in the little apron at my waist. He'd taken me to Gil's last night to get Mia, then dropped me off at my apartment. I swear he only said a handful of words after I told him what Bogie had told me. He didn't react at all, just nodded. Then he'd asked me if that was all. I had told him it was and he put the car in drive and took off again down the road.

"Joe sent me out. He said you needed to talk to me?"

"I don't know why he'd do that," I say, turning slightly. "I didn't even know you were at the diner."

"I don't know. That's just what he said." He doesn't leave, instead Colt pushes out the door and stands by the picnic table. "About last night. I'm sorry I kind of spaced out, went left of center. I'm still trying to digest what you told me. Dad was the only one who called me Horsey Boy. You know, like a colt. Hearing you say it was like getting a fist in my gut and a hug at the same time. He must have known something was wrong to say that to the guy, right?"

"I don't know. I do know he said there was a lot of talking around your dad's voice. He was clear that your dad didn't jump from the plane. We didn't get to talk more, somebody pulled down the road."

"Yeah, the guy died, you know that, right?"

I rub my forehead. Yes, I'd heard it on the TV in the diner this morning. They are still trying to put out the fire.

"Yeah, God Squad. He was a nice guy."

"You thought about going to the police about it?"

"No."

"Okay, I get it. You get off in a few hours. Want to hang out?"

"I can't," I tell him. "I've got stuff I've got to do." He looks at me like he doesn't believe me. So I sigh. "And I don't want your girlfriend chasing me down right now because she thinks I'm trying to hit on you or something. I mean, considering her daddy is a cop and already wants my butt in jail. I'm not pushing any buttons on her."

"I thought maybe you could show me what you've been working on with the murder stuff, with the plane wreck. We could watch some TV."

"You've got everything I've got," I tell him, hold out my arms to my sides.

"You think? Listen, Taylor doesn't need to know we hang out. I'm not telling her."

"I'm not that person you think I am, Colt Lucero," I tell him softly. "I'm just not. Sorry, no sneaky, no slumming tonight."

"I wasn't implying we do anything more than talk," he backtracks quickly. I roll my eyes.

"Listen, I appreciate you bailing me out from the

crap I get myself into again, I really do," I tell him. "But we're obviously not very good at just talking to each other. Either I say something stupid or you say something stupid or—"

"That was good, right?" he interrupts. "I mean until the part—"

"You found out you just slept with the woman you'd sworn to destroy?"

"Yeah, pretty much." He forces a smile, shrugs. "Does it mean anything if I don't feel that way anymore? I'm trying to be a little more open?"

I hear Joe hollering from inside telling me my break is over. I don't answer Colt, just shrug while I go back through the doors.

CHAPTER 38

GETTING BUSTED BY GIL

Katie sews. She grew up Amish and said she'd been sewing since she was five or six. So in return for me teaching her daughter, Kendra, and three other little girls a bit of ballet, she is fixing my tutu so the tulle material isn't dangling from a few threads to my knees.

She is sitting in with me and the girls while I show them the proper way to stand. They are sweet and attentive, big eyes looking up at me even after Mia shoved four year-old Tia on the ground for giving me a hug. I went to Gil's house and trudged through his attic again looking for some of my kid-size tutus Anna's stored up there. I think Gil must believe I'm trying to find some old family treasure because he came up the stairway behind me and hovered at the opening the entire time I went through the boxes.

"Where'd you get that truck?" he asked me. "Do you have to park it in the driveway so people think it's mine? Park it in the street. No, maybe don't do that. The trash guys might pick it up."

"Ha ha. Not funny," I returned. "I bought it from Rocky." I did. It was eight last night before I knocked on his door. Rocky had been sleeping all day, getting ready to go into work for the late shift. He was grumpy and scratching his head. His hair was sticking up and he looked like a chubby eight year old who'd gotten awakened in the middle of the night. He told me his truck was old, ugly, and beat up, but it worked. I told him that I wasn't looking for a boyfriend so it was exactly what I wanted, something that actually worked. Age and beauty came down a far second and third from my experience with men—and vehicles.

I picked up the truck and Rocky was right. It used to be a candy apple red Chevy truck. At least when the first owner pulled it off the lot in 1952. Now the paint is almost skinned off down to the primer so it is a dull gray and spotted like an Appaloosa horse. Rocky bought it to fix up and between working at the bar as a bouncer and trying to keep his dad's car shop afloat, he never got the time. "It's kind of like a horse, Tango, you hate to see it go out to pasture and never get ridden." He did look like a sad cowboy when I drove it out of the lot.

Rocky also eyed Zane curiously. He told me if I was into picking up stray pups, I should just go to the pound. The boy was bad news. I guess he'd seen him hanging around the bar, panhandling. I'm surprised he recognizes Zane. He looks like an all-American boy after he's cleaned up and shaved and wearing some of Kevin's jeans and a t-shirt I dug out of the closet this morning. He's got this reddish-blonde hair and freckles and he's always grinning at me like he's getting ready to tell me the punch line to a joke. Despite Kevin and Rocky's warning he's kind of difficult to be angry toward. When I came home from work, he's got peanut butter and jelly sandwiches, canned chicken noodle soup spooned into bowls, and chocolate milk all set on the table and ready for us when Mia and I walk through the door.

"So when were you going to tell you were delivering for Jessica, Zane?" I ask him while I take a sip of the tepid soup. I look up and catch his eyes before they fall away. His face pales. I'm learning he's very mild and gentle. In fact, I think he was terrified to leave the couch today. I suppose I identify with him. My dad hit me without reason or with very little reason. I believe he has gone through similar situations as me. I think he is testing me. I'm like his newest owner in a long line of abusive owners. He doesn't want to get hit, but he is trying to figure out that line that I will hurt him. It's a tightrope walk.

"Do you want me to leave?" he asks.

"No."

"I—I get it. You don't want me around your little girl. I don't do drugs. I promise. I just delivered stuff for her," he tells me. "I mean, I did smoke weed with her a couple times at her house, but that's it. I was sleeping at the park and I hadn't eaten in a few days. She gave me burgers and fries and paid me ten or fifteen bucks to drop packages off at people's houses. There was a couple times I met people in cars." He stands up, knocks the table and all three soups wiggle back and forth, spilling noodles and broth on the old wood. I jump up to catch Mia's before it pours to her chair.

"Crud, I'm sorry. I'm so sorry. I did stuff for her. I can do stuff for you. Anything you want. Just show me—"

It happened so fast, I hadn't even had time to say anything to him. I just stop there. I had reached over to snatch up a towel while he is bumbling around trying to push the liquid from the edge of the table. I can hear his hands slapping on the broth.

"Just let it go," I tell him. But he's like freaking out and now trying to get the soup from where I was sitting. "Zane, just let it go!" I yell it and it is loud. Mia jumps and Zane comes to a complete halt. Only the sound of the soup dribbling off the table and pattering on to the drab linoleum floor fills the air. I have to let him know I don't take shit, but I won't hurt him. I walk the same tightrope. We have to meet in the middle, figure out how to pass each other or one of us gives and backtracks to the other side. I have a good feeling Jessica didn't need to pump this broke pup up with drugs to have him coming back to her. He'd do tricks for a hamburger, I guess.

He thinks I'm mad at him. Zane's eyes are wide. He steps back, gets a look like he's sizing up the door and the trying to figure out the consequences of passing me on that tightrope and bolting out the door.

"Look, it isn't hurting anything," I say softly, point to the little pools by the table legs. "There's three years of that stuff caked in there from Kevin and me and Mia dumping our cups of orange juice, dropping our cereal bowls, and once, I even dumped an entire gallon of milk on it because the plastic jug slipped out of my hand. You did what you had to do to survive, do you hear me? My dad beat me across the kitchen and into the living when I was five for dropping a bowl on the floor. I'm not that person. I'm telling you right now, you can go into the kitchen cabinets and break every plate I've got and I'll stand right here and watch you do it. I'll be hurt. That is all. Do you understand?"

"Yeah."

"Now, you stop doing that stuff," I tell him. "From now on, you don't smoke weed. You don't deal drugs. Because you are in my house, you have to follow my rules. Not—not crazy-ass rules, but normal rules. And the only thing you have to do with me or for me is don't let the dishes in the sink get too high. You're here. You are safe and can stay here as long as you want. Like a family, okay? Like a little brother."

"A family." He seems to nibble on this. "What if my dad finds out I'm here."

"You're eighteen, right?" I ask him and he nods.

"I just turned eighteen last week. I still have another year of school."

"Okay, so you're a big boy now. He can't make you go home." I see Zane kind of roll his gaze like he knows that isn't true. "And I've got a baseball bat, a can of bear repellent, and a really, really bad attitude. Just ask any guy I've ever dated. Even some I haven't. I'm not afraid to use any of it or all of it."

He thinks this is funny and laughs a little even though he is still shaking. I tell him we'll figure something out, get him to another school if his dad is teaching at Hensley Grove High School. He just needed to lay low for a couple weeks, not leave the apartment. We finally sit down and eat soggy peanut butter and jelly sandwiches and talk about stupid stuff. I'm trying to figure out how I'm going to feed an eighteen year old who probably eats more food than a diesel truck sucks down gas. Then I go get the truck, stop by Joe's diner for the day's leftovers, and head up to the old mill. I swear Zane to secrecy and he looks a bit overwhelmed when Big Bob gives him a stinky bear hug. Everybody is still stuck here. Their homes or makeshift tents along the river are still sopping wet or under water. So they sit around in broken lawn chairs, stuff their mouths with the food I brought and watch me dance with the girls.

"Car outside!"

I don't know the warning, so I'm standing there with wide eyes when the lanterns all go out. I suppose being the closest adult, Tia and Kendra bolt to me thinking that I know to flee through the side door and out the back. I don't. I'm almost dumbstruck by the sudden darkness. Mia and the smaller three start yowling. Of course, not being a local to this little community, I wasn't made aware of the escape plan. Nor was Zane. He has the intelligence to disappear into the dark corner. However, when the front door explodes with people coming inside, I'm standing dead center in the middle of the room huddling with five little girls in tutus.

I'm blinded by flashlights, four of them. They are the big ones like Poppy uses when the electric goes out. A huge shadow comes between me and the lights and I see the silhouette of Big Bob coming to save us and swinging a two by four plank in both his hands.

"Umph, attack! Help! I'm being attacked!"

Oh, God, I recognize that voice. Then I'm jumping up and screaming for Big Bob and an old man who is brandishing a pink lawn chair to stop because it is Gil they are getting ready to beat to a pulp on the ground. I can see him faintly wallowing on the ground with his arms and legs flapping in the air like a turtle turned on its back.

"It's my brother! Stop!" I'm wagging my own arms in the air, traipsing between them like a horror show ballerina in my black tights and an old lime green tank top.

While the dust settles, I push away the flashlight shining in my eyes and stare down a Gil with my hands on my hips. I can hear Mia sniffling behind me before she runs over and clambers up into my arms. I hear assorted echoes of sobs from the little girls while Katie slips into the room with a lantern and swoops over to the girls.

"What the hell?" I spit down at him while he pushes himself to his feet. I look up to see Colt stepping back and of all people, Adrien looking a bit ashamed in the rear and—oh, my gosh.

"Poppy, is that—you?" I can see him slithering through the door with a lurching step over the old boards. His eyes are darting around like he's a lizard looking for a fly. Even he appears to be confused gaping now at the little girls crying and the chairs along the wall knocked over. The food everybody was munching on along with the paper plates and plastic silverware had been dropped to the floor. Two lanterns have toppled and are spinning in slow motion.

"Did you—" I grunt at Poppy, turn my head to Gil. "—follow me here?"

They are all silent for a moment. Eyes blink like a

herd of deer suddenly caught in the headlights of a semi truck. I don't think they had a plan to fall back on which completely ticks me off. They must have just jumped in a car and sped off into the night, dead set on saving me before I shoved a dirty, used needle in my arm.

I know why they are here. And I can see them looking from Big Bob to me and then Katie and the girls. The sudden impact of it hits me in the belly like a hard fist.

"Oh, sweetheart." Poppy looks confused, his head snapping back and forth. He looks me up and down, must see my tights, see Mia in her tights. "Gil said—I don't understand, we thought you came here—oh."

"Gil said what?" I snap my eyes over to my foster brother while he stands, sloughs off the dust from his pants "Is my life so bad that you think I need to go somewhere and shoot up or buy weed or whatever smack druggies do?"

"Oh, c'mon, Tango," Gil intercedes. "Don't act so surprised. You've been acting squirrelly all week. I ran into Kevin at the gas pumps and he even said you were acting strange. That says something, doesn't it? What are you doing here?"

"She's been bringing us food." That's Katie and I turn. She smiles at me and then turns angry eyes to Gil.

"Squirrelly?" I hiss. "Is that how you describe me? You should assume," I walk up to him and poke him in the chest, "that I've got enough sense in my head to be like *perfect* you! But no, nobody ever expects you to do something like sneaking off and doing drugs Gilbert Baldwin, you ass. Why would you question my intentions? Because I have never given you or anybody any indication that I do drugs. You just assume because it is me, because you think I can't do shit with my life, because I'm working at a diner and can't get my classes finished. Well, you don't know anything about me and I don't want you to know anything about me!" I yell it and it echoes off the walls. "Get out of here and leave me alone!"

"Well, you're here." He waves it off with his hand, looks around the shabby room and shoves off any embarrassment of his intrusion and lack of trust in my morals. "Illegally, I presume."

I don't say anything. Mia is stuffed into my shoulder. I glare at Poppy. I can't even look at Adrien and Colt. I know they are shoved up by the door and keeping quiet to save their butts. I don't even want to know why they are there and what was said about me to get them to this point.

"Please leave," I say.

"Come on, Rae," Gil grunts, leans in to me. "Normal people don't hang out in abandoned buildings. I'm not leaving until you get in your truck and leave."

"Normal people don't stalk other people," I retort. I'm almost embarrassed for his forthrightness. I turn to Katie and see her cringe. I see Colt finally coming around Gil, pushing a hand on his shoulder. "Come on, she's fine."

I know Gil is just looking for a way out of the situation. He nods to Colt, drags his gaze back to mine. "See, Whiskey Tango, it is stuff like this that left you stuck with your stupid nickname. You know," he looks at Mia, then back to me. "Stuff like that."

"Gilbert!" Poppy eases past Gil. He's looking around the room. A couple people slipped back inside. Most are gone. "Poppy," I pull at his sleeve. "I'm begging you to make Gil keep this quiet. Please."

"This place isn't safe for these people, Rae," he says softly. "It isn't just that they are staying here illegally. The building is falling down—"

"They've got no place else to go, Poppy," I groan. "No place."

CHAPTER 39

BLACK STAR

"So this is where my mysterious girl with the black star conceals herself when she is not spying for whatever menacing agency is paying her the highest tip." Adrien looks around my little dance floor. "Étoile Noire." I tip my head, questioning. "Black star." He reaches out and lays a hand on my arm, turns me slightly and pokes a finger at my scrawny shoulder. "Why do you dishonor such a beautiful body with a tattoo?"

"I didn't," I tell him with my chin high. "I'd like to tell you it is a symbol of an elite club of emissaries for the government. You obviously don't like to play much so I'll be direct. It's not. My daddy's drunk buddy did it with an ink pen and a needle. Not the dad who was here tonight, my birth father. I didn't have a choice. I was five or six. It hurt. My ex-boyfriend said he can always tell when I talk about my dad, I rub it with my fingers."

"Five or six." He turns me more. I see him grimace. Shit, my shoulder blade scar. I know my tank top is exposing it. "And the scar?"

"Another choice he made. Dropping me on a whiskey bottle when I was two or three." I push him away, stand up straight, and wiggle my tank top higher. "I hate the sound of athletic tape because it makes this grating sound when you pull it." I cringe. "It's the same sound the masking tape made that he used to adhere my skin together over the cut. You want more of the imperfect me?" I ask. I don't wait for an answer. "If you see me pull my lip, it means I'm lying. I started doing that when daddy told me he'd beat the hell out of me if I told the cops he hit me." I don't know why I'm telling him this. I suppose it makes most people's eyes turn dull, makes them go away. *Control Burn,* that's what Colt called it. They just don't know how to react, don't know what to say. Then, they walk away as fast as they can. "I don't know why I'm telling you this. I know I'm not perfect. That's one of the many reasons I dance here in a dingy old building instead of where other people will judge me. You don't understand. You are perfect. I'm sure every dancer you dance with is perfect and whole and beautiful."

"Yes, they are."

He doesn't apologize for my dad like most people do or say he is sorry that it happened. He doesn't deny I'm imperfect and he is perfect. It is humbling. I just want to pinch him.

"And that's why you use me. I get it." I look toward the door. Mia is playing with one of the little girls on a blanket on the floor. "Shane used to do it to me too, make me his crash test dummy so he could complete his masterpieces without banging them up."

"These masterpieces, who are they? It is Taylor and Alexandra?"

"And Delia. I guess Hannah, too, back then," I add. "He never wanted to drop them, leave little bruises to show for the competitions. He told me that all the time. Me, I was already dinged up before he came along."

Mia comes running across the floor and I snatch her up with tickling fingers on her neck.

"Well, I hope we don't do this again," I tell him, wiggle my finger in the air. "I've got to get her home. It's bedtime."

"You don't want to dance tonight? Can't she play with the little girls? We can dance right here."

"No, Adrien, I already danced by myself and I'm

completely worn out." Then I turn and wiggle my eyes. "Please, in honor of the Society of the Dark Star, don't send your Russian mafia friends after me. I would hate to battle them this late at night."

I think it pisses him off. He is used to getting his own way, having girls fawn all over him, beg to get him to dance. Billy said Delia and Taylor were in tears when they heard he was coming to the school. Now, he just stares at me like the high school football captain would stare at the ugly girl with frizzy hair, a big nose and pimples sitting on the bench who just turned him down for a dance. He thinks it incredible that someone as bent, broken, and poor as me would reject him.

"Go pay your teacher, give her a hug before she goes." Katie's voice echoes in the air. She has the girls dressed. They are their daytime clothes. I know what it means. I give the girls a big hug in my arms. One of them already has tears coming out of her eyes.

"I'll miss you," I tell them softly.

Adrien, he is visibly upset when we walk out the door. He doesn't say anything until we part halfway to our cars. "Why were they crying?"

"Because I won't see them again."

"Why won't you see them again?" He sounds like a little kid asking me these questions. "You are their teacher."

"Because they know my Poppy is going to call the police and try to get them into a shelter. He means well, but there isn't a shelter for a good hundred miles. And they are afraid they'll take away their kids."

"Where will they go?"

"I don't know. Back to the river, maybe another abandoned building. The viaduct under the highway."

Colt is leaning with his back against the driver's side door of my new used truck. We both know he is blocking my escape. He's swinging his keys around the long lanyard holding them. His posture isn't defensive, but his eyes have taken on a dull, cynical glint. I stop too late to tell Zane to duck back into the shadows. He's attached to my side and I don't think he's going anywhere soon.

"I tried to talk them out of following you." Colt looks up, eyes Zane with what appears little surprise and settles his gaze on me. "Just so you know."

I stop just short of where his foot is sticking out, turn long enough to wiggle my finger at Zane and tell him to get inside.

"Really?" I shift Mia on my hip. "Because I've personally seen you convince way too many cops to dig a little deeper in their heart, their conscience and think how their reactions might affect everybody around the people they were going to arrest. I think you could talk a horn off a unicorn if you thought it would save the world."

He tries to hide a bleached out laugh, shakes his head. "You've got me wrong."

"I just know because this happened, my friends in there, they are going to be gone and it is my fault. They aren't going to stick around. They are scared Poppy is going to call the cops. They've got no place else to go."

"It isn't your fault."

"It is my fault." I toss my hands out. "And what were you thinking dragging Adrien here? My God, he's probably never seen the inside of a grocery store, much less—" I turn and wave a hand at the dilapidated factory behind me. "—this."

"He was waiting for you at the theatre again after his class with Shane when Gil called. I think he said he's there for a couple days. I know he's working with Taylor and Alexandra, trying to get them ready for some tryouts in New York. He heard me talking, wanted to come along." Yep, I'm still the trial-run, ballet punching bag. He jabs a thumb behind him. "I rode in his rental car. I was hoping you'd give me a ride back to my car."

I roll my eyes, wiggle my head, and stick out my tongue when he says Taylor and Alexandra's names.

"You know you get that same expression every time somebody mentions Taylor or Alex," he points out with a bit of soft laughter. He pokes me in the shoulder. "Don't tell me you're jealous of the attention they get from Shane."

"Why would I be jealous of Taylor and Alex?" I know he is going to laugh again because he's right, I spontaneously make a face when I mention their names. But it isn't Shane's attention I don't want them to get. It is Adrien's. Shit.

"I don't know. Because I've seen you dance with Adrien Moreau and I've seen both of those girls dance with him." He reaches out, twirls his keys right in front of me so they bang against my folded arms. "He's going through the motions with both of them like he's bored stiff. They are like robots. It's like they know the moves, but they just don't know how to use them and express themselves at the same time. When you dance with Adrien, you two are in love, mad passionate love."

"Ha ha, mad passionate love." I laugh. "Thank you. But since you're dating—I'm not sure which one it is this week," I divulge. I'm not sure. I could have sworn I saw Alexandra holding his hand once and Taylor trying to fit snug under his arm another time. "I find it odd you're telling me this."

"Okay, so you noticed that too?" Colt steps back, then bangs me hard with his keys. "I'm not sure either. They've got this weird thing going like I'm either with one or the other. If one is doing something, the other is with me. I'm not sure which one I'm dating. They tow me round like a puppy on a leash. At least, that's what your brother says when he makes fun of me about it."

"Is this where I'm supposed to say: *attaboy*?" I think my remark came out more scathingly than it had played out in my head. Colt snaps his attention away from his keys. When he does they swing wide and high and belt me in the elbow.

"Ow!"

"Crud, I'm sorry." He pushes out his hand, stops and wipes a palm down his face while I rub the sting away. "I didn't mean to do that. And I didn't say I liked it. It's like I said, weird." He stops, looks up at the night sky. "Small towns. They kind of suck with their small gene pool. Taylor's the chief's daughter. I work with the cops all the time. Alexandra's stepdad is my boss at the mission. I'm kind of afraid if I don't walk the line with those two, I'm out of here. Then I think it doesn't matter. I'm not getting anything done here, I'm just running circles over and over."

I laugh. "Yeah, well, I think you're wrong about not getting things done. You helped Zane."

"And look where he is." Colt cocks his head toward the truck. I rock back and forth on my feet.

"He's safe. And happy. I mean, staying with me and Mia isn't exactly the perfect fake family, but—" I wave my words away. "You still a little messed up about your dad's message to Bogie?"

"You can tell?"

"It's a lot to swallow. Maybe you need to set new goals," I shrug. "Did you want to tell me something before we got in?" I ask him. Zane was in the truck making faces at

Mia. I can hear the two laughing.

"Huh? Oh, yeah." He almost tears his eyes away from me. I don't know how else to describe the look he gives me. He is concentrating on my face so hard all of a sudden it is like he is focusing on a picture and I think I caught him off-guard with my question.

"You know you're putting a stick into a wasp nest messing with Jessie, right?" Colt says softly. "She doesn't want anybody messing with her boys."

"Her boys?" I laugh. "How would you know? Don't tell me you buy drugs from her too."

"No, but I get to clean up the messes she leaves with the families, Tango." He stuffs his hands in his pockets. Now he's rocking back and forth on his feet. "And I'm not talking about just a few like your buddy in there."

"Is that what you thought you were doing tonight, God Squad? Before you answer, I already feel like I've got a knife in my gut seeing my Poppy here. Everybody tells me to trust and that I've got to open myself up a bit and let people in. And you know what? I'm the one that keeps getting dinged by everybody doing this kind of crap, thinking I'm on drugs. Choose your words wisely before you answer. This is a deal breaker."

"A deal breaker?" Colt does that thing where he rubs his hand through his hair. But this time, he's got both his hands on his head and he's looking up at the black above us. "You're unpredictable. You're reckless. You disregard laws like you think you're above them and you flaunt it in paint from one end of town to the other. You're like the most talented person I've ever known, dancing and with your art. But you waste it in old buildings and before empty seats. You're batcrap crazy one minute and—" he waves a hand toward the factory building behind him. "—frigging feeding all the people who needed my help that I didn't even know exist. You're a wildcard, Tango—"

"Enough. Shut up. You're not answering the question." I push my hand out. "I know my weaknesses. Please get in the truck. I've had a bad day. I don't need you adding—"

"No, you shut up," Colt says sharply and catches my shoulder just as I turn. "Everything I just said, they aren't weaknesses or I wouldn't have said them. I just don't want to answer and I'm rambling. I guess what I'm saying is I can't answer the question if it is a deal breaker, alright? I don't want to be wrong."

CHAPTER 40

LOVE ON THE BATHROOM SINK

It's the bathroom this time. It's the only place I've got in my two-bedroom apartment that's private tonight. Zane is in Mia's room laying on her teeny bed and watching a movie on my computer. Mia's sleeping soundly in my bed. It's amazing how easy it is for a man to get me in bed (well, the bathroom sink) with a few twists of words spit out like a politician evading questions with more questions instead of what he'd really like to say. Because after Colt said those words and after he'd run his hand through his hair a thousand times like he's a nervous seventeen year-old waiting for his homecoming date, I just kind of blurted out: "Do—do you want to come over and let the ice cream melt on the floor again?"

"Is that code for—something?" he asks. "Because now you're talking riddles too."

I laugh. It is my laugh that sounds like a witch cackle and a whoop and it is loud and almost as bad as my snort that sneaks out sometimes.

"Is that your laugh?" Colt pokes me in the belly. "Because if we are talking deal breakers—geez, don't look at me like that. I'm just kidding."

"Oh, my, it is. Poppy always warned me to get in a couple weeks of dates with a boy before I let that cat out of the bag." I'm feeling really stupid I even said what I said. "Never mind, I was just meaning that we could—"

"I know what you are suggesting." Then he is all serious. "You're talking to a guy that goes back to an empty house. I don't even have a cat, just a bunch of messages on my answering machine telling me to call my mom."

And so I close the door behind us forty minutes later and we stand there looking at each other awkwardly. I changed into a pair of soft shorts and a t-shirt and Colt keeps reaching out and tugging my shorts, dragging me toward him. I keep pushing away. "You do realize what our dates are that lead up to—this each time, right?" I ask softly, leaning against the sink while Colt steps back, leans against the bathroom door. "Fighting. I'm not sure if these are the best tools in building a relationship." Then my face turns red because I feel the heat beating from forehead to neck while I take a good stare at the shower. "I mean, if you want a relationship. I mean, maybe you and Taylor-and-slash-or Alex are already in a relationship."

"Do you really care?" Colt just takes two steps across the gritty linoleum floor. He reaches around my shoulder, tugs me right up to him by my shirt and kisses me softly on the lips. "You've got the most beautiful eyes, Tango," he whispers. "I think they are purple?" He pulls his head back enough so his eyes dart back and forth between my own. "I stare at them, then I realize I'm staring at them like I can't pull away and you probably think that sounds creepy."

I'm lacking words which says a lot for the way he's looking at me. I'm caught up in the way his hair is falling across his own eyes. They are darker blue tonight basked beneath the two yellow lights of three above the sink that aren't burned out.

"Say something," he says. I blink.

"Like what?"

"I don't know."

"Um, I like your jeans?" Oh, that sounded ridiculous. There is a lull then.

"Okay," Colt says quietly. "Ask me if I care if you're going out with that Sasquatch you were dancing for at the bar." I look up, see him smiling down at me.

"Do you care?"

"Crap, you weren't supposed to really ask it." He does that thing of rolling a hand through his hair again. "Yeah, I do. You on the back seat of his Harley riding off into the night with your dress hiked almost up to your hips makes me just a bit envious. He probably would have laid Kyle Matteson flat instead of getting the crap beat out of him across the lawn."

My heart makes a flip-flop jump in my chest. I wasn't expecting that. I can feel Colt's fingers tugging at the hair behind my neck, tickling around back there. Goosebumps trickle up my arm and I shiver, lean into him with my forehead on his chest.

"Well, okay, I seem to recall seeing Finn with a black eye when I went on the second date with him. And I heard, from good sources, that you dragged him from one end of Poppy's house to the other."

"Oh, you had to bring that up," Colt throws his head back, groans. "If Ralph Edward ever gets wind of that, I could get my butt booted out of here."

"Well, luck is on your side with that. I don't think his stepdaughter wants you gone." I laugh. "And, by the way, the Sasquatch is Rocky Merino," I divulge. "He's my next door neighbor and Kevin's best friend. He's not my type, a little too rough around the edges for anything more than friendship. He thinks I'm too skinny. I'm not dancing *for* him by any means. I don't want to dance alone, so he goes and catches a few winks while I do."

"I don't know how a guy could sleep through that. Holy crap. Is he dead inside?"

Colt gives me such a funny face that I stifle a giggle. Then I tickle his sides and look up to see if he smiles. He does and man, I like his smile. "Here, I know you're a player, Tango. You like lots of men. It's fine. What we have here, it's fine," he says softly and grabs me around the waist. He picks me up, plants my rear on the sink. I don't get to deny the charges. I'm not a player. I know he is. I don't know why he's throwing that back on me. I suppose, right then, it is the least of my worries. He's kissing my neck and I'm wrapping my legs around him, dragging off his shirt.

"You still looking for a muse?" he asks me while I run my fingers along his chest, slowly until they stop just short of the muscles on his shoulders. I look up, take him in.

"You made it pretty clear at the water tower that night you didn't want anything to do with—"

"Well, I suppose it depends on the situation. Don't think I didn't see the four horses of the apocalypse down at the tracks, I think you already used me—" Colt stops, shrugs it off and sighs. "When you asked, I didn't know what a muse was and then, I felt like an idiot. I didn't know you. I only knew about—the Tango porn and people told me you're kind of wild."

"I'm wild?"

"I had to look it up. I thought you meant like some kind of a sex toy or something. I didn't know it was somebody you use for inspiration."

"Oh." I stifle a giggle. For some reason, I feel comfortable with Colt right now. I don't feel like the awkward one like I do with everybody else, bumbling around for the right words, tripping over the last stupid thing that came out of my mouth. Right now, he's the one swallowing hard, stuttering and looking everywhere but at me. "Yeah, like the graffiti at the church. So you really did look up the pictures?"

"Oh, yeah." Colt mumbles, then looks over my head. "Who could resist talk about Tango porn? The label alone could lure a bee off the last flower on earth."

I'm scooting up, kissing his chest and getting wrapped up in his arms. "So I'm getting the feeling you're a closet bad-girl addict," I throw out at him. I'm sliding off my t-shirt, unsnapping my bra. His cheeks are suddenly burnt red and he's bumbling around like he wants to say something, doesn't know what.

"Answer me, Colt." I settle on the sink, then jerk his head down and lay into him with a hard kiss.

"Yeah, maybe?" His voice is hoarse. His eyes are a little wide. I don't think he was expecting me to kiss him again before I grab on to the belt at the waist of his jeans and jerk him foreword. "Well, you chose to visit wisely," I whisper. "Because I'm feeling bad girl tonight."

"What are you doing?"

I'm back to being awkward again while we sit on the couch eating a bowl of popcorn with only the light of the TV covering us. I'd plopped down on one end, Colt sat down hard on the other. Then about five minutes into a 1980s sitcom with boxed laughter, he scoots over and snatches up my right hand in both of his hands.

"What does it look like?" he answers. "I'm holding your hand."

"You better watch it," I tell him. "I'll think you like me."

"I do like you."

He says that and I tell him when you like a girl, you don't hold hands like that. I take one of his and slide my fingers between his, twining them together. He shifts back and we sit there holding hands. It isn't discomfiting, just different than what I'm used to doing. Kevin didn't even bother to hold my hand as an attempt to get me into bed. Shane pretended he didn't know me outside of class, so holding hands was never an option.

"I like it." I announce it and Colt swings his head around.

"The show?" I know he keeps watching for Zane to come out of the room. I know that even if he does like me, he doesn't want anybody else to know. Then I kind of get the feeling in the back of my head that he's just using me to get something he can't get from Taylor or Alexandra because God knows they don't think of anything but ballet and themselves.

"No, holding hands." My phone goes off and I slide my arm to the couch stand and pick it up. Gil.

"Hey, so dad's upset," he tells me on the other end. "You need to talk to him. I think he feels worse about busting in on you and finding you were feeding a bunch of poor people than if you'd been shooting up."

"Hey, I'm upset, Gil," I mutter, turning to roll my eyes at Colt. "I'm really hurt that you'd assume I'd be shooting up. Listen, in eighth grade, who was it that talked you out of going to Janie Karnes house to smoke weed, huh? Me. When you got drunk in tenth grade, who got Poppy's car and picked you up?"

"You didn't have a driver's permit. You almost got us killed."

"That's a valid point for another conversation subject, not the one I'm focusing on now," I tell him. I hear Colt snicker next to me. I know he can hear what we are saying. Still, he is leaning forward, dragging my hand with him. "But I really don't want to talk about it."

"Did Colt talk to you?" He shot that out and I see Colt

roll his hand along his face uneasily. Then his eyes slide over to mine and I question his own with my gaze. He shakes his head back and forth.

"No?"

"That sounded more like a question. He was supposed to talk to you." Gil sighs on the other end, my eyes work over to Colt who is nodding his head up and down and looking a bit pale. "I don't know what's going on with you two. Obviously something. You don't need to be hanging around with him, you understand? He doesn't need to be hanging around you. I talked to him and he agreed. I don't want to see any of my friends hurt and Taylor's a nice girl. Colt's a nice guy. Don't be pulling the whiskey tango trick on us again. Mom and dad can't do this again."

"They are nice, but I'm what? White trash?" I want to hang up the phone. I feel the anger tickle my shoulders. "This isn't the eighteenth century, Gil. I can choose my friends." I tug my hand away, scoot up in the seat to rise. I'm trying desperately to move far enough away so Colt can't hear.

"Listen, I'm not an idiot. I know Mia's dad is Shane Delgado. I was the one that used to pick you up from your classes after I got my license." Gil's voice drops. "Raeanna, you are what you are. I can't change that. God knows dad and mom tried, but can't change you. I'm just asking you to stop being—well, *you* for once and think about everybody else and how your actions impact them."

Too late, I hang up. Colt is standing up when I turn. I'd only made it two steps away.

"Was that still within earshot?" I cringe.

"What do you want me to say?" Colt is shoving his hands into his pockets.

"Just tell me the truth."

"The truth is I'll tell Gil anything he wants to hear so I can sit around the couch and hold hands with you," Colt says. "And you know I knew about Delgado."

"I'm not the whore people make me out to be," I say softly. "I'm not. I didn't know what to tell them, so I told them I didn't know who the dad was. I mean, I didn't want them chasing down ghosts or some poor boy who didn't do anything. My head was spinning and everybody was yelling at me. So they all assumed I was doing every boy who came along. And yeah, I knew he was married. I was just stupid and fifteen going on sixteen when he started keeping me after class. I thought it was cool, all the attention. Anna thought I was some brilliantly, gifted protégé to Shane. I was, God Squad, nothing more than someone Shane could pour on the complements to get an easy lay."

"You are gifted."

I look up, surprised he wasn't wagging a finger at me like I felt everybody else did. "No, Colt," I shrug. "I was about as naïve as they come. I thought I was just special. I didn't even think about him having a wife. I just wanted to please him." Colt doesn't say anything and we're standing there in silence.

"So, you want me to leave?" Colt asks.

"Do you want to leave?"

"No, not really. I mean, it's late—" He puffs out his cheeks. "No, I don't want to go. Let's watch another show."

CHAPTER 41

NICK GRADY

"You're Nick Grady, right?" I'm staring at the back of a man walking into Hane's Liquor Store in a strip mall in Ashton, Kentucky about an hour from Cincinnati and two hours from Hensley Grove. He's got his hand on the door and it's more like a bear paw—huge and bulky.

"Who wants to know?" He turns, takes an aggressive step toward me, and I want to shrink back. He's probably six feet and seven or so inches of big, mean and scarred up from battles past. His face is weathered and his nose has been broken so many times, it is nearly even with his cheekbones.

"M—me," I stutter and want to kick myself. If there was one good thing that my daddy taught me, it was to never shrink back, never show fear. He told me once it was better to jump into a bonfire, than to shy away from a candle flame. So I jump into the bonfire. "Me. I'm Raeanna, well my dad called me Starr. I'm Dell Smythe's daughter. You were friends with my dad when I was like three or four."

I suppose I'm giving him a wide margin when I say he was my dad's friend. I only remembered them fighting in the front seat of the car when I'd sit in the back seat. I remember playing in his dingy mechanics shop and daddy would sit on an overturned bucket, drinking beer and talking to Nick while he worked under the cars. I can't remember what their conflicts were, I was too little. I suppose it was stupid stuff because daddy liked to fight.

But I was laying up last night and staring at the ceiling and heard Missus Finch yelling at the door of Kelsey

Riddel's apartment because it was two in the morning and she was fighting with the newest boyfriend. Fighting. Then I thought of daddy and Nick always fighting. I sat up straight in bed.

"Bethel." I'd said it aloud while I tossed my legs over the side of the bed and listened to Missus Finch yowl. Daddy had a friend somewhere near Bethel. I remember passing the road sign off the highway, spelling it out each time when I was five or six.

I hopped up out of bed and rifled through the copies of the police files Billy had pulled off my phone. He had gone to the store, purchased a three ring binder and on the front, there was a little clear plastic opening where a cover could be inserted. There, Billy had tucked a map he had made for me showing the places the girls had lived before they died with a little red dot, then the location each had been found, he labeled with a blue star. Inside, he had color coded the information on each girl including interviews with their families and friends.

I suppose what caught me tonight was that Billy had posted a little yellow Post-It note on my front door. It said: *Found a note that said all four girls soaked in bleach. Found two girls in Indiana (unsolved) soaked in bleach after death.* Bleach. The image of a white bleach container popped up in my head. Daddy always had like six or seven huge bottles of bleach in the kitchen. Bleach. The scent reminded me of somewhere, an old garage we used to visit somewhere over in Cincinnati. The garage had a gross little bathroom and there was bleach by the toilet—

I had stuck the Post-It note on the binder and now I rub it down with my fingers. Then, I poke the little red star at Bethel where Tammy Lynn had lived. Bleach. Uncle Nick's garage. Nick Grady. I look up Nick Grady's old garage address online. Sure enough, Nick Grady lived and worked only four miles from where Tammy had grown up.

Now, Nick looks me up and down. His upper lip twitches ever so slightly. "So he's coming to collect, sending his kid?"

"Collect?" I ask him. I shake my head back and forth. "No, I just wanted to ask you some questions. I wanted to know if you knew where he was."

"Dead, I hope. We all better pray he's dead, right?" He laughs and starts to turn.

"Can I talk to you? Just five minutes. Five questions. I need to know if he's still alive, still around."

"How'd you find me?"

"I found an old number online and it was your ex-wife. She told me you worked here."

He seems to contemplate my answer, turns and looks over my shoulder. "I seen them talking on the news about the dead girls showing up in Hensley Grove. That what you're trying to find out?"

"Yeah."

"Well, if you don't remember, they let him out after they couldn't match his DNA on any of them, couldn't match anything on those girls."

And I know from Billy's notes, that there is a new thing they have in common that only the cops know. They were all washed clean inside and out and soaked in bathtubs of bleach before being dumped. "And he had an alibi for—Tammy's death, right? Tammy Lynn. You lived near Bethel, Ohio where she was abducted. She was at a concert in Cincinnati." I reach into my purse, tug out a copy of the newspaper clipping I pulled off the internet at about three in the morning. I open it to expose a picture of the man in front of me on the front page. There is a tiny woman walking with him. "That's you, right? And your mother is walking next to you. You were his alibi. That's what the front page said on the Cincinnati newspaper. You said he was at your house all night. Your mom did a polygraph test and passed it saying he was working on a car in your garage."

"Why don't you just let sleeping dogs lie, girl," His voice is as gruff and rough as his features. "Just let it lie. You go stirring up trouble and if he's alive, he's going to come at folks like he's got rabies."

"Did you know Eddy James, the man that took Tammy and her friends to the concert?" I ask him. "Because I found another newspaper about Tammy's death that said he was a worker at Grady's Tire and Battery. I remembered you owned a garage back then. I remember jumping on the tires in the back of the shop." I do. It was damp and dark and smelled like old oil—and bleach. Daddy laid down three tires for me to play on and I jumped from one to the next over and over.

Nick's head tips slightly left. He hones in on me and I take in a soft breath because he looks like he's going to lunge at me. His shoulders shift, he drops the door knob. His face is devoid of expression.

"He did work for me at the garage."

"In 1972?"

"You want me to answer that?"

"Yes. Please."

"Why don't you just ask me if your daddy murdered that girl, huh? Ask me if I lied on the stand and my mom lied on the stand in court and then passed a lie detector test that said he was in the garage with me behind my house. I mean, those are the real damn answers you want. I don't get why you're not asking them and you're going in circles."

"Because I didn't think you'd answer."

"Yes, because I'm not an idiot. I won't just like I won't answer any of the other questions you asked!" He starts to yell, wag his finger at me. A woman getting out of her car in the parking lot slams her door and looks over at us. I see his eyes widen. They are angry red when he drops his voice and works a fist at me from his waist. "I'll tell you the same thing I told the cops. He was with me that night. We were in the garage—"

"—with a girl named Tammy Lynn," I added for him sharply and loudly. "I believe you. But I also think you were with him that night and she was with *you* that night. Because I read an interview with her friend and her dad. I think she called the garage from a payphone because she was probably afraid to call her mom or dad when she couldn't find her friends. She skipped school. She went to the concert without their permission. She was supposed to stay the night at Janie Dickson's house. That was the plan, at least. Janie said she was staying at Tammy's. Tammy told her mom and dad they were staying at her house. They had an entire afternoon and night all covered without parents."

"Stop, or I swear to God I will—"

"Kill me?" I ask him.

"It wasn't me, dammit, it was your dad. Fuck. Fuck!" He holds his hands over his head. "Eddy was working for me and I paid him under the table so I didn't have to pay taxes. You get it? That bitch was always over here with that little Janie flirting it up and getting high while he worked. Eddy didn't have a phone. So she called from a payphone looking for a way to get ahold of him because she couldn't call home. She said her parents didn't know she went to a concert. So we went to pick her up and she was too damn scared to go home so she sat in my garage and drank beers with us. I told her to go get a piece of gum and chew it so her breath didn't smell like beer, then go home, tell her mom and dad she and Janie got in a fight. They didn't need to know more. She was listening to the radio with your dad, dancing and carrying on. She was young and stupid and flirting with him. I think she probably thought it was safe because he was her dad's age, like in his thirties, and she was jailbait. She passed out about two in the morning. I went in the house and went to bed. Your dad, I just assumed he took her back in the morning. They were both gone when I came into work. I didn't know anything until a week later when I saw she was missing in the newspaper. I didn't have a clue he could have touched her or even murdered her. Dell, he didn't touch her while I was there. My hands are clean of whatever happened. You go to the cops and I swear to God, I'll deny it. Then, I'll kill you."

CHAPTER 42

DANCING CLOSE WITH ADRIEN

"You are literally killing me," I tell Adrien. I'm laying on my belly on the floor and my chin rests on my wrist. He is twisting my leg above me making the toes touch far beyond my head.

"I haven't even gotten started with you." He's serious. At least his voice sounds unsmiling. His dank expression really hasn't changed since he'd pushed himself through the broken door of the Cannon Bread Mill factory and stood there staring across the floor. It was empty except for me and Mia and a bit of light seeping through the broken windows above. Oh, and a few pigeons flapping once in a while. I was dancing alone. Every one of the people living in the old building had disappeared. Gone. He'd just stood there while Colt slid in behind him. "The dancer will find a place to dance if she has the passion for dance," he said and dropped his bag. "Why didn't you show up at the theatre again?"

It was a good question. I look around his shoulder to Colt. "I told you I'd let you in. You didn't show."

Ah, he didn't know. "It's because I was removed from the property by Fields Community College police at eight-thirty this morning for trespassing."

"Trespassing?"

"Yes." This morning I got a call for a meeting at the Field's College dean's office. I'm thinking that they are wondering why I didn't sign up for classes next year and why I was just a little late on my tuition payment. But I'm sitting in Dean Paulson's office and Shane Delgado comes in the door. He points a finger at me and tells the dean I'd been sneaking into the buildings at night. Then he goes on to say I was using the room in the basement to teach a dance class.

"Shane told the dean I was breaking into the buildings and I was teaching dance classes there."

"You were teaching a dance class?" Colt shakes his head. "That doesn't make sense."

"Well, yes, it does in a manner of speaking," I answer. "I've been working with the Fields Acapella Club for the yearly competition. I don't get paid. I'm doing it for Billy. They never win. Nobody ever wins but Shane's students. It's true. Billy looked it up. So I told them I'd show them some dances."

Adrien didn't say anything up to this point, just plopped his bag down and looked around. The dust is sifting around my feet and I'm standing there in what remaining beam of light is left in the room in my usual attire, black tutu, faded pink tights, and worn-out legwarmers. I think I must have looked like a wild, stray kitten sitting in an alley.

"The poor and the oppressor have this in common— the Lord gives sight to the eyes of both." Adrien sighs and slips off his warmup jacket. I'm tipping my head, not quite getting what he is saying.

"If a king judges the poor fairly, his throne will last forever," Colt adds and looks at me. "It's from the bible, Proverbs. Shane isn't going to be around forever if he keeps doing stuff to those he believes are beneath him."

Adrien waves a hand in the air like he's trying to bat the dust away. "Okay, let's get to work then."

"Here?" I'd asked him. "Did I not make it clear I didn't want to be a test dummy?" He held up his hands and gave me a funny face like it was a stupid question. He was in a bad mood tonight. I saw that from the start. He dances one way, I go the other. He yells at me for improvising some modern dance. I tell him he's a prude. I'm tired of plain old ballet. I want to knock it up a step. He wants me to try to balance on just one arm while he holds me up. I try and try and just can't hold the position. Then he gets really mad and yells at me while he is lifting me up. "You are unbending, that's what you are! Straighten your arm!"

"No, you are unbending! Why can't you break the rules once in a while? Try something new?"

"Because it isn't the way it is done! Are you the stupid, clumsy girl Shane says you are?"

I just let my entire body free fall while I'm basically doing a one-armed handstand on his shoulder. It was a stupid move and Adrien has to bend to catch me.

"Don't you dare throw that in my face," I growl.

"You could have hurt my back!"

"And don't insult me and yell at me! This is my place! MY PLACE!" I am screaming it with my hands to my sides. I drop my voice, see Adrien just staring at me expressionless. "I dance here to feel good and I dance alone because I don't want assholes like Shane to judge me." I am so infuriated, I can't even think of the words. "I am not Shane Delgado's cast-off, second hand doll. His stupid crash test dummy. Nor am I yours. I do not care what he calls me. Either dance with me without being a dick or leave and don't dance with me at all. I DON'T NEED YOU!"

"You know what, Tango? I don't need you either," Adrien says quietly. He walks away. I can hear him muttering words like he is talking himself down from a fight. "You are insolent."

"What?" I ask his back with a smart-alecky twist to my neck. "What'd you say? Say it to my face."

"It is none of your damn business."

"No, I heard it. You called me insolent. Nobody uses that word anymore."

"Okay, the only other word I know to describe you is bitch. You're a big bitch."

I cross my arms. I am so angry I shiver. He walks away from me and it makes me even madder. However, what ticks me off the most is that I don't want him to leave. Every step he is taking away makes me want to run after him. Yet, I don't. I just pivot on my feet and walk the opposite direction.

I really thought he was going to leave. He doesn't. He just returns, opens the bag he is carrying, and pulls out a mat. Then he comes back and stands overtop me while I'm sitting with my legs crossed on the floor. No apology, no remorse. He unrolls the mat and points to it. "You need to have more bend." That's where we ended up stretching on the floor and him bending my leg in an awkward, painful move. I think he is just taking his anger out on me.

"So, you are an artist. What is your dream?"

It is a simple question. I don't know if anybody has ever asked this of me. It is always somebody else's dream I seem to be living. "I don't know. My Anna wanted me to be a prima ballerina. Poppy thought I should be a gymnast in the Olympics. Between the two, I was doing dance classes for three days of the week and gymnastic classes for two and—"

"I'm not asking you what other people's dreams are," Adrien pushes hard and I grunt. "I'm asking what you want to be when—"

"I grow up?" I laugh. He doesn't. "Okay, I want to paint the world," I don't hesitate. "I want to put graffiti on a wall in every country of the world. Just one wall. Then leave in a big cloud of dust because the cops from every nation are chasing me."

"Ah, you like the life of adventure like your—alter ego, my American spy contact. Why don't you do it?"

"Because you're going to kill me first?" I ask him holding my breath while he bends me nearly in half.

"Quit holding your breath."

"Quit bending me in ways that are not humanly possible."

"You are out of shape," He tells me. It irritates me. I hate it when people harass me about how I look. Shane used to do it all the time in front of the class. It was humbling. "You need to do these exercises, lose two or three pounds by not drinking those sodas you have at the diner. You need to lift weights, get more muscles in your arms—" He reaches out, pinches my upper arm at the tiny bulge of muscle there.

I start to push away, "What are you going to do, spank me if I don't?" I sass him. I see his head lower. He's not used to anyone telling him what to do. He's a big guy and one that's used to everybody kowtowing to him. Adrien tips his chin in the same way Poppy yields his head when I talk back to him.

"You need to respect me, Tango," he says suddenly his eyes looking angry. He's got that *I'll-just-get-up-and – leave-your-sorry-ass* twist to his lips. "Don't talk to me like that. I'm your teacher."

"I thought you were my dance partner. And I didn't ask you to be here," I say back, giving him the same twist of chin. "Because I'm not sure what we're doing here. You're slumming, right?"

"You're not good enough yet to call yourself my dance partner."

Ouch. Every fiber in my body wants to stand up and

stomp off. I realize that's what he is expecting I'll do because he's pushing his hand on the floor to give himself leverage to rise. I'm torn. Am I just like all of those girls that follow him around begging for him to simply notice them? Or am I the one that says screw it and never gets to dance with him again. Because for the first time in my life, I feel like I want to dance outside the walls of an old vacant theatre when I'm with him. I like to feel the muscles of his arms when he lifts me. When he lifts me I feel like I'm a butterfly and he's releasing me to the wind from his cupped hands. I like to look down and catch his gaze, pretend we really are spies and on some grand adventure.

I suddenly feel small while I retrace my steps, realize he is right. I realize that it would be my loss and even if he is using me as a stupid crash test dummy, I'm having fun. And even if he isn't, I am just a poor, clumsy girl who has been dancing by herself in an old, abandoned building. I swallow my pride, something I don't do often.

"I'm sorry, *учитель*." I give him the name for teacher in Russian that we learned when Shane brought in a ballet student he had worked with. It sounds like *ucheetal* and I know I drag it raggedly across my tongue and it is as ear-splitting as the sound Poppy's riding lawn mower makes when he accidently scrapes the blade along the edge of his sidewalk. "It won't happen again. I will be your—what are the Russian words for: *most attentive student*?"

"No, you won't, Tango," he says flatly. "But the word you are looking for is élève, student. I am French, not Russian."

"Oh."

"Hmm," he reaches out and spins his finger around for me to lay back down on my belly. "Maybe le chouchou du professeur."

"What's that?" I cringe, do as he says and wait for the pain to start again.

"Teacher's pet." He taps me on the leg and I turn. Then he pulls me up and makes me sit instead. I don't look at him. I can't tell if Adrien is being mean like Shane, or silly. "You know, there are a lot of students who would have looked that up online to impress me." He tugs one of my legs out to the side and makes me bend to the left. His hands guide me and are so gentle. "Because they do. I get to hear all about me—" He's so haughty. I bet he likes that. The thought makes me irritable.

"Do I need to impress you?" I ask him with a roll of my eyes. "I mean, really. Barring that I would hope my skills on the dance floor would be enough to dazzle and amaze anyone, it is just my cover." I kid him. He does not have my sense of humor and gives me a sour look.

"Cover?"

"For my spy work."

He sighs so deeply, shakes his head. "Now, most attentive student, answer me. Why can you not dream?"

"Because I can't even afford a car that would go far enough to get to the airport. Because I have to work every second I'm not in classes to keep my electric from getting turned off." Adrien doesn't say anything. It is quiet. "So, Adrien, what is your dream?"

"Ha, that's funny. Nobody ever asks me that. You know why?"

"Why?"

"Because they believe I am living my dream. And, I think I've lived all my dreams. Now I'm just kind of, um, riding along in—what the cars have, cruise control. I've been in every ballet company worth being in, every competition worth competing in. I'm not sure now what is left to be."

"So that's why you're here, trying to feel that same thing you felt when you were at the very bottom?"

He looks around the dingy room, stops at a lantern. His face is shining in the light. He's got a slight smile. Adrien is rugged, handsome. The perfect form of the male dancer. He's got the chiseled features of Greek gods. "I was never this low," he says and sighs. "Still, I'm trying to bring back that feeling, that sensation of life—"

I swear I feel my muscle pop right then. I pull away from him, roll over and kick him hard in the shoulder. "Shit on a stick, Moreau, that hurt!"

"Yeah, that," he points at me and laughs, rubs his shoulder where I kicked it. "The spark you have," He wiggles his hands at my irritated eyes. "Not everyone has it. A few have it. Hmmm, maybe just you."

"I did it again, didn't I?" I sniff at him. "I am sorry, teacher."

"I did push a bit hard. Don't call me teacher."

"What do I call you, then?" I yawn out loud.

"Um, Mister Moreau is good. When you earn more than being—this," he waves a hand at me. "You can call me something else."

"Well, Mister Moreau, you still have something in you. I feel it when you dance."

"When I dance with you, Tango," he says. "You breathe life into me. I have been everywhere in the world, I think, dancing. Dancing with one girl, then another. Hundreds and hundreds of tiny dancers and big dancers, but all the same inside. Music box girls going around and around. I teach and teach and teach. Now, I have been dancing full time with Svetlana Mikhailova for three years. She is a head master teacher of dance at Academy of The Dance with the Conciergerie Ballet Company. She teaches the new ones coming into the company. Dancing with her is a routine, like dancing with a pretty doll. She's plaster-faced smile, rigid and unbending from the rules. It is boring and the crowd is bored by her and by me. Her students, they are just like her. We are worse than two spinning tops out on the floor, drab and just going around and around. It is the same thing over and over and her expressions are always the same. Not like this," He reaches over and grabs my cheeks in his hand and squeezes my mouth. I slap his hand away. "I keep coming back to this place and thinking it is going to go away, that feeling, that life. And it scares me that I'm going to suck it out of you with my everydayness. Dance, it has gotten so monotonous nobody wants to watch it anymore, nobody wants to do it anymore. It is like those worn out reality TV shows. It is always the same performers, the exact same shows. People don't get it."

"So change it," I'm almost whispering and he leans in and ruffles my hair like I'm a two year old.

"Baby, it isn't that easy," he says softly back to me. "It is in the soul, Tango. You can't take off a soul and exchange it for a better one."

"I want—" I start to say. Because I'm thinking that if there was one thing in the whole world I'd like to do, it would be to step out of my soul and into someone else's. Somebody's soul who wasn't marred like me, wasn't dinged up and broken and had a bit of a mean daddy in it who murdered girls and hit me. And when I get up on that dance floor, I'm not me. I am dancing in someone else's body who isn't scrawny and freckled and has frizzy hair like me. I want to be in someone else's soul who hasn't been tarnished by a thousand mistakes. "I want to believe you can, Mister Moreau," I tell him firmly. "Because every time I dance, I am baring my soul to everyone in the audience. I feel naked in front of them, naked in front of you. And still,

I feel swan beautiful in my ugly duckling skin. So maybe you can't really exchange a soul in here," I push my hand up and touch his chest, "But when you are dancing, you make-believe up here so it is—almost true."

We have a moment then. I'm staring at Adrien so swept up in his passionate words, my eyes are wide and unblinking. He's just looking at me. I'm just looking at him. Locked, our gaze is. I'm not sure how much time passes. It is like time stands still. Suddenly, Adrien rips his eyes away and blinks. "The student teaches the teacher," he says softly. He stands up quickly like he's dazed. "Um, we should do our Whiskey Tango before I leave, right? So you can roll your eyes and make goofy faces at me? My part of the deal so you're not feeling swindled."

I sniff a half-laugh. "I think the word you're looking for is cheated," I say. Our Whiskey Tango. Each time he dances with me, after he's concluded the session, he holds out his arms and we dance. I know he knows this is the part I like. No rules. It is this strange mix of modern and ballet, a pinch of the tango and I think we waltz somewhere between. I can flip and jump. Sometimes, I do my own thing and he rolls his eyes or wiggles a finger at me like he's thinking I've gone too far. He holds out his arms and I walk into them, look up and cross my eyes. He shakes his head.

Tonight, though, about halfway through, he stops. "I better leave. I'm going to miss my plane." I do feel slighted. He just drops my hands and I realize I was leaning into him maybe a little too hard, his eyes dead set on mine. I brush it off, rub my hands together and nod.

"You got the tickets, the application to work with Svetlana, right? You are going to try out for the summer program?" I nod dumbly. Svetlana. That's his dance partner who has been contracted to lead the audition. I want to tell him it is a joke. I'm not good enough. He just stares at me like he knows what I'm thinking.

Adrien snatches up his mat and makes a beeline to the side of the room, grabs up his duffel bag. I can see Colt standing in the shadows. I don't know how long he has been in the room. I had not heard any foot shuffle near the door.

"I'm leaving too."

"Okay." I stand up a bit dismayed. I'm feeling lonely like a lover has pulled away just as we begin a roll beneath cool sheets. I think he might be mad at me. He doesn't even say anything when Adrien gives me a wave and leaves out the doorway. But he doesn't leave either. And it is silent.

I walk over, snatch up my own worn out bag. I'm quiet. It is warm in the room and it smells like the oil the people who lived here used in their lanterns.

"It's too quiet in here," I note.

"They left, I see. You were right." Colt sighs, looks around at the odd array of decorations still clinging to the walls. "I'm so sorry for that."

"Me too. I miss them." I lug the bag over my shoulder and take a step toward the door.

"I've never love-hated something so much in my life," Colt says. I turn. He is standing just within the light of one lantern. He's wearing jeans. I know he must be hot.

"What do you mean?"

"He is right. Watching you dance, Tango, does something to people. You aren't the usual dancer, kind of doll-like and fragile and like a dollar store knockoff. You're real and unique and—I don't know. I've never seen or felt anything like it. You couldn't pay me a million bucks to go to a ballet. I like baseball. I watch football. But you, you've got something I've never seen. I'd pay a million bucks to watch you dance. And he sees it so I'm not crazy."

"I just think I'm his dance whore," I grunt, tossing my bag over my shoulder and turning toward him. "I'm kind of your whore too, aren't—?"

"Stop it," Colt takes a step forward and gives me a light shove with his hand on my shoulder. "You're not anybody's whore. I'm thinking he's your whore. Maybe me too. Who flies from New York to Kentucky three times a week to dance two hours with someone in an abandoned warehouse? Geez, this place is disgusting. And—and you're talking dreams. You dance like you're six minutes from making out on the floor. He couldn't even take it tonight. And I don't even want to go into how I feel when he's laying there on top of you—you know, stretching and calling you *baby*."

I was getting ready to step toward the door leading to the main room. I stop there, adjust my bag and nudge Colt with my knuckle. "I think when he said baby, he meant like childlike. Sometimes, his translation is a little off. Regardless, I like you too. I don't understand this relationship between you and me because it isn't quite what they write about in paperback novels. But if you want to be with me in whatever capacity we are in and plan to be in, or want to be in—if you want to be in a relationship with me, then you have to understand *he* is there too. Not like you. Not close how you and I are close and working on holding hands without having a panic attack, but close on the dance floor and we have to be open and communicate there just like you and me—share stuff, personal stuff."

"So you don't mind if I share stuff with Alex, then? Personal stuff, stuff that makes us close." He says this a little cocky-sarcastic. I narrow my eyes, take him in.

I look at him. So he's settled on Alexandra. She is the prettier of the two. He is irritated with me. I don't know if I can make him understand. "Let me tell you this," I say. "I think that is Adrien's main problem with his ballerina now. They are like two statues never talking. And he might figure that out and be gone tomorrow. I'll still dance in whatever dirty building I can find. It will be by myself and I will feel a horrible loss, but I will go on because for the first time in my life, I understand how dance and passion collide. He is— um," I look up. "I can't even describe how he makes me feel on the dance floor. Like I'm not—me. Like I'm the princess from an old storybook. Like I never screwed up. But off the dance floor, I don't feel that passion. Because he doesn't show that same passion off the dance floor. I am assuming he shares my interest in men. And I like having you around." I shrug. "Maybe I shouldn't. But you're talking to the girl who is standing by while you date my archenemy."

"Standing by? I don't see it that way. We don't have a choice. You don't seem like the jealous type," he says it like he is testing the water with his toe. "Or the type that needs a man around to feel whole."

"I'm not," I say it too quickly. "However, I like having *you* around, God Squad." I stop and poke him with my finger. "Like a half hour before I find double chocolate ice cream dripping down the table and on to the floor."

"What does that mean?"

"Figure it out."

CHAPTER 43
SECOND BEST FRIENDS

"You know, Billy is my best friend, but you can be my second best friend."

I plop down next to Adrien so we are facing each other. We are in the new theatre. He told me to come here to dance tonight. Nobody was supposed to be in the building tonight. It was raining and the road to the mill was mucky and muddy. And all the dankness in the old mill was making him come down with a cold.

"Who is Billy?"

"He's my next door neighbor. He goes to school at Fields. We both don't sleep well. So we hang out at night on my back porch or his." I'm not comfortable being here. I know if Shane walks in, he'll call campus security and maybe the town cops. Still, it seems like I don't want to go a whole day without being with Adrien. I don't want to admit it, but he's growing on me.

I've got a little, brown paper sack in my hand from Hart's Pharmacy in town. I wiggle it above my palm and a little box comes out. The price tag of $24.99 is showing and I turn it around. "Don't look at that. It is not the actual box," I look up and smile slyly at Adrien. He is just staring at me. "It is priceless or at least forty bucks pawned off at Hensley Pawn and loan." I open the box, tug out the two matching teeny necklaces inside. "Here. You get one and I get one." I have to untangle the chains, then I wiggle my fingers so he holds out his palm. "Both of them say: BFF Best Friends Forever. You can wear it or hang it from your bag. I never know if you're coming back so I figured I'd better get them before it's too late. Something for you to remember me by.

Something for me to remember you."

He takes it and wiggles it around in his fist. I'm thinking he is going to put it in his pocket. He doesn't, just holds on to it.

"I know it's cheap," I shrug. "You don't have to do anything with it. I just saw it and thought about you. You probably get crap like it all the time. Probably expensive stuff, too, from old and rich ladies. And young and rich ladies. Or men. Maybe you are—it doesn't matter. Yeah, I guess it was stupid." I hold out my hand palm up, give my fingers a wiggle. "Here, give it back. I'll save you the agony of trying to figure out what to do with it."

"No, I don't think so, Tango," he tells me. "So what's it take to be your number one best friend?"

"You mean my best-best friend?" I think about it a second, wiggle my head. "I suppose Billy knows all my secrets, all the skeletons in my cupboard. He likes me anyway. He understands I'm annoying and calls me on it all the time. He makes me feel safe." I'm starting to get stiff, so I lean over to my right and stretch toward my toes. "It's kind of one of those positions that if Billy left, it'd be empty for a long time. It's kind of hard to fill."

I look up. Adrien is just looking down at me with his head tipped just a little to one side.

"What?" I ask him.

"I don't know." He shrugs my question off. He reaches out his hand to help me up and tugs until I get just about to my knees so we're face to face. I have to stop, balance myself because I was getting ready to stand. My hand falls on his upper arm and I kneel there, wavering a bit, thinking he must have a cramp in his calf or maybe his phone just rang and I didn't hear it.

"You've got something in your eye," I say that. It was

supposed to be a joke to break up whatever lull was happening here. I'm starting to grin. Gil used to do it to me all the time, tell me I had something in my eye and then pretend to poke me with his forefinger. I'd blink and ask him: *what?* and he'd laugh and say: *My finger!*

I don't though. My hand comes up. And my gaze lights on Adrien's face. He cringes so I'm sure he was expecting me to poke at him. But there is like this sadness in his eyes that strikes me just plain dumb.

"What is it?" he asks when I don't poke him. I can see it in the way they gaze at me, the way his lips turn like a mopey Mia before her nap. Instead of feigning a poke, I stretch my hand out and let my palm rest gently on his cheek.

"Sadness?" I whisper. He doesn't stop me, push my hand away. He doesn't do his usual hands-off policy of letting go as soon as we stop whatever dance we are doing. I touch his face and his chin and his neck and then I run my palm down his arm. That's it. That is all. It is just a gesture, a fond one, and I'm not sure exactly what it means.

I start to stand, feeling stupid, I suppose. I stepped over my bounds. Why don't I have this trouble with anyone else but him? Just as I pull my leg up to rise with a mumbled apology, his fingers jerk me back. Adrien's hand comes up, alights on my face in the same way I cupped his cheek, then his chin. His fingers roll downward along my shoulder and then my arm, elbow to wrist, and leave a trail of goosebumps that make me shiver.

"Is this what second best friends do?" he asks me quietly. His voice is hoarse.

I shake my head. No, it is something lovers do. I don't say it aloud though. "I don't know," I tell him instead. The words are soft, echo off the walls. "I should leave. I'm afraid Shane will come. It's making me tense tonight. I almost kicked you twice and I start another job tomorrow. I want to get some sleep."

"You are working another job?"

"Just until Joe can find somebody else to cover my shift," I tell him. "My brother got me a part time job at the high school cleaning rooms from seven to eleven. When I quit Joe's, they are taking me on full-time."

"From seven until eleven. Then when do we meet?" he asks me.

"I don't know." I'm frustrated and hold my hands to my head. "Gil and Anna are right. I can't keep living with no food in the cabinets. My electric is shut off more than it is on. I can't even afford new underpants, for God's sakes. I mean, look at what I'm wearing." I wave my hands in front of my makeshift tutu, my t-shirt that is ripped. "I have to think of the future."

"On the salary of a part-time janitor."

"I'm an artist, Mister Moreau. I'll paint when I'm home with Mia between work—I don't know. Not everyone is as gifted at their career as you, the child prodigy of ballet. Buy me a frigging hundred pair of underpants and maybe I can reconsider." I shrug. "I don't know. You will leave soon, not come back. I can't live my life being your free crash test dummy for a week or two months, whatever it is. It's not fair for me. I can't give up a paying job to do this."

"I can pay you. I'll buy your paintbrushes."

"You'll pay me. For what?" I laugh softly. "People pay you what, a couple hundred dollars an hour to teach them? I can't imagine what the college is paying you right now if you're on commission. I mean, let's be honest. Delia, Alexandra—Taylor, they can all do what I'm doing right now. The janitor job is steady work and for as long as I can keep it. Even as we sit here, I'm worried I drop Mia off at Anna's too much."

"You should dance."

"She had her chance to dance and blew it."

I look up to the open doorway to the theatre, Shane is tromping his way down the aisle. He scares the shit out of me. I'll be honest. He knows how to manipulate me. He threatened to tell Poppy and Anna that it was me who came on to him, that I had Mia on purpose. It wasn't anything like that. He touched me first. He flirted. Then he told me if I stopped, he'd fail me in class and tell everybody I was a whore.

"I have to go." I know my eyes are wide while I stand up, snatch up my duffel bag.

"You don't have to go. I asked you to come here." Adrien rises too. He's eyeing me curiously, then he looks over at Shane.

"Yes, you do, Raeanna, get the hell off my stage," Shane is waving his arm, making these marching-tromping steps. He's almost to the stage and goes slightly to the left to come up the steps leading to the wooden floor. "I've had it with you sneaking around like a little cockroach."

"Why does she have to go?" Adrien asks. "I want her here. I asked her."

"Because she is not a student here anymore. It is against the rules. If you aren't a student or teacher, you aren't covered under the campus insurance. Such, she is trespassing on Field's Community College property." Shane comes up in front of me. He turns his head enough to take in Adrien, then looks back at me. "Raeanna, one more time and I'll have you arrested. And I believe if I heard correctly from some of my students, you don't have the luxury of being safe if you are arrested, right? Because of that stupid,

stupid prank you played on the police chief. So I would think you would be following the rules. Trust me, Adrien. You don't want to be involved with this one." Shane shakes his head. "You don't think I don't know it is you painting all the graffiti in town? You want me tell the cops that?"

"No, I'm leaving." I start to turn. "Adrien, just forget it. Please." I shake my head, hope he sees the urgency to my eyes. He nods and walks across the room to snatch up his own bag. Shane leans in, calls me a slut in the softest of tones. It isn't loud, but it reminds me of daddy while he gives me a nudge with his hands on my arm.

Shane escorts me to the back door. He stops, leans in with his eyes to the vacant area behind us. "One more screw up, Tango, and I'm turning you into the cops. I know they've been chasing you down for three years. All's I have to do is show them some of your graffiti with the star and it is all over for you. They will arrest your sorry ass." Then his voice rises so it sounds childlike. "Then, I'm going to tell your Poppy how much of a *wittle* whore you were six years ago. You don't screw with Shane Delgado and get away with it. In fact—"

"Stop." Adrien must have kept step with us. I didn't hear him. However, he is there and thrusts out a hand, gently pushing Shane back. "You aren't throwing her into the dark parking lot alone. I'll escort her."

Shane stares solidly at Adrien, then he gets this wily smile to his face. He throws his arms into the air. "Oh, I see how this works. I get it what's going on—" He doesn't finish, just steps back. "Tango likes the teachers. Go. Walk her to her car. But I'm telling you, it's not worth the free lessons—"

Adrien gets this funny twist to his body. I see him turn his head toward Shane. "What, sir, are you implying? And be careful about your words."

"Adrien, no, just—just drop it, please." My face is red.

I've never heard Shane imply any relationship with me outside my own ears. To add to the insult, he has the audacity to snicker like a twelve year old boy who has just snuck his first, accidental boob touch. I know it is because I blundered by his standards, overstepped my bounds and called Adrien by his first name. Shane requires his own students to call him Mister Delgado.

Now Adrien's face is red. I'm not sure if he is clenching his fist to hit Shane or simply trying to talk himself down.

"Please. Just walk me to my car." My voice is hoarse like a palm rubbing sandpaper. Adrien pushes on the door handle and a blast of warm summer night air hits our faces. We are halfway to my truck when he tries to stop me with his hand on my shoulder.

"So is there something you need to tell me about your relationship with Shane?"

"No, because there is no relationship," I say. I'm all scrunched up, hugging my duffel bag. I feel him catch my arm, cause me to pause. "Why do you need to know? It's none of your business."

"It just became my business. His allegations were unprofessional, Tango. I don't want to be in the middle of something that would hurt my reputation."

I stop, turn. "He's the father of my daughter." I just say it.

"What?" He's looking at me with shocked apprehension. "How does that happen?"

I shrug, try to force a smile. It falls flat. "Um, do I have to explain the birds and the bees to you—?

"Be serious."

"I don't know." I can't look him in the eyes. "It starts with your teacher driving you home and putting his hand on your knee, I guess. Then feeling too stupid to tell anybody because you're young and naïve and should feel safe with him, right? It will stop there. Then—then being threatened about getting a bad grade or kicked out of class if you say anything. And being scared crapless to tell the two people in your life that ever believed in you that this is happening when you're so deep into it and they think you're some sort of child prodigy for all the shit the teacher is pouring on them."

"I don't want to ask this—how old were you?"

"Fifteen."

"Holy shit."

"Can we stop talking about this?" I want to walk away. "My Poppy and Anna don't know, alright? Please don't tell anybody." I sigh. "You know, that's the kind of stuff second best friends do. Keep horrible secrets."

"Stop, please," he says when I am jamming my key into the lock of my truck.

"What?"

"You are going tomorrow? To the audition?"

"I've got to start my new job."

He nods slowly, looks like he is going to disagree. "You would have done great, la belle. But you will be a good janitor too."

I stop, eye him with a furrowed brow and a teasing glare. "La belle. You are calling me the French word for idiot, aren't you?"

"Um, no."

CHAPTER 44

GUILTED INTO AN AUDITION

I've never ridden in a plane. Poppy preferred driving every yearly vacation to Myrtle Beach. I suppose, in retrospect, the same fear of flying Poppy carried from the plane crash on the Black Street Bridge probably doomed the dreams of many kids from Hensley Grove who wanted to fly in a jet. However, Kevin loved b-rated disaster movies so I've watched all the shows where they crash. They seemed so stupid when I watched them. But when you're a million miles up in the air and just hanging there without a string, it's amazing how realistic it is that both pilots could have heart attacks at the same time in the movies and there's nobody to land the plane. Hence the reason I came off the jet in New York dizzy, pale, and with nothing more than an empty stomach and my duffel bag.

Honestly, I hadn't planned on flying at all. After Adrien and I parted ways, I went to bed, got out an old pair of jeans and a t-shirt, and readied myself for the minimum wage Hensley High part time janitor position in the morning. Then, just as Mia falls asleep in the cleft of my arm in bed, she says: *Mama, I want to be what you are when I grow up.* And I'm thinking, what? You want to be a woman with shattered dreams that can't find her way out of a bucket? You want to be a waitress, a janitor, a— frigging ballerina dancing in dirty buildings who sleeps with losers just to feel whole? Then she has the audacity to cup a palm to her lips and just barely, sleepy-whisper: *Anna says you're—um, fearless. You're not afraid of anything even if it's hard. I want to do lots of stuff and not be afraid like you—*

So I don't even wait for my little motivational speaker to fall to sleep before I snatch up my stuff and head over to Poppy and Anna's. Anna just blinked at me sadly and patted my hand. "And if you don't get it, you can be an artist still." Huh? She didn't ask where I got the tickets or the audition form. I called Rocky to check on Zane. Then Poppy drove me to the airport in Cincinnati. He over-talked the entire drive. In my boredom while he whistled out two or three songs, I made the mistake of pulling up some pages on the social networks.

There's a great big salute to Taylor and Alexandra who headed the same direction I am going to the audition two days earlier with a gazillion encouraging comments. Then came the punch in the gut when I skidded over to Taylor's page and she's got tons of pictures of her and Colt. Some are at the country club, others are on a porch swing. I mean, there's a picture for every outdoor setting. It appears Taylor and her family left two days ago to take in the sites of New York. She's got pictures of her saying goodbye to Colt at the airport. And finally, a collage that states: *And to my wonderful and incredibly handsome boyfriend who supports me through this crazy dream. I love you, Colt.*

I forgot to get my suitcase which I assume is in some back storage room at the airport. I really was so sick and freaked out by the time we landed, I decided I could walk back home tonight instead of taking the return flight. Thank goodness I was running late dropping off Mia at Anna's or I wouldn't have stuffed my dancing ensemble of tights and shorts into my shoulder duffel bag instead of the suitcase.

My tummy hurts. My audition is at two. It is a big building and looks like an old high school. It is impending and even more so that there are seventy or eighty women there. Nobody bothers to tell me there are warmups involved and I need to make it there by one-fifteen. When I get to the sign up booth, to check in and get my identification number to attach to my shirt, everyone has already been there and each are divided into their groups of five to practice the first round of cuts—double pirouettes and a jump. They were already halfway through calling in the seventy or so girls. Some were leaving in tears, others were screeching in happiness when they left the room. I'm lost. I have no clue where I should be. I lean against the wall, watch the other girls in the hallway working together or alone to get the combination correct.

I walk through the crowd. They ignore me, so focused on their own practice for the audition. They are all talented. I can see that. They are all so well dressed. Me, I'm still in my street clothes of stretchy jeans and a t-shirt. I try to stop a couple women who appear to be working for whatever company is setting up the audition. They ignore me or wave me away with a hand.

"Hi, I'm Raeanna Baldwin. I'm here for the auditions with Svetlana Mikhailova." I finally bumble into a room and too late, realize it is one of the rooms for auditions. There are three tables side by side and surrounded by chairs that are filled with sixteen or seventeen men and women.

"Well, you're an hour and fifteen minutes late." A woman is looking over papers. She is gorgeous like the women on the glamor magazine covers. Her complexion is perfect. I think she might be of Asian descent. I don't know. I only know she is shooting nails into me from head to toe. I get the feeling I came in the wrong door. She rolls her eyes at one of the men attached to her side. Oh, shit. It is the Dark Witch herself, Sorcière Noire, Svetlana Mikhailova. It is like a huge mistake on my part. "Get her out of here."

"I have all my paperwork. I got lost coming out of the airport. Adrien Moreau sent me."

Silence. I look around the room. There are nine

women standing still and in mid-audition whose eyes stray cautiously to Svetlana.

"Oh, this ought to be funny," she says and I see something on her face that reminds me of my daddy. It is just a hint, a glint in her eye and a grind to her teeth. It is there and then, it is gone. I see her snatch up a paper, run her finger down the page. "No, you are not on here," she says. "What makes you feel so special?" she asks me, turning her head upward. "I didn't approve your audition."

"I don't know. I thought they were open. I have my application here," I tell her. "I—I didn't know it had to be turned in ahead of time. I figured they were taking applications at a front desk or something."

There is muffled laughter around the tables. It is cut quickly by Svetlana's angry glare. "Oh, my God! Nobody does that. We cull hundreds of incompetents to get to this point and—" she adds, "many talented." She wiggles her fingers at me. "You are funny. Let me see your application."

I take the long, silent walk across the room. Then I hand her the tiny folder I have with my dance pictures Billy took last night with his phone and then printed them out to his computer.

"Let me just start out." Svetlana stares at my packet, barely looks at what I have to offer. Within, I have my performance resume and a full body photo in arabesque position. "This is your portfolio, your pictures? It looks like you took them with your phone, not by a professional."

"I did." More soft laughter follows. My face is burning red.

"This is unacceptable at any level. Adrien usually sends me the boys he sleeps with who are at least somewhat experienced, not the girls off the streets," she sniffs derisively, rolls her eyes and waves a hand. "I suppose I have to at least look at you or he will be angry. Join this group. I will see what you've got."

She berated me for not knowing the combination. Svetlana laughed at me and pointed out how stupid I looked in jeans and t-shirt trying to keep up with what she called *the big girls.* "You are like a child," she tells me. "You know what a baby ballet dancer knows. No, less. You are clumsy and inept." I see the other girls look at me while Svetlana destroys every last shred of my dignity when she leans out the doorway. I am following the other girls, trying to not feel like I'd just been beaten with a whip. "You forgot your score sheet, Miss Wallace."

"Miss Baldwin," I correct her. She slaps a paper, a score sheet, at me. I am the only one who receives one now. I look at mine. She doesn't even bother to score me. It is quieter in the hallway. I know each of these girls are looking at Svetlana with eager eyes and bated breath, stopping in mid-practice as if she might notice them. But no, she notices me, raises her voice so all can hear: "You, my dear, are an embarrassment to the art, to ballet. Go home. Find a poor little man with a shop and raise children. That, my little bitch, is the only thing you are good for."

I can't find my duffel bag or my purse stuffed inside. In my desire to get out of the audition room, I left it on the floor. I'm told I have to wait until the end of the auditions to get it. When I re-enter the room four hours later, it is gone.

There is only one man remaining there and I ask him if he has seen it. It has my return flight ticket, my phone, and the one-hundred dollars Poppy slipped into the side for lunch and supper and a taxi ride to the airport.

I'm woozy with fear when he states he will go ask if anyone has seen it. It is late. My flight leaves in two hours. When he returns five minutes later, he tells me Svetlana has sent for a car to get me to the airport. He says I just have to tell them that I lost my ticket. They will be able to fix it there. So I play right into her trick, not knowing even after a car pulls up to the walkway in front of the building that I'm never going to make my flight.

The man in the car is a personal driver for Svetlana. We drive for thirty minutes and I try to peer up at the lights and the buildings and take in New York because I know I'm not coming back. I'm sad and lonely and wishing I'd never come. I hate ballet right then. I wonder if Adrien did not set this up with Shane to make me a laughingstock. Suddenly the car stops. I wait, thinking we are caught in traffic or stopped at a light. But it is dark where we are and dingy and dirty. It is a vacant back alley with dirty garbage dumpsters and six or seven blankets holding homeless people laying slumped on the pavement.

"This is your stop, where Svetlana told me to let you off."

"I thought she was sending me to the airport."

"Sure, it is just one block up. You have to walk from here because they don't allow personal vehicles."

If I knew he was lying, it is probably a question to my sanity why I got out. And yet, without my purse and my phone, I do. And I stand there in the bleakness of a dingy street in the deep of New York City not knowing where I am, but seeing the ratty neighborhood around me. I know she sent me to the dankest section of town while I blink against the first of many raindrops to batter my eyes. And I watch the car lights fade away into the darkness.

CHAPTER 45

TINY CHAINS LEADING TO A CLUE

"You going to be alright?"

That's Kevin saying those words a few seconds after he pulls up to the curb in front of Poppy's street. It is eleven o'clock at night and he still guns the motorcycle engine twice before he turns it off. What can I say? He was the only one whose number I could think of who would pick up the pieces of my broken dreams all the way from Kentucky to New York and back again, all twenty hours of driving on Rocky's borrowed motorcycle.

"Yeah." I linger there. It had been warm and cozy pushed up behind him, like old times. I still have his scent on me and it is leaving a melancholy burn inside my chest. I want to reach out, beg him to stay with me tonight. "It's hard moving on, Kevin."

"Yeah, I know that," he tells me. I figure he doesn't get off his bike and drag me into his arms so he's already passed me on the moving on issue. I guess he'd never do that anyway. "Thanks. When I get paid, I'll get you money."

I'm standing there watching him drive off. Poppy's front door slams. I snap my head over to the lights in the windows. I see Anna with her hand on her chest and Poppy pushing around her like he's heading for the door.

"Jesus Christ, where have you been?" Gil is yelling at me halfway down the driveway. "We've been worried sick about you. Do you not own a phone? Why weren't you on the return flight? Dad waited there six hours—"

I'm just tired. I haven't slept in two days. "I got lost and my purse got stolen," I just say. I'm thinking it is a thing with Svetlana, maybe. I remember that is how I met

Adrien. Someone had stolen his wallet. He later mentioned his partner had it. I thought, then, he was just playing a game with me. Perhaps not. Poppy's almost running down the driveway. "Was that Kevin? Sweetie, where have you been? Everybody's been searching for you. They said you left the auditions and just—disappeared. Joe called from the diner, said you were supposed to work. You didn't show."

"They called in a driver for me because my purse was gone. They dropped me on the wrong side of town. I didn't have flight tickets. I didn't have cash. I didn't have my phone. I walked for four hours in the worst part of the city. I went into a little grocery store and the guy let me use his phone. One call. I called Kevin."

"Why didn't you call me?" Poppy peppers me with questions.

"Can we talk about this tomorrow? I need to sleep." I pass Anna on the porch. "I hope that stupid janitor position is still open. Can I crash here tonight?"

"Of course, Raeanna," she tells me. From the look in her eyes, they have already heard how the audition went. It is humbling. I take the steps and stop just outside my old room that is now the place Mia sleeps when she comes to Anna's for an overnight. I lean against the doorframe, peer inside. "Mama, I waited up for you," the whisper is soft, sweet, and sleepy. "My eyes keep shutting." She flaps her little fingers to imitate her eyes trying slowly to close. "Then bam! I open them. Are you a ballerina now?"

My heart jerks hard while I slide in the door and slip off my shoes. "I missed you," I tell her. I'm glad I didn't do well at the audition. I'd rather be with her. "So bad. And I'm already a ballerina. I don't need to be with a company to be one." I lay down, feel her little arms wrap around my neck.

"I love you like a fat kid loves chocolate cake."

My eyes widen. "Huh? Who taught you that?" She giggles. "Colt. He said to tell you that when you get home."

"Well, don't say it around Nanna Anna."

"Okay."

Hmm. When did she talk to Colt? That is my last thought before I just fall to sleep.

At three in the morning, I wake up. Guilt. It pours into me. I opted out of paying my cell phone bill so I'd have extra cash for my little trip. I failed once again. I sit up in bed, hunch there for three or four minutes in a half-awake daze. My eyes wander over to Mia's little pink overnight bag. Her clothes are tossed on top and the little box is laying half on and half off her tiny tennis shoes. It is the shoebox from daddy's that Poppy said belonged to my mama that she carries with her like a treasure box. I push myself up, trudge over to the box and pick it up. The lid is open and the contents spill out to the floor—among them, the doll, a marble, and a few other things Mia added to this new treasure box. And the tangled mess of necklaces.

I snatch up the doll and shove it in. Then, I reach over and grab up the necklaces. I blink and see a prism. It shimmers against the hallway light while I sit back and take it in. I recognize it instantly. It is one of the little baubles daddy hung from his rearview mirror. I remember sitting in the back seat of daddy's car and he was always poking at that prism dangling with a handful of other trinkets, a soft smile playing on his lips. I wiggle the jumble of tiny chains and a bit of black fabric twisted with it.

A tiny turquoise heart wiggles near my fingertips. Turquoise heart. Black velvet choker. I blanch and hold my palm flat, digging through the snarled mess. Tammy Lynn was wearing a black choker with a turquoise heart on it.

"Shit," I whisper while I dig. SAINT AGATHA PRAY FOR US. Oh, crap. Cathy Schuler wore a Saint Agatha pendant. It was missing when they found her.

I dig more. I see a chain with a tiny gold heart. It has a hole for a key in the center. It doesn't ring a bell. Just as I stare at that one, I poke my finger deep and work out a tiny pearl set in a gold bell cap. "Lisa Tatum. She was missing a pearl necklace. Oh, my God." I stare at the necklaces before I sit back and feel the sweat forming on my brow.

It isn't until the next evening, I can stop at my apartment and snatch up Billy's folder and dig through it, look for the two girls in Indiana that he found had been bathed in bleach. Twenty minutes later, I am staring at a little silver dolphin that belonged to Leanna Erlstein from Lafayette, Indiana who came up missing eight years ago walking home from school. Then, I find the class ring dangling from a chain belonging to Erica Bell of Indianapolis who disappeared while jogging ten years ago.

"Oh, daddy, you crazy, crazy idiot. How many more are there?" Billy was right. If I found the killer's trophies, I'd find the killer. He'd collected the girls, then collected these from them, tiny trophies to hang on his rearview mirror. I clasp them there in my fist. I can only say there are a lot more in the pile than just four. And now, I really don't know what to do.

CHAPTER 46

CONVINCING CHLOE

"Okay, I got a good feeling my dad killed those girls." I am standing outside Chloe Murphy's house two days later. She is standing inside a screen door, her arms crossed. "As much as I want to deny it, I can't. Look." I'm holding up the intertwined necklaces, waving them at the door. "This morning, I looked up stuff on Susan James that was murdered in 1958. Her boyfriend gave her a heart necklace for Valentine's Day. It was one of two matching chains with separate pendants. He kept the other, it was a key. I read it in a newspaper yesterday. They had a picture of him holding it up, begging for whoever took Susan to return her to him, bring back the one he'd given his heart to."

"Stop, Tango, this isn't happening."

"Yes, it is," I tell her. "Please listen to me. Here's Cathy Schuler's Saint Agatha pendant," I hold the thumb-size silver trinket up for her. "It was supposed to protect her. Obviously, it didn't. And—and here's Tammy's choker and Lisa's pearl—"

"Tango, I said stop!" Chloe hisses at me. "Every one of those is common. You've got a whole handful. Just go—go away."

"He used to hang these from his car mirror, Chloe! And, no, I won't. I don't understand why you won't listen." Chloe doesn't move even while I hold a folder up, open it wide and poke a finger at the map. "Look, I have more. From Indiana. Billy found them and—"

"And I'm three days away from getting back to work, Tango. They want to drop it. I'm not on the case anymore. I'm not taking any chances. And I think everybody's already established that he's a murderer."

"Chloe, not just for the old murders. The two new ones." I hold out a hand while she starts to close the door. I poke at the class ring. "Please, please, please, just give me five minutes. Five. I promise if this doesn't hold your attention, you can—"

"What's up, babe?" I see another woman come up behind Chloe. She's a bit more bulky from what I can see beyond the screen and looking from Chloe to me. "You want me to call the cops? Oops, you are the cops."

"I'm a cop and won't be if she doesn't leave, Reagan. Stay out of this."

"A good cop or a bad cop?" Reagan says and she is smiling like Kevin used to smile at me when we had some inside joke.

"A good cop."

"Well," Reagan is munching on a sub. I can see her bringing it up to her mouth, smacking her lips together loudly while she takes a bite and chews. "A good cop listens if there might—" She stops to swallow. "—be a lead on the bad guy, right?"

"You didn't hear the whole thing, Reagan," Chloe turns, eyes upward. "She is the bad guy. She's Dell Smythe's daughter. The chief of police, he told me to drop it all. It is done. Closed."

"No, way," Reagan interrupts and says it like it's a cool thing. She pushes on the door, sub and all in her hand, and sticks her free hand out to shake. "You don't look like a serial killer's daughter."

I shake her hand. I really don't know what to say to that. "I don't—look like one?" I answer slowly then look around her to Chloe. "Okay, the map. I was looking at it last night and trying to figure out a route to walk for Susan

James, the librarian who was found dead—" she's starting to close the door. "Please, please, please, two minutes." I press the folder to the screen. "Look. It is a star. Do you see it?"

It's true. I went to the Welcome Viaduct last night with a red paint can because, you know, I'm freaking out about this whole thing trying to decide if I should go to Chloe or the FBI. I don't want to be implicated in all this. I just want—to paint in the dark and dance in the dark. Alone and without people beating down my door to interview the serial killer's daughter.

I'm standing there getting ready to spray the crap out of the bricks when I catch the faint scent of someone grilling burgers or steaks. The scent makes me melancholy and I pause trying to recall the reason I'm getting a sensation of Déjà vu. Then, I remembered. Daddy used to cruise through this section of town. He'd pull over to the old hotel cattycorner to the viaduct and just stare at the viaduct. There's a little picnic shelter in the center of town that has a grill. I remembered the scent from when I was little standing at the exact same place. He always told me he was looking for trains. "Starr, baby, watch for the train. Here it comes!" He liked to hear them grinding along the tracks. But I can't remember ever seeing any trains there. It was just me and daddy, and him staring at the stones with a longing twist to his lips. *Starr.*

I remembered them all, then—all of Daddy's favorite places. Parking by the viaduct where Susan James' body was found in 1958. Fishing at the Black Street Bridge where Lisa Tatum came up missing in 1963 and then was dumped at the ballfields. He used to take me to the mill at almost the exact spot where Tammy Lynn's body was discovered 1972 so we could watch the logs roll by when the floodwaters came. *Look at the water, Starr. It is getting higher.* Cathy

Schuler's body was found in 1983 on that front yard along Second Street. Once in a while, daddy would cruise past the area, tell me he grew up there. *Starr, this is where daddy lived when he was a little kid just like you. Right here.*

Starr. Starr. *Star.* I had felt the spray can slip through my fingers. Star. It's my stupid graffiti signature, a black star with WT on either side. I couldn't get home fast enough and Zane eyed me like a crazy woman while I tossed papers all over the place to get to the map on the outside of the folder. I took a pencil in my hand. I drew a line from the mill where Tammy Lyn's body was found to the Welcome Viaduct. I stopped. Then I brought it back up to stop at the place Cathy Schuler's body was found in 1983 on Second Street. Straight across was the place they found Lisa Tatum's body at the ballfields. Then back down, was the place of Hannah Lafferty's body.

"Chloe, it's a star. Starr. That was my name. My dad used to take me to each of those spots to hang out." I wave a hand at the map. "Do you see it?" I turn, slap my back. "Dad had some guy put a tattoo on my back when I was six. A star."

I think she gets what I'm saying. She leans in along with the woman who is standing with her. I hear a car pass.

"Star," Chloe says. "A black star like the signature of the perp who has been vandalizing public property and painting graffiti all over town for the last five years."

"Well, more like three years."

"W—T," Chloe whispers more to herself than me. "Whiskey Tango." Oh, she looks really, really angry.

Reagan laughs out loud. It is louder than my own. However, I'm not laughing. "This little, scrawny thing is the criminal evading you for years? God, that's funny, Chloe."

It is quiet a moment while Chloe seems to take in

what I've told her. Her face is red. I'm not sure if it is anger or embarrassment. A car passes, then another. I've heard one or two while I've been here. This time, however, Chloe looks up and watches it go by.

"Crap. That's what I was afraid of."

I turn, let my eyes slide toward the road. It's a small car, black with tinted windows. I recognize the dent in the passenger side door instantly. It's the same car that showed up at Bogie's right before his trailer blew up.

"You need to get out of here, Tango. They know you're here. I'll contact you."

"No, you need to listen. Hannah's brother doesn't think those were Hannah's clothes. Look, look, look," I hold up my copy of the crime scene photo. "He says this isn't her. Maybe it isn't. All the girls, Chloe, were kept alive for six or seven weeks." I try to tell her while she drags Reagan back through the door. "What if she's still alive?"

She stops, her eyes following the car driving away. Then she looks at me. "Baldwin. I'm just going to say this once. That car you see, it's one of the drug impound vehicles. They confiscated it after they arrested a bunch of families making meth in town. You get where I'm coming from? Those are the cops. The cops are following you. That's all I can say. And if anybody asks, I sent you away."

CHAPTER 44

WHAT IF HANNAH'S ALIVE?

Billy is banging on my door at eight in the morning a day later. It is Saturday and my day to sleep in until ten. I bust out of bed in a dead run at the sound of his fist against metal thinking surely there has to be a fire. I'm dragging anyway. Zane wasn't home so I spent two hours trying to find him. He seemed to completely disappear off the face of the earth then just showed up looking guilty. He wiped out everything in my refrigerator so I had to stop at the store and pick up more groceries. Then I painted storm clouds and tiny hearts all over town at the tops of the buildings near each of the places they found the murdered girls.

"What?" I'm squinting at him through the crack in the door. The sunshine beats into my eyes, begging me to close it. He's dressed in a button up buttoned to his chin and khaki pants. He's got this new stylish haircut that's sticking up on top and he's wearing new glasses. These, he is shoving nervously up his nose.

"Tell her no." He waves a hand over his shoulder and I look up to see Amy Goddard elbowing her way past Billy. She's in theatre and always has the lead in the productions put on at Fields. She's tall and blonde and wears lots of makeup. And she's dragging three of her entourage from the drama club.

"We want in," she says forcefully, then turns her head and looks at me funny. "Do all dancers look this bad when they wake up in the morning?"

I glare at her. "Maybe." But I doubt they do. I think women like perfect Svetlana must plug themselves in at night because they are robots. "You want in on what?"

I'm still not awake. I'm still in t-shirt and shorts and scratching the frizz of hair from my face. I watch Billy's eyes roam straight over my shoulder. I follow. Zane is standing behind my couch rubbing the sleep from his eyes. Crap. I didn't want half the college to know he was here. I don't want his family knocking on my door trying to get him to come home.

"Is that your boyfriend now?" Billy asks me right out of the blue.

"No, he's just renting a room. I can't afford the rent myself." I don't know where that comes from, but it seems to work. Billy mulls it over in his head, then he nods.

"He's a boy. You know that, right?" he divulges. "My mom says boys rent with boys, girls rent with girls."

"That's not true," Amy says with exasperation. "What century was your mom born?"

"This century. But the rent is high here," he announces, then shakes his head and seems to toss it aside. "And Tango likes boys—"

"Where is this going, Billy," I interrupt. I'm not thinking it is going to end well.

"The show," Amy answers for him. "We heard that you're doing the competition with the dweebs." She shoots a hot glare at Billy. "There's no way we'll even place if they've got a dancer."

"I'm not a dancer. They consider me a visual art student and not in the performing arts—"

"Do you dance?"

"Well—"

"Tango," Billy sidles up so he's the closest to me. "We've already been approached by Jenny Fields who is in fashion design and four of the graphics designers. Everybody wants in on this. It's crazy. I don't want it. It's not normal." I find it slightly amusing that Billy, who only a few weeks ago did not even want to join the acapella club, is now so defensive of his little group.

I can see Missus Finch peering out her doorway. I hold up my hand. "I don't see how we're going to make this thing happen in a week, Billy. Most of the students competing have been working on this since it ended last year. Four days. I don't know if I can even come up with a music mix in that amount of time. I've got to get ready for work. Can we discuss this when I'm awake?"

Somehow, the debate gets dragged down to Joe's diner. I see the entire acapella club coming through the doors all at once. Then, a few here and there of the theatre club and others, I figure are those focusing on the graphics and fashion design. They pull four tables together in the center of the restaurant and their discussion is loud and animated. It is already starting to get crowded with the lunch folks and I feel like with Joe, I am kind of walking a tightrope. I'd talked him into hiring Zane to wash dishes and help him cook. Joe was hesitant, said he'd give it a try for two days. I gave him a two week's notice and then, I missed the janitor job the morning of the audition. So I asked him if I could have my job back. He nodded, but I know his feelings were hurt. So now, he's a bit grumpy because he hates training new people and he's showing Zane how to flip burgers on the grill. I cringe when he leans out of the kitchen window.

"Okay, Tango, you're a pain in my ass today and apparently a dweeb magnet. I assume that this meeting going on out there has something to do with you," he tells me. "So go tell that little group if they are staying, they are buying. They are taking up paying customer space."

So I go out and poke my little pencil to my pad of

paper. "Joe says you have to buy food if you're going to have a pep rally in here." It doesn't seem to be a problem. The menus are flying as are the orders. I don't stop bringing out French fries and sodas, burgers and chicken legs for nearly an hour and a half. It is now like they are competing on who can buy the most food during their discussion. They lay it all out in the middle and they are stuffing their faces. And with every idea they pour out, they look to me for advice I simply can't give and juggle the orders from my tables.

"What can I get you," I'm asking the entire line at the counter. "Please tell me it is just coffee. My feet hurt, my head hurts. I've got two more hours before I'm off. Then—"

"A coffee." It is a man's voice behind those at the counter. The three men there just give me a funny look over their menus. I recognize the voice and cringe because I know it is Hannah's brother. I don't feel like dealing with his anger issues right now.

"Okay," I turn sharply, snatch up a mug and a cup and set it down on the counter. He's just standing there looking at me. "I need to talk to you," he says softly. "Can you meet me later tonight?"

I'm getting ready to pour the coffee and realizing he really doesn't want any. "Yeah, sure." What am I supposed to say?

"I can help with them, you know, find a common ground. I'm good at that." Mark takes the cup of coffee I hand him. I know he's trying to extend a hand, help me out while both our eyes veer toward the raucous chatter of the college students.

"You fix that group and I'll be your slave," I say a little too quickly. I see everyone in earshot snap their gaze at me and then Mark while I bumble through a stuttering jumble of words that is supposed to remedy my insinuation, but probably only makes it worse. "I—I mean that in the most *not* literal sense. I won't really be—be your slave like you'll be my master and I have to do stuff that is inappropriate—not that I wouldn't because you're not attractive or anything because—oh, hell."

Laughter. Good gosh, I recognize that damn laugh. I look over to a table butting up to the counter. It's the church crowd. And among them, Colt Lucero. He's sitting with Alexandra and Delia. To his left is Taylor and she's shooting darts at him while he's nearly doubling over. I see them all laughing at my words and suddenly Mark looks over and gives them all a nasty stare. "Leave her alone, Delia."

Delia just loses the smile and nods like a subservient child who was just warned with a time out. There's like a moment they are staring at each other, then Delia turns her gaze away. It's strangely akin to something an alpha male wolf would do to a lower pack member.

"They are a bunch of idiots," Mark says to me. "I need to talk to you as soon as you can."

As soon as I can is three hours later. He waits for me, sipping coffee and watching every move I make. It is strangely not awkward, but worrisome at the same time. I know he is dying to tell me something. I don't trust him especially with the looks I could see him shooting Delia once in a while. When I snatch up my keys at Joe's desk and scoot out the back door, he is right behind me.

"Chloe Murphy called me. She told me what you said about Hannah being alive. And she told me what was on the body. Those weren't my sister's clothes, Tango."

I'd stopped at the back door to wait for him to catch up. "Huh?"

"They won't let us go through her belongings—the stuff she was wearing when they found her." He stops me with his hand. I turn, look up at him. "Gabe at the police department told me that there just isn't enough left of her or her clothing. What they have, they are keeping as evidence. However, Chloe showed me pictures of what they had cleaned up—I got to look at the sweater."

"Are you okay?" I ask him.

"No, not really." He takes in a deep breath. "I have never seen Hannah wear a light blue sweater. There were pieces of blue sweater. I've never seen her wear brown leather shoes, have you? I mean, they were dorky, old-lady, looking. Hannah was a lot of things, but dorky—"

"Did the sweater smell like bleach?" I ask.

"No," He shakes his head. "Should it? You're the only person in the world that agrees with me that it isn't her."

He's leaning against the doorframe. I'm one step away, rubbing my head and trying to think it out, trying to say the right words. "All the other dead girls were bathed in bleach. So we don't think it was Hannah's clothes and even if they were, they weren't bleached. DNA. Can't they test that on the body?"

"They are so sure it is her, they aren't even sending it off. I'm crazy, right?" Mark is bending low like he's trying to see my expression. "It is her. I'm wanting to believe it isn't."

"No, stop," I say softly. "So what if it isn't—Hannah they found at the tracks. Let's just go this side of crazy and say it isn't." I look up at him. "Where is she?"

"I don't know."

"Here's the bigger question." I close my eyes. I don't want to look at Mark. "Nobody will believe me that I think it was my dad that killed all those girls. Yeah, everybody whispers to everybody else that he did it. But the cops, they turn their heads, look away. So—where is *he*? If we can find him, maybe we can find Hannah."

CHAPTER 48

THE TRUTH ABOUT COLT

What if Hannah is still alive? I can't get the idea out of my head. It has been almost six weeks since she came up missing. I pour through the papers, trying to find a time base between the abduction and murder of each girl. Estimates are all I can find placing the time each girl was kidnapped to the time she was killed at about six to eight weeks. And if the girl at the bridge isn't Hannah, who is she?

"Rae, you remember Bella Price, here, don't you?"

"Well, for a couple weeks it was Bella *Lucero*," she says quietly. "I changed it back to my maiden name."

I'm having breakfast buffet with Poppy at the country club the next morning. It used to be our thing. He'd take me out to have Saturday breakfast at Uncle Lion's country club from the time I was six, to about the time I turned seventeen. Poppy asked me if I wanted to celebrate old times and stop in. How could I say no? I wanted to pick his brain a little about how to deal with Zane. He's dealt with plenty of wild boys. Rocky said Jessica was looking for him, then he thought he saw Zane at the playground at midnight. He just looks guilty when he's around me.

I was heading that way out of town anyway. I told him I just wanted to make one stop on my way. And it was along Second Street. Second Street. I pass it on my way out of town, thinking there must be some reason a body would be dumped in a yard. There's a fifty- fifty chance maybe it was random. Somebody kills a girl, freaks out and dumps the body on the way out of town. Cathy had been dead, the coroner estimated, almost a year. Or maybe the body was dropped there on purpose. But what purpose?

I decide to go with the latter. I take a quick detour to meet Poppy and drive up Second Street and make a right on Baker Avenue to make a run-through again. Baker takes me to Black Street. I make a right and start back toward Second. Then it hits me—Baker Avenue. My heart pounds. Taylor Peirce's grandpa lives on Baker Avenue. I remember Colt telling me that when he brought the food pantry box with the girls.

It only takes me three minutes to pull off the road and look up John C. Peirce on Baker Street on my phone. 61534 Baker Street. Sure enough, his name pops up. I pull up the GPS on the phone and make another round, follow the directions until I am matched up with the little pinpoint on the map. And I slide past a cute little white house.

"Where does Taylor's dad live?" I call Chloe. I am sure she is kicking herself in regret for giving me her cell phone number on that tiny business card.

"Good gosh. Tango, leave me alone."

"Just answer me, please."

"Chief Peirce has a huge log cabin at the old quarry," Chloe says. "You know the one when you drive out of town. It is kind of hidden, but it's sitting on Gilman's old quarry."

I have seen it. It's one of those places that just gets etched into your mind because it is built into the Hensley Grove scenery for so long. You can see it from the highway. It's like a fortress and castle.

"That's a frigging mansion," I murmur. "He works for the city and can afford that thing?"

"I don't know. Maybe somebody left him some money."

"His dad lives in a tiny house on Baker Avenue."

"I don't know, Tango, I think if you're trying to tie Chief Peirce in, you're reaching for it. Like if you think your dad is paying him off for not telling about the murders, that's reaching for it."

"What if he's the one that stole the money from the plane?"

The conversation ended with her sighing big and telling me to quit calling her.

And so I am sitting with Poppy at our little table in the rear and I'm downing a donut the size of my plate. I look up and see Uncle Lion stopping just short of the table with the same lithe brunette who cornered me outside the bathrooms on my revenge date with Colt. Bella.

"I wasn't quite formally introduced, but we crossed paths," I stutter. I rise up and shove out my hand. I have not heard from Colt since the day before I left for the audition. Strangely, I don't feel a huge loss. I mean, my heart hurts a little and my pride is dented, but I just don't think my soul was ready for a new investment right after Kevin.

"And this is Ralph Edward with the Wesley Outreach Program." Poppy is the one who introduces Ralph. I am getting jittery and hope my hand isn't showing that when I shake his.

"He is not the man he tells you he is," Bella tells me right off. I am standing awkwardly in front of the table with my back to Poppy before I sit back down. He, of course, rises up and snatches an empty seat from another table and helps her sit down. Ralph Edward sits between Bella and Poppy. He is watching Bella, nodding his head up and down.

"Colt Lucero," she says, scooting her chair up while Uncle Lion sits down on her other side.

"Raeanna, you need to hear what Bella has to say," Ralph tells me before I can even dismiss her.

I bob my head slowly up and down, put down my

fork and sit back in my chair. I look to Poppy who is watching Bella intently.

"He isn't here to do mission work. That was never his goal. Never." Her eyes are steady on mine, but I can tell she doesn't think I believe her. She looks to her right at Ralph and he pushes a hand on her shoulder.

"Just tell her what you told me," he says softly before he turns his attention to me. "I told Colt to stay away from you. I was worried from the beginning there were ulterior motives to him signing up at the outreach program here. But he seemed so eager to redeem himself from his past, to help those in the community. He was so—convincing. I thought—I really thought he was being truthful. And I couldn't just tell you then. We have so many privacy rules. I had to protect both you and him."

Bella takes in a long breath, releases it. She nods her head up and down and looks tired. "Listen to me, Colt and I met when *I* was doing mission work. My dad talked me into helping build homes for a weekend. It was in Ohio and a handful of TV celebrities came to the event to promote the stations and movie companies they work for—"

"Yes, I saw it on TV," Uncle Lion tags on. "Communities Together. That's the name of the program.

"Well, one of the celebrities who came was a Paul James who has a band. There was some big scandal about him getting caught with drugs in his car when he took his two kids to school. Colt was there for his father's magazine, undercover, of course to get the story on Paul James. We met. He told me anything I wanted to hear about how much he wanted to help the poor, how much he wanted to save the world. All's he *really* wanted was to get the inside on Paul James. We hit it off, Colt and me, and within three weeks, we were married. All of his work with Communities Together was a big scam. When I found out, I called him on it. He said he still loved me. I told him he based our entire relationship on a lie. I got the marriage annulled."

"So, he's a scammer," I say flatly.

"Not just that," Bella looks over at Ralph Edward and he nods as if to tell her to go on. "He is obsessed with finding the money. I mean, not just obsessed, but possessed like a demon."

"The money?" I ask. "What money?"

Uncle Lion sighs. "The money that has always been rumored to be on the plane."

"He thinks it was his dad's pay for flying the plane."

"Which says something about his father," Poppy eyes me cautiously. "Why would someone get paid a million dollars to fly a plane?"

"Agreed." Uncle Lion tugs on his chin.

"Yes. He's afraid somebody else has it." She smiles wanly at me. "They gave him a box of belongings they found in the plane. Inside, there was a set of keys that the family believed unlocked some lockbox. This is how odd he can be. Colt has this little frame he keeps by his bed. In the frame is a picture of his father. He hangs the keys on this frame. One night, I was reaching over him to get my phone on the bed stand. My hand accidently touched the picture. He screamed at me like I'd touched some sacred cross. The family has always believed that the suitcase is what Dell Smythe took from the plane. Since he did not have it on his person when they arrested him for robbery ten years ago, he must have put it somewhere else safe. And who would you trust more than anyone? Family. You, Raeanna. "

Keys. I force myself from looking at Poppy. Because I can almost bet the keys belong to a Tringle Double Case suitcase. Now my mind is churning and I can't pull Poppy aside and ask him right there. Oh, but when I swing a gaze across them all, he's paler than a ghost. Assuming the keys fit the suitcase, why would my law-abiding, sweet and gentle, church-going Poppy have it?

I suppose it is a heavy pill to swallow for me. I realize I like shutting people out and shutting completely down when I get used and tossed aside like a worn out, rummage-sale shirt. Damn, I thought Colt was sweet. I thought he was sweet on me. Obviously, Bella felt the same. I see the pain in her eyes when I look up. I guess I'm kind of numb. Yeah, I hadn't known him that long. I should have known he was lying about a relationship when he didn't want to be seen with me in public.

"I'm so sorry." That's what Bella says. I mean, I guess after dealing with Delia and her lot, I expect most girls to be mean. She reaches out, gives my fingers a hug with hers. "I feel your pain."

"What made you decide to tell me this?" I asked. I am curious. "I mean, you could have just let me get hurt."

"And let him get the last laugh on both of us?" she laughs, shakes her head. "No, I'm hoping I can follow him around to every woman he uses to get from point A to point B and ruin his relationships at least for the next ten years." Bella sighs, then. "There is something I'd like to ask you. My dad, he has done nothing but talk about your paintings in your uncle's office. Would you paint one for his birthday from me? I'm sure we could come up with a price we agree on."

I nod and smile. "Sure." I should be ecstatic. I just want to be alone, not think about sleeping with an idiot. Later, when we get into Poppy's car, I turn to him while he slides his key into the ignition.

"They key matches the suitcase?"

"Yeah, Raeanna, we need to talk."

CHAPTER 49

DEALING WITH JESSICA

"Jessica didn't show up for work yesterday or today." Rocky is telling me this while he chomps down on a grilled cheese at my table. Zane is sitting next to me looking from Rocky, to me, and then back again. "Her neighbor said she tossed three bags of clothes in her car and took off down the highway at six in the morning. Weird. We're hiring somebody new to head the bar."

"Why are you looking at me like I did something?" I ask Rocky. "I've been busy painting my very first, big girl consignment." I had to toss that in. He just hard-stares me.

"So, Zane," I say. "Can I rely on you to get to work on time at Joe's?"

"Yes, ma'am." I know he must know something. He looks a bit scared when he blinks at me.

Zane wasn't safe yesterday. I can guarantee he is today. I'm not sure at what point he was going to tell me Jessica had been picking him up every night while I'm working on the Edna Fields Performing Arts Contest or while I was at work.

"I'm eighteen. Leave me alone," he told me two days ago. "Do you want me to leave? Because Jessica said I could crash at her place."

"Do you want to stay with her?"

"You just don't understand." He just left, slammed the door behind him. But I do understand. I had to take a class in business management at Fields and I learned about market systems. Market systems are good things if set up properly. Jessica Pelletier has set up a market system with buyers and sellers of just about every drug known to man and also a few rolling brothels with twenty year-old girls giving blowjobs in the back seats of old men's cars. Her system is based on addiction so she's got lots of people coming back for more and more, whether it is coke or weed or sex. It is also based on greed. Her own, that is. Therein, lies her problem.

I know all this because the third night in a row Zane doesn't get home until two in the morning, I ask Poppy to come over and watch Mia for me while I find out where he's going. I'm used to hiding in the dark and not just because my daddy made me break into houses. I'm always just one spray paint can away from getting caught by the local police. I've learned to blend. It seems he borrowed six-hundred bucks from Jessica to help his mom leave his dad. Now there's a certain interest rate involved.

So I ask the two prostitutes standing outside the bar and find out he is paying off a debt. The fourteen year-old who is waiting for some weed in the parking lot tells me Zane brings it to him and twelve or thirteen of his buddies. He looks their age. Nobody bats an eye when he shows up at the ballfields with a bat and glove. And the fear that Jessica is going to send some big dude to hunt Zane's mom down and kill her if he doesn't pay her back sends him out again and again.

I suppose I wouldn't be slapping a bag down on the bar counter four hours later if I didn't see the flaws in Jessica's plans to be the drug monopoly queen of Hensley Grove. Because I have my own little league and it is having an alleged serial killer for a daddy.

"Okay, here's how it works. You see this paper, Jessica?" I ask her, scooting a small white piece of paper around so she sees a list of women's names.

"What do you want, Tango?" she says flatly with a roll of her eyes. She was sopping up some beer residue on the counter and stops, looks at me with the cocky flair of someone who has a couple big-boy bouncers to protect her and plenty of money to pay them.

"I want you to take a look at the paper." I poke a finger and she glances at it. "If you'll notice, there is a list of women's names. Susan James, Lisa Tatum, Tammy Lynn and Cathy Schuler. I added a few more the cops don't know about." I let my finger skim to the bottom and a little line I put in there at the end. "You see the blank space at the bottom?"

"Tango, if you don't quit bothering me, I'm going to call the cops."

"I find that hard to believe you're going to bring the cops down here. Might be bad for business, huh?"

"Then I'll call the bouncers up and have them drag you out of here."

"One second, please." I snatch up a pen from my pocket. I carefully write down: Jessica Lynn Pelletier, 614 Pike Street, Apartment 6. "I turn the paper around and let her eye it carefully. "You see, these girls all have three things in common. Their doors were locked, their windows were shut tight. But the night before they died, they each found a gallon of bleach with a pack of cigarettes sitting on their bed stand when they woke up in the morning. But most disturbing, they were all found dead holding burnt cigarettes in their fingers six weeks later and all smelled like they had been bathed in bleach." I smile a little. The kind of smile crazy people do with wide eyes. "I know the cops want you to believe it is a random act." I lean in and drop my words to a whisper. "It's not, Jessie. I can call you that, right? I talked to your little grammy today in Wheaton, Pennsylvania and she was the nicest old lady. Grammy told me you used to love to run around the house naked. Oh, by the way, you know I'm Dell Smyth's daughter, right? And

Dell, he doesn't like to see his little girl get angry. So here's what I'm saying to you. Leave Zane Hill alone, or you could, quite possibly, end up smelling like bleach. Maybe Grammy will too."

"I'm getting ahold of the cops."

"That's your call, Jessie," I say with a shrug. "But I heard you get your stuff from a guy named Cody Simms. I talked to Cody last night—well, I didn't just talk to him. I left him some presents. I sent some pics of you walking into the Hensley Police station, talking to cops right before his people got raided for drugs. It is so funny now the dates coincided. All six of them." At least, the dates on the pictures Kevin gave me that he had on his phone. "I also told him you've been informing cops about him so you've got the monopoly for all of southern Kentucky." I pat the counter. "Just saying. You might want to give the coroner in Wheaton a call, too. Make sure Grammy's okay. His name is Dutch Madison. You want his number?"

She didn't call. At two in the morning, I climbed up the fire escape of her apartment. I slipped through the window and set a pack of cigarettes and a gallon of bleach next to her bed. I can't believe she slept through it. However, there was a half bottle of rum sitting next to her pillow and a little gun I think she would have used on my daddy if he would have showed up. And I know she thought he would.

CHAPTER 50

ADRPEN RETURNS

"Is this yours?"

I'm sitting in the old theatre at Fields. I'm fiddling with the pay-as-you-go cell phone Poppy bought me until I can afford a new one. I'm trying to text Zane. He's not answering again. I figure he's eighteen. He should be able to run and do whatever he wants. But Poppy says if he is living with me and Mia, he needs to follow my rules. What rules? I don't have any house rules.

You need me? Finally he answers.

Where are you?

Just hanging out. Do you need something?

No, I really don't. I can't complain he left dishes in the sink because he keeps the house immaculate. I can't tell him to go home and clean his room. He makes the bed every morning. I just sit there thinking nothing, then I sigh.

I need to know you're safe.

I'm with your poppy. Big G's Pizza. Getting lecture.

That's when I hear the voice ask if something was mine. I am pushed down in the chair with my feet on the seat in front of me and my hoodie over my head trying to be as unobtrusive as possible while Mark Lafferty calmly listens to the one-hundred and seventy-eight students seated in front of me, so he can come up with a choreographed program for them. They are all allowed into the theatre. The school is allowing them to practice for the competition. I'm not supposed to be in the college. The dean was quite clear if I was caught there, he would have the police arrest me.

I know Mark would rather be out banging door to

door to find out if his sister is still alive. I told him it wasn't feasible. He needed a break. It is like dipping our hands into the water and trying to catch a minnow. We just keep coming up empty handed. We have spent the last two days culling through every file I had, every file on the internet trying to figure out where my dad is located now or if he is even alive, and sifting through the known felons living in town.

I peer up through my hoodie at the whispered voice. It is my duffel bag Adrien is setting down on the seat next to me. He is standing one row back in a t-shirt and jeans and plops down on one of the seats behind me when some of the people in front of me turn to take him in. Then he leans in and lays his arms on the back of the seat to my left and rests his chin on his arm. He's got his hair tied back. He's clean-shaven. He smells sweet and musky like the kind of expensive athletic aftershaves they sell at the high-end shops at the mall.

"So I guess your teaching doesn't stop at the dance level," I mumble to him, not even bothering to acknowledge him with my gaze. "You're teaching me life lessons too? Like distrust and fear—" I want so badly to tell him I am doing a painting for someone. Then, it pisses me off I want to impress him so badly now.

"Don't."

What is it with that word? "Don't say *don't*. I've heard it before and it got me in a mess of trouble with my—" *Heart.* I don't want to say it. I just close my mouth. "If you're wanting to rub your little joke in, you'll have to get in line behind the long list of other people who have crapped on me this month."

"I don't know exactly what happened—"

"I do," I say and turn slightly. "Your dancing partner made a laughingstock of me in front of everyone there, dropped my self-respect down to a minus ten. Then she took my duffel bag and had a car drop me off somewhere in downtown Brooklyn."

"I'm sorry. I had no clue Svetlana would go to such great lengths, Whiskey Tango."

I think the entire front row is Billy's acapella club. I think they recognize Adrien because they keep turning to gape at him. My face is red.

"It is just Tango," I grunt, sliding down more. "And great lengths to what? Have me murdered?"

"Don't disrespect me."

"We are not in the classroom," I hesitate, unsure how to address him and make a point. I settle on: "Mister Moreau. We are in the audience. When we are on the dance floor, okay, I'll have the highest reverence for you if you want—hell, I'll worship the very ground you walk on—"

He pinches my shoulder and it hurts a little. "Ow!" I say a little too loudly and rub my skin after his fingers fall away.

"No, I'm not talking about respecting me as a teacher. I'm talking about insulting me because you think I would do anything to hurt you."

"You just did."

"God, you are such a diva."

He says that loud enough everybody can hear him. Mark looks up from the paper he is feverishly writing on and I shove my hand across my forehead. Soft laughter fills the air while every head turns to take us in.

"Can we take this outside?" Adrien says staring down the third row eyeing him again. I'm not so sure I'm the diva in our relationship. I think he is. I look up, give him mean eyes and then roll them around to push the exaggeration.

"Okay, *Tango*," he stresses the name as if he is pointing out he is saying it properly while I follow him out to the dark hallway. "First of all, I had nothing to do with what happened with Svetlana. In fact, when I heard from one of her girls what happened, I got my contract out and tore it up in front of her. Second, it was your janitor, that I found out was not a janitor at all, who came up with the whole idea with her. You know he used to date her, right?"

"Colt dated—?"

"Svetlana Mikhailova. Yes. Colt Lucero. He nearly ruined me with a story he did five years ago writing for that stupid *Celebrity Magazine*. I thought I recognized him last month, but who would think he would be sweeping floors in Kentucky? He's one of those asses whose life is so bad, he tries to bring down everybody else to his level. He slept with her to get to me. But she always excuses herself that he really liked her. And she believes it. He wouldn't have slept with her if he didn't love her. Sadly, she didn't care how it hurt me professionally. It was love, she says, primal and passionate."

He must see the acknowledgement in my eyes right then. I mean, I knew Colt had used me. I'd heard everybody else—Poppy, Gil, Bella. I don't think I quite digested the whole thing or maybe I just didn't see the magnitude.

"I am sorry, Tango. You—?"

"Well, he wasn't that good to be primal and passionate as far as I'm concerned. He was kind of—clumsy," I mumble. "Yeah, he slept with me. Don't ask. Bad move, bad timing. I just broke up with my boyfriend and he told me I was beautiful. Sadly, at that point, I think a guy could have told me I look like a wilting daisy and I would have gone out with him." I look up. "But this isn't about you. It is about me. He didn't sleep with you, did he, to get information about me?" It is light teasing, but Adrien's face turns a deep shade of red.

"No."

"Well. I do care, Mister Moreau, about your reputation. It isn't happening again."

"Svetlana played me like he played you. I suppose that is why I need you to respect me."

"I'm sorry about your contract," I say softly. "You were trying to help me, give me a second chance I really don't deserve. I'm sorry you got caught up in this whole mess with me and Colt Lucero and Shane—"

He steps back, gives me a funny look like I just said something crazy. "I'm not sorry. Are you kidding?"

"No."

"You know," he says those two words and suddenly, he looks like a different person to me. I don't know, like a young man his age and not like I had been seeing him as old and rigid like Shane. It is like, suddenly, twenty years is washed off his face. "You weren't right when I rode with your father to the old factory. You said I'd never seen the inside of a grocery store. Yes, I have but only if I was lucky and my mama had enough to send me to go buy some bread. I'm not that person everybody makes me out to be. Svetlana tells me to hide my past because I grew up with my mama and three other families all smashed into a little brick apartment in the city. We barely had enough to eat most of the time. I'm not proud that I denied it. But I did. I did everything she told me to do. Now, I don't know what to do. For so long, I get stuck with plastic dolls and suddenly, the real thing comes along and I—" He draws out a long sigh. "We should leave it at that."

"At what?" I'm confused. It is just too much. I think my head is going to explode.

"A professional level."

"In comparison to—?" He doesn't seem to be focusing on me as much as the loud chatter in the theatre behind us. They must be finishing up inside. I reach out and poke his arm. "Tell me."

"Enough. You heard what I said."

I nod. "I did." I did. I know what happens when two people collide on the dance floor. When one uses another. But why, then, does his face take on a sense of sadness, loss? I shrug it off.

"So is that it?" I ask. "You aren't going to dance with me anymore? Because I'm not good enough. Because I didn't even make the first cut with Svetlana? Okay, I get it. I never wanted to dance with you in the first place." And hell, yes, I did. I hate how things come out of my mouth in anger to quickly like a defense mechanism shooting out darts before my enemy can even load.

He looks like he is going to say something. Adrien opens his mouth, then clamps it shut, closes his eyes.

"What?" I ask. "Just say it. You're moving on."

And crap, everybody picks this time to push their way out of the doors, a herd of cattle leaving the pen. They are all eyeing us as soon as they pass. Billy sidles up next to me, tells me he still doesn't like the idea of singing in front of a crowd. And he has a solo. I tell him we'll work on it.

"Are we still on tonight?" That's Mark, slipping from the throng and stopping in front of me with his hands stuffed in his pockets. It is twenty-four-seven trying to find his sister. He surpassed thinking she might still be alive and is now positive she is out there somewhere.

"Yeah," What can I say? "I can't do an all-nighter again. You're killing me. I got to work in the morning."

He gets this funny smile on his face. It is like the first

time I've seen him not fake one. "What?" I ask.

"I think that sounded sexier than you meant it to sound."

Oh. I blink, roll my eyes. "You know what I mean. I'll text Zane and tell him you're coming over. I made meatloaf tonight so if you're hungry, there's leftovers. Grab a bite to eat. I need just another minute, alright?"

Okay, Mark gets the hint. Billy does not. He's rocking back and forth on his heels about three steps away like a five year old who knows he shouldn't interrupt, but he's busting at the seams to tell me something. Adrien is eyeing him warily like he's wondering how the hell he's got the position as second-best friend over the goofy guy bouncing around the hallway and glaring at me.

"Go ahead, he's like a seven year-old who wants a cookie. Ignore him. He'll wait," I tell Adrien.

He looks at the stragglers leaving, looks at Billy apprehensively. "I don't know the first thing about relationships. I'm such a geek, Tango. I've always been able to maintain a certain amount of professionalism as an excuse. And you've got pretty boys stashed everywhere around you. Every time I turn around, you're wearing a new one around your neck. Where you are like a pup, unafraid and chasing and snapping at your little butterflies, I am the pup that's too afraid of the one butterfly I want to catch to run after it. Then when I do chase the butterfly, I don't know what I'd do if I caught it."

His words make my tummy jump. They are picturesque like a detailed drawing. Tonight, his demeanor is different and I notice it right then. He isn't all *quit being goofy, Tango*. He's like talking to me like a normal person. I'm not sure if I'm comfortable with that. It is a whole different atmosphere between us. I'm staring at a stranger, I suppose.

"And still," I pause and reflect on his words. "You've managed to come back three times a week from New York to Kentucky to dance with me. And I've waited three times a week for you to get here so I can dance with you."

"Half the time, you don't show."

I look over and Billy is waving his hands at me. It is annoying. I flap my hand back at him and shake my head.

"Most of the time, Colt would not open the doors for me," I mutter to Adrien. "Listen, I'm sick of dancing by myself. I would dance with you every night of the year, professionally speaking, of course. But I'm walking a trail of broken relationships in every capacity and I'm always looking for an excuse to walk away. It sounds like you came to break up with me. I get that. I really screwed up at the audition. I'd be embarrassed to dance with me too. So here's your chance. Tell me I'm not good enough to dance with you so I can make an excuse and walk away."

"I can't be your teacher anymore."

It hurt so badly. It was a nice way to put it. I just stare at him and I suddenly realize I just got my heart broken for real. Maybe for the first time. I swear, I feel it just smashing inside my chest like sharp shards of glass.

"Well, I never wanted to be your stupid student in the first place." Oh, my God, I'm crying when I reach out my hand and gently give him a push on his chest. Adrien takes a step back. My tears are hot and flowing. I don't know how to deal with it because I haven't done it since I was four.

"Tango!" I hear Billy and he's waving his hands while I swipe my wrist on my eyes.

"What, dammit!" I whisper-scream at him. He is waving at the darkened hallway.

"It is Shane Delgado and he has the campus security! I tried to tell you—"

CHAPTER 51

GRANNY PANTIES

"It's a Friday night. Don't you go out and dance?"

I'm surprised. I didn't even hear Adrien come into the theatre. Mark had practice a third day in a row for the competition. They are all day. I snuck in at six to help him. Shane is busy with his girls in the new theatre. Mark's nice and lets me dance after everybody leaves.

I left the door ajar. It is hot and muggy inside. We didn't part ways well which is kind of becoming our thing. I am stretching. My feet are literally going to fall off, I think. They ache. I lean over, unlace one smudged, pink pointe shoe at a time and tug each off. Ug. Big red blood blisters.

"So the thing is, no, I'm not going out tonight. It's not my usual way of spending an evening. I got two and a half hours while Poppy takes Mia to a gymnastics class. So I'm enjoying every second—alone. I'm popcorn, a glass of cheap wine, and an old movie—" I look up and he's staring at me quietly taking me in. He's from big cities and all-night clubs. I'm from a mid-size, rundown town with one strip bar and a coffee-club-bar. I'm sure he doesn't understand. It is discomfiting so I cut it short. "I guess tonight I've got the granny panties on." He acts as if he didn't even say mean words to me. He doesn't seem to care that I bawled my eyes out all the way home and partway into the night.

"You're wearing your grandmother's underpants?"

I lean in slightly to look at him. He tosses his duffel bag up next to me and plops it down in front of me.

"No, Adrien, I'm not. It is just a matter of expression." He reaches out and slips his hand around my foot and drags me gently toward him. "You know, a girl doesn't want to wear her old panties out dancing in case she hooks up with a guy. Can we drop it?"

I have to walk with my hands behind me, scoot on my butt until my leg is slightly turned in his lap. Damn, this is sexy. His fingers are gently massaging, turning my foot. "Butt ugly dancer feet," I point out, poking my knobby toes.

"Naw, beautiful dancer feet," Adrien corrects me, grabbing some athletic tape from his bag and two Band-Aids. He makes a concerted effort to slowly peel the tape away so it doesn't make the scary sound that reminds me of daddy. And he looks at me with knowing eyes. He looks up and smiles. "Mine, on the other hand, are big and ugly." He's so gentle taping my feet, gives me just enough of a foot massage while doing it that under less professional circumstances I would have offered sex in return for another five minutes of the bliss. "You need to wear those boot slippers the girls wear instead of those high heels and sandals." He pats my ankle so I slip my leg off his lap.

He yawns, throws his hands up like a little boy stretching his arms over his head. He is so young looking. I wonder how he got parts in the big ballets looking like he was thirteen. I guess you just have to be ten times as good.

Adrien falls back and lays on his back on the floor. "Jetlag. It gives me pneumonia."

"You mean insomnia?" I ask him, stifling a laugh.

"Yeah, I can't sleep." I stop and lay back next to him so we're side by side. Then, I realize the cement hurts my head, so I scoot around and lay my head on his belly.

"So, what do granny panties look like? Is there like a special store that sells them?" He asks and his belly vibrates with his words. I shift my head to look up at him to see if he is sincere. He's all unsmiling and serious, his brow is furrowed while he looks down at me. I laugh out loud. I can imagine the image he is conjuring up in his mind of the same kind of huge white underpants big-butted Missus Finch hangs off a string in her balcony apartment.

"Well, I guess we are going to discuss this whether I want to or not." I sigh, turn my head toward the door like I can escape. "They are just your old underpants. The ones you wear every day, not the cute, sexy thongs with lace and bows you set aside in case a gentleman wants to see them."

"Men ask to see your underpants?"

I think he is serious and roll over so I am laying with my bent elbows and chest on his belly and thinking he couldn't be that naive. "Excuse me?" I mumble, lacking for words. Then Adrien does my cross-eyed stare at me.

"Goofy girl. Svetlana keeps a tight rein, but I'm not that inexperienced."

"Keeps a tight rein? I don't know what you mean."

"She doesn't want me to see other women, dance with other women except the students. I've been dancing with her since I was a baby. She's like ten or twelve years older than me and I know—I know she won't admit it but she can't dance like she used to. She has arthritis in her knees and I don't know how many times a month she sees a doctor for her feet. She has kind of raised me. She says it takes the passion away from our dance if I'm thinking of another woman. Focus is the key."

"Forever?" I ask him. "There's a huge world out here. What if you meet someone you love? Or even someone that will, like in my case, eat popcorn and watch old sappy movies with you at night."

"I just don't."

"Damn, I bet you get lots of offers too." I shake my head. He smells good and I try not to think about the sweet scent of his sweat and the cologne he is wearing. "You're like an old married couple from one of those churches that don't believe in sex. Or do you have sex?"

"Tango, don't ask that."

"Sorry. I'm just curious."

"No, we don't. She's kind of a stepmother, I think."

"A wicked stepmother. What a waste." I pat his chest, shake my head. "That could be a new twist on a fairy tale, the wicked stepmother and the prince."

"You dance while your bodyguard sleeps, no less."

"You've got a point," I agree with him. I haven't felt this close to anyone, not even Kevin. It seems so flawed that our relationship is like two people staring at each other through a glass window. We can't do much more. "But you're going to go through your entire life trying to dance with passion and emotion with a woman who is cold and uncaring enough to stop you from finding love. So, in all reality, you will never actually experience what you are trying to get an audience to feel. How does that work?"

He reaches up, playfully pushes the hair away from my face that has unraveled from my hair tie. His eyes are sleepy. He's got these perfect full lips that curve downward. Shit, I want to grab his hand, twine my fingers with his. I want to feel his hand in my hair, tugging me forward. I want to see if his lips are as soft and full as they look—

"It doesn't. But it doesn't matter. Everyone I meet is shallow." He gives me a little push, sits up, and rests his elbow on his knee. "They just want to dance because I'm famous, because I'm—" *Boom.* The moment is over.

"God, I have the same problem," I interrupt him with a sassy bite to my words. "Men fall at my feet, want to be with me because I'm talented." I roll my eyes. I'm looking down at him on the floor. "You are so arrogant."

"No, Tango, I am not. I try to be. I'm just—not. The shallow people bore me because they are fake. I thought you saw that, maybe you don't."

"You're right. I'm just like them. Let me fawn on you, oh great one, mighty one." I hold up my hands, clasp them together and fall to my knees next to him. "What is the saying on your shirts? *Adrien Moreau, Mon Chéri.*"

"Stop it!"

He is angry. I clamp my mouth shut. I drop my arms to my side and sit down across from him.

"I'm sorry," I say. I try to read his eyes. They are cool. I wiggle my fingers. I just expect him to take them. Billy does it all the time. So does Rocky when his friends aren't around. He, too, latches on. We sit there staring at them.

"Billy always brings me down with something like: *Gross, Tango, you know you have huge a pimple on your forehead,*" I divulge. "Or *your zipper's been down all day. Did you know that?* It's like, why didn't it occur to him to not point out the pimple or just tell me when he sees me at seven leaving for school that my zipper's down? What I'm saying is that friends point stuff out and sometimes we figure it's okay because—"

"Tango, I can't be your friend. We dance." He wiggles his fingers from mine. I'm just humiliated and dumbstruck.

"Are you even capable of a relationship outside dancing?" He's got on this stone face. "Svetlana, she's made you a board. You feel—nothing. And that is why your partners are like dancing with boards, Mister Moreau. You are like dancing with a board." I smack my hands together and right in front of his face. "Two boards."

"I don't have to put up with this dollshit." His face is livid. *Dollshit?* Um, I don't point out his misuse of words that would be comical in any other situation. "I don't need you." He says that, grabs up his bag, and simply walks out. "I'm done with you, Tango. Done."

CHAPTER 52

I DID A BAD, BAD THING

I did a bad, bad thing on Wednesday. And for that, I'm not proud. I'm standing outside the new theatre doors watching Adrien do some basic lifts with a girl. I don't know her name. She's one of Shane's chosen few, a freshman who will probably be quite talented, but still lacks a certain refinement. In my opinion, of course. Adrien can make a garbage bag full of trash look good dancing.

She is young and pretty and unemotional in her expressions. But she performs them tonight with Adrien with soft doe eyes and the obedience of a well-mannered, paper-trained pup. She's a hundred sorries and please and thank yous and the perfect student. She listens, doesn't complain, doesn't mouth him like I do. I figure, she's his spare tire, my replacement. She's certainly prettier and clings on Adrien's every word. He probably won't drop her.

It's when she clings a little too long on his arm that I do the bad, bad thing. I've never really felt jealous. The night I tore apart the apartment when I caught Sophie with Kevin, it was anger that I'd been feeding and clothing the idiot for the last year. This, this is a new explosion in my chest that I have no tools from past experience to use to tame it. It just hits me like a spray of gasoline hits a lighted fire and explodes hot coals in my chest.

She doesn't see it coming when I strut across the stage and simply push her down with both my hands. She's surprised. She didn't see it coming. Hell, I didn't see it coming. While she scoots across the floor on her rear in a panic to get away from me, I am matching each of her spider-crawls with a step and my arms crossed. The poor thing is dazed, looking at me like the little bluebird that hit the glass window in Anna's kitchen, stunned and not quite sure why she is suddenly dizzy and sitting on the ground.

"Tango, what are you doing?"

He's so calm it makes me more irritated. I don't even know why I went looking for him.

"Am I that replaceable? I'm like a frigging disposable plastic razor, am I?" I hiss. My eyes have not left his perfect student on the floor. She's wide-eyed, glancing from me to Adrien who is behind me and to my left.

"Shauna," he says, snatching up a towel and swiping at his face. "Can you go get a drink of water, take a break?"

I don't even turn. "Don't bother. I'm leaving."

"No, you are staying, telling me what this is all about," he demands. "And you are going to give her an apology." I know he must have waved her out with a hand when I don't answer. "Tango, you said you didn't want to dance with me anymore."

I did. Yesterday, he walked out. Then the door slams back open and Adrien is standing there again.

"What are you doing here?" I ask him flatly.

"I am not done with you."

"You said—you were done with me."

"Just shut up," he says hotly. So we're working on the one arm handstand yesterday. It is only a ten second hold where Adrien lifts me in the air, turns my body around in a circle and then, I flip my legs upward. For just five seconds, I linger there, then I twist my legs around slowly and fall into his arms. He's in a rotten mood already and rigid. We have danced long enough together, I can recognize it in the tightness of his moves, the expression on his lips, eyes and brow.

"Tango, you have to hold it there without shaking."

"I don't know how to *not* shake."

"You have to work out, strengthen your arm. Dammit, I thought we talked about this!" He gives me a little push upward. I'm not sure if he is angry or just frustrated when he does it. I wasn't expecting it. My elbow simply buckles and I just collapse straight downward, headfirst and like a rocket spiraling a million miles an hour toward earth.

He can't catch me with any grace. I slap the ground hard, thank God, on my right side instead of my head because he slips a hand over and moves my head to the right. My body still makes a sickening thud to the floor. I just lay there, trying to figure out if there is anything broken. I wiggle my toes, my fingers, waggle my neck.

"Oh, shit. Oh—shit!" Adrien is freaking crazy next to me. "What the hell were you thinking? What were you doing, stupid girl!" He falls to his knees and he's leaning over me with his hands out like he's just dropped his mom's two-hundred year-old heirloom vase and it has shattered into a thousand pieces on the floor. "My God, I broke you. Why do you never listen to me? You need to work out—"

The truth of the matter is I have been working out. I've been working out an hour in the morning and an hour after I get Mia to bed. Hard. No soda pop. Lots of salads. I lift with Kevin's old weights and stretch and practice with an old banister Rocky screwed to my bedroom wall.

"Screw you." I just say it. "I'm done. I don't want to dance with you." I roll and push myself to my feet, a dizzying event that leaves me clinging to Adrien's arm until I find my balance. "You yell at me. I don't want to be yelled at. I'm doing you a favor, you get that right? You treat me like dirt. I don't want to be treated like dirt. You're the friggin' diva, you get that right?" I waggle my hands in the air. "Oh, Adrien Moreau, he's so beautiful, he's so perfect.

He knows everything about ballet. He's got girls and boys lined out the door for lessons. Well, as I see it, you're arrogant and spoiled and maybe there's a hundred little dancers that would let you treat them like shit just to be tossed around like you, be your crash test dummy. But I'm not one of them. I'm tired of being your freebie, your dollar store dance whore. So lay off. Find somebody else!"

I push off of him and swagger toward my duffel bag.

"Your nose is bleeding, Tango," he says softly. "What is wrong with you? You are acting— angry." I know that. He tries to snatch my arm, I jerk it away. I am cupping my hand above my lip catching the blood until I can grab up my t-shirt and stuff it there. "I said get off of me! I don't want to dance with you!"

So he's right. I'm acting angry. I'm stressed. I started my janitor job and it is lonely and sucks. I can't keep dancing. I finally get an art consignment and I will hardly have time to paint. I won't have the time now. To make matters worse, Mark gave me a picture of Hannah and me when we were little and posing for a play together. *Why?* I asked him. *Because it is the only way I know of to keep her alive. You are the only one that believes me and you're not doing anything.* While I pivot on my feet in my stretchy running shorts, an old tank top and the tennis shoes Colt gave me, I'm wagging my head peeved none-the-less and trying to shove away Hannah's tiny face on the picture pressed to mine in a silly kiss on the cheek. Adrien grabs up a towel and swipes it along the back of his neck.

"Do you just want me to stop dancing just because you got mad at me for dropping you? I teach. That is what I do." He reaches out, runs his finger along my arm. There's a big black, red, and blue bruise forming between my shoulder and my elbow. It tickles. I get goosebumps. I hate him for making me get goosebumps, for wanting him to touch me like that again.

"You know I'm not mad at you for dropping me."

"Then what?"

I don't answer.

"You need to apologize to Shauna," he states. "Before you leave."

"Okay," I say it so nonchalantly, I know he is gritting his teeth, expecting the worse when I slam the door open. He probably should. I was going to scream *I'm sorry!* right in her face, watch her cower.

"Hey, Tango." I turn my head slightly while my hands are still on the door. He is shaking his head, laughs softly. "Why don't you do that to Svetlana for me, eh?" He reaches out his arms, pretends he is giving the air a push. "She's the only one I have to answer to like I'm an indentured slave."

He's rolling his head around his neck. I know it is a nervous gesture. I spotted it the first time I met him. *Svetlana.* Yeah, I bet he does that when she's around. I bet she does this kind of crap to her girls. I realize, I don't want to be anything like her. I bet she won't let him leave as easily as tearing up a contract.

Shauna is standing right at the doorway like a mouse waiting for the cat to paw at her. I simply stop and look at her. "I'm sorry. I shouldn't have pushed you."

He's sitting at the same table in the back of Joe's. I'm not taking his table today. I find out from Gil who found out from Colt who found out from Delia why Adrien was so moody yesterday. I guess Shane has been making remarks about me in class. You know: *I had a student, who shall remain nameless* (then he'd slip my name here) *who did it this way which is wrong,* and *do it right, you don't want to turn out a failure like Raeanna Baldwin, do you?* Adrien has always just stood back and remained expressionless whenever he ridiculed me. Then two days ago, he pushed up a hand and told Shane Delgado if he made one more unprofessional remark about me or any other student, he was not going to offer his services any longer. Gil said the room was completely silent. They both left and there was a heated discussion in the hallway that included cursing. Only Shane returned.

So, Cassie Jones offered to take his table. If there's a cute guy, she wants the table. I was more than happy to oblige even though I am still cleaning up after her because she never cleans the table right, always gets the order wrong.

The only thing I ask of her is to drop a note at the table, lean over, and tell Adrien: "This is classified. The man in the kitchen cannot see it. He is an assassin. Burn the letter when you are done reading it."

And the note says: *Je suis désolé, I'm sorry. You are right. I don't show I respect you. I do. So I will be like the other girls and prostrate myself before you and worship you with fervor. I will be obedient and keep my mouth closed and try to impress you like the others— So here goes. You were born on a little farm outside Domfront, France. Your maman moved to the city when you were little to be closer to a hospital because you were sick. That was when your papa left. The doctors said you weren't going to walk again and she said: C'est des conneries, bullshit. (Bullshit not dollshit) My boy will run. But you had to learn to walk again and your sister's dance instructor said she could help. You didn't like dancing at first. Your first ballet class was when you were six. It was at school and it was supposed to be for one of your sisters,*

Frankie. She was mad when you were chosen for a scholarship. She ended up working as a nurse and still holds the grudge today—

"How do you know this?"

I am ringing up a customer at the register when Adrien barges past the man and waves my little note at me.

"I looked it up." I tell him, counting out the man's change in dollar bills. "You know, online. You said your fans looked up stuff online to impress you—"

"No, nobody knows this—all of this."

"Oh, okay," I thank the customer with a wave and close the register while he walks away. "I used my secret agent skills and called your mom."

"You what? How did you get her number—hell, how did you talk to her? She does not speak English."

"I know that too. I paid Chad Evans, you know the guy in the wheelchair, twenty bucks to translate. He learned French when he was stationed on a post somewhere in Afghanistan with French troops. Your mom's funny."

"You need to learn boundaries. This is—" He is staring at the note, shaking his head.

"Impressive, I know. She also said you haven't called her in two months. She has to find out about you in the newspaper or online. Anna would hang me out to dry if I didn't call her at least once a week and I told your mom that and she agreed," I tell him, turning to grab a tray Joe is handing me out the window. "But I suppose this is another control tactic Svetlana has on you. Or another excuse not to call your mom. Or dance with me outside the shadows of dark, dingy rooms like—you know, the dollar store dance whore." I sigh, pass him by. "But you should be nice to me. Because I *don't* know boundaries, I got her recipe for stew."

CHAPTER 53

FALLING IN LOVE IN FRONT OF A FAKE CAFÉ IN FAKE FRANCE

"I think you like this, running from the police."

That is Adrien Moreau and I know he can't see my eyes are big and wide with that *oh-shit-we're-gonna-get-caught* look. I'm shoved up beside him in an overlap of the gate to an old flood wall, trying desperately to keep the toes of my red shoes from being the focal point of the spotlight zooming in and out of the window of the Hensley Grove Police Department cruiser.

"Cripes," I whisper over the cruiser radio, "can you be quiet, please?"

"I was just pointing it out," his voice drops to a whisper. "You were laughing like a hyena when we were sprinting down the street."

"Well, I'm not now, am I? I was drunk on fake love and wine. Not only is this awkward—" I wave a hand between us, "but I can't get dragged down to the police station again. For one, we aren't on what you could call good terms, the cops and me. Two, they'll figure out it is me who paints this town in graffiti."

"What did you expect?" Adrien is standing with his back against the wall. I was pressed into the corner against his side. When the light bounced six inches from my feet, I made a quick turn. It left me facing him, well, his belly button because that is where my chest is pressed. "Besides, this isn't that awkward. You dance with me all the time. We get closer than this, look into each other's eyes." Yeah, he's right. I like looking into his eyes, holding on like we're just about to kiss, then don't. Of course, in my mind, we do kiss.

"Dancing is your profession. When we dance, we are working." I peer left to right. I can barely hear the cruiser tires rolling over the gravel on the street.

"Right, now we are partners in crime."

He's right. We are. I mean, at least I am. It took me three days, but I paint a little panorama from an online map view I pulled to street level of his city. It is an old stone street that matches a tiny brick alley by the Welcome Viaduct. I even added the tiny outside scene of a little coffee and butcher shop called Café Alain I can see on the map. Poppy cut a little A-frame, hinged storefront sign from some plywood he had in his garage. I painted it to closely resemble the café sign. Anna surprises me with some paint. Gil gives me an old plastic table and chairs from Layla's last yard sale that didn't sell and I stick them in front.

Alma Bean delivers the note. She's in theatre and plays the part of an informant for me. She doesn't question my motives. However, she does ask me if I'm really dating Billy. I tell her no and she looks pleased. I tell her if she delivers the note without letting anybody know, I will have her over for ice cream this weekend with Billy, Mia, and me.

The note says: *You must meet me. It is urgent. I have info of your lover. I will be wearing red. Corner of High Street at the Welcome Viaduct. 10:00 pm. Wednesday. WT*

So I'm there at nine-forty-five with Chad Evans who is playing watch out at the welcome sign. I like him because he's okay with me being weird and doing this stuff. He says he's bored anyway, sitting in his apartment all alone watching TV.

I'm figuring Adrien either shows or he doesn't. I'm only out the eight dollars and ninety-two cents I paid at the second hand store for the sultry red dress, pumps, and black flapper cloche hat with red silk ribbon and a brim that dips over my right eye. I got four dollar's worth of cheese at

Jenson's, crackers and I pilfered a bottle of wine from Gil's liquor cabinet. I'd curled my hair, plopped the hat on my head and set up the little café table in the shadows. And I wait in the shadows. Of course, he doesn't show.

By ten-thirty, I'm leaning against one of the green antique gas lampposts the city revamped in the historic district of town, which is anything north of the Welcome Viaduct. The orange light makes black butterfly shadows on the ground. Chad and I have passed the bottle of wine back and forth twice. It is a quarter of the way gone.

"We can take the party over to my apartment if you want," Chad nods down the dark street. "Because if the cops come by and see you like this, you're going to get arrested for prostitution."

"Are you making a pass at me?" I tease him, tossing my hand over my head and turning my face to look upward like I am being coy. "Because flirting with me in this dress costs my johns fifty-bucks."

"You know my heart is broken. I was saving myself for Hannah." He tries to play it off like he's making a joke. I see the hurt in his eyes. "But whatever. I was just thinking we could play some video games."

"I'm good with that," I shrug, plug the wine bottle and stuff it in my duffel bag. "I got an hour and a half until I pick up Mia from Anna's. I don't want my fifteen bucks for all of this to go to waste. Plus the twenty I'm giving you. She thinks I'm cleaning grills tonight at Joe's." I start to push away from the lamppost.

"Is that the guy you're meeting?"

"How'd you know he was there?" I can see him, a dark shadow walking fast along the sidewalk. It rained this afternoon and the lights from the hotel and the lamps shine off the wet asphalt.

"I heard his steps." Chad wheels around. "I guess our date is off."

"Okay, so there are two viaducts. I have been standing at the other viaduct for forty minutes," Adrien is walking up to me fast, talking at the same time. He gives Chad a quick wave and a curious gaze while he wheels off. "Who is he?"

"My look out. So we don't get caught."

"Oh, for what?"

"I told you in the note. It is official business, secret. No one can know. Now finish what you're saying."

"Oh, it's just that a guy finally drives up and asks if I needed help. I say, yes, this is the Welcome Viaduct, right? So he sets me straight. I am here—" He looks me up and down like suddenly he is taking in what I'm wearing. "Holy hell. Is that what the expletive is for—what I'm seeing?" He waves a hand at me with wide eyes.

"Don't Holy hell me." I reach out my hand, wiggle my fingers. "We don't have much time. Come with me."

Adrien, he just stops me with his hand even before we get to the table. "What the—" He narrows his eyes, stares at the painting, the table, and then the little sign.

"It looks kind of like your town, right? The one you grew up in?" I'm standing a step behind him. I'd released his fingers. He steps away from me and just keeps gazing at the wall, stepping left to right and seeming to take in every little detail. He walks straight up to it, touches the door to the café, then steps back and breaths out a sigh.

"You did this, Tango?"

"I did. Sit down, I have news about your—"

"Stop." He just says it, yanks his eyes away and glares at me. "Why are you doing this?"

"Are you mad at me?" I'm furrowing my brow. He is looking at me like Poppy glared at me when I went off the paper once in a fit of artistic fervor and colored the entire dining room table. "It's just a wall."

"Answer me."

"I don't know. Because." I hold out my arms to my sides and think about it. "Because I like you. You're my second best friend. I think of you in a lonely hotel room reading a book with the fan on in the bathroom. It's fun. I like playing spy with you."

"Um, I like it too."

"You do?" I ask slightly incredulously. He ignores my question. He turns again and does the staring thing. I can see him rubbing his chin. He nods to the wall. "I could—I feel like I could just walk up and go inside. I know Paul Alain whose grandfather owned the café, then his father, and now he owns it. We played together as children. I didn't want to be in ballet, did I tell you that?" He turns and smiles at me. "I wanted to be a butcher. He wanted to play American soccer. He texts me once in a while and he talks meat and I talk dance. We are so different now."

"Well, yeah, sit." I walk over and snatch out the crackers and cheese and wine and set them on the table. "I have news of your lover—"

"Can I take some pictures of you with my phone in front of the painting?" I start to balk. But Adrien gets a soft smile on his lips and shakes his head. "This time, with clothes on should not be difficult?"

"No," I groan. Those stupid Tango Porn pictures again. "You saw those too? Is there anyone in this entire state that hasn't seen them?"

"I don't know how many people live in Kentucky. But you have two-hundred and fifty-thousand views. Two-hundred and fifty-one if you count me. It gets lonely sitting in gloomy hotels. I spend a lot of time on the computer."

I just give him a classic roll of my eyes, then shake my head. "Of course," I say and with airs of a model, I pose a dozen ways—looking covert, backing into the wall with my arms at my side, sitting at the table and eyeing him coyly. Then I make him sit down and we eat crackers and talk silly spy stuff and drink wine beneath the gas lights. I tell him I am undercover this time as a lady of the night and the man I slept with knew of his lover's trail into the unknown.

"So where is my lover tonight?" he asks me, taking a swig of the wine straight from the bottle.

"She had made it from Florida, through Alabama and Tennessee. That is what my john told me. She was delayed there to stop some terrorists who were boarding a plane. After that, the homeland security took her in for questioning and they saw she had an alias. But there was a Russian spy among them and he helped her escape."

"And now?"

"That is all I know," I whisper. I see him pulling up his phone. He turns it toward me with a picture of me. "La belle," he says. "Beautiful." It does look cool. I lean on my elbows to see closer. The painting comes alive with the yellow gas lights, the colors deep and vibrant.

"It is."

"No, it is you," he corrects me. "You are a beautiful woman."

I'm caught off-guard. I try to shrug it off. It is difficult. Is he playing our game? He is smiling and I know I fall easily and then shove up a fence around me. Still, even if I don't show it, my heart plays havoc when no eyes can see.

"If I did not think my lover would murder you, I would take you away from this life of espionage and lack of underwear for your low pay."

I laugh. I should never have used the example of not being able to afford underwear. "We could still leave your stupid lover," I tell him boldly. "We could run away, change our names, find a new country where no one knows us."

"And dance and paint graffiti, just the two of us forever."

I snatch the bottle of wine from the table, take a swig.

"That is so spicy," he chuckles. "You're drinking like the man sitting with the blanket on the corner that I passed at the wrong viaduct."

"Oh, that's Tom Burg. He is a watch out for me sometimes too."

He reaches out suddenly and pushes his hand on my cheek. I look up from my hat. Our eyes are just about to meet. At the exact moment, I hear Chad give a good, loud whistle between his fingers. "Cops!"

"Do we need to run?" Adrien snaps to attention, cranes his neck to see Chad falling sideways in the wheelchair at the curb. "Oh, no, your friend, he just fell—" He jumps up ready to run toward Chad. I grab his arm. "No, monsieur, this way. He is paid to cover for me. He will keep the cops for a few so we can get away." Adrien is looking at me like I am crazy. "You're not serious."

"Yes. I am."

And that is how we end up at the floodwall twenty minutes later, sandwiched together.

"You do this a lot?" he asks me.

"I do. Usually alone. Sometimes with Mia. Half the time with Rocky. Never with a fake spy. You're having fun?"

"I am." I can't tell if he's kidding. The siren runs loud, two long drawls and then a bleep-bleep. I can hear the radio they are so close, see the red and blue lights rolling across the wet asphalt. I feel Adrien push back against the wall as far as he can. He pushes his arms around my shoulder, tows me with him. I don't have a choice but to press my head to his chest. It is clumsily comforting.

I can hear the cop cursing. I try not to giggle. Adrien chuckles and his chest jiggles. I realize they are making their way down farther, turning on another street. Relief. "So this is where we part ways, no?" Adrien asks me softly. "I will miss you, Étoile Noire, Black Star."

"I know how to find you, Russian Mafia."

"And you will?"

"Perhaps," I sigh with exaggeration, look upwards to Adrien's eyes. It isn't easy with the hat bobby-pinned to my hair. "But we have tonight, this moment, right now—"

"This moment," he says softly and he reaches up, tips my chin back. I know we are both caught in that moment. I look at him and he says something in French I do not understand. Then he brings up his free hand and rubs his thumb across my lips. "La belle," he says softly. "You are so mysterious, my mischievous little dancer with the perfect grande jeté in a dark hallway of the police station behind the police escorting her to a cell. And you don't have two sides, a fake and a real. You are spicy all across the board, I saw that in you when you held your ground with those silly girls at the art show, right? Then you are spicy to me even though you should be like them and put on bogus smiles. I think of the scent of your skin on sleepless nights and it is every night now. I see your eyes the color of lilies. Now I will have the image of your full red lips stuck in my mind and the feel of your body pressed against me."

I'm like dizzy with his words. I am drunk, but not as much on the wine as feeling his eyes on mine, his hand cupping my chin. His body pressed to me.

"Adrien, we need to—stop this," I say suddenly, push

back with my hands, step away. "It is going too far with me. You are making me—break out into a sweat."

"Too far?" He pushes to one side. "You tell me to play with you and when I do, you push me away? You are just too crazy here and crazy there for me. At least with Svetlana, it is straight down the line unemotional and detached. I know what to expect and what not to expect."

"Do not compare me to Svetlana," I hiss between my teeth. "And you know what? If that is where you want to be, with your stupid bitch Svetlana, then go be with her. Don't come back to me. Everybody tells me I push people away. Not this time. It isn't me. You are the one who pushes me away. You say you don't want to be my teacher and you still come banging at my door three times a week to dance. And I try everything in my power to be there at that door waiting for you. You do understand that, don't you? I wait for you. Because, dammit, I didn't want to dance. I really, really didn't want to dance for anyone anymore until you came along. And then, you did. I give you a necklace to show you how I feel and you never wear it. I look into your eyes and you turn them away unless you are playing some part in the dance. But when I look at you, I am feeling emotion, not just faking it. I'm feeling—shit, love and you—you don't want to give it back because it is inappropriate or whatever because you are my teacher. Well, Mister Moreau, if you don't feel like being loved, then leave. Get out of my life. Because I love you and I can't stop. I can't just pretend I don't like you just because you're a teacher. I don't need another man for a one night stand and I definitely can't just dance with you. So don't be my damn teacher and stay or go back to Svetlana and leave me alone!"

I realize what I'd said far too late. I don't know if I've ever just bared my soul so easily. I stand there blinking. I take off down the street. I hear him calling me. I don't turn.

CHAPTER 54

FINDING MY CRY AND FREAKING OUT POPPY

Sometimes I think the only person in the world I can trust is Poppy. Then again, I'm finding out there's a bit more to him than I thought. I drive straight to his house in a blinding rain of tears. Thank God, Anna had already laid Mia down in her little bed.

"There's—there's this girl," I sob, "who likes this boy, but the boy doesn't like the girl. The girl didn't know she liked the boy and it—it doesn't matter because the girl was trying to *not* act like she liked the boy. Now—now he's gone. And it didn't matter because I'm broken and my heart is broken and—" While I sob in his arms on the couch and make no sense at all blubbering about everything wrong in my life and he pats my back a little too hard thinking something horrible, horrible has happened because I never cry, he tells me a secret about the suitcase.

"Your dad gave me that Tringle Double Case," he says thirty-two minutes into my weeping that are now snuffles. He hands me tissue number eight and waits for me to blow my nose. "Oh, that's a lot of snot," he says to make me laugh. I force a little smile. Then he says this: "Back about twenty years ago. Your dad said as long as I kept it safe and hidden and gave him fifty bucks a month, I could keep you. He said he'd come back for it someday and he'd know if I messed with it."

"You're telling me you bought me on a payment plan?"

"He did what he could to make you safe, Raeanna," Anna tells me. She has just come into the room and although it is eighty degrees outside, she has made me a warm cup of chocolate milk.

"You are still paying him? He's still alive?"

"Yes." Poppy looks at Anna and she nods. "I send a letter each month to a post office box. None have been returned so I have to assume he's still alive."

So he could still be murdering girls. "You don't know where the other suitcase is?"

"I have no clue."

"What's in the suitcase?" I ask and just then, there is a knock at the front door. Anna has her arms wrapped around her chest and she turns to go answer it. Poppy sighs one of his deep, deep sighs and pats my shoulder. "We don't know. I was afraid to open it, couldn't open it. Maybe he couldn't either. That young woman, Bella, said Colt Lucero keeps it in a box by his bed. It never leaves his sight."

"Is he still hanging around Gil?"

"He was over the other night with his girlfriend," Poppy tells me. "She's the cutest little thing. They played some board games until about eleven. What a fun bunch they are."

I don't say anything to Poppy about my past relationship with Colt. Nor does he seem aware that Taylor and her coven have spent most of my life trying to make it a living hell. I'm only culling around in my mind how I can get my fingers on that damn key and open up the suitcase. Barring breaking into Colt Lucero's house—

"Sweetie, you have a visitor." Anna has this really strange expression on her face. She almost looks like a balloon that is going to pop. Her eyes are bulging and her smile is being smothered by biting her lower lip. I sit up a bit, let my head sway to the right. It is Adrien Moreau and he's holding my duffel bag up in his hand. He towers over Anna and makes her look like an elf standing next to a giant.

"You know," he says with a nervous smile at Poppy and then me. "I think most commonly people assume the princess is going to leave a shoe instead of an old— rucksack." Rucksack? His accent isn't that deep, but once in a while when he scrambles for the proper word, he slides back into a thick version of his own.

I know my lipstick is smudged. My lips must be puffy and I'm dragging a tissue across my nose to swipe off the snot. "I'm not a princess," I tell him. "You made that perfectly clear. That is a duffel bag—there are no shoulder straps like a backpack. Please just leave me alone."

"I told you I wasn't good at this. I am used to Svetlana telling me what to do, telling me who to be with or without. She doesn't even want me to talk to my mama. You have to know that. You talked to my mama."

Anna and Poppy's eyes are going back and forth between me and Adrien. "No, you tell me I am horrible at dancing. *Quit being goofy,* you always tell me. Well, I'm goofy. You could have saved me a whole lot of grief, recognized that, and left me alone in the first place."

"You're killing me, Tango." He is looking right at me. His voice is low and his cheeks are pink. I can't tell if he's angry at me or embarrassed because Poppy is taking him in, maybe sizing him up to drag him out of his house. "I want to dance with you and that is the problem. You are here, I am there. We're a million miles away." Then he reaches into his shirt and tugs out the necklace I gave him. "I take it off only when dancing, Tango. That is why you didn't see it. We were dancing. How can you think I don't care? Do you know how much money I have spent flying back and forth two and three times a week just to dance with you? Screw Shane and his program. I stayed to help because I wanted to dance with you. I wanted to set you up with a program in New York so—so we could dance. That's why I sent you that information. I did not know the extent Svetlana would go to make sure I did not have another dance partner, on stage or off. If you would just give me time to explain I don't want to *teach* you, I just want to dance with you."

"You know, if you just put in *be with you* instead of *dance* each time the boy who doesn't like the girl talks, it might make better sense to you, Raeanna," Poppy says slyly. Anna giggles like a four year old. Obviously she has some dance magazines stashed beneath her bed like Kevin used to hide his porn under the mattress. "Am I correct, son?"

"Yes, sir. I mean, I like her," Adrien has this head roll he does after a dance, stretching out his neck. He does it right then, a nervous gesture. I can literally see Anna get goosebumps while she ogles him. Adrien doesn't seem to notice, but blows a puff of air out of his lips and gives me wide eyes. "I like you. I probably love you. Is that weird to say? I called my mama like you guilted me into doing. She says I must love you on the phone that's why I'm tripping around like a clown and I've lost three pounds."

"It's not weird at all," Anna answers for me. My mouth is open, I hadn't quite been able to push words into my lips. She snatches up a tissue and I swear she is dabbing her eyes. I'm sure she's got me married off in her mind, with three kids, fenced-in backyard and a seasonal above-ground swimming pool.

"I like you too. The only thing weird right now is these two being a part of this conversation," I wag a hand at Anna and Poppy. "Can we talk out on the porch?"

"Oh, my," Anna waves her used tissue in front of her face when I come back in to get us some waters.

"Yeah, please don't get excited, Anna," I whisper. "I give a lot of leeway for bolting until they find out my past. Kevin is the only one who has stuck around."

Poppy has a swing on the front porch. It is wooden and has chains attached to the ceiling. I sit down with two glassed of bleach-smelling Hensley Grove city water and hand one to Adrien. We're like two high school kids on a blind date. I'm not sure how to act around him when we're not dancing. I think he's the same.

"So—this is awkward, right?" I ask Adrien. He laughs and shrugs. "No dancing, just sitting."

"I don't know, maybe," he answers, takes a fake sip of his water. "Awkward isn't bad." Silence. Holy shit. I really, really like him. I mean, I can't ever remember looking at a guy and thinking anything more than *why the hell does he like me?* Now, I'm thinking *How the hell can I make sure he doesn't see the real me and run like hell?*

We swing a little, our feet banging on the floor. "You want me to show you how to do the slow Whiskey Tango?" I ask him.

"What exactly is that?"

I snatch the phone out of my back pocket and I flip on a slow song. Then I stand up and wiggle my finger at him. "Well, it's a bit of a slow dance, a tango in slow motion with my usual breaking away from what you call *the program* and doing—"

"Your own thing?" Adrien puts his glass of water on the white painted railing. "So you realize you're taking me to the dark side of dance, don't you? The one that is whispered about, but rarely spoken."

I hold out my hand. "And this is the point that you can walk away or take my hand. This is the point that will create or disintegrate our relationship."

I see him take a look behind him to the sidewalk leading to the street. It is slow and deliberate. Then he laughs when he turns his head back around. He doesn't hesitate, takes my hand. Then he draws me close underneath Poppy's yellow porch light with the bugs buzzing around. I feel his right hand slide up around my shoulder and to the back of my neck. I push my own to his waist. It is funny. I lean in and we're not doing anything more than two middle school kids on a dance floor, just rocking back and forth like neither of us have ever danced before. I press my head to his chest because he's a good foot taller than me and catch his scent while we sway there making small talk and just enjoying each other's company.

"So, am I just the flavor of the week?" he asks me. I think for a moment he is being mean. "This man you are doing all-nighters with—"

"You probably heard about Hannah Lafferty being murdered, right?"

"Yes, everybody thinks your father did it."

I feel a little dizzy. "You know about that?" I am holding my breath. I know he knows it. He always feels it even before I recognize I'm holding my breath while dancing.

"Look at me, Tango," he says softly and snatches my chin up so I'm forced to look at his eyes. "My father was an alcoholic that abandoned my mom with one boy and six girls all under the age of twelve when I was sick and everybody thought I was going to die. I am not my father. I would have gone to work in a coal mine if my mother hadn't seen me watching my sisters at a ballet show at school. Why ballet? Because I had the chicken pox and my legs weren't working right after it. My sister's ballet teacher recommended it. She worked three jobs so I could do what I do. I am like my mother. Maybe you are like your mother. Now finish."

"That was Hannah Lafferty's brother, Mark. I am trying to help him find her. He believes she is still alive. I do too. We're just trying to figure out where she could be. He gave me a picture of us when we were little with our arms around each other at some play. I can't get it out of my mind—do I still call you Mister Moreau?"

"No, Adrien. Then what are we doing here?" he asks. "Do you need to be with him?"

"I want to be with you."

CHAPTER 55

ADRIEN BIDS ME ADIEU

I get a text from Zane halfway between home and Poppy's. *A lady named Chloe is here. She's a cop. She wants to talk to you. No uniform.* I'm not sure whether to be relieved or scared when we pull into the parking lot.

"You sure you want to be a part of this, don't want to head out of here?" I ask Adrien who is pushing his rental car into park. "I don't mind. You probably don't want to be involved—"

"I'm *involved* already. I've invested a lot of time in you."

"Great, I've worked up from crash test dummy to an investment scam," I mumble. Twenty minutes later, I'm trying to convince Chloe Murphy I'm not crazy like she thinks I am. Somehow, her girlfriend has persuaded her to take a chance and listen. She is standing behind Chloe, arms crossed and *uh huhing* me while Chloe stands stoic and expressionless watching me. On one side of me is Mark Lafferty and on the other, Adrien. Zane is munching popcorn on the couch and Billy is sitting next to him giving me a strange glare.

"Okay, so what I was trying to tell you the other day is that I can't tell you where he's hiding the girl, but I can tell you where he's going to dump her. And maybe since there is a thought-out process to placing the murder victims in certain areas, there is like a relationship to where he is keeping them," I announce, laying the map down where I had marked the star. "In 1972, Tammy Lyn was dumped at the Cannon Bread Mill. That's the top of the star. On the left side is Lisa Tatum who was found in 1963. On the right point," I poke a finger on the map, "Cathy Schuler's body was dumped in a front yard. Bottom left, it was Susan James who was the first known murdered girl in 1958. She was found at the Welcome Viaduct. Right down the street and the right bottom edge of the star was who the cops say was—" I pause and push a hand on Mark's arm. "Hannah. But we don't agree with the cops. Mark says the clothing doesn't match Hannah's. Another discrepancy is that each of the girls murdered were missing six to eight weeks. The body that is allegedly Hannah's was found within a week." I don't want to look at Mark. I'm still touching his arm. "So exactly halfway between the top of the star and directly heading to the bottom left side, Tianna Mills' body was discovered along Black Street. I am guessing that the next victim will be directly across from her on Black Street—"

"Hannah, you mean, she's the girl, right?" Mark is gritting his teeth. "So how the hell do we get from where she is going to be dumped to finding her alive?" I think he is going to break right then. I know my eyes are wide because his voice is loud.

"I don't know."

"Well, you got this far, dammit, figure the damn thing out!"

I'm standing there staring at Mark. I am blinking and not sure how to react, what to say. I know everybody is looking at me, blaming me for what is happening. My cell phone tings where I've plugged it into the outlet in the kitchen. I simply turn from the anger and walk in, check my message box. There are like seventy messages from people that I haven't answered because my phone was in the duffel bag and drained of battery.

Hey, what are you up to? It is Colt and I stare at the message. Really? He thinks it wouldn't get back to me that he had a part to play in dropping me in the worst part of the city? I decide to play along. I mean, he's got the keys to the suitcase.

Just sitting here watching TV with Billy.

Want to fool around?

Can't tonight. Have to work early. Tomorrow?

Naw. Water pipe broke at home. House flooded. Taylor's mom told me I can stay at one of their cabins. Thought it'd be fun. You mad at me? Be back tomorrow hopefully. Text me if you change your mind.

"You okay?" I'm leaning with my elbows on the sink staring at the phone. I jump at Adrien's soft words. "This is—intense. I think that is the word. How long have you been researching this information?"

"I don't know. Since I thought Hannah was killed."

"You really believe she is still alive?" Adrien looks out into the living room. Chloe has a hand on Mark's shoulder talking to him. Whatever she's saying has something to do with me. I see him look into the kitchen, catch my eyes. He looks guilty like Mia when she tells me a fib.

"I do."

"So you are meeting him?"

I don't realize he can read the text. I know I can lie and tell him *no, not really.* I know I can lie and tell him that I am just leading Colt Lucero on for some sort of revenge. I'm damn good at lying. I look up at Adrien Moreau. And I *can't* lie—

"It's fine. No big deal," he tells me, forces a smile. "Maybe I was wrong about him—"

"It's just complicated. Like Svetlana." I reach out my fingers to tickle his belly. He looks at me, doesn't laugh.

"Oh, my gosh. We're going to have to work on that," I say, tugging my fingers away.

"I'm not tickles."

"It is ticklish," I correct him. "But everybody is ticklish somewhere." I lean in and it is like suddenly, he's back to his old self, all stoic and standoffish. He holds his hands in front of him.

"Can you just—" I start to make an excuse for the text. But his phone buzzes. He looks worn out after he takes the phone out into the parking lot, then returns ten minutes later.

"Svetlana demands that I return tonight. I have to return. She has her attorney coming in."

"Okay. Her attorney?"

"Yes. I can't just walk out of a contract, she says. I have classes to teach. She can't do it alone. I'm so sorry."

"No, I get it." I do get it. How did I explain it to Colt? If we were in a relationship, so was my dance partner. "Your partner, she comes first. It is, Adrien, your life." It's been the same in every relationship I'm in. I'm just not enough, I suppose. For Kevin, for Colt, for Adrien. So, in the end, Sophie or Taylor or Svetlana are going to win.

"It is just that I have obligations. She has reminded me of them. Complications like your Colt. I can't expect you to just drop your life. I shouldn't have taken off without speaking to her."

"Hey," I try to kid with him, hide the knowing he wasn't going to come back. "Your lover, she awaits you in some God-forsaken place desperate for you to find her. If I hear from her, I will pass the word to your Russian informants. Adiós."

"Um," he shakes his head. "I'm French, I told you that, right?"

"Yes."

"Adiós. That is Spanish for goodbye. I think you mean: Au revoir. That is *until we meet again*. Or adieu.

SHAY LAWLESS

That is goodbye. "

"Adieu. That sounds sad and pretty final," I was smiling. Now my smile drops. "Which one is it, Mister Moreau? Au revoir or adieu?"

"Adieu, Tango."

CHAPTER 56
THE SHIT HITS THE FAN

"Zane, let me ask you something," I lean over the couch on my elbows. I changed from dress to pants and t-shirt. He looks at me kind of sadly like he knows something is amiss with me and Adrien. "When Colt sent you out of town to the safe house, where did he send you?"

"Actually, it wasn't that far," he tells me, stifling a yawn with his elbow. "It was one of Chief Peirce's cabin rentals along the Rocky Fork Creek. I saw the sign. Big Chief Cabins. He's got a bunch."

"Like how far out of Belleview from where Colt met with the folks taking you in?"

"I don't know. I only stayed with them one night before Chief Peirce came to get me. Belleview's not that big. It took us maybe ten minutes."

"Did the police know you were there?"

"No, I don't think so."

"Did anybody come by like Chief Peirce?"

"Yes."

"Chloe, come here a minute," I wave a hand over and Chloe Murphy breaks from the papers she is sifting through. "So, I guess I knew Chief Peirce had cabins. At least, I knew his wife ran some cabins," I say. "Zane, here, was telling me he stayed in one when we were trying to get him away from his dad."

"Yeah, so what?"

"I mean, you're a cop, right?" I scratch my head. "Did it occur to you at all that Chief Peirce might have my dad in one of these cabins?"

"Why would you think that?" she asks. "Why would he rent to a felon? There's hundreds of rentals here in town and even out of town that could have rented to him."

"I don't know," I mutter. "He's been following me around, he told me to get out of town—"

"Because he probably thinks you're dealing drugs or something, Tango," Chloe tosses her hands up. "He tells that to all the—" she stops and blows air from her lips.

"Say it," I order her. "What am I?"

"I don't know. You break the law with your graffiti."

"Mia's asleep, Chloe, you mind watching her while I take Mark for a drive to get a pizza. We need to talk. I need supper. Can I trust you with my kid?"

"I shouldn't have blown up on you." Mark hops into the passenger seat of my old truck. I'm already turning the key. He looks down where I am pulling up a GPS tracker on my phone while the engine grinds. "I know where State Route Pizza is. You don't need a map."

"That's not where we're going." I put in the name of Chief Peirce's cabins and a map comes up showing the different areas he has them. "We are going here." I poke a finger along the edge of Rocky Fork Creek between Belleview and Hensley Grove. "And we've got to do it fast. I'm not so confident leaving Chloe with Mia for long. My dad used to stay in an old cabin right here. That's where I grew up until Anna and Poppy took me in."

"You're kidding me, right?"

"No."

"Is there a reason you didn't tell Chloe this?"

"If your sister is alive, I know where she could be. I didn't tell Chloe where we were going because I know that she knows my dad used to rent a cabin over there along

Rocky Fork Creek. I saw it in her notes. She just denied it. I'm standing there telling her this and realize she's going to call the cops with the info." I shake my head. "She refused to help me when I stood on her front porch the other day. Suddenly, she shows up at my front door? Mark, somebody with vehicles from the impound lot have been following me. I was there when that trailer blew up outside town. Somebody who has access to those cars did it. I know it. I have to assume it is the cops. So right this moment, the only person I trust is you. And let's be honest, you don't like me. I know that. It goes way back. But I trust you because we both have the same common goal. And we are the only two who actually believe that Hannah is alive."

"Why don't you think Chloe believes you?"

"I think she does. I think she thinks like a cop. Her mind is locked into that bigoted everybody's-a-criminal mode. I was raised by a criminal for six years of my life. I must be a criminal. I think, Mark, she is covering for her boss. Why? Because nobody has lifted a finger to check out his cabins. Every time I say something to somebody, their feet drag. I mean, I really think somebody told Delia to lie about that picture I drew. Maybe she was next if she didn't make it look like I did it as a joke. That's what bad guys do."

"They do."

"I'm more into romance books than suspense novels. But wouldn't you check out a guy if somebody drew a picture and said he might be part of a crime? They laughed at me at the police station. All of these things that I've found out about the murders, they were easily accessible for the cops. In retrospect, I think that envelope with all the information on the murders was planted in my car. By whom? I don't know. Chloe was the last one I saw with it. As soon as I start digging stuff up and forcing it in their faces, they locked the doors on all the information."

We drive for about a half hour with the radio low. I can almost feel the tension in the truck. There's small talk about the competition. Billy's afraid to sing in front of the crowd. The design team making the backgrounds are taking too long. Two days. It's all we have until the performance.

"They want you to dance."

"You know, I don't want to dance anymore," I just say it. "I really liked Adrien Moreau. I liked dancing with him. I'm sick of dancing alone." Actually, my chest hurts so hard now, I think my heart is broke. "He left saying he had other obligations."

"You don't think I want to do the same? But I can't just stop life right now. If Hannah is alive or dead, she wouldn't want me to do it. So I'm kind of doing it for her. I think everybody is."

He makes me feel guilty. I nod. "Whatever. I don't want to be the ass that doesn't."

"That's the old team spirit!" Mark pumps his arm and he makes me laugh softly.

About three miles outside Belleview, I turn right along an old dirt road. There are ruts in the old mud, now hard and thick and almost to the middle of the wheels. The truck jogs left and right along another two, slow miles until we turn again.

"You ever think it's strange Colt Lucero showed up just a few months before Hannah came up missing?" Mark asks me. "I think it is odd how he comes off as being something different to Alexandra and then to Taylor and pretty much, everyone he meets. Alex thought she was dating him. Taylor thought she was dating him."

"Yep, I think he's playing everybody." I also know Colt went to great lengths to gain my trust—taking the job as a janitor to let me into the theatre, beating up Finn. I have to assume he had Svetlana send Adrien here. I can only imagine the reason was to bring one more person into the pot that would criticize my dancing so Colt could be the one to fly in like a superhero and save me. There were so many little intricately laid out details to his plan, it scares me. "*Les plus sombres,*" I let the words roll off my tongue. Mark tips his head, shakes it like he doesn't understand the meaning. "It means *The Dark Ones.* It is what Colt told me they nicknamed Adrien and his partner, Svetlana. She is known as *Sorcière Noire*, the Dark Witch and Adrien, he is Homme de L'ombre, her shadow."

"I don't understand."

"I don't know," I shake my head. "I want to believe Adrien Moreau danced with me because he saw something unique in me. I don't want to believe he was just another piece to this puzzle coming together like maybe Colt setting this whole thing up for his magazine and using them as tools to get information."

"So I'm not the only one. I'm just not sure how the puzzle all fits together."

"Yeah, right?" I bob my head up and down. "It gives me a headache all the crap going on. It's like someone has tossed a couple puzzles down the stairway and I'm picking up the pieces thinking I'll never be able to sort the two out." I raise my hand, point to a grassy pullover. "There. That's the trail."

I remember when I was nine or ten sniffing one of Anna's lilac bushes she plants along the front path to her house. It smelled so sweet and I took it in, closed my eyes to bask in the wonderful scent. What I didn't know was that there was a ground hornet's nest tucked beneath a rock on the walkway. Just as I breathed out of the scent, I felt the first of six cruel bites into my skin.

Whenever I look at lilacs even to this day, I wince. Even the fake scent of lilac candles leaves me shuddering. I suppose I feel the same way about daddy's cabin on Rocky Fork Creek. We hike down a hillside and then up again. When it opens up to a small overgrown yard and the cabin enveloped in only the shine from the moon, a whole lot of bad memories rush forward and the faint scent of old wood smoke still fills the area around it.

My feet just stop a stone's throw away. "Give me a second." I have sweat beading on my forehead. Mark gazes down at me. I know I must be pale white against the dark. The blood is draining from my face. "I just—I just remember this place." My fingers rub over that damn tattoo. I can still feel the needle grind into my bone.

But Mark looks almost fevered like he senses something. Maybe it is just hope. I wag my head, take those steps toward the cabin. We try to keep to the shadows. Then he takes off at a lope and stops just short of a partially opened door to the cabin. I can see there isn't any glass left in one front window. Peering inside, the old bed and mattress are there and a wooden table lays on its side.

Mark pushes open the door with both his hands. I can hear his feet crunch on little bits of stone and twigs that have blown in the door. I follow behind, pushing my hand on his arm. I know he feels my fingers shaking. "I hate this place," I huff. "I just hate this place." I sniff, smell the lantern oil. Then I freeze, realizing it is fresh. "Shit," I hiss, tighten my grip. "Someone's been here, Mark. Smell it. It is lantern oil."

There are tracks at our feet. I open my phone, turn on the light and let it spray across the floor. We follow them, stop short of a small door.

Please, please, please go away. Let me go.

"Holy shit." It is all Mark says at the words. They aren't coming from the room at all, but beneath our feet. Both our heads drop. Mark jerks me back and falls to his knees. "Your light!" He shakes a hand toward me while he's peering at the floorboards. "Hannah? Hannah, is that you?"

"Oh, Mark! Is that you? Help me!"

He called her serial killer bait. Hannah tells me that when we pull into the little garage behind Chad Evans' apartment. Chad knows we're coming. He's wheeled himself to the darkened doorway waving us in. He's the only one I trust will protect Hannah until we can figure out what the hell is going on.

"Chief Peirce told me that I was being stalked by a serial killer. He said he'd let my family know I was going to a safe place. Chief Peirce took me to Colt that night. Colt said he would be there with me the whole way." I've been trying desperately to get ahold of Chloe, but I couldn't get cell phone service until we hit the highway. Then, there is only a full voicemail box message.

"And you believed him?" Mark is harder on her than Gil is on me. "What the hell, Hannah?"

"Oh, my God, don't get mad at her. She's been living in a well for three days." I groan.

"Mark, I've known Taylor's dad for as long as I remember. He coached my soccer team in third grade. He played his guitar for us around a campfire at his house just a couple months ago," Hannah says softly. "He's a cop. I believed him. It was fine for the first couple days, then I realized they'd locked me in the cabin. Then a few days ago, a man came and brought me to the little hole in the ground."

"For serial killer bait."

"Yeah, Tango," Hannah looks at me for the first time, locks eyes. "Your dad never showed up. Why do you think they did this? Do you think they were trying to get him to come here?"

"They found two dead girls, Hannah," I break the news to her. "They said one was you. I just need to get home and get Mia. Then I'll come right back and we'll figure out what we need to do." That was when my phone tinged. Chloe. I sighed in relief. I shouldn't have. *Can't get ahold of you. It got late. Colt stopped by and said he'd watch Mia for you. Called Anna and she said that'd be fine with you.*

"Oh, shit." I waver there, feel the blood drain from my face. I barely let them get out of the truck before I'm shoving it into reverse and barreling through the parking lot. Colt has my daughter. The only thing I've got to barter is the stupid suitcase behind my seat.

"And the keys," I say softly to myself. "I'm going to get the keys."

CHAPTER 54

DADDY

"Daddy?" I'm numb standing just inside my door at ten-thirty-two. I blink almost hysterically, my eyelids batting up and down. It's my dad. I know it is. I remember his face. I remember the way he used to sit with his elbows on his knees and his cold face staring hard to whomever he was talking. He is doing that right now. I stare at the man I haven't seen in maybe fourteen years. Poppy wouldn't let me go see him in jail. But one time, when I was eleven and riding my bike along the sidewalk, I saw an old car drive past slowly. I know it was my daddy inside staring at me. I told Poppy and he wouldn't let me ride my bike out of the driveway for weeks. Then, Poppy stood guard there with his arms crossed watching the road when I went out to play. Daddy's face is the same, round and with thick brows nearly covered by the gray hair he's got hanging to his shoulders.

"Starr, look at you all grown up."

I shiver. My heart is racing. My cheeks are numb with fear. The crunch on the old linoleum floor in the kitchen forces my eyes over the couch. Zane is sitting uncomfortably in the recliner. I see blood on his lip and a red mark on his cheek. He is pale. Oh, no, his nose is bleeding. There is a full beer on the side table next to him. His eyes follow my own to Colt Lucero standing just inside the doorframe of the kitchen. Colt's got a beer in one hand.

"She is grown up." Colt holds up his beer like he's making a cheer. "Been a long time since you've seen your daddy, huh, Starr?"

It's strange when he says my old name. I mean, I thought I knew Colt. But he's like an entirely different person right now. "And look who I found," Colt smiles and pats Mia's head. God, it is sinister. He just walks across the room, pushes his hand to the door behind me so it closes. I look down. He's got my little pink pistol tucked into the waist of his jeans. So glad I slept with him, showed him that. I hold out my arms to take her. Mia balks. She does that biting dinosaur thing she did with Colt before clapping her thumb and fingers together. "Gonna, gonna—" she says.

"—eat you," he finishes for her. "Yeah, I am. I'm the big bad wolf that's gonna gobble you up!"

Shit. She giggles and so does Colt. But he looks up at me with a sly glare. He frightens me. He looks like a wolf grinning white teeth at me. I didn't see that coming, the idiot befriending my kid with ulterior motives.

Daddy looks at Mia. "Sweet thing, she is. Always wanted another after you grew up." He gets this funny half-smile on his face and catches Mia's attention. "Baby, go get granddaddy a beer."

"She doesn't know how to do that," I say quickly. She doesn't know how to get a beer. *Baby, go get daddy a beer.* How many times did I hear that as a little kid? Maybe three or four times a day. I drop my purse right there just like I used to drop my raggedy doll or whatever toy daddy had snatched up from some house we robbed. And quickly. Because he would have to tell her how to do it each step. She doesn't know he'll grab her up by the arm, drag her into the kitchen and shove her face against the refrigerator like he did to me. All the while he banged me against the refrigerator door, he was explaining it to me: *It's this easy. Bring me a fucking beer. You walk into the kitchen, you open the fucking refrigerator and you get out a fucking beer you stupid, ugly shit.* And she doesn't know he'll cuff her with his fist once she brings it. *That'll teach you to be faster next time.*

"I'll do it." I find myself walking to the kitchen and trying really hard not to close the refrigerator too loudly or make any noise. It always made daddy mad.

I snatch up a beer and walk it back inside and hand it to him. I feel the wet condensation on the bottle. I should have wiped it off. I feel four again. I'm numb. Numb.

"What do you want from me?" I ask. I feel a dribble of sweat on my forehead. My mouth is dry and feels like I've got cotton balls inside. "What the hell is going on?"

He just stares at me about ten seconds. He works his eyes from the top of my head, down my chest and to my legs. I feel almost sick to my stomach at the way his eyes work back up, stop again at my chest.

"Well, you might find this funny, but I got a call from Colt, here, asking to do a story on me. I told him no, of course, because my attorney said it would be legal suicide. He actually used that term." Daddy sighs. "But then I get this call from my ol' Buddy in Cincinnati." He winks at me. Oh, no, no, no. That's not a good sign. It's the mean daddy coming out. He's wearing a raggedy button-up shirt and gray cargo pants and he rises. "This buddy—Nick Grady, you remember him, right? He tells me you've been knocking on doors, asking about those girls they say I killed. You could leave well enough alone and we wouldn't be having this conversation. I say, no, my little girl wouldn't be doing that to her daddy." He is standing above me. I knew I should have stepped back. I didn't. I don't know why, but I had turned. It was ever so slightly, but my eyes fell on Zane right then. He knew. He knew what was going to happen right then even before Daddy raised his fist. And I know he sees the subtle shift of my head. He knows I know. We've both been there. Done that. *Don't.* I mouth to him. Because I know he's going to get up and try to protect me. He must know that if he does, it is only going to be worse. On me. On him. Because he just looks up to the ceiling with a strange glaze to his eyes, holds back the urge.

"Everything's going good for me! Why'd you fucking do that, huh? Stir up trouble for your old man!"

Man, he slugs me on my left ear so hard, I whirl around. My head is numb, my jaw tingling. I'm standing one second, the next, I'm on my hands and knees on the ground. Then comes the kick in my ribs. Daddy's signature assault. He knows how to kick hard enough to hurt, but not enough to crack a rib. *Bang. Pop.* That's what I always remember about him. He'd hit once with his fist in the head. That was the *bang*. Then when I'm down, he'd kick me—scoop me up with the toe of his shoe and flip me on my side. *Pop.*

"Jesus Christ, you didn't have to hit her so hard." Colt's eyes are wide. He's got a sneer working up on his lips. "I bet that—" I know he's going to say *hurt*. But Mia gasps, then she all-out screeches: "Mommy!" I know that makes daddy mad. Crying. I see daddy's glare work up to Mia.

"Please don't hurt her." I grunt, lay there a second catching my breath. Zane is halfway out of his seat when Colt takes the three steps toward him. He's still holding Mia and she's got her hands over her ears, eyes as wide as fists. "You want to go this route again, little dude? I'll flatten you to the floor again."

I realize daddy is hovering over me. He kneels down next to me and grabs me by my hair and shakes my head to the squeals of Mia and the sound of a blow while Colt punches Zane in the side of the head, sends him reeling.

"I came for the suitcase, sweetheart. That damn cop's not going to get this one. He ain't gonna get both." My dad jerks my head to the side, kind of tows me up so I'm supporting myself with bent elbows and face to face with him. "Colt, here, said he's got the keys. I tried to open the damn thing for weeks after the plane went down. Then it disappeared when they took you away from me. I figured, well, the social services agency got it when they ransacked my house the day they took you. I was wrong, wasn't I? I figured the Hensley chief of police got his hands on it like he got the other half of it. That bitch. I watched him pull it out of the water. When he saw me, he tossed a second at my feet. Our little secret. Not one person questioned it when he got rich quick, did they? There must have been a mint in that suitcase. I figured he got greedy, that's why they used you as a ploy to get into my cabin and find the suitcase. It was only a matter of time. But I hear from this boy right here—" he points to Colt. "Ray Baldwin snatched it up when he came to get you. And now, you've got it. Is he right?"

"Yeah." My mind is churning. "It's in my car. Take it. Please leave, daddy." My cheek is burning and Mia's sobbing is scaring the crap out of me because I know daddy has no qualms about hurting her. Daddy looks at his hand. It is red from hitting my face. A bit of blood is dribbling along the knuckle of his middle finger. He shivers, smiles.

"Shut her up!" he yells at Colt. "Or dammit, I will!"

"I'll keep her quiet." Zane reaches out. Colt just lets her go, almost drops her. He snatches her up, sits back down does a funny rocking back and forth with her. I can hear him whispering in her ear while she sniffs. I know he's telling her if she is quiet, the odds mama will get hit again are slimmer. I'm sure that's what his mama used to tell him.

"I'll leave when I damn well want to leave. You want to be like them?" he asks me. "Those girls, they came to me, you know. The one at the river, the one on the bike. That stupid one in Ohio that asked me for a ride. They were there for the picking. I didn't hunt them down. They came to me. Just like you are now. You understand that, don't you? And each one of them, they asked me in the end to kill them.

Begged me. So I did. God, you bring out the worst in me."

Daddy releases my hair, stands up. "Regardless, I was a good boy after your mama left you. You were a sign."

"A—a sign?" I stutter. I'm on my knees. I'm going to rise slowly. I know at any second, he will shove me back down. "Did you kill my mama too?"

"Naw, baby, your mama was dead already. She was sucked downstream. You came from the heavens and God dropped you in my lap," he says. "I wished upon a star and said I wanted to stop making more dead girls. Then, you came along. My Starr. " He points up to my cob-webby ceiling. My eyes follow like I'm going to see some night sky.

"I don't understand. When mama left you?" I am staring at him while he comes to his full height. "You're not making sense."

"I found you in the Rocky Fork Creek that night the plane wrecked, Starr. I saw a lady pop up out of the creek. She was bloody and just laying there before a tree or a log hooked her. You were shivering and holding on to a piece of the plane wing. You were right at my feet. I didn't see you at first. I bundled you up, brought you home with me. You kept saying *star*."

"Huh—?" My answer is a huffed breath and my words skid off my tongue curiously unintelligible. "Are you—kidding me? No. You found me—*what*?"

"He's telling you that you were on the plane," Colt groans. "You told me that Bogie guy told you that there were six people on the plane. You and your mom must have been the two extra. He found you in the wreckage. Pretty wild, huh? Who would have known?"

"He's making that up," I turn to face Colt. "It's not true." But now my mind is whirring. I'm dizzy. "Is it true?" I ask the man who is staring at me. Daddy. I take my wrist, swipe my nose. "Why are you telling me this now?"

Oh. It is true. Now, I think I'm seeing the light. I know it inside. I remember Mama. Vaguely. I remember her pointing out the window. *Look at the star. Go to sleep. When you wake up, you will see your daddy.* It was a plane window. I don't remember much but falling to sleep. Then, I woke up and—went into daddy's arms.

"I never really fell in the creek, did I?" I ask slowly. I know the answer.

"I made it up in case you told somebody."

"Why—why did you take me? Why didn't you just leave me?"

"Because—I could," Daddy says. "You were free for the taking."

I see it now. I didn't get it twenty-five minutes ago when I squeezed through the back window of Colt's house and snatched up the key sitting on the suitcases partially packed and ready in his room. I get the feeling he never even unpacked most of his bags. He was living out of suitcases the last six months, ready at any time to escape.

The keys, I took to my truck and with bated breath and trembling fingers I opened the Tringle Double Case suitcase and exposed the contents inside. Clothing—there was nothing but a couple modest 1980s dresses, makeup bag, a pair of sneakers, women's blouses and two pairs of jeans. I stared at them. But it wasn't long. I knew I didn't have much time. I had been strangely fascinated and not disappointed there wasn't oodles of money inside. But when I dumped the clothing into a few brown plastic grocery bags I keep in there to use for trash bags, I watched as two little pink dresses tumbled out along with a little teddy bear and a handful of pictures. I didn't have time to think about it in the dark of night on the off street I pulled into to sneak to

Colt's house. I stuffed these beneath the truck seats. Then, I closed up the suitcase and placed it back behind my seat. The keys, however, were a different story—

Bang. Bang. Crap. Right then, I can hear Billy banging on his bedroom wall.

"He's starting up again," Zane's voice is hoarse. He turns to Colt. "Do you want me to knock back?"

"He'll get over it." Colt rolls his eyes. "I already banged back. You banged back. Dumbass stopped for a while. Now, here he goes again." He puts down the beer. "So where's the suitcase. I can't get out of this shithole town quick enough."

Bang! Bang! His bangs are louder and more desperate. I try to ignore them. I can only stare at the man who I thought was my dad and who isn't—my dad. He—he kidnapped me.

"Don't head out so quickly now." My dad—no, my ex-dad says. "You're not leaving until I'm somewhere safe. That was the deal."

"No, the deal was that I leave you the girl, Dell, and the money for the story," Colt says. "Now, you're on your own. You've got a hundred-thousand dollars in that duffel bag. Just go."

The girl. Hannah. My heart is pounding. I don't know what's coming next. I see daddy shift. He must have a gun. He has to have something so we don't run to the cops the second they leave.

"Come here, sweetheart." I look over, see my daddy—no, my ex-daddy wiggling a finger at Mia. "Come here, sweet thing, you're going with me. You don't got a daddy, do you? I'll be your daddy."

Both Zane and I jolt in shock. "No," I say in a whisper. "No way. You're not leaving with her."

Colt beckons Zane with his hands. "Give her up so he can get and go, dude."

"No—"

Now, somebody is banging on my front door. Colt snaps his eyes upward and over my shoulder. "What the hell?"

"It's Billy, Colt." I swing my head toward Colt. "I'm sure of it. I just need to let him know I'm okay."

"Then do it." Colt steps back. Zane has a wild look to his eyes. I'm not sure what he's planning, but I step across the floor. Colt's stepping over toward the bedroom.

"I'll take care of it." That's Ex-Daddy. He's lumbering across the floor and he slides between the door and the wall so when it opens, he is hidden behind it. Yeah, he has a pistol, a little black thing that he wiggles from his belt and holds up so it is pointed at me. "Watch yourself, Starr."

"Wipe the blood from your nose." I hear Colt say and I turn, acknowledge him. I wobble a nod. Then I swipe my wrist above my lip and open the door.

"Hey, babe, Billy texted me." I'm staring at Kevin. Right behind him, Rocky is rolling his eyes like he's saying; *I told you she was fine.* "Said you didn't answer him. Please tell me you're dying so it gives me a justification for the speeding ticket coming over here—"

"I'm fine." I pluck my lip. "Everything's fine. I'm just getting ready to go to bed." I reach over touch the star on my shoulder. Then I open my eyes wide, let them roll to the right. "Billy's being an ass. I banged a hundred times back," I mutter hoarsely. "Just tell him to go to bed." I wave them away, start to close the door slowly.

Then I do something that Gil would most likely call Tangoofy. I almost close the door, then I take every bit of my one-hundred and three pound frame and slam it back on the man behind it. I hear the gun hit the door. I hear my ex-daddy curse before his head slams hard into it. But I don't stop there. My ex-daddy hit the curtains and the back wall. His fingers grasp at the curtains while I swing the door almost closed again and start to shove it once more. Bam! Bam! Bam! I'm slamming it again and again until Kevin wheels around me and straddles the door. He just leans over and I can see his elbow coming up and down, hear the smacks of fist while he is just waling on the old man behind it. There's a struggle and I'm kicking with my feet until Rocky grabs my arms and pulls me back.

"Get, now!" He's accessing the situation, then just takes two or three steps and leans over and grabs my dad around the neck and drags him out with his hand on ex-daddy's wrist bending it until the gun just falls to the floor.

I'm oblivious to what is going on behind me until Mia's soft sobs fill the air. It is quiet save my ex-dad yowling to release him and the curtains from my bedroom doorway slapping at the wall that leads out on to the deck. I had turned, see Zane staring at them. He looks as surprised as I do while the sound of sirens fill the air in the parking lot. He's clutching Mia like an old teddy bear.

"The fire escape," he says.

I look at Kevin who is sitting on ex-daddy's legs while Rocky grasps his arms around his back. He is face down on the floor. I know they are trying to figure out what to do about Colt's escape. I know as I stand there he's getting the suitcase out of the back of my truck.

"It's okay. He's not going far. I tossed the keys up on the catwalk of the water tower. There's a note on the suitcase telling him that. If he wants to open the suitcase, he's going to have to climb the ladder to the tower."

CHAPTER 58

THE AUDITION

"My name is Raeanna Baldwin. I've been dancing since I was six. I've been to Fields College of Dance—"

"I see that. You know this is for ten weeks on-site."

"I do."

"You have a child?"

I can see the assistants flipping through my papers. Can they even ask that? There are three women and two men. There was six. I saw Adrien Moreau get up and leave the theatre just as I walked in and set down my bag. I'm hurt. He is the artistic director, the head of this new ballet company, and his team have already culled out those who don't define what they are looking for when they placed us in groups this morning and sifted us down throughout the day. I'm assuming they, alone, went through the paperwork and he just found out I was there. He looked a bit dazed like he wasn't expecting me. From the information Anna pulled off her tablet before she snuck it under my nose two weeks ago, Adrien Moreau purchased the building as an offshoot of the Academy of The Dance with the Conciergerie Ballet Company. Svetlana Mikhailova is not involved with this company. He is starting from scratch, but will use the school to employ his staff. It is a huge point against me.

They are down to the last forty women and twenty-five men. Maybe it is a relief I do not have to perform in front of him. But it is no reprieve from the ache in my gut telling me I should not have come here. That all along, Adrien was a part of Colt's plan to get his story.

Nobody does these one on one auditions anymore. It is too intimate for me if he is one of the few watching. The rest of his artistic hiring team, they look bored, detached. Suitably so, they've been looking at dancers for four days, culling hundreds out. I'm just another face in the crowd doing the same pirouettes, the same style, the same old thing they've seen a hundred times.

"I actually have two people I support," I answer. "I've got a three year-old and I'm also taking care of an eighteen year-old until he finishes high school. I've worked two jobs, got a dual-degree in art and dance, fed a lazy boyfriend for two years before I booted him out. I'm used to juggling and I've got support from my family. I just finished my first painting consignment. I need a break. This is my break."

"Did you choose a partner you'll be working with today? Or would you like us to choose a dancer?" a woman asks. "We would just like to see how you work with a partner." She is wearing glasses and pushes them along her nose. I remember her from early this morning when I made it through the third of eight cuts. She kept coming past me, eyeing and I swear she was going to thumb me out the door. She didn't. But still, I didn't know any of the other dancers in the auditions. Yet, they seemed to know each other well. Well, enough, to know what partner to dance with if called.

"No. I am dancing alone."

"You don't list partners in your references. Do you prefer to dance by yourself?"

"No. I used to like to dance by myself," I tell her. Then I realize I haven't had any triple-chocolate days since I'd been dancing with Adrien. "Now, not so much anymore."

"Are you afraid to fly? We plan on flying a lot to different countries."

Am I afraid to fly? I suppose I'm terrified. Tucked inside my mind somewhere, I think I relive that last flight with my mama. It's just a dark space there, but I feel it right when we take off. It's a certain panic like I think the only way I'll get out is straight down into water.

Seventy-two hours earlier, I sat on the plane focusing on the movie Anna had on her tablet. I wasn't listening. I wasn't watching. My mind was on anything but what was going on around me. I shut out the two year-old crying and the man seated next to me who kept tapping out a beat with his finger on the armrest to whatever music his earphones are plugged into. I shut out Chloe standing at my door the day after they dragged daddy away to the prison and telling me she was sorry about leaving Mia with Colt. She said they were still trying to find out if daddy murdered the girl from Columbus they found along the river a couple months ago.

Chief Peirce had kidnapped Hannah. He pilfered the body of an elderly woman from the morgue and tossed her on the tracks to make it appear like Hannah had committed suicide. He was going to trade her to Dell Smythe for the suitcase Poppy kept for him. At the same time Peirce was planning a trade off with Dell Smythe, Colt Lucero was secretly interviewing him about the serial killings. Dell Smythe told Colt about Peirce's deal. And that was when I came into the picture, unfortunately for all of them. Each is getting jail time. The Hensley Grove police are sorting through the necklaces and jewelry I gave them from Mia's shoebox. So far, three other cold cases with missing women who lost jewelry have matched.

"I'm sorry how the newspapers wrote it up, Tango," she tells me softly. But I don't think she was sorry at all. They pegged it as *Detective* Chloe of the Hensley Police solved the Kentucky crime of the century all by herself. What a joke. I dragged her kicking and screaming across that finish line.

I try to bring up the good things. Chad Evans texted me yesterday and told me he was going out on a second date with Hannah Lafferty. I guess she feels safe with him. Mark told me she hasn't left Chad's side since she stayed with him that night. The Lafferty's paid for my plane ticket to the audition as a thank you for finding Hannah alive. I have a new friendship with Mark who has decided to use his scholarship money to learn dance choreography at Fields. He says I've been whining too much about dancing alone.

Daddy's in jail again. He's not getting out anytime soon. I got the last laugh with Colt. They found him clinging to the top of the Hensley Grove water tower after he called 9-1-1 to help him down. He climbed up there to get the keys to the suitcase. Of course, the suitcase was empty. The clothing I stuffed in bags beneath the seat, however, tell a different story.

I am Bosnian. At least, my real mother and father were. Mama was just a middle class wife in a nice apartment complex when the war in Bosnia broke out. My father was a school teacher and he was beaten to death by a Serb soldier when they took their home. My mother and I were taken to a detention camp near Sarajevo. Somehow, she managed to get word to a cousin in America who was in the military and helped her get out. This is where the details of my ending up in Hensley Grove are gray. How my mama got the Tringle Double Case suitcases and who placed five-hundred thousand into one of those suitcases to get her to safety is a mystery. I will, most likely, never know the whole story. My family in Bosnia are either dead from that war or have flown like seeds to the wind. Only the wife of the American cousin who helped her escape is living. I only have the five grocery store bags of our clothing to remind me of them. And, curiously, my mama's sweet scent of rose perfume. I can still smell it on her jacket.

"Sweetie, are you nervous about the audition?" Anna was sitting next to me holding the tablet. She smiled softly, reached out with her free hand and patted my arm. "You've done this before. You go in and do your best. It is just a small ballet company and it is only for a few months. After the show two nights ago, I know you can do anything you put your mind to do. I tell Mia you are fearless."

"I know," I smile fondly at her. But it is not just any ballet company. It is Adrien's new company that tours internationally during the summer. And I have not seen him since the night all hell broke loose three weeks ago, not after his goodbye. No phone calls, no texts. Only one box sent through the post office and sitting on my doorstep two days ago. It was a hundred pairs of high priced panties, a beautiful and very expensive custom-made ballet outfit and fluffy sheepskin slipper boots and a tiny matching set for Mia. And a six-pack of professional graffiti spray paint, the expensive stuff. Underpants? What does that mean? He hasn't even shown up at the new theatre where I am allowed to practice once again.

"I didn't do it by myself," I say softly. I reach into my purse and I pull out a little picture and frame. I found it among the clothes that were in the suitcase. It is a picture of a man and a woman. The woman is holding a little girl in her arms. They are young, but the woman looks almost exactly as I drew her in my painting for Neil Wright's class—my mama in jeans and a button up blouse and high top tennis shoes. On her wrist is the rainbow snap bracelet I gave to Zane. He seems to cherish it and never takes it off. I couldn't ask for it back. My daddy's wearing dark blue jeans and a t-shirt. He wore glasses. His arm is around her. I think the tiny one he is looking at is me. I look up, note that Anna is peering from the picture to me so I tuck it back into the purse.

"I just painted and danced a little," I mutter. "Mark Lafferty threw his heart and soul into the competition. He made history, you know." He did make history at the college. For the first time, a dancer didn't win the Edna Fields Performing Arts competition. They couldn't win because there was no way they could compete with what Poppy called the *utter grandeur* of the program Mark put together. By the time the show went on, there were four-hundred and twenty students involved on our team from every aspect of the college. There wasn't a single class not represented. The entire time, I painted a backdrop while the acapella group sang and the other groups performed whatever embodied their program. It was amazing.

Mark even had dancers planted in the audience and outside the doors that came in on the grand finale. When the dust had settled, Dean Paulson announced that Mark had won the scholarship and money. Shane's dream team of Delia, Alexandra, and Taylor were so mad, they stormed out. Shane, in his anger, pointed out that I was not to be on school property. He wanted our group to be disqualified. Then Billy, who still does not have a shutoff valve, strutted up to the dean and announced the reason Shane didn't like me. I got called into the Fields Community College offices three days later with Uncle Lion's attorney. When I came out, Shane was no longer working for the college.

"You are the one who brought everybody together," Anna says softly. "You taught the dances and some of those young men and women looked like they usually couldn't find their way through a lighted hallway. And I think that is wonderful that the dean wants you to help teach classes when you finish your degree Fall semester. You did that all by yourself."

"No, Anna, you did it. You took me to a million dance classes and gymnastic classes. When I made a mistake, you corrected me. You know, I don't call you mama. I always felt like I would hurt my birth mother's feelings if I called you mama. Now, I don't think my real mama would think that way. You're the one that's been here for me no matter when I make mistakes or not. You took her place, but only because she couldn't be here. So you're my family, my mama. I call you *my* Anna so much everybody thinks that it is your name. It's like Poppy said when Adrien kept saying he wanted to dance with me and he really wanted to say he wanted to *be* with me. Well, My Anna is mama. That's how it is in my head. I love you." I look over and she's digging through her purse for a tissue. "Please don't cry."

She's just sniffling and nodding, patting my hand like it is me who is sobbing, happily, I think. "I'm not," she fibs.

"So, Adrien didn't call, hasn't done anything to let me know he wants to be with me since he left that day. He just—bid me adieu and left. What if I get up there and he laughs or leaves or—"

"Did you text him?"

"Of course. I asked him how he was doing." I lied. I texted him six times. *Hey, I heard from my informants in Brazil*— Stupid stuff like that, stuff you can't erase from a text once sent. He probably passed it around to everybody in his dance company and told them about the stupid, poverty-stricken girl who danced in an old mill. "I'm sure, Anna, that he read the stupid article in *Celebrity Magazine* that Colt Lucero wrote. If the stuff before it didn't freak him out, finding out I lived with a serial killer probably did."

"Well, we don't look at it that way. We are proud that you were the one that outshone the Hensley police even when they were—" she breathes in a sigh, presses a hand to her chest. "It just sends a chill down my back knowing they were stalking you, that our own chief of police was nothing but a common criminal who stole from dead people."

"He shall pay for his crime," I say half-heartedly, holding up a finger in the air like a flag. "Along with eighty-thousand a year for six years in compensation to me—" I stop, sigh. It just makes me sad what he did. I drop my hand. Chief Peirce found four of the bodies caught up along the bank three days after the plane wreck. My mama and Colt's dad are thought to be among them. He buried them and kept telling the historic society they were from an Indian burial mound. "Kevin saved my life. I feel like— oh, Anna, I was with Colt a couple times," I whisper softly, roll my eyes so she understand the capacity I was seeing him. "Adrien saw a text the night he told me how he felt. He thought I was going to see Colt. I couldn't lie to him. I was going to see him, but not for a—um, date. To get the key to the suitcase."

"Well, you need to tell him the truth. Because I think he will understand. You need someone to love and cherish you, Raeanna, not just somebody to have one night stands with or who's going to take out the trash. Kevin was seeing another woman while you were supporting him. Good men, they require a bit of work from you too. You know, from what you told us, your Mister Moreau showed up night after night to dance even after you stood him up several times. He flew, Raeanna, hundreds and hundreds of miles just to dance with you. He could have danced with Delia or Taylor or any of those girls. He could have danced with any of the girls at the academy where he worked. He didn't. He found something in you that kept him coming back. Perhaps you can return the favor to let him know how you feel."

And that is what I am doing standing by myself on a little stage that was once an old movie theatre. It is dark and dingy, but has some echoes of beauty in its past. It has a new sign out front that says: Adrien Moreau Dance Company. The chairs are a deep red velvet, the stage floor is pocked and scuffed, but it is a light-colored old wood. And there are balcony seats and curtains.

The lights flicker and I realize I'm daydreaming while

they are slapping my papers together. We all look up.

"You better go before the lights do," a girl laughs.

"Or the place falls down around us." A man rolls his eyes, but he has a smile on his face. "Probably the worst place you've danced?"

"No, no I've danced in places where I had to turn on the flashlight on my phone to see because there's no light." All of them look up and stare at me. I scratch my neck, prepare myself to begin. "I like the ambiance. This place, it has—a spirit, character. I think I can feel the energy of hundred other performers and their audience with me." I can. It is old and reminds me of the Fields Community College theatre. I feel at home. "You don't feel that in any new, sterile auditorium."

"I'll dance with her."

I turn slightly, see Adrien coming up from the side. He's dressed in his warmup pants and tank top. He isn't smiling, just comes up behind me like he does when we practice together in Hensley Grove. I have my arms to my sides and he places his hands on my wrists and gently pulls them into the air. Then he drops his voice, "Even though the diva here does not return my calls, tell me she is coming, or show up at her old haunts."

I work my eyes up at him as we begin to dance. "I am not a diva," I have to whisper-yell for him to hear when he steps back. "I texted you—"

"Um, Svetlana threw my bag out the window when she found out I bought this place. I had to get a new phone. It took two days. Still, I went back to that old factory when your dean at the university, he asked me if I could fly in. When I did, he asked me to teach Shane's old position. I thought it was exciting. But you were gone."

"Mister Moreau, You told me goodbye—*forever*.

Adieu means goodbye—forever. I looked it up. You were clear it was not *au revoir* which is *until we meet again.*"

"Because you were still planning on seeing Colt Lucero. I took the hint." He lifts me up and tosses me high, flips me over with the really advanced throws we have practiced. "How is that working for you?"

"I wasn't going to see him. Period. I didn't want to just say no and he figured out that I knew something was going on with him." I drop my eyes to his. "I thought you were a part of his stupid plot to get the story."

"No."

I stop while he interrupts to tell me what he wants me to do. I perform the task, a simple pirouette. I stop and face him.

"You could have told me that."

"I tried. Then you told me Svetlana was making you come back. I didn't want you to—have to choose—"

"Between the woman I hate and the woman I love?"

He tosses everything at me that we worked on together straight to down to the grand jeté where I jump into his arms and he turns me while I twist and turn again and again. Not just once, but twice. Then he tells me to go into a cambré press. I am out of breath, he's out of breath.

"I talked to your Anna," he tells me with a grunt. "She said I shouldn't chase you." He is almost gulping his breaths. "It makes you run away. Poppy, he said to let you come to me. That's what he did when you hid in the woods and they couldn't find you when you first went to stay with them. He sat on the porch until two in the morning with a melting bowl of ice cream with a piece of fudge Anna made. And you finally came out. So—I wait. And wait. And wait."

"Mister Moreau, you need to learn boundaries." I fall down in front of him, look up into his eyes. I don't say anything, look away.

"You have been working out. You are bending so much better," he huffs.

"I bent just fine before."

"No, you didn't. You were lazy. Look at me."

"I'm am not lazy. I'm mad at you. I don't want to look at you."

"Tango, listen to me. Look at me—"

"Okay." I do look at him and I give him the snarkiest face I can come up with. I finish off with an eye cross and my tongue sticking out.

I don't know if Adrien Moreau has ever dropped a dancer. At least not because he snorted a laugh. It was mostly my fault. His eyes got really wide when I made the face at him and I felt his arm quiver. I snapped up, the worst thing you can do and ended up rolling sideways. I hear one of the girls in the seats gasp. Of course, it won't be the first time we ended up on the floor.

"Oh, my God, I think you broke me." I'm laying on my back trying to sort through my aches to make sure they go away in a reasonable amount of time. But I'm laughing flatly while he's poking my wrists and ankles like he can identify a break from prodding me.

"You are kidding me, right?" Adrien says.

"Except for your jabbing me, I'm fine." I narrow my gaze. "Unless you aren't really Adrien Moreau and instead, his double sent to assassinate me. Oh, no, you are—"

"Get up. This is done. You are being goofy, Tango."

"Done? You mean, I'm out?" I don't realize until he pulls me up with his arm, his entourage has broken from their seats in a panic thinking I was hurt.

"Is this—the Tango you were talking about?" someone says. I nod. But I'm upset.

"Yes, the one and only." Adrien wipes off his pants.

I shouldn't have been so goofy. He's right. I'm thinking that Shane Delgado is right. I'm just not cut out for anything more than little town dance classes. I take a quick curtsy and thank them. I snatch up my bag just outside the hallway. There is a stairway I have to descend to get to the back door. I don't want to pass all the others finishing their auditions. I just want to go home.

"Where are you going?"

I look up and see Adrien standing at the top of the stairway.

"Home. You said I was done."

He makes quick steps down the stairway. "Did you get my gifts?"

"The one with the underpants?"

"Because you said you couldn't afford them, right? You said if I bought you a hundred of them, you would reconsider not taking the janitor job. You would dance instead."

"Oh," the word sifts from my lips. He's right. I did say that in a rant. "It didn't matter. They fired me for not getting my work done. I spent too much time in the school auditorium at night—"

"Dancing," Adrien finishes for me. I nod. "Did I hear you say you finished your first painting consignment?"

"Yes."

"That is so good, right? Why didn't you tell me you had one?"

"I wanted to. I didn't think you would have cared."

"I care. I have a picture of you at our fake café on my office wall. I love that you are talented." He stretches his neck. He's nervous. "Um, wait," He's digging in the little pocket of his workout pants and he pulls out a piece of paper, opens it. "When I said you were finished, I meant the audition was done. You were flawless, Tango. You already had the job. I saw it on my staff's faces. They were as speechless as I was the first time I saw you. That's what the dance outfit was—to wear at our programs. And the paint—so we can paint every city we tour in and do your graffiti." He wiggles the paper while he stops beside me. "Volim te."

"I don't know French, Mister Moreau."

"It is not French. It is Bosnian."

I stop, tip my head to the side. "Bosnian. So you read the article in *Celebrity*?"

"I did." He shrugs it off.

"Volim te, what does it mean?"

"I love you," he says.

I know I get this goofy smile on my face. "Volim te," I say back to him. "Did you know I was coming to the audition?"

He kind of looks uncomfortable then, shrugs and gets a red face when he looks at the paper. "No."

"You've been carrying—"

"Yes. I've been carrying it around."

"We haven't even kissed. Maybe you—"

And holy hell, Adrien just leans over and snatches me up. He slips his hand behind my neck and gives me this incredible, mind-blowing kiss that leaves me breathless.

"God almighty," I whisper, my fingers touching my lips. Then he stands back and gives me a boyish grin. "I was just waiting for you to ask." He holds up a finger. He squints at the paper in his fingers. I'm just reeling while he makes a raggedy spiel of words: "Here's another one: hoćeš li se udati za mene?"

"This place is falling down around us, right?" I tease him, work my gaze to the ceiling. Oh, no, actually I notice it is beautiful with a chandelier.

"No, it is what I can afford, what my investors can afford. We can work on it together? I am asking you to marry me."

I'm thunderstruck. I just blink dumbly up at him. I can actually say I was almost less surprised to find out I wasn't the daughter of a serial killer than I am at his words.

"I've got a ring, Tango, if that is what is stopping you. Or do I have to get what is it you called it, a crash test dummy to try things out on?"

"Oh, no you're not," I hold up a hand. "You saw what happened when you did it once before, right?" I fake-glare at him. "I'll lay her flat."

"So all this—" he waves a finger in the air. "This building that's falling apart and not knowing what's coming around the next corner, I'm hoping you're okay with it?"

"It is beautiful. You—are beautiful."

"And you're okay with working for me? I want to travel like you said, so you can dance and do your art, right? With Mini-Tango. I'm not forgetting her. We can all run from the cops in every country so you can do your graffiti until we get tired and settle down. You will be my principal dancer."

"Is it a *yes,* you are waiting on?" I ask him. I don't wait for him to answer because he's not going to stop throwing in stuff like *I'm* the one that needs convincing. "Yes. I want to marry you. Yes, I want to dance *for* you and *with* you every pas de deux. I want to run from the cops in every country we can think of and spray graffiti on the walls. Yes, Adrien, would be the answer from the moment you dropped your stupid duffel bag on the dirty floor of the cruddy old mill and without question danced with me. Yes."